Lords of th

In a remote fortress in Bud.   warriors—
each more dangerously sea
bound by an ancient curse nor
    When a powerful enemy returns, they will travel
        world in search of a sacred relic of the gods—one
                that threatens to destroy them all.

Gena Showalter's
LORDS OF THE UNDERWORLD

continues with

THE DARKEST SEDUCTION

Also available in this series

THE DARKEST NIGHT
THE DARKEST KISS
THE DARKEST PLEASURE
THE DARKEST WHISPER
DARK BEGINNINGS
THE DARKEST PASSION
THE DARKEST LIE
THE DARKEST SECRET
THE DARKEST SURRENDER

Dear Readers,

At long last, I'm pleased to bring you the story of Paris, keeper of the demon of Promiscuity. Yes, I finally feel like I've tortured him enough. After all, since the LORDS OF THE UNDERWORLD were first introduced, Paris has:

1) Lost the only woman he was able to bed more than once

2) Given up his chance to find her by choosing to save one of his friends instead

3) Formed an addiction to an illicit substance

4) Choked out any light of goodness inside himself

5) Turned into a war/fighting machine.

His road to happily-ever-after has been paved with blood, sweat and tears. Mostly mine. Fine. Mostly his. Whatever. *Semantics*. Anyway, I knew he deserved something—and someone—special. In fact, I had an idea for him and sat down to write it. Four tries later—with three hundred pages in the trash—he showed me exactly what he wanted. OK, fine (again). I finally gave in and did things his way. And you know what? He got the "special" I wanted for him.

The characters had so much more depth than I expected, and as they interacted the puzzle pieces began to fall into place—I saw why he wanted what he wanted, and for the first time in a very long time I heard Paris laugh. (I heard this in my head, of course, but laughter is laughter.) He'd found his "mine," and she was and is exactly what he's needed all along.

Will I ever stand in my characters' way again? Well, yeah. (Hey, at least I'm honest.) But this one time, giving in proved to be the best thing I could have done.

I hope you are as satisfied with Paris's story as he is.

All my best!

Gena Showalter

GENA
SHOWALTER

THE DARKEST SEDUCTION

MIRA is a registered trademark of Harlequin Enterprises Limited, used under licence.

Published in Great Britain 2012
MIRA Books, Eton House, 18-24 Paradise Road,
Richmond, Surrey, TW9 1SR

© Gena Showalter 2012

ISBN 978 1 848 45097 4

59-0312

MIRA's policy is to use papers that are natural, renewable and recyclable products and made from wood grown in sustainable forests. The logging and manufacturing processes conform to the legal environmental regulations of the country of origin.

Printed and bound by
CPI Group (UK) Ltd, Croydon, CR0 4YY

Throughout the years I've learned that family matters. I've been blessed with one of the most amazing families EVER. They love me, support me, and they are always there when I need them. The bond you see between the Lords, as well as the bond between the Harpy sisters? That's what I have with my family, and I am beyond grateful. So this one is to my husband and children, my mom and dad, sisters and brothers, in-laws (who are so much more than that), nieces and nephews, and crazy aunts and uncles. I love and adore you all!

ACKNOWLEDGEMENTS

From family to friends, I am blessed. To Jill Monroe, Kresley Cole and PC Cast. I love you, ladies!

I speak, and the humans tremble in fear. I speak, and my people rush to obey—and yet still they seek to destroy me. My salvation rides the wings of midnight, and my burden she carries. My rage she unleashes, delivering damnation to all with a single swing of her sword. I speak.
—A passage found in the private journals of Cronus, king of the Titans

Speak all the hell you want. I'm taking what's mine.
—Paris, Lord of the Underworld

PROLOGUE

"His rage…"

"I know."

High in the heavens, Zacharel watched the world below him. Watched as the once genial Paris murdered yet another of his enemy, the Hunters. How many victims that made in the past hour alone, the angel could not say. He'd long since lost count. And even if he paused to do the tally, the answer would have changed a second later as yet another body fell to the slick, blood-coated blades the warrior wielded.

Of course, the panting, sweat-soaked Paris spun to engage two others, his motions fluid, lethally graceful… as unstoppable as an avalanche. At first, he played. A punch, cracking bone. A kick, smashing lungs. Laughing, spouting the worst of curses. Soon none of that was enough for the demon-possessed soldier, and he danced his blades over the tendons in their ankles, hobbling his prey for easier elimination.

Paris had made himself Bait to purposely draw these Hunters to him. They'd come eagerly, happily, intending to steal the vile demon tethered inside him and finally end him. So Zacharel could not fault the warrior for what he did to defend himself, even as several new bodies joined the already mountainous pile enveloped by a sea of crimson and black. And yet, he could not commend the warrior, either.

These were not mercy slayings or even carried out in the name of a cold and calculated vengeance birthed in the bowels of an equally cold rage. No, these were a spew of fire, hate and desperation hotter than anything hell had ever created.

"He is like a poisoned apple," Zacharel said to the angel beside him. And because Paris was bonded to the demon of Promiscuity, his pruning belonged not to the humans he lived amongst but to the Deity's angels, who policed different realms of evil. "Poison of this nature spreads slowly but corrupts absolutely."

Beads of ice fell around Zacharel, as they always fell around him these days, his breath misting in front of his face. Every crystal was to be a reminder of his own crimes, so recently brought to his attention. But unlike Paris, he did not wear misery like a winter coat, hugging it close to his body, relying on it, feeding it, helping it grow. Zacharel cared for nothing, not anymore.

In his quest to destroy the demons that had ruined his life, he had slain "innocent" humans, and this was to be his punishment—to carry his Deity's displeasure with him always.

"As succulent as others consider this particular apple," Lysander proclaimed, "they will be willing to taste any-thing he offers."

Zacharel moved his gaze to the man who had taught him how to survive on the battlefield. The elite warrior was a muscled tower of unwavering strength. He wore a long white robe, his majestic wings like rivers of molten gold. Zacharel's ice raged around him, too, though not a single flake dared land on the man. Perhaps, like myriad other creatures, the crystals feared him—and rightly so. In their world, he was judge and jury, his word law.

"Do we remove temptation?" Zacharel asked. For centuries he had acted as Lysander's executioner.

"I will not order his assassination, no," Lysander said, resolute. "At the moment, Paris is redeemable."

Unexpected. Even with the great distance between the heavens and the earth, Zacharel could hear the grunts and groans Paris elicited, the screams of his enemies. The pleas for mercy that would echo into eternity, forever unheeded. And as determined as this Lord of the Underworld was, this was only the beginning.

"What will you have me do, then?"

"Paris searches for his woman, intending to free her from the Titan king's enslavement. You will aid him, protect him and protect the girl. The moment her ties to Cronus are cut, however, you will bring her here, where she will live out the rest of eternity."

Even more unexpected. The command smacked of leniency, something Lysander had shown to only one other demon-possessed immortal in all the millennia of his life: Amun, Paris's friend. And only because Bianka, Lysander's Harpy mate, had asked.

She must have requested this second favor, as well, for it was widely known that Lysander was powerless against her wiles. But even a besotted groom, tasked as he was with governing the heavens, responsible for all that transpired there, should not have asked another angel to do this deed. Aid a demon? Bring another here to live? Horrifying.

Zacharel offered no objection. And despite the fact that he had never experienced desire himself, he would do his best to cure Paris of his so that, when the inevitable break with the female came, the warrior would not return to his rage.

"Paris will protest her loss." After everything the warrior had done to find and save her already, everything he would soon do…oh, yes, he would protest—using those dripping blades to make his case.

"You must convince him that he will be better off without her," Lysander said.

"Will he be?"

"Of course." There was no hesitation in the pronouncement, lending it an edge of fiery truth. An unnecessary edge, for Zacharel knew Lysander would not, could not, lie.

"And if I fail to convince him?" He had to ask, needed the penalty riding heavy on his shoulders, driving him to succeed.

Eyes of pitiless navy frosted over, revealing the iron depths of Lysander's warrior core. "We are lost, for the greatest war the world has ever known now brews. The girl will lead us to our victory—or our enemy to theirs. It's as simple as that."

Very well, then. When the time came, Zacharel would take her. No matter how Paris was affected.

Paris would hate him, and would, perhaps, do more than rage. There was no stopping that, not when so much darkness swirled inside him, a rot in his soul, far worse than any spiritual poison. But that wouldn't stop Zacharel from fulfilling his duty.

Nothing would.

CHAPTER ONE

PARIS TOSSED BACK THREE fingers of Glenlivet and signaled the bartender. He wanted an entire hand and by
right or might, he'd have it. Except soon after the single
malt was poured, he realized an entire hand wasn't going
to cut it, either. Fury and frustration were living enti-
ties inside him, frothing and bubbling despite his recent
fighting.

"Leave the bottle," he said when the bartender made a
move to help someone else. Hell, suddenly Paris doubted
every drop of alcohol in a ten-mile radius would do the
trick, but hey. Desperate times.

"Sure, sure. Anything you say." Shirtless Boy Wonder
released the bottle and beat feet.

What? He looked *that* dangerous? Please. He'd washed
off the blood, hadn't he? Wait. *Hadn't he?* He looked
down. Shit. He hadn't. Crimson streaked him from head
to toe.

Whatever. He wasn't in a human bar, so no "authori-
ties" would have a beef with him. He was in Olympus,
though the heavenly kingdom had recently been renamed
Titania. Once only gods and goddesses had been allowed
here, but when Cronus reclaimed the realm, he'd changed
things, allowing vampires, fallen angels and other creatures of the dark to come and play. A nice little screw
you to the previous king, Zeus.

Call the bartender back, Promiscuity said. *I want him.*

Promiscuity—the demon trapped inside him, driving him. Irritating him. *Remember when I wanted fidelity? Monogamy?* Paris replied in his mind. *Well, we don't always get what we want, do we?*

A familiar growl sounded in his head.

Whaa, whaa, pout, pout. He downed the second alcoholic offering and quickly chased it with a third. Both scorched so good he enjoyed a fourth. The potent alcohol razed his chest, burned holes in his abdomen, and flooded his veins. Nice.

And yet, his emotions remained as dark as ever, the edges of that bone-deep fury and frustration unsmoothed. His inability to save a not-so-innocent woman he should hate—*did* hate, at least a little—but also hungered for, body and soul, drove him, a constant whip against his flank.

"If I asked you to leave, would you?" a monotone voice said from beside him. A voice accompanied by a blast of arctic air.

He didn't have to look to know that Zacharel, warrior angel extraordinaire and infamous demon-assassin, had just joined him. They'd met not long ago, when the feathered axman had come to Buda to off Paris's friend Amun. Had old Zach actually succeeded, two crystal blades would have been drilling into his spine at that very moment.

I want him, the demon said.

Screw you.

Finally. We're on the same page.

Really hate you right now.

Once upon a time, the demon had spoken to Paris with annoying frequency. Then the stupid sex fiend had stopped, merely urging Paris to bed this person or that person, no matter their gender or Paris's own feelings toward them. Now, the talking had started up again and it was worse than before, because he wanted everyone, *especially* the ones Paris felt no desire for.

"Well?" the angel prompted.

"Leave, when I had to beg Lucien to bring me here and I know he won't be so accommodating next time? No, but I'd damn sure want to know why you gave a crap about my location."

"I do not care about your location."

True story. Zacharel didn't care about anything, a fact you learned real fast in your dealings with him. "That's my point, so get lost."

As Paris nursed a fifth whiskey, he studied the smoke-stained mirror in front of him, covertly panning the area behind him. Bejeweled chandeliers hung from the ceiling. The walls were rose-colored marble, veined with glittering ebony, the floor a sparkling stretch of crushed diamonds.

Throughout the room, men and women talked and laughed. From minor gods and goddesses to fallen angels trying to work their way back into their saintly fold. *Good luck with that in a bar. Morons.* Anyway. There was probably a demon or two sprinkled among the masses, but Paris couldn't tell for sure.

Demons were as sneaky as they were evil. They could skulk around in their own scales, proudly showcasing their horns, claws, wings and tails—and getting decapitated by warrior angels like Zach. Or they could possess someone else's body and skulk around in *their* skin.

Paris had thousands of years of experience with the latter.

"I will leave, as you so succinctly suggested," Zacharel said, "*after* you answer another question for me."

"All right." Something else Paris knew from experience: angels were freakishly stubborn. Better to hear the guy out, otherwise he'd find himself with a new shadow. He turned, facing the dark-haired stunner with eyes the color of jade, and sucked in a breath. Never ceased to amaze him, how magnetic these celestial beings were. No matter their gender—or how mind-numbingly dull their personalities—they drew and held your attention, every damn time. For some reason, Zacharel did so with more intensity than most.

But the magnetism wasn't what caught Paris's attention this time. Majestic wings arced over the angel's broad shoulders, a turbulent fall of winter clouds with streams of gold winding and curling throughout, snowflakes raining from the tips like glitter in a globe.

"You're snowing." *Captain Obvious, that's me.*

"Yes."

"Why?"

"I can answer you, or I can ask my question and leave." Dressed in the long white robe that was customary for his kind, Zacharel should have looked innocent and prissy. Instead, he looked like the Grim Reaper's evil twin: emotionless, as frigid as the snow he shed and ready to kill. "Your choice."

No thought necessary. "Ask."

"Do you wish to die?" Zacharel said it as simply as he'd said everything else, mist crystallizing in front of his mouth, creating a dreamlike haze and reminding Paris of the breath of life. Or death.

Definitely ready to kill, Paris mused. "What do you think?" he asked, because honestly? He didn't know the answer anymore.

For centuries he'd fought to live, but now, now he constantly threw himself into the fire and waited to be burned. *Liked* being burned. What kind of sick prick had he become?

Unflinching, the angel held his gaze. "I think you want one particular woman more than you want anyone—or anything—else. Even death…even life."

Paris pressed his tongue to the roof of his mouth. One woman in particular: the not-so-innocent one.

Her name was Sienna Blackstone. Once a Hunter and always his enemy, for Hunters were an irritating army of humans who hoped to rid the world of Pandora's demons. Then fleetingly, she'd been his lover. Then dead, gone. *Then* she'd been brought back from the grave, her soul merged with the demon of Wrath. Now, she was out there. Somewhere. And she was suffering. Cronus had enslaved her, thinking to use her demon to punish his adversaries, and now that he'd lost control of her, he thought to torture her into submission.

Paris might dislike the things Sienna had done to him, and yeah, as he'd already admitted, part of him might even hate the woman herself, but even she did not deserve the cruel, vicious—eternal—punishment being meted out.

I will find her, and I will *save her.* From Cronus… from himself. Right now, Paris simply couldn't get past the fact that she was suffering. Once that part of the equation was dealt with, he would stop thinking about her. He had to stop thinking about her.

"So I want her," he ended up saying to the angel. Sienna was not up for discussion. "BFD."

"I will pretend I know what that means." Zacharel shook his wings, more of that pure, glistening snow raining down. "As for you, I think that, despite your own desires, your demon wants anything with a pulse."

"Sometimes even a pulse isn't a requirement," he muttered, and damn if that wasn't the truth. Sex, as he'd taken to calling his dark companion, wanted anyone and everyone—but only ever once. With the exception of Sienna, Sex would not allow Paris to harden for the same person twice.

Why could he have Sienna again? No damn clue. "But again, so?"

"I think, even though you crave this particular woman, you slept with your friend Strider's future wife. He is the demon of Defeat, and your actions made his courtship of the Harpy very difficult."

"Hey. You're entering dangerous territory here." Not that Paris had anything to apologize for.

The one-nighter had happened weeks before Strider and Kaia hooked up. Or had even thought about hooking up. Therefore, Paris had done nothing wrong. Technically. And yet, he now knew what Kaia looked like naked, and Strider knew that he knew, and that meant all three of them knew Sex tossed out naked images of the girl every time they were together. A consequence Paris loathed, but couldn't stop.

Zacharel's dark head tilted to the side in a reflective pose, all the more mysterious because of the mist that continued to form with his every exhalation. "I meant only to point out that you have clearly moved on to other conquests and that you are hardly discriminating in your choices, which makes me wonder why you still pursue your Sienna."

Because Sienna had been Paris's one and only shot at monogamy. Because he'd inadvertently brought about her death. Because he'd felt like he lost *everything* when she died.

"You're annoying," he snapped. "And I'm done talking to you."

Still the angel persisted. "I think you feel guilty about every heart you break, every dream of happily-ever-after you crush, and every bit of self-loathing you encourage when your partners realize how effortlessly you overcame their reservations. I also think you are overindulged and pathetic, and that you have no business crying about your problems."

"Hey! I've never cried." Paris slammed his glass on the counter with so much force the bar split down the center and the cup shattered. Blood welled from the slices in his palm, but the sting was minimal. "And you know what? I think you are seconds away from finding pieces of your body scattered in all the corners of this bar."

Then, while he's down, we can have him!

Zip it, Sex.

"Uh, here you go," the bartender said, Johnny-on-the-spot with a clean rag he thrust in Paris's direction. His arm shook. He was still afraid of Paris.

I want—

I said zip it! "Thanks, man." Paris fisted the material, applying pressure to the slivers of torn tissue before anyone could scent him and the oh-so-special pheromones his demon excreted.

One whiff of the intoxicating aroma, and everyone around him would become unforgivably aroused, uncaring about where they were or who they were with. Mostly their hunger would be for *Paris,* and though that would have been an especially craptastic outcome tonight considering he was operating under a time crunch, he would have enjoyed rebuffing the males with his fists.

Except…the pheromones never enveloped him. He frowned. Sex wanted everyone he'd spotted tonight. Why not take advantage of his ability and force the patrons to want him back?

Paris returned his focus to Zacharel, wondering if the angel was somehow responsible.

Those eyes of the rarest jade narrowed to tiny slits. "I think you hope to save your Sienna, and that is a good thing. I think you mean to keep her, and that is not. No matter how intensely you crave her, no matter that she might be your only chance at forever, your demon will eventually ruin her, for humans were never meant to battle demons, and at heart, she is still a human."

"What about her own demon?" he snapped.

"If one is bad, two is surely worse."

"Enough!" If they continued on this path, his fury and frustration would rise up and consume him. He would lose sight of tonight's goal. "I'm not going to keep her." He would. He *so* would if given a chance, and if she would have him, of course, but hell, she wouldn't have him.

"Good. Because this particular woman would not like the man you have become."

Snorting, Paris shoved his free hand through his hair. "She didn't like who I was." And now, after he'd irrevocably stepped over the line between right and wrong? Please.

He'd known his actions were reprehensible, and he'd stepped over anyway. He'd killed, callously. Seduced, methodically. Lied, cheated and betrayed. All of which he would do again and again.

"Yet you still rush to save her," Zacharel said.

Yeah. He was as big a moron as the fallen who frequented this place. Whatever. He *knew*. Didn't care. "Look, I don't answer to you. I don't have to explain myself. And what's with all the questions? You said you only had one more."

"I have asked only the one. The rest have been observations, and I have one more of those to offer." Zacharel leaned into him and whispered, "I think, if you continue on this destructive path, you will lose everything you have come to love."

"Is that a threat?" Paris fisted the collar of the angel's robe. "Go ahead and try something, winger. See what—"

Air. He was fisting and yelling at air.

Little growls sprang from his throat as he lowered his arm to his side. The only reason he knew Zacharel had been here was the temperature of his hands. They were practically frostbitten.

"Uh, who were you talking to?" the bartender asked, faux casual as he cleaned an already clean counter.

If an angel didn't want to be seen, an angel wouldn't be seen. Not even by his brethren, fallen or otherwise. So only Paris had seen Zacharel this go-round. Great. "Myself apparently, and we prefer to chat without an audience."

Was Zacharel still here? Paris wondered. Or had he materialized somewhere else? And what was the purpose of all that talk of Paris needing to stay away from Sienna? The angel shouldn't care.

Paris dropped the rag and turned the rest of the way to face the crowd. Several warriors were scowling in his direction—why?—dangerously close to ruining the room's elegance with the blood they were tempting Paris to spatter. He massaged the back of his neck, forcing thoughts of Zacharel and his threat into hiding. He had bigger and badder to deal with. He was here for Viola, the minor goddess of the Afterlife and keeper of the demon of Narcissism. She should have popped in already.

Maybe she'd heard he was coming and bailed, and if that was the case he couldn't blame her. He and his friends had once stolen and opened Pandora's box, unleashing the evil from inside. As punishment, they were cursed to host the demons they'd released within themselves. Unfortunately, there'd been more demons than naughty boys and girls to contain them, and when the box had disappeared in the chaos, the leftover evil spirits had needed homes. What better recipients for the Greeks to select than the unlucky, unable-to-run inmates of Olympus's—*Titania's*—immortal prison, Tartarus?

So, yeah, Paris was partly responsible for Viola's dark side. She'd been one of those unlucky prisoners. He wasn't entirely responsible, though, considering the girl was a criminal once considered dangerous enough to be forcibly kept away from the very gods and goddesses who were often praised in mythology books for their most vicious deeds.

What crime Viola had committed, he didn't know and didn't care. She could slash him to ribbons, as long as she gave up the information he craved. The final puzzle piece needed to at last save Sienna.

According to the Hunters he'd slain just this morning, Viola came here every Friday night to hustle immortals at pool and rave about her awesomeness over a few beers. Apparently, said Hunters had been watching her, intent on nabbing her and "persuading" her to join their ranks. So, in a way, she kinda owed him.

Where the hell is she? he wondered again, searching for the telltale long blond hair, eyes the color of cinnamon and a killer body that could—

Appear in a puff of white smoke.

There, in front of the bar's only entrance, stood a luscious woman with long blond hair and eyes the color of cinnamon. Paris straightened, his nerve endings zinging with anticipation. Just like that. Prey located. Target acquired.

CHAPTER TWO

I WANT HER, SEX SAID as Paris studied Viola.

Of course you do, he replied dryly.

The tendrils of smoke that had marked Viola's appearance now curled away from her, thinning out to reveal a slinky black dress. The thick straps on her shoulders veed to frame heavy cleavage before dipping past her pierced navel. The micromini skirt stopped just below the hem of her panties.

Was she even wearing panties?

Paris yawned. He'd been with gorgeous women, ugly women, and everything in between. One lesson he'd quickly learned: beauty could hide a beast, and a beast could hide a beauty.

Sienna belonged to the beauty-hiding-a-beast category—at least to him. While he'd been crazed with desire for her, she'd been plotting his downfall. And maybe he was as bad as his demon because part of him found even that side of her sexy. A reed-thin female had bested a battle-hardened warrior, and he thought that was hot as hell.

And okay, yeah, she considered herself plain and maybe once he would have agreed, but from the beginning, there'd been something tantalizing about her. Something that drew him, held him captive. Now, anytime he pictured her, he saw a flawless gem with no equal.

Concentrate. A command from the demon, who still wanted the minor goddess, and a reprimand from himself.

Viola flipped the length of her silky hair over one sun-kissed shoulder and scouted her surroundings. Men openly gaped. Women tried to hide their jealousy with (unconvincing) blank masks. She paused on Paris, looked him up and down, her lids narrowing, and then, shockingly, she dismissed him and continued her visual sweep.

The last time his demon had failed to attract a potential bedmate, he'd met Sienna shortly thereafter. Could that mean...what if... His anticipation intensified until his bones vibrated. He would get his answers—*tonight*—no matter what was required of him.

He closed in on Viola, schooling his features to reveal only admiration as he went over his plan. Charm first, if he could actually remember how to be charming. Force second, and yeah, he definitely remembered how to go that route.

Ignoring his approach, Viola bent down and slid a glittery pink phone from inside her black leather boot. Moans of approval erupted behind her, and men high-fived each other, as if they'd just received a glimpse of heaven. Even immortals could be childish. *Never me.* Unaware or unconcerned, she danced her nimble fingers over the phone's tiny keyboard.

Paris frowned. "What are you doing?"

As an opener, the question totally blew, as did his accusing tone. But if she thought to summon help, someone to fight him, or even a Hunter to kill him, she'd soon find herself his hostage, *as well as* his informant.

"I'm Screeching. That's the immortal version of twittering or tweeting or whatever you lower beings want to call it," she said without glancing up. "I've got over seven bazillion followers."

O-kay. Not what he'd expected. He'd spent a lot of time with humans, and knew they enjoyed sharing their every inane thought with the world. But a Titan who did so—that was new.

"What are you telling them?" Was Cronus among the seven bazillion? Was Galen, the head honcho of the Hunters? And how many was a bazillion?

"I maybe might be kinda sorta telling them all about you." A grin lifted the corners of her plump red lips as she continued type, type, typing. "'Lord of Sex is filthy and looking to score. I'm not interested, but should I help him rack up points with someone else?' Send." She focused those haunting auburn eyes on him. "I'll let you know when the results come in. Until then, is there anything else you want to know about me before I walk away and ignore you?"

Lord of Sex, she'd said. Sooo. She knew who he was, *what* he was, but she wasn't running from him, wasn't tossing insults at him and wasn't screaming for his execution. A great start. "Yes, there is, and it's a private matter very important to me." Subtext: *don't you dare Screech about it!*

"Ohhh. I love private, important matters that I'm not supposed to talk about but do, because I'm such a giver. I'm listening."

Despite her convoluted confession that she meant to tattle, there was no more typing. Good. He proceeded. "I want to see the dead. How do I make that happen?" Sienna was a soul without a body—a soul he couldn't sense in any way. Only those who communed with the dead could see, hear and touch her. But rumor was, Viola knew a trick that rendered the ability unnecessary.

She blinked, and he noticed that her lashes were painted a glittery pink to match her phone. "Let me tell you what I just heard. Talk, talk, talk, *I*. Talk, talk, talk, *I*. Well, what about *me?*"

His jaw clenched. There was being charming, and there was being a sucker. He wasn't a sucker. Well, not all the time. "I'll tell you about you. You can see the dead. Now you're going to teach me how to see them." An order she would do well to heed.

Her nose wrinkled. "Why do you care about seeing souls? If they're still here, they're causing trouble and—oh, oh, wait." Clap, clap, jump, jump, twirl. "I've already figured this little mystery out because I'm highly intelligent. You want to see your slain human lover."

Instantly his fury flashed to the surface, hot enough to blister. He didn't like anyone speaking of Sienna in any fashion. Not Zacharel, and certainly not this strange minor goddess with a penchant for gossiping. Sienna was his to protect, even in that capacity. "I—"

"Tsk, tsk. No need to confirm my genius assumption." Viola patted his cheek, all syrupy sweetness for his mental handicap. "Especially since I can't help you."

She tried to walk away.

He caught her wrist. "Can't or won't?" There was a big difference. The first he could do nothing about. The second he could change, and if she pushed him, she would discover the lengths he was willing to go to, to do just that.

"Won't. See ya." Oblivious to the rage she threatened to unleash, she jerked from his hold and practically skipped to the back of the bar, her perfect ass swaying, the heels of her boots clicking.

Incensed, he followed her, shoving aside anyone who got in his way. Grunts, groans and growls abounded, the predators in the crowd taking exception to his brute-force tactics. No one attempted to stop him, however. They sensed a far greater predator in their midst.

"How do you know who I am?" he demanded the moment he reached Viola. They'd start there and work their way to the mind changing, just in case one was dependent on the other.

She performed another twirl, making a production of it, as if she were a model at the end of a runway. He was a tall man used to towering over women, but Viola was a tiny fluff of five feet nothing and he *dwarfed* her.

Sienna, on the other hand, was just the right height. Standing, or on his knees, or lying down, he'd reach all the best parts of her, no problem.

"I know everything there is to know about the Lords of the Underworld," Viola said. "I made the entire horde of you my business when I escaped Tartarus and learned you were responsible for my condition."

She *did* blame him for the demon she'd been stuck with, then. And she smelled of roses, he realized with a jolt, the gentle scent suddenly clinging to his sinuses, very nearly drowning him in a warm sense of peace.

Lucien, the keeper of the demon of Death, could do the same thing to his enemies, calming them just before he struck a life-ending blow.

Paris's fury and frustration quickly chased that peacefulness away. "Stop that."

"Wow, that's a dark scowl. And not a very good look for you, I must say," she added, then caught a glimpse of her coral-painted fingernails and studied them in the light. "So pretty."

Touch her.

He tuned out his demon and decided he'd give the charm/sucker thing one more shot. Because, honestly?

He had yet to intimidate this female in any way. If this next attempt failed, he would let loose his beast in full force—and he wasn't talking about Sex. There was darkness inside him now, so much darkness, and that darkness would drive him to do what was necessary, no matter how vile.

He had no one but himself to blame, for he'd opened himself up to it. Just a fraction at first, like a crack in a window. But the funny thing was, once you welcomed in a breeze, there was no stopping what came next. A wind, a storm, thunder and lightning, until you could no longer reach the window to close it—and didn't really want to anyway. That's what this new darkness was. Evil in its purest form, an entity very much like Sex, urging him on.

Lie, cheat, betray, Paris thought. Here, now, like all the other times before.

He leaned down, softening his expression, forcing his demon's desires to seep through his pores. Forcing his blood to heat and the musky scent of arousal to drift from him, as sultry as champagne, as heady as chocolate. If Sex wouldn't use those pheromones, Paris would. He hated doing this, because, like everyone else, both he and Sex became mindless, flesh-hungry beings at the first whiff. Worse, the memories of what he forced people to do…to crave…

"Viola, sweetness. Talk to me. Tell me what I wish to know." His tone was a sensual caress, blissful and sure, and yet, even with the pheromones affecting *Paris,* he wanted only one woman and Viola wasn't her.

"I meant to thank you for my demon," she went on, as if he'd never spoken. As if he did not currently smell like pleasure walking. "He's the best! But then halfway to Budapest to track down your fortress, I forgot all about you. I'm sure you understand." She fluffed her hair, looking away from him as she waved to someone at her right. "So, anyway, now that you're here, thanks. Feel free to relay that to the others. Now you'll have to— Argh! Who put a mirror there?" she ended in a screech.

Undiluted rage blazed from her expression for a single heartbeat, followed by rapturous ecstasy as she studied her reflection.

"Look at me." She angled one way, posed, then angled another and posed again. "I'm *gorgeous*."

"Viola." Seconds passed, but she never stopped admiring herself. She even blew herself a kiss. Fine. They'd do this the other way. "I can make you beg for my touch, Viola. In front of everyone. And believe me, you *will* beg. You will cry, but relief will never be yours. I'll make sure of it. But do you know what else? That's not even the worst of what I'll do to you."

Several seconds ticked by, but she never offered a reply.

Fury...

Frustration...

Darkness...rising... He wanted to strike, to hurt, to kill.

He inhaled, held, held...smelled an infusion of roses... released the breath. Okay. Good. This time he was able to allow both emotion bombs to fizzle before detonation, calming him.

Perhaps Viola couldn't help herself, he realized suddenly. As he knew very well, all of Pandora's demons came with a major flaw. This could be hers. She was Narcissism, after all, a lover of self.

Testing his theory, he stepped in front of her, blocking her view of the mirror. Her entire body stiffened. Her gaze darted left and right, as if searching for interlopers who might have tried to harm her while she'd been incapacitated. No one had approached, and the tension drained from her. She breathed easier.

"I will *gut* the culprit!" she whispered fiercely.

Bingo. Her flaw, and one she clearly reviled.

"Concentrate on me, Viola." He gripped her by the shoulders, squeezing harder than he'd intended and shaking her until those cinnamon eyes rose to meet his. "Tell me what I want to know and you'll walk away from this unscathed."

Still not the least bit intimidated, she shrugged off his hold. "*So* impatient. I should be used to it by now, but alas. Men falling all over me…still a burden."

"Viola!"

"Fine. Let's see what my worshippers have to say sooner rather than later, shall we?" She lifted her phone and read the screen. "Four hundred and eighty-five votes for *Help him by giving him my number.* Two hundred and seven votes for *Are you stupid, climb him like a mountain,* and one hundred and twenty-three votes for *He's mine, bitch, walk away.*" She looked up at him, another smile taking root. "The little people have spoken. Yes, I will tell you about the souls."

Urgency overrode his relief. "Tell me, then. Now."

"Hey, you. Demon scum." The harsh voice rang out from behind him.

Annnd one of the guys Paris had bumped into earlier was finally acting out. Paris ground his molars. His hands returned to the female's shoulders. "Viola. Tell me." She would tell him, and he would leave, finally beginning his search in truth.

"Get your hands off my female!"

Or not. Unleashed aggression dripped from the male's

tone, and the need for violence quickly resurfaced inside Paris.

Restrain yourself, common sense counseled. *Victory is within reach.* "A friend of yours?"

"I have no friends." Graceful fingers reached up and hooked several tendrils of hair behind her ear. "Only admirers."

"I'm talking to you, demon." The male again.

Need rising…higher and higher…a thick black cloud that would not dissipate until blood ran in rivers at his feet. "If you want this admirer to survive, flash us out of here." Popping from one location to another with only a thought always made him sick, but sick was better than distracted.

"I don't," she said. "Want him to survive, that is."

"Are you listening to me, demon?" The tone was harsher, and far more determined. "Move away from her and face me. Or are you a coward?"

The cloud enveloped his mind, a single thought suddenly consuming him. The male was an obstacle in his path, blocking him from Sienna, and obstacles were to be eliminated. Always.

Another small voice of reason whispered through him, a beacon of gold amid an endless stretch of midnight. *Zacharel… Current path… Destruction…*

"Look at yourself in the mirror, goddess," the male commanded. "I don't want you to see what I do to the demon."

Even as a curse tore from her mouth, Viola obeyed, angling around Paris as if she couldn't help herself and hated herself for it. Just like that, she was once again enraptured by her own image, pinkie-waving and blowing kisses.

The golden whisper was destroyed. Death became in-

evitable. Paris pivoted on his heels to glare at his opponent.

Soon, blood would flow.

CHAPTER THREE

PARIS HAD GOTTEN ONE FACT wrong. He didn't have an opponent. He had opponents. The knowledge caused a heady rush of eagerness to flood him. The day just kept getting better. Earlier he'd slain a handful of Hunters, and this hour's selection—aka dessert—was a trio of fallen angels, each one bigger than the last. They were without shirts—the new fashion?—their scarred backs visible in the mirror at the top of the wall.

The frothing trio formed a solid wall of muscle on the other side of the bar, their arms crossed over their chests, their legs braced apart to evenly distribute their weight. A classic I'm-about-to-hurt-someone stance.

I want them, Sex said, as if that were some big surprise.

"You will not walk away," he warned the men. Lately, he couldn't afford to leave survivors. They had a nasty habit of returning for revenge.

"I've seen you around," the one on the left said. "You smile and women fall at your feet, but I'm gonna change that when I rip your spine out of your mouth. *Then* I'm gonna tell your enemies where you are. Yeah, I know who you are, Lord of Sex. I also know the Hunters want the privilege of killing you."

The one on the right flashed a grin, total I've-lost-my wings-and-I'm-glad evil. "Yeah. I like that idea. Maybe

I'll sign up with them, just to watch what they do to you when we're finished, you dirty—"

The one in the middle, the biggest one, placed a hand on Rightie's shoulder, silencing him. He had a bright white halo tattooed around his neck. That could mean he was only recently fallen, that he still had ties with the angels or that he liked to reminisce. Whatever. He would experience the same fate as his friends. "Less words, more pain."

"Yes, more pain," Paris agreed. He unsheathed his two favorite daggers, the clear, crystal blades glinting like rainbows in the light.

"Hey, no arsenals allowed inside," the bartender bellowed. "Only fists."

The entire bar stopped and quieted, clearly intent on watching.

"Feel free to try and pry mine from my grip." That would mean more opponents, more bloodshed. More satisfaction.

"Unfair advantage," someone else called.

Exactly. If you weren't cheating, you weren't trying. But, all right. Even lost to the decadent taste of violence as he was, Paris knew how to pretend to play nice. He commanded the blades to vanish from view while still remaining in his hands. Magical as they were, they obeyed.

"I don't care what weapons you use," Halo said.

"You shouldn't have come here." Leftie unfolded his arms. "This is our territory, and we're taking it back."

"Now, we'll make sure you never return." Rightie fisted his hands, cracking his knuckles. "This is gonna be fun."

"Fun. Yes. For me." Paris approached.

The trio approached.

All four met in the middle. The moment Paris was

within reach, he kicked Leftie while punching Rightie. Leftie hunched over, gasping for breath. Rightie died. Paris had punched with his invisible blade, sinking hilt-deep into the bastard's carotid.

One down. Two to go.

Halo swung a meaty fist, but the low, straight line Paris had made with his body caused the former winger to encounter only air, the momentum spinning him around. By the time Paris jerked upright, Leftie had regained his stamina and jumped on him, attempting to rip out his trachea with claws that hadn't been there a moment ago. Through dumb luck or talent, Leftie managed to angle his wrist when he realized Paris was shifting position, hitting the tendon that ran from neck to shoulder instead. There was a brutal rending before Paris shoved him off, the bastard taking hunks of skin and muscle with him.

Paris didn't release him, though. He held on tight, even as Halo got back in the game and hammered at his face. He stabbed Leftie with a quick *jab, jab.* Kidneys first, to shock and disable. Heart second, to kill. Leftie died just like his friend.

Two down. One to go.

Paris released the now-lifeless body, heard the *thump* as it landed. Grinned. All the while, Halo continued to whale on him. Crack, crack. Pain in his eye, pain in his lip. Blood cascaded down his chin, stars winked through his vision, and Sex retreated to a hidden corner in his mind. Each new point of contact threw him backward into tables, knocking down glasses, chairs and people.

Finally he managed to dodge one of those fists. He regained his balance and spun low, intending to slash Halo in the back of the knee and hobble him. But the once heavenly being was used to dirty demon tricks and spun as well, darting out of the way just before contact.

An arm's length away from each other now, they straightened and glared. Paris had yet to land a single blow on the man. He wanted to land a blow. *Would* land a blow. Then, when Halo was immobilized, Paris would slice him from navel to neck.

From the corner of his eye, he caught a flash of alabaster, a ripple of molten gold amid the feathers of an angelic warrior, and the snow that had become Zacharel's closest companion.

The man desires his woman as you desire yours. You would punish him for that?

The words drifted through Paris's mind, rays of light scented with hope. To his shock, the darkness thinned and he thought, *No, I don't want to punish a man for going after the woman he craves. Even if I'm the obstacle he faces.*

"I'll probably regret this," Paris said, gripping the invisible blade hilts tighter, just in case, "but I'm willing to let you leave. This is a one-time offer. Leave and live. That's it. No negotiation."

Halo scowled, his chin lifting, dark gaze narrowing. Whatever his name, there was no denying his punk-rocker appeal. His hair had been dyed the same pink as Viola's phone and lashes. Tears of blood were inked at the corners of his eyes. A ring of steel protruded from the center of his lower lip. "I'm not leaving. She's mine, and I will not allow you to have her, to use and discard her when you finish with her."

Everything always came back to that, Paris thought, disgusted with himself and his demon's need for sex. But then, the guy had said the one thing guaranteed to demolish his no-negotiation boast, so they'd try this a different way. "Does Viola want you in return?"

A hiss of fury. "She will."

Same thing Paris had once thought about Sienna. Still did, if he were being honest. He hoped that there was something he could do or say that would change her mind about him and she would come around, want him the way he wanted her.

Did the fallen angel have a chance at success? Did *he?* Females were the most stubborn creatures ever created.

"Just so you know, I don't want Viola." He stepped to the left, again and again until they were circling each other, every second bringing Paris back to the man he used to be: honorable, concerned, valiant. This wouldn't last, he knew, but he ran with it while he could.

"You lie!" Halo's nostrils flared with the force of his inhalation. "I, who never before craved a woman, could not resist her. *Everyone* wants her."

"Again, not me. I'm here for info that will help me save *my* woman. That's it."

A heavy pause as Halo flexed and unflexed his fingers, debating the truth of Paris's claim.

Circle, circle. "Information only," Paris reiterated. "I swear."

"No." He gave an abrupt shake of that pink head, his stubbornness a rival to that of a female. "I do not believe you. You carry the evil nature of a demon. You won't be able to help yourself. You will lust after her, take advantage of her. Bed her."

No, he wouldn't. He was too close to Sienna, and he would wait for her as long as he could and survive. Fine. So maybe the truth was—he might. Survival had caused him to do terrible things. Maybe he should point out that

Viola carried a demon, too. But then, Halo was past the point of thinking logically.

Paris sighed, the darkness rising again. "We finish this, then."

Paris...

"No!" he gritted, blocking Zacharel's voice from his head. "I tried your way. It didn't work."

He and Halo leapt at each other, meeting in the middle. Just as before, those meaty fists hammered at Paris. While the beating felt like stampeding demon hooves on his face, Halo's midsection was left wide-open. But rather than take the kill stabs as Paris had done with the others—some of Zacharel's light must have stuck around after all—he swept his arm low and sliced into Halo's thigh, barely nicking his femoral.

Still the beating continued to rain, the fallen never registering the fact that he was going to bleed out if he didn't leave and stitch himself up. Arms swinging, legs kicking, they fell into a table, toppled to the ground, rolled. Broken glass cut at Paris's arms, his back. He landed several searing blows, accidentally slicing with his blades, until finally he sent Halo stumbling backward, out of range.

Halo stood, gasping for breath as he stepped forward once, twice. Then he stopped and frowned with confusion. At last his knees gave out. He dropped like a stone in the ocean. His once-tanned skin blanched to an unnatural chalk-white, his tattoos dimming. His eyes were suddenly fever-bright.

Fallen angels did not heal like immortals. They healed like humans: slowly. Or not at all.

"You...you..."

"Won." Done, done and done. All three were felled. "Get some help, and you should recover just fine."

"But you…" Incredulity bathed Halo's punk-rocker features. "You won through cheating. That was a blade I felt. Multiple times!"

"Hate to break it to you, big boy, but cheating happens a lot. You might want to try it yourself. Besides, you said you didn't care what weapons I used."

There was muttering behind him.

Paris raised his arms and spun in slow motion. The crowd had yet to disperse, more concerned with collecting bets than escaping notice. "Who's next?" Blood dripped from his still-invisible daggers, pooling on the floor.

Suddenly they all had somewhere else to be. The sea of faces parted, giving him a direct view of Zacharel. The angel had his arms crossed over the wide expanse of his chest. His expression was troubled.

"Still here?" Paris arched a brow in challenge. "You want a piece of me, too?"

Frowning, silent, Zacharel vanished.

Seriously. Why the interest?

Does it matter? Urgency shooting through him, Paris stomped to Viola, who still studied herself in the mirror. He sheathed his weapons and jerked her toward the door. "Come on."

It was definitely time to go. One, he didn't want to risk anyone else deciding to fight him. Two, seeing him talking to her might be more than Halo could handle. And three, she might have changed her mind about telling him what he wanted to know. He'd have to get physical.

Halo watched her with longing in his eyes—and just before the door closed behind Paris, hatred. Yeah. The dude would be back for revenge. *Shoulda killed him.* He still could. But Paris opted not to return to finish the job.

If Zacharel reappeared and kicked up a stink, his game plan would be screwed.

"Hey," Viola said, at last snapping out of her trance. She tugged at his hold. A cool wind blew past them, caressing the silky length of her hair along his arm. "What do you think you're doing?"

I want her, Sex said, peeking from the shadows of his mind.

On a mission here. "I'm getting you to safety," he lied. "You don't want your admirers to swarm you, do you?"

She tugged harder. "Of course I do. Here's a lesson about women. We like to be admired from afar, and then complimented up close."

He seriously did not need lessons. "I meant your admirers weren't paying you the proper homage. They don't deserve your exalted presence."

And wouldn't you know it. Her resistance ended there. "You make an excellent point."

Of course, she'd missed his sarcasm.

He arrived at an abandoned alley and stopped. Perfect. The moon was so close he had only to reach out to trace the soft, orange-yellow edges. Clouds were closer still, enveloping him in a fine, dew-scented mist. Though the area was well-lit, no one passing by would see what transpired within the narrow space.

He rounded on Viola, pressing her against the solid gold bricks of the building, invading her personal space to gain her full attention. Except, her attention had already moved to her phone, her fingers flying over the keyboard.

I want, I want, I want!

I hope you rot and die.

"'Lord of Sex is bloodier than before and...ick... swollen. My eyes are not amused.' Send."

He claimed her phone and, rather than smashing it as instinct demanded, returned it to the inside of her boot. "You can Screech about this later. As for right now, you're going to talk to me. What can I do to see the dead? Remember, your worshippers insisted you tell me."

A pout of those lush lips, but she said, "Burn the body of the soul you wish to see and save the ashes. Speaking of, did I ever tell you about how I once saved the ashes of a—"

On and on she droned about what she'd done, then about herself, her life, and Paris tuned her out, a curtain of hope forming around his mind. He'd already burned Sienna's body and saved the ashes. At the time, he hadn't known why he'd done so; he'd only known he couldn't part with what remained of her. And ever since, he'd secretly carried a small vial of those ashes in his pocket.

Somehow, he must have suspected he would need them.

When Viola at last quieted, he said, "There's more to seeing a soul than saving the ashes." There had to be. A few weeks ago, Sienna had escaped Cronus, had hunted Paris down, yet Paris hadn't seen her.

He never would have known about her arrival if William the Ever Randy, another being who could commune with the dead, had not been with him and casually mentioned the dead girl at his feet. Of course, Cronus had swiftly tracked her down and dragged her back to her prison.

An act the Titan king would pay for.

"Duh, of course there is. Mix the ashes with ambrosia and tattoo the rim of your eyes," Viola said. "You'll see her, I promise. If you want to touch her, tattoo the tips of your fingers. If you want to hear her, tattoo the flesh behind your ears, blah blah blah. I remember a time when I—"

Once again he tuned her out. This he could, *would* do. Tattooing one's self with the ashes of the dead might be disgusting to most people, but Paris would have done a lot worse. "Will I smell her? Taste her?" he asked, interrupting Viola's monologue.

"Only if you tattoo the inside of your nose, lips and top of your tongue. One time, in Tartarus, I—"

"Wait."

Enough! I don't want her, Sex suddenly piped up. *Find someone else.*

Well, well. For once they were in agreement. "Is there anything else I should know? Any consequences I should be aware of—"

"Paris."

The familiar voice came from behind him. Paris whipped around, sickness already churning inside his stomach. Whenever Lucien visited him, bad news was quick on his heels. "What's wrong?"

CHAPTER FOUR

LUCIEN, KEEPER OF DEATH, stood tall and strong, a powerful presence even through the haze of mist that enveloped him. Like Viola, the warrior could flash from one location to another with only a thought. His dark hair was a mop of tangles sticking out in spikes. His eyes— one blue, one brown—were bright with concern. Dirt smudged his scarred cheeks, and there were rips in his wrinkled shirt and pants.

"Since I told you not to come back for me until I texted you, I take it that's not why you're here." Out of habit, Paris palmed his blades. "You better start talking."

Lucien's gaze strayed to Viola. "Get rid of her first."

The "her" in question straightened her spine with a jolt. "Oh, no, he didn't. I'm not some pretty a man can just toss aside whenever—oh, hey. You're Anya's man." The indignation left her, and she waved happily. "Hi! I'm Viola. As if you couldn't guess. My reputation for awesomeness precedes me, and I'm sure Anya has mentioned me countless times."

She knew Anya, the minor goddess of Anarchy? A woman who had more balls than most men—because she'd cut them off the guys stupid enough to get in her way and kept them as souvenirs. Well, of course Viola knew Anya. They might have "minor" in their respective titles, but they were both major pains in the ass.

Lucien's dark brows drew low. "No, she never—"

"Stops talking about you," Paris rushed out, halting his friend before he insulted the egomaniac. He ran his hand along the front of his neck, his fingers taut as a blade, the universal sign for *cut that out or die*.

"Yes," Lucien lied, frowning. "She mentions you all the time."

Viola laughed, a tinkling sound of amusement. "No need to state the obvious, you darling boy. As if I'm not aware of how often I come up in conversation."

"You should probably Screech about seeing Anya's man," Paris said. "Maybe describe him. Post a picture. Whatever."

Expression serious, she said, "Ixnay on the picture. Those are reserved for *my* image, otherwise my fans get twitchy. But the other thing...totally. Description is one of the many areas I shine in, since I shine in everything." She grabbed her phone and typed away. "Hair of indigo and eyes of crystal and chocolate, he stands before me..."

Paris met Lucien's confused stare. "She's the keeper of Narcissism, and she only registers conversations about herself." Clearly. "You can talk freely with me."

Lucien's eyes widened, and he studied Viola anew. "Another keeper? How did you find... Why isn't she...? Never mind. Doesn't matter right now." His focus whipped back to Paris. "I'm here because Kane's missing."

The sickness returned to burn a path up Paris's chest, stopping to play a game of tonsil hockey in his throat. "How long?"

"Just a few days. He and William were together. Someone captured them, took them into hell to execute them. Maybe Hunters, maybe not. Another group attacked the first. William says the cavern they were in collapsed and knocked him out before the men could do anything to him. When he woke up, he was in a motel room in Budapest. Without Kane."

Paris rubbed a hand down his face. "Is Kane still... alive?" He had trouble speaking that last word, much less thinking it. If his friend had been slain while he'd been chasing tail, he would never forgive himself.

"Yeah. He is. He has to be."

Because they couldn't stand the thought of living without him. "You putting together a posse to search for him?"

"That's why I'm here."

"Who do you have so far?"

"Amun, Aeron, Sabin and Gideon."

Nasty fighters, all of them. If Paris were missing, he'd want the same guys looking for him. Seriously, the only team capable of getting better results would be Jason Voorhees, Freddy Krueger, Michael Myers and Hannibal Lecter.

Amun was the keeper of Secrets, and there was no greater warrior to have on your side. The man was like a worm in your brain, able to ferret out in seconds information you'd buried for years. In fact, there was *nothing* anyone could hide from him. So Kane's location? No prob.

Aeron was the former keeper of Wrath. He'd recently been beheaded and given a new body, and that's when his demon had merged with Sienna. But even without his darker half, Aeron liked to make his prey squeal before he moved in for the kill. Anyone who'd hurt Kane would pay. Repeatedly.

Sabin was the keeper of Doubt, a warrior of unparalleled strength and determination, and he had a vicious streak that caused hardened criminals to soil their pants in fear. He got into your head, reminded you of your weaknesses, and basically turned you into a slobbering bag of self-recrimination before he savagely murdered you—with a grin on his face.

And Gideon, well, he was the keeper of Lies. He dyed his hair blue, was tattooed and pierced, and had a warped sense of humor very few others got. His new favorite game involved casting his demon from his body and into his enemy's, then sitting back and watching the human destroy himself as the evil consumed him.

Paris almost felt sorry for whoever had taken Kane.

Almost.

"So, you in?" Lucien asked.

"I—" *Hate this.* He wanted to say yes. He did. He loved his friends. More than he loved himself, even more than Viola probably loved *her*self. (Speaking of, the damn woman was still typing, and from her mutterings, she was telling the world how the Lord of Death found her far more attractive than the goddess of Anarchy.) His friends had fought beside him, bled for him and always had his back.

They'd do more than take a bullet for him. They'd take a life—even their own. But... "I can't," he said, whether he'd be able to forgive himself or not. "Not right now. There's something I have to do first." His resolve, that cloud of darkness, still swirled inside him, driving him. He'd come this far; he couldn't back out now.

Lucien nodded without hesitation. "Understood." There was no trying to change Paris's mind, no making him feel guilty, which meant there was no better friend. "You want help with your mission?" he added, and damn if Paris didn't start to feel guilty anyway. "If you're headed into something dangerous, I'm happy to volunteer William."

William, Anya's best friend and someone Lucien

would love to see stabbed in the back. And heart. And groin. Willy wasn't possessed by a demon, but according to gossip he was the devil's blood-brother, as well as related to the Four Horsemen of the Apocalypse.

Gossip was probably right. Nothing scared William. Nothing bothered him. And the cherry on top? If Willy ever opened a closet door and the boogeyman jumped out, it was only the boogeyman who'd be scared.

"Bring him to me," Paris said. "He owes me." William had let Cronus take Sienna without a fight. As far as Paris was concerned, the guy was now his slave for life.

"Done." Lucien's gaze shifted to Viola, who was *still* typing. "What about her? We can't let her run around on her own. Cronus *and* the Hunters would doubtless love to snatch her."

Cronus hated the Hunters, and the Hunters hated Cronus. Both sides were searching for the remaining demon-possessed immortals, each hoping to recruit more than the other, and neither would shy away from using brute force to get what they wanted. Paris enjoyed the idea of screwing both parties over.

"Take her," he said, placing his hand on Viola's shoulder, meaning to shake her and gain her attention.

The action, innocent though it was, startled her, and between one heartbeat and the next, she went from gorgeously angelic to looking like the demon inside her. Two horns extended from her scalp. Red scales replaced her skin, and her eyes glowed like radioactive rubies. Sharp, deadly fangs protruded over her lips. Her nails grew into claws. The scent of sulfur overpowered the scent of roses, a scarlet mist wafting from her, stinging his nostrils, making *his* demon whimper like a newborn baby.

With a roar of white-hot rage, she sank those claws into Paris's wrist and tossed him so hard he smacked into the building next door, its solid gold bricks cracking and plumping filigree into the air.

Oxygen abandoned his lungs. Stars returned to his line of vision. What. The. *Hell?* When he was able to focus clearly, he saw that Viola was Viola again, exquisite, blonde and innocent.

"Oops. My bad." With a tinkling chuckle, she stuffed her phone into her boot. "Touching the merchandise isn't allowed. Ever. Now, did you need something from me?"

Lucien pinched the bridge of his nose. "This is gonna be fun. I can tell."

"Do you mind going with Lucien?" Paris asked her as he lumbered to his feet. Every new breath scraped his lungs against his ribs. Worse, the wound in his neck had opened. With one toss, she'd done far more damage to his body than the three amigos inside the bar had. "He'll take you to Anya and you two girls can, uh, catch up." He'd thought to force her to go. Now? He'd beg if necessary.

"Seriously?" Viola clapped, twirled and threw herself into Lucien's arms. "Yes, yes, a thousand times yes! I'm going with you, but only if you promise to stop and pick up my pet, Princess Fluffikans, on the way. Small word of warning, though. You're about to fall madly, passionately in love with me, and Anya will be utterly heartbroken."

It was far more likely that one of the other—single—warriors would fall madly, passionately in bed with her, but now wasn't the time to point that out.

Lucien fought off her octopus-like arms, scowled at Paris, and vanished with Viola jabbering about her majorly awesome awesomeness. Paris didn't bother staying where he was. Death could follow the spiritual trail he left behind, easy, and meet him somewhere else.

Time to do a little tattooing.

The mortal and immortal worlds were scarily alike. Titania was a thriving metropolis of shopping centers and restaurants, brimming with entertainment of any and every kind. Didn't take Paris long to gather the necessary tattooing equipment and a spare set of clothes, and settle into one of the motels he'd been amused to discover existed here. Apparently even immortals liked to have secret assignations.

As he waited for Lucien, he ate because it was de rigueur. A sandwich, and he had no idea what was strapped between the bread. He got himself off because that was necessary for his demon. He hadn't had sex today, and the orgasm was like an injection of strength. Strength that wouldn't last, not like the adrenaline rush that accompanied intercourse, but whatever. He'd take what he could get.

He showered, cleaned off the blood and the wealth of other things clinging to his skin. A lot of humans had died under his blade today. Hunters, his enemy. Mostly males. More and more, they were recruiting females. Paris wondered what would have happened if he'd met Sienna on the battlefield, or if he'd ever attempted to interrogate her.

If she'd lived long enough, that's what he had planned to do to her. *After* he'd bedded her again. Would he have hurt her? He liked to think no, but…damn. He couldn't be sure. She'd known things she shouldn't. Where he was, why he was there. How to distract him, what to use to drug him, an immortal unaffected by human toxins. Now he knew she'd gotten her info from Rhea, Cronus's wife and the true leader of the Hunters. Not directly, he didn't think, but filtered down through the ranks. But even if he hadn't known, he wouldn't have concerned himself with questioning her this time around. He just wanted her.

Safe, right? You just want her safe? A sneer from Sex.

Whatever. Paris toweled off and looked himself over in the steam-fogged mirror. He'd lost a little weight, had bruises under his eyes, a few scratches on his cheeks and neck. His hair wasn't exactly even. He'd trimmed the strands himself, just kind of chopping anytime a piece fell into his eyes. What would Sienna think of him now? Despite everything, she'd been attracted to him before. Would she still be attracted to him? Right now, he might be a little too feral for *any* woman. Very mountain-man meets post-traumatic stress survivor.

But what if the impossible happened and she did, in fact, want him again? For real, with no hidden agenda. What if she simply craved his body inside of hers? After all, she'd fought her way free of Cronus's prison and come looking for him.

Lowering his guard would be stupid. He couldn't trust her. Not really. He could take her, yeah, that was still on the menu. If he could still get hard for her while he was around her. Only time would tell. And if he could—and he thought he could, considering he was hard merely from thinking about her—maybe he could even stay with her a few days. If so, would his hunger for her finally wane? Or would it continue to intensify? Would he be able to let her go when the time came?

What if she *wanted* to stay with him?

He yearned for that. So damn badly he yearned for that. But like Zacharel had said, Paris would ruin her if he kept her. Not for the reasons the angel had given, but because if he and Sienna were ever separated and he couldn't get to her, he would cheat on her. He would have to. His other choice would be death, and on the scales of life-versus-death, cheating—surviving—won every time.

He knew that firsthand, had once tried to sustain a relationship with a woman. Susan. He'd had her, knew he couldn't have her again, but had craved something more and had pleased her in other ways. He'd genuinely liked her, had enjoyed her company—but had ultimately cheated on her, hurting her worse than anyone else ever had.

And here was another slap of truth: if he cheated on Sienna, he would destroy everything they had managed to build, as well as her heart, her sense of trust and any hint of innocence. He would be worthy of every dark deed she then committed against him—yet still he wanted her.

The situation was *so* messed up.

Scowling, he slammed his fist into the mirror. Jagged pieces of glass fell, shattering further when they hit the floor, surrounding his discarded weapons and glistening like diamonds in a sea of destruction. Blood dripped from his knuckles as he palmed and sheathed the blades at his wrists and ankles and holstered the guns under his arms. At this rate, he'd soon be carving himself up like Reyes, the keeper of Pain. Anything for release, for a moment when he didn't have to wonder or worry about anything but his injuries.

Whatever. He'd gotten used to wondering and worrying. They were his constant companions now, and without them, he'd be utterly alone. Paris dressed in the new clothes he'd bought, a black shirt and black pants. Where he was going, night reigned no matter the time of day. He needed to blend.

Not long ago, he'd snuck into Cronus's secret harem

and seduced one of the concubines, trading sex for information. Paris now knew Sienna was being held in the Realm of Blood and Shadows, part of Titania but...not. The realm was a kingdom within this heavenly kingdom, invisible to most and protected by evil. To enter was to die, blah, blah, blah.

Paris could find the realm on his own, no problem. He'd gotten very good at bribing his way through the heavens, even the hidden areas. Finger-combing his wet hair, he padded to the desk in the living-room-slash-bedroom. He sat down and spread out his new tattoo equipment. Part of him wished he was out there, killing Hunters or already making his way into the Realm of Blood and Shadows. These delays sucked.

To his immense relief, Lucien found him a short while later, appearing in the center of the room. "I felt bad for stiffing you with Willy, so I brought you a prize."

Death shoved the drenched, protesting William in Paris's direction, then motioned to Zacharel, who stood at his other side. The "prize," as though he was something out of a Cracker Jack box.

"Actually," Zacharel said in that cold voice of his. "I brought myself. Lucien was hunting you, and I saved him the time and trouble."

Paris popped his jaw. "Thanks tons," he said to Lucien, ignoring the angel. "Mean that."

William, my sweet William! I want him, Sex said, practically spraying drool through Paris's mind. Sex *always* wanted a piece of the guy. Not that Paris had ever admitted that aloud. Not that he ever would.

"So sad I can't remain," Lucien said with mock pity. "By the way, Viola's pet, Princess Fluffycakes or whatever, is a Tasmanian devil *and* a vampire. You're lucky

I'm leaving without slitting your throat." Once again, the warrior vanished.

As tiny snowflakes swirled around him, Zacharel eyed the room with distaste. "What are you doing here?"

"Seriously man, it's a dump," William added. "When I'm in the heavens, I only ever stay at the West Godlywood. Can we at least request a suite?"

No, they wouldn't be playing either man's version of the Q-and-A game. They would be playing Paris's. "Why is it always snowing around you lately?" he demanded of Zach.

"There is a reason."

So not helpful on any level. "Will you share it?"

"No."

"Are you following me?"

"Yes."

At least he didn't try to deny it. Not that he could have. Angels spoke the truth, and only ever the truth, which made Zacharel's earlier threat to kill him all the more real. "Why?"

"You are not yet ready to hear the answer."

Paris loved that kind of cryptic crap, he really did. "If you're going to stick around, make yourself useful and tattoo the rest of me." For the lines around his eyes, he needed a steady hand. "Then you can help me kick ass and not bother with names."

Zacharel leveled him with a frown as fierce as the flurry of snowflakes storming from the ends of his wings. "I have never tattooed anyone before. I'm likely to mar you."

And yet, he would still do a better job than William, no question. "The worst you can do is poke out my eyes, but that's hardly a concern since they'll grow back. Eventually."

That frown deepened, minutes ticking by. "Very well. I will do this for you."

"Yes, you make yourself useful, angel boy. Meanwhile, I'll be in the bathroom." William's jet-black hair was dripping wet and plastered to his face. There was a fluffy white towel wrapped around his waist, displaying muscles that rivaled Paris's own, and a tattooed treasure map that led to his man junk. Looking at him, you could see the makings of a temper so savage anyone who miraculously survived an encounter with him would end up needing therapy. And diapers. "I've *got* to finish deep conditioning my hair."

Or maybe *not* so savage.

No matter. Paris had never been closer to finding and saving Sienna. With these two warriors at his side, he'd succeed. Guaranteed.

CHAPTER FIVE

Sienna Blackstone, newly crowned Queen of the Beasts, Princess of Blood and Shadows, and Duchess of Horror, stood with her back pressed into the crumbling stone wall of the castle she unwillingly called home. Her wings were heavy, constantly pulling at recently formed tendons and bones, making her ache, cringe and, humiliatingly enough, sometimes cry.

The wings arched over her shoulders and draped down her sides in a cascade of midnight, their spiky tips now reaching the floor. She remembered seeing these very wings on Aeron, the previous host for the demon of Wrath. On his muscled, grimly tattooed body, they had appeared soft, gossamer, as weightless and beautiful as storm clouds. On her slight frame, they overpowered and overwhelmed and she had trouble finding her balance.

Sadly, that wasn't the worst of her problems. Cronus, god of gods (according to him) and all around asshat (according to her), paced in front of her, ranting and raving. Saying he was "upset" would be the equivalent of saying the Atlantic was a rain puddle.

When she'd first met him, he'd looked like a codger of an old man, complete with gray hair, wrinkled skin and stooped shoulders. Now he was *GQ* flawless and barbarian tough. Dark chestnut hair hung to strong, wide shoulders. Skin of the smoothest texture was tanned to the perfect shade of bronze. He'd also ditched his prissy toga in favor of a black mesh shirt and black leather pants.

The change was gargantuan—and creepy. She wanted to ask why he'd gone this route, then offer to punish his stylist free of charge. Did she dare? Heck, no. The ranting and raving would morph into a straight-up savage beating. At least, that's the impression he gave.

"I saved you," he snapped, death in his timbre as he stomped one foot in front of the other, back and forth, back and forth. "I strengthened you. Gifted you with your demon. And how do you repay me? By constantly refusing to obey me. It's unconscionable!"

Gifted? *Really?* If the new definition of *gifted* was *cursed forever and ever with misery and pain,* then yeah, he had. "I obeyed you," she reminded him. *At first.*

"At first," he said, parroting her thoughts. *His* was an accusation that lashed like the sharpest of whips. "And only because you were compelled. You've since learned to block me."

True. And that she had was a testament to the iron-hard rigidity of her stubborn core. With only a thought, this huffing, puffing being could render unending pain. With a wave of his hand, he could vaporize entire cities. Something she would do well to remember.

Sienna chose her next words carefully. "To be fair, you tricked me." Okay, so maybe she hadn't chosen carefully. At least her tone had been as flat and unaccusatory as possible.

A narrowed flick of his gaze nearly buckled her knees. "How so?"

She pressed more of her weight into the wall. "You promised I would see my younger sister."

You look so pretty, Enna.

Really?

Really. You're the prettiest girl in the whole wide world!

Skye, her only sibling, a little girl she'd adored with her whole heart, had been abducted years ago, never to be seen or heard from again. Sienna missed her terribly, prayed she was healthy, whole and that she hadn't suffered incomparable cruelties.

"Yet you merely teased me with a glimpse of her," she added, rubbing her stomach as she always did when she thought of her sister, reminded of yet *another* girl, someone else she'd loved and lost, the— She cut that thought off before it could form. *I won't break down in front of this creature.*

Cronus ground his molars. "That glimpse... I should have known it would come back to haunt me." He paused, a low growl bubbling from his throat. "I guess I should at last admit the truth, then. I showed you an illusion of your sister, nothing more."

Wait, wait, wait. An *illusion?* Sienna bit her tongue. Why would he... How could he...? No matter the question, the answer was simple. To play her like a piano, as Paris had once said to her *about* her. *Bastard* wasn't a vile enough word for this beast.

Steady, calm. "Is she even alive?" Sienna gritted out.

"Of course."

There was no *of course* with Cronus. He lived by his own set of rules, and he didn't always abide by those.

Every time he appeared before her, her demon showed her the despicable things he'd done throughout his life. The lives he'd taken, striking down not just his enemies, but his own people, humans, *anyone* who dared defy him. And he'd stolen, oh, had he stolen. Ancient artifacts, powers that belonged to others, women. He had no shame. No limits.

"How do I know you're telling the truth now?"

"You won't. Your demon will."

A suspended moment as she searched inside herself. Wrath was calm, not worked into a frenzied need to punish him for lying. That glimpse of Skye had indeed been an illusion, but Cronus did believe she was still alive. Sienna gritted her teeth, saying, "Bring her to me, the *real* Skye, and let me keep her, *then* I'll do anything you ask."

"No."

"Why?" She stamped her foot. It was childish, sure, but she had no other way to express her displeasure with this man. "Do you, a supposedly all-knowing being, not know where she is?"

In a blink, he was a mere whisper away, scowling down at her, his breath fanning over her. "Enough about your sister! Aren't you curious why I gifted you with Wrath? You, a fragile, dearly departed female who had upset one of my strongest warriors? Aren't you curious about my desire for your willing participation in my war?"

Do not suggest the king of the Titans needs a breath mint. She gulped. *And don't you dare think about the warrior you upset. Don't you dare think about Paris.* Oh, no, no, no. "Y-yes." And now she was stuttering? *Grow some lady balls, Blackstone!*

Red flashed in Cronus's eyes. Demon-red. A fiendish crimson that made her think of blood mixed with nuclear toxins. Not only was he the king of the Titans, but he was also possessed by Greed—and right now, his demon was at the wheel, driving his actions, his words. Around her, the castle shook, his anger rattling its very foundation.

"You know the Hunters. You know how they operate. You were once a part of their cause."

"I know." As if she could ever forget or absolve herself. Once she'd even borne the symbol of infinity on her wrist, their mark. A permanent reminder of their "goals." In this spirit form, she had no tattoos but the butterfly around her wings, and for that, she was immensely grateful. "The same is true for thousands of others."

Except those thousands of others actually had no idea they were fools, or that they were expendable, nothing more than puppets on strings. Like she had been—until she'd gotten a bitch slap of truth and clipped those strings with brutal proficiency.

Soon after Wrath's possession of her, Cronus had whisked her to a Hunter compound. Because Cronus could shield himself from prying eyes and humans could not see her, no one had noticed them. Just as she'd seen the king's sins play through her mind, she'd seen the transgressions of the Hunters. Thefts, rapes, murders, all in the name of "good." That she had once been a (supposedly vital) part of their cause, that she had once aided them...

Punish them... Steal, rape, murder...

There he was. Wrath. Her dark companion. Even remembering what he'd seen, and being worlds apart from those responsible, he urged her to seek vengeance against the Hunters. To show no mercy, no forgiveness for even the innocent among them, for all the harm they had caused, to hurt them far worse than they had hurt others.

Punish...

Cringing, she covered her ears with her hands. "Shut up, shut up, shut up," she chanted. Sometimes she could resist him; sometimes she could not. That's when he would overtake her, and her world would go black. For a little while, at least.

Though she was cursed to remain inside this deteriorating monstrosity of a castle, somehow Wrath was not. When he was in control of her mind, they could leave. He would use her body to castigate others however he wished.

Days later, she would wake up with blood on her hands, coating her skin. Of course, memories of what the demon had done would then deluge her. Sadistic, stomach-curdling things. And yet, nothing—*nothing!*—he had forced her to do was more disgusting than what the Hunters were doing to innocent humans.

Humans. How odd her new vernacular was to her. Once *she'd* been a human. Such a foolish human. *How could I ever have thought the goal of the Hunters was the* elimination *of evil?*

Well, okay, that was easy. As a teenager, she'd seen a vile demon in action—or what she'd thought was a demon—and the experience had freaked her out, convinced her that such evil was the reason her sister had been taken. Combine that with the shock of learning that humans were not alone, that there was an entire world of creatures at work around them...

The whole other-world thing had proven to be true, at least. But the rest, the demon she'd seen? While they did in fact exist, she hadn't encountered one that night. Her Hunter boyfriend had drugged her—his preferred method of recruiting—created the perfect atmosphere to elicit fear, and her hallucinating brain had filled in the rest. Afterward, he'd fed her fear with stories of the evil they could fight and the good they could do, saying she might even be able to find and save her sister.

What he'd failed to tell her: humans made their own decisions, influenced by demons or not. They decided to embrace the dark or run into the light.

Not all Hunters cloaked their malevolence with righteous determination; she knew that, she did. Some were genuinely sincere in their desire to rid the world of evil, and wouldn't create their own to do so. But the fact that she had once willingly contributed to such a warped cause, well, she would never get over that fact. Worse, *she* had hurt Paris, a warrior who would give his life to protect the ones he loved.

There was no stopping the next flood of thoughts, each revolving around the man she had once harmed beyond repair. She had struck at Paris when he was at his weakest. Worse, she would have aided in his cold-blooded murder if he hadn't escaped with her.

During that escape, she was shot down and she'd even blamed him for that, thinking he had used her body to shield his own. Oh, how she had despised him. Now, she despised only herself.

No, that wasn't exactly true. She also hated the Hunters and everything they represented.

Cronus wanted her to punish them. Her demon wanted to punish them. *She* wanted to punish them. But Cronus refused to simply unleash her. Instead he demanded she return to their midst and spy on Galen, the leader's right-hand man, as well as the keeper of Hope. Yep, a demon was second-in-command of the demon slayers, and none of them knew it. They thought he was an angel.

"As devoted as you were to the Hunter cause in life, Galen will believe you wish to rejoin him in your death," Cronus said, as though reading her thoughts. Maybe he had. "He will welcome you with open arms."

"He won't be able to see me."

"He will. Leave that to me."

"He won't wonder why I'm demon-possessed? *How* I'm demon-possessed?"

"He knows. My wife, *his* leader, told him. But he is overly confident of his appeal and his strength, and he will think *he* is watching *you*."

"In that case, he'll never tell me anything."

"No, he'll feed you false information, and the truth can be garnered from that."

"What if he asks me to prove my loyalty to him?"

"He will."

And she would be forced to comply to continue her ruse. Would he ask her to hurt the warriors she now wished to aid? To hurt innocent humans? Well, the answer to both was the same. Never!

Look at me. Once a human who didn't know about the supernatural, then a Hunter in the midst of it all, hating the demons I chased, and now I'm one of those demons— and hoping to aid the others. "Sorry, but I'm gonna have to stick with my first answer."

Another flash of red streaked through Cronus's eyes, brighter than before. If she was intelligent, she would view that red as a stoplight for her resistance.

Why start acting like a smartie now? "That's a big-time no, in case you forgot," she said more firmly.

"Your human superior ordered you to sleep with Paris," he growled, "and you did. Do not try and act self-righteous with me."

Yes, but her attraction to Paris had been immediate and overwhelming. She had yearned for him.

Yearned for him, even though she believed his demon was responsible for infidelity, the breakup of marriages, teen pregnancies, rapes and the rampant spread of STDs. Even though Paris had been, and would always be, at the head of a never-ending parade of lovers. A fact driven home by a coworker who had watched him for days, snapping pictures of all the women he bedded, then showing those pictures to Sienna after she'd brought him in. And yet she'd still had to fight a wave of jealousy, an emotion she never should have felt in the line of duty.

Had she mentioned her mental incompetence?

"If he asks you to kill for him, seduce him into bed instead," Cronus said. "That will save you from having to do something unpleasant."

They certainly had different definitions for *unpleasant!* "You'd be better served demanding I bring you Galen's head in a magical box of starlight while riding on the back of a Pegasus through a rainbow, because he won't want me sexually. I've never been the type to attract a man's attention."

She knew what she looked like. Hazel eyes too big for her face—ordinary. Lips also too big for her face—unappealing. Freckled skin—unfashionable. And wavy brown hair that was neither silky-straight nor perkily curly—ordinary, unappealing *and* unfashionable.

Cronus remained undeterred. "You're right. You haven't."

The truth can't hurt you, she told herself—while hurting.

"But then," he went on, "your looks will not matter. Galen will be attracted to your demonic power. He'll want to control you, to feed you all that false information, to use you. Yes, the more I think on this, the more I like it. You will sleep with him."

She ran her tongue over her teeth. "Killing Galen will destroy the heart and soul of the Hunters far more effectively than pleasuring him."

"Yes, but dying is not his fate."

"What's his fate, then? What is it, exactly, you think he can do for you?"

Silence.

Deep breath in…out… "Okay, there are two problems with your plan. Galen's a douche bag, and I suck in bed." Wait. That hadn't come out right. "I mean, even if he only wants me for my demonic power—" just saying the words grated "—or because he thinks he can feed me false info, or control me or whatever other reason you think up, he'll never come back for seconds because we'll both be embarrassed by our performances, and the entire plan will be moot."

The only reason she'd garnered Paris's interest was because he'd been desperate to get laid—by anyone!—in order to survive. "Galen is more likely to laugh at me than tell me his secrets."

Perfectly trimmed brows arched, fixing the king's features in a patronizing expression. "You can be trained."

"So can dogs, but they'll only bite you." She would do far worse.

A beat of silence as he absorbed her taunt. "Woman, you frustrate me! I'm not asking you to willingly submit to torture. I'm merely asking you to allow a man to have you in the name of duty—as you have allowed before."

"That's too big a commitment for me. I kill him, or I do nothing to him."

"Galen is an immortal warrior who has spent thousands of years on a battlefield. How do you propose you kill him, hmm?"

"Just leave that to me," she said, mimicking his earlier words. "And, hey, here's another idea. Why can't *you* kill him? I thought you were all-powerful."

"Enough!" With a scowl as dark as a moonless night, Cronus slammed his fists on either side of her temples, creating holes in the wall and causing bricks to fall and dust to plume in the air.

Rattle…rattle…

Great. The entire castle was shaking again.

"How dare you, a slave, question me? I am your master, your owner. The arbiter of your fate. I answer to no one."

Except to your wife. With the royal sovereigns, hurting one always hurt the other, pain slithering across the bond between them. But Sienna wasn't going to remind him of that little gem. "I don't care who you are. I will not align myself with Galen."

Before she could so much as blink, Cronus fit his hands around her neck and squeezed until she could no longer breathe, until her lungs burned and her throat felt scaled by acid. *Rattle, rattle,* went the walls, as if the entire structure might collapse from within. "I can be the executioner of your soul, and you will cease to exist in every way, or I can be your savior, granting you a measure of peace at long last." Tighter…tighter…then, abruptly, the pressure eased. "Remember that, for you are the one who will decide your ultimate fate."

She barely curbed the urge to feed him both of her knuckles. "Whatever I decide," she snapped, uncaring of the consequences, "you're still an asshole."

Surprising her, he gave a grin full of teeth. "Aren't I, though?"

At one time, Sienna had been mild mannered, afraid of hurting anyone's feelings, desperate to smooth any and all ruffled feathers. Maybe the demon's bad mood had bled into her. Or maybe the waspishness came courtesy of knowing just how worthless her entire life had been. Either way, she had never had more to lose—or cared so little.

"You should have picked someone else to host Wrath. Because…wait for it…*my answer is still no.*"

Rather than adding fuel to the seething cauldron of his

temper, her words seemed to make him back down. His features softened, the murderous rage draining from his gaze, his taut lips sliding back over his teeth. He lowered his arms.

Shocking.

"No," he said, gentle, so gentle now. "There was no better choice than you."

Her heart drummed fitfully in her chest. Though she was dead, her spirit self had developed a heartbeat, a need to breathe, the moment the demon had entered her soul-body. Unfortunately, this meant she could feel pain and if cut she would bleed.

"Why me?" she finally asked. "You have to tell me *something.*"

"Do I?" He turned, offering his profile and ignoring her question. "In this realm hidden from the rest of the heavens, where no one will ever find you, I don't *have to* do anything."

A muscle drummed rapidly in his jaw, and before she could reply he added, "Do you enjoy living here, Sienna?"

"No." Not because she was magically compelled to remain inside this castle, but because he'd done what he could to make her time here a misery. Including digging deep inside her mind and yanking out the worst of her memories. Those memories played out like movies in every room, a never-ending stream of persecution, guilt and shame.

Every day she relived Skye's abduction. How she'd failed to save her sister from the man dragging her away. Every day she witnessed the loss of the baby she'd been unable to bring to term, something she *hated* remembering, would never willingly dwell on. Every day she saw her foolish betrayal of the beautiful Paris. How she'd hurt the first man to ever make her crave *more*. How she'd condemned him simply because of his race.

"That's too bad. Because you will remain here until you agree to return to your flock and become my spy."

Back in the air went her nose. "If those are my choices, I'll stay here forever."

Cronus tossed her another grin, a cruel twist of his lips that lacked any hint of amusement. "Is that so? What if I told you that I picked you *because* of your sister?"

"I would demand to know why." Her eyes narrowed to tiny slits, the king of Titans in their crosshairs. He was tricky, without morals and utterly devious. She had to be careful. "I would also point out that you could have played that particular card sooner."

"Not if I feared you would obsess over her and forget my purpose. Now, however, you have left me no choice."

She feigned nonchalance and buffed her nails.

He hissed at her. "What if your precious Skye once lived with Galen? What if she bore him a child?"

Take me swimming, Enna. Please, please, please. I'll never ask for anything ever again.

"I don't believe you." The denial gasped from her, a croak of dismay. *He's lying. He has to be lying.* "Show her to me." She forced herself to add, "Please," though the word was gritted.

He wasn't done. "What if Galen is the only one who knows where they are? What if he tortures them? What if becoming his whore is the only way for you to learn the truth? The only way to save them?"

"I—I—" Had no answer. *He's lying!* The scream of desperation echoed through her mind—her own, not her demon's. She had to stay strong. Had to insist he present at least a modicum of proof before she reacted.

"Think about all I have told you, my darling Sienna. I

will return soon and we will discuss any new duties you might wish to take on." With that, he disappeared, there one moment, gone the next.

Sienna sank to her knees, her strength leaving with the king. Her eyes burned, her chin trembled. Her wings pulled and folded in ways they shouldn't, and a sharp cry escaped her. *Every* damned *day* was a new lesson in horror for her.

Tears trickled down her cheeks, scalding her skin. How much more could she take? How much longer until she broke?

For Skye, she'd do just about anything, and Cronus knew that. Skye was all she had left, having somehow become both sister and daughter in her mind. Made sense, though. She'd only known her sister as a little girl, and the baby she'd lost, a girl as well, had never gotten the chance to grow out of infancy. And the possibility of a niece or nephew? Yeah, she'd do anything.

Cronus knew that. No wonder he'd reined in his temper. He didn't have to hurt her physically to get what he wanted. No wonder he'd chosen Sienna for his games. She was still a puppet, the strings she thought she'd cut anchored to another master's hand.

Worse, there was no way to fight this one.

CHAPTER SIX

PARIS SPRAWLED IN an unfamiliar bed, one hand at his side and gripping a crystal blade, the other draped over his forehead, shielding his eyes. After a few days of traveling, closer than ever to his goal, he was in another motel in Titania, with Zacharel...somewhere, and William snoozing peacefully on the bed beside his.

In quiet moments like this, Paris's mind always hopped the Memory Train, taking him back to when he'd first met Sienna, and tonight was no different. He remembered walking the streets of Rome, in desperate need of a lover, every woman he encountered shooing him away as if he were repugnant. Then someone had rammed into him from behind, and weak as he'd been from the lack of sex, he'd nearly fallen flat on his face before he'd managed to right himself.

"I'm so sorry," he'd heard her say, the sensual rasp of her voice thrilling him on every level.

He turned slowly, afraid that if he moved too quickly he would frighten her and she would run away like the others. Papers were scattered around her feet, and she crouched, trying to gather them. First thing to register was dark hair curtaining a face hidden by shadows.

"That'll teach me to read and walk at the same time," she muttered.

"I'm glad you were reading," he said, bending down

to help her. "I'm glad we ran into each other." More than she would ever know.

Her heavily lashed lids lifted, and her gaze met his. She gasped. He reeled. She was on the plain side, with eyes and lips too big for her face and skin dotted with uncountable freckles, but she possessed a grace and presence so few mortals could ever hope to attain.

"Your name doesn't start with an A, does it?" he asked her, suddenly suspicious of fate and master plans. Maddox had recently become a sap for a woman named Ashlyn. Lucien had abandoned his manhood for Anya. Paris refused to do the same for anyone.

Her brow puckered in confusion, and she shook her head, that fall of dark hair waving around her delicate shoulders. "No. My name is Sienna. Not that you care and not that you really asked. Sorry. I didn't mean to just blurt it out."

"I care," he replied huskily, thinking he would have the best time stripping her. One, her clothes bagged on her, hiding the secrets of her femininity. Two, she was skittish, her babbling charming, and he expected a similar reaction in bed. "You're...American?"

"Yes. Vacationing here to work on my manuscript. Again, not that you asked. I can't place your accent, though."

"Hungarian," he said, giving her the simplest answer. The Lords had been living in Budapest for a while, and there was no way to explain—without sounding crazy—that he spoke languages she'd never even heard of. "So you are a writer?"

"Yes. Well, I hope to be. Wait, that's not right, either. I *am* a writer, but I'm not published yet."

Now, of course, he knew the truth. She wasn't a writer.

The pages of her romance novel had merely served as a launch pad for their sensual conversation, nothing more.

When she'd next asked him to grab a coffee with her, he'd said yes, already throbbing with need for her. They'd talked and laughed the entire time, and he'd enjoyed every moment of it. He'd relaxed with her, something he hadn't been able to do with very many others. But she had a contagious smile, a keen wit, and that grace of motion that matched her demeanor.

Meanwhile, his demon shot out wafts of his pheromones, so there'd been no great difficulty in convincing her to rent a hotel room with him. Or so he'd thought at the time. Along the way, she had pretended to change her mind. Or hell, maybe she *had* changed her mind. Maybe she'd fallen in like with him, too, and had decided not to hand him over to her Hunter brethren. But sex fiend that Paris was, he'd pressed her for more, dragging her into an abandoned alley and kissing the breath out of her.

That's when she drugged him, using a needle hidden in one of her rings. He'd woken up strapped to a gurney, naked and groggy. She had crouched in front of him, and he'd assumed the Hunters had taken her prisoner, too. Until she'd said four little words that changed the nature of their relationship.

"*I* locked you up."

His brilliant reply? "Why would you do something like that?" He still hadn't wanted to believe this woman he so craved had something to do with his current circumstances.

"Can't you guess?" she asked. She angled his head to the side, and, studying his neck, traced a fingertip over a sore spot. Puncture wound, he'd realized, the answer to her question slipping into place, taking root.

"You're my enemy."

"Yes." Then she'd added with a frown, "The wound isn't healing. I didn't mean to jab you with the needle quite so forcefully. For that, I'm sorry."

His eyes narrowed on her, feelings of betrayal and disbelief whisking through him. "You tricked me. Played me like a piano."

Again, "Yes."

"Why? And don't tell me you're Bait. You're not pretty enough." He'd said it to be cruel, but now, remembering, he cringed. No wonder she had later done what she'd done, said what she'd said.

A blush stained her cheeks. "No, I'm not Bait. Or rather, I wouldn't have been to any warrior but you. But then, you don't care who you screw, do you, Promiscuity?" Every word had dripped with disgust, his charming, babbling romance writer long gone. But the grace... oh, that she couldn't banish.

"Obviously not." When her blush deepened, he added silkily, just to taunt her further, "Aren't you afraid I'll hurt you?"

"No. You haven't the strength. I made sure of that."

Her newfound resistance to him, no matter how poorly he acted, irked. Females adored him, always. Well, almost always. "You enjoyed yourself while you were in my arms. Admit it. I know women, and I know passion. You were on fire for me."

"Shut up," she snapped.

Good. He was getting to her. "Want to give me a go before your friends show up?"

After that particular jab, she had stomped away from him, but she hadn't left the room. Remaining a safe distance away, she admitted her status—Hunter—and detailed exactly what her friends planned to do to him.

"We're going to experiment on you. Observe you. Use

you as Bait to capture more demons. And then, when we find Pandora's box, we're going to draw out your demon, killing you and trapping the monster inside."

Warrior that he was, and as many battles as he'd fought, he'd known to show her only indifference. "That it?"

"For now."

"You might as well kill me then, sweetheart. My friends won't surrender themselves to save little old me."

"We'll see about that, won't we?"

When he realized antagonizing her wasn't helping his cause, he switched to seduction, his default setting. He projected sexual images into her head, something he hated to do. *Didn't* do anymore. He couldn't live with himself afterward. And as she had pictured what he wanted her to picture—the two of them together, naked and straining toward climax—her breathing became choppy, her nipples hard underneath her shirt. A white shirt that did nothing to hide the lace of her bra, proving she had a secret sensual side.

He'd almost had her, but in the end, she'd wised up. He'd made the mistake of continuing to call her sweetheart, an endearment he'd used on countless others, and she'd known it. After that, it hadn't taken her long to figure out he used the term because he couldn't remember her name—or anyone else's.

Finally she'd left him for real, only returning a few days later when he was a few breaths away from death. That's when she at last stripped for him, at last pleasured him.

That's when he killed her.

CHAPTER SEVEN

THE NEXT MORNING, Paris stood at the highest edge of a cliff overlooking the Realm of Blood and Shadows, his body poised for war. Finally, he'd found his destination, hidden in a far corner of Titania, its portal invisible to everyone but William. What do you know? The guy had his uses.

Now Paris would find Sienna.

His blood boiled with the fury he'd suppressed for far too long. His muscles burned with startling ferocity, and his bones vibrated with the need to act, to hurt someone. Multiple someones.

Soon.

Sharp gusts of wind blustered, doing nothing to scatter the shroud of thick, black mist surrounding him, seeping inside of him. The scent of aged copper filled the air, leaving a moist film in his nose. Muted shrieks echoed from every direction, so many shrieks of pain. Above, the moon formed a sallow hook, its ends frayed, hemorrhaging into an endless expanse of unforgiving night. Below, an ocean of crimson tears frothed and hissed, creating a second symphony of anguish.

And there, in the center of it all, perched a nightmare of a castle. Dark stone crumbled. Withered ivy with dagger-sharp tips climbed the walls, every leaf reminding him of a spider. The roof knifed into several points, a body staked through the heart and hanging from each, dripping blood onto the glass panes of every window. There were several balconies guarded by multiple gargoyles of every size.

Gargoyles that would, apparently, come to life.

Writhing shadows, slick and oily in appearance, hovered around the entire structure, but they didn't touch a single stone. They maintained a generous distance, as if a rod of iron held them in place. The moment they heard the starting bell, whatever that was, Paris suspected they would burst free and attack whoever happened to be nearby.

"She's inside," he told his companions. "I know it." He wanted to go in, guns blazing. Was desperate to go in, guns blazing and knives slashing, but he couldn't. Not yet, not yet. Information had to come first.

Death was in the details.

"That's great, wonderful, but why am I here again?" William asked, scratching his head. He consumed the space at Paris's left, dressed for the runway rather than the front lines. Silk suit, no weapons. A bottle of conditioner in his pocket. Yeah. Conditioner. Again. For split ends. A little jaunt into hell had "damaged some of the precious strands," so he now carried his "necessary daily treatment" *everywhere.*

Annnd hearing his voice caused Sex to purr like a kitten. It was disgusting.

"I'm still recovering from agonizing physical and mental trauma," William added. The warrior had barely escaped from his encounter in hell, true, but being crushed by boulders and clawed by flesh-hungry fiends was hardly agonizing.

"Just, I don't know, consider this your punishment for abandoning Kane," Paris said. How many gargoyles would he have to battle? He did a quick head count. Fifty-nine from the front. Probably a similar number waited in back. Half of them were as big as dragons, but some were as small as rats.

As William could probably tell him, size didn't always matter. Which of the creatures would cause the most damage?

"I didn't abandon him. Per se." William brushed a piece of lint from his shoulder. "I was pummeled by falling rock and woke up in a motel in Budapest. In my compromised mental state, I thought some demon damsel in heat had taken one look at my amazing body and rescued us, but then Kane thought to remove her from my rugged animal appeal, and so he dragged her out to get coffee, not yet realizing he was simply energizing her for the mattress marathon to come. A marathon with me, in case I wasn't clear on that point."

Paris didn't bother rolling his eyes. Clearly William was Viola's male counterpart. Wasn't that a nice little bouquet of roses?

"Actually, you're here because you owe Paris a favor." Zacharel flanked Paris's other side, the snowstorm now brewing above him. The change had happened the moment he'd stepped into this realm. He still wore his robe, but blades were now strapped all over his muscled body. He was definitely warrior-appropriate. "More than that, you are avoiding your girlfriend."

William gasped with outrage. "First, I don't owe *anyone* a favor. Second, I don't have a girlfriend, you pansy-ass winged piece of shit."

"Don't you?" A blink, all innocence. Zacharel didn't seem to care about the name-calling. "What is young Gilly to you, then?"

Gilly. A human with a crush on William. The warrior claimed they were just friends and nothing more, but if anyone could see secret longing in someone's gaze, it was Paris. And William definitely had a lot of secret longing going on for that girl. Shockingly, though, he hadn't done anything about it. Had only coddled and babied her, which was why Paris hadn't gutted him. Gilly had been through enough in her short life without William turning his lethal charm on her.

Dangerous as a lightning strike, as lethal as a pair of crisscrossing short swords, William whispered, "You're about to find out how your liver tastes, my friend."

"I have tasted it already," Zacharel said, his voice its usual monotone. The snowflakes began to fall in earnest, tiny at first, but growing in diameter. An arctic wind blustered around him. "It was a bit salty."

How the hell was a guy supposed to respond to *that?*

Apparently William didn't know, either, because he gaped at the angel. Then, "Maybe if you added a little pepper?"

O-kay. It was official. William had an answer for everything.

"Enough," Paris said. Just then, he had his inner darkness on a leash. That could change at any moment. This was the closest he'd ever come to saving Sienna. To seeing her again, to touching her, and urgency had him in a vise grip. Which was stupid. He knew it was stupid.

He didn't know her, not really, had only interacted with her those two times, and yet, looking back, he was certain he'd never felt so connected to anyone in his life. He could still remember the delicate rasp of her voice. Soft and lyrical, washing over him, entrancing him. Could still smell her sweet wildflower scent. Could still feel her soft body pressed against his harder one.

Now he wondered if he would even like her on any level but a sexual one. Would he find her annoying? And what about her—would she still view him as evil, even though she herself now carried a demon?

"Let's focus, ladies." *That includes you,* he added for his own benefit. If he could bypass the outside line of the fortress's defense completely, he'd be in perfect condition when he got inside. "Zacharel, you will flash me inside the castle."

"No, I will not."

He scowled but didn't bother asking why. As always, his ears picked up the web of truth woven through the angel's tone. Zacharel couldn't or wouldn't flash him; the reason didn't matter. "William?"

"I've only recently begun to flash myself, and yeah, I'm damn good for a beginner—not that I need to tell you that since anyone with eyes would have noticed— but I'm still honing my amazing skills. There's no way I can cart your carcass anywhere."

Paris stifled a sigh. No flashing with William, either. "Is the water swimmable?"

"Nope. Not only is the water poisonous, but the fiends inside it have a hankering for flesh." William motioned to the dilapidated bridge leading to the front entrance, thick, arched double doors covered in spikes with a clear liquid dripping from their tips. "You have to use the drawbridge, and you have to let the guards carry you. There's no other way."

"I have never battled a gargoyle before." Zacharel shook his head, a dark lock of hair tumbling into one emerald eye. Damp from the melting snow, the hair stuck to his skin. He didn't seem to notice. "But I am certain these will murder Paris before willingly carrying him inside."

As if he were the only intelligent life form left in existence, William splayed his arms. "And the problem with that? He'll still be inside, exactly where he wants to be. And by the way," he added, blinking at Paris with lashes so long they should have belonged to a girl. "Your new permanent eyeliner is very pretty. You'll make a good-looking corpse."

Do not react. He did, and the teasing about his ash/ ambrosia tattoos would never end. "Thanks."

"I prefer the lip liner, though. A nice little feminine touch that really makes your eyes pop."

"Again, thanks," he gritted.

He wants us!

Stupid demon.

William grinned. "Maybe we can make out later. I know you want me."

Tell him yes!

Not another word out of you, or—

"Paris? Warrior?" Zacharel said. "Are you listening to me?"

"No."

Zach nodded, apparently not the least offended. "I enjoy your honesty, though I believe you suffer from what the humans call ADD."

"Oh, yeah. I definitely have attention deficient demon."

"Now, changing subjects, since I'm not listening to the angel, either," William said. "Since we're going with my diabolically genius plan, you're gonna have to scale down the cliff and step onto the drawbridge." He tented his hands and drummed his fingers, contemplating the bridge from every angle. "The moment you do, the gargoyles will come to life. They'll attack you. Oh, and the more you fight them, the harder they'll bite and claw you. So, if you remain relaxed, they'll only hurt you a wee bit before they cart you inside to chain to a wall. In theory."

Wonderful. But this was what his woman had to deal with every day. He could do no less. And if the gargoyles had broken her...

Broken... In, out, in, out, he breathed, oxygen scalding his throat, blistering his lungs. He twisted his head left then right to pop the bones in his neck. His fury bubbled to the surface, riding the waves in his veins. He would save Sienna and torch the castle to the ground—along with every living creature inside it.

Zacharel folded his arms over his massive chest, the snow so thick now that none of the flakes had a chance to melt. His hair now boasted strands of glistening white. "How do you know so much about this place and its protectors, William of the Dark?"

William of the Dark? That was new, yet fitting. "Yeah. How do you?" Paris studied the gargoyles in question. They were hideous. The big ones were winged, with ram-like horns, fangs as long as sabers and probably just as sharp, and daggers for nails—on both their hands and their feet. The small ones just looked hungry. Oh, and infected with rabies.

Another piece of invisible lint was brushed from William's shoulder. "Maybe I was once co-ruler of the underworld and sought out all the hideaways of Cronus and his followers, intending to blackmail them, and discovered this little love shack. Or maybe I see the future and knew we'd come here one day. Or maybe the gargoyles once served me, calling me Master Hotness."

Paris read between the lines. "Maybe you once nailed a gargoyle, and she had a big mouth." If there was a bigger he-slut than Paris, it was William.

William gave another shrug. "Or that."

White wings threaded in gold lifted, shook and returned to their place of rest against Zacharel's back. "And what makes you so sure your Sienna is in there, demon?"

Do not react. "I just am." Arca, the goddess he had seduced in Cronus's harem, the one he'd vowed to rescue after ensuring Sienna's safety, had told him there were only two possible locations for her. If Sienna had been taken to the other, her soul would have withered within days. Therefore, she was here. End of story.

"I'll provoke the guards," he said, thinking out loud, "but I won't enrage them. They'll cart me inside, planning to lock me up. I'll free myself before they can, search for Sienna, find her and escape with her. Simple, easy."

Yeah. Right.

"I'll stay here and act as lookout." William nodded, clearly satisfied with the idea. "If you don't return in, say, the amount of time it takes my conditioner to penetrate my scalp, I'll go for help." He snickered. "I said penetrate."

For freakin' real. "Knowing you, you'll forget all about me and head to a salon for a mani-pedi." More than that, Paris wasn't sure Zach would have his back— or stab it. "So, guess what? You're going in with me. Zach will act as lookout."

"Perhaps you've been living in Hungary for so long you've forgotten English and didn't understand what I was saying." First in French, then in Spanish, then in Russian, he said, "I'm staying here, and that's final." William tangled a hand through his indigo mane, frowned when he encountered a snag. Scowling, he whipped out his conditioner, squeezed a few drops onto his fingers and combed the creamy mixture through until he achieved the desired smoothness. "I'm a lover, not a fighter."

"Guaranteed you stabbed your mother seconds after she birthed you. So do me a solid and strap on your big-girl panties because here's the deal. If you walk away now, I will follow you for the rest of your days, seducing every woman you desire away from you."

A heavy pause, rife with fury as cold as the angel's snow. "Fine," William eventually muttered. "I'll go with you, but only because I'm in need of a decent cardio workout."

Good. Paris had meant every word. He hadn't come this far to welcome defeat. He would lie, cheat, destroy, whatever it took. Now, and until Sienna was safe.

He did a quick pat down. All of his blades were in their sheaths. A visual check on his guns ensured the safeties were off.

"Bullets won't kill them, you know," William said. "They'll only cause hissy fits."

"Don't care." Bullets would buy him a few seconds, surely, and sometimes that's all a guy needed to bring home the victory.

William slapped him on the shoulder, sending Sex into rapturous convulsions. "Before we do this, I've got one question for you. And you can't lie. This is too important."

A bit sick to his stomach at what such a debaucher could want to know, Paris cast his attention to the black-haired, blue-eyed he-devil. "Ask."

"Are you going to suggest I kiss you for good luck or strength or whatever it is your sex demon needs?"

That earned the warrior a two-fingered salute.

"So that's a no?" William asked.

Paris worked his jaw. "Here, let me help you off the cliff to the drawbridge." With no more warning, he shoved William over the ledge. He thought he heard a fading, "*So* not cool," from the bastard as he fell…fell…

Splat.

Sex gasped in outrage.

"Not exactly a nice thing to do," Zacharel said, but there was a gleam in his eyes, one Paris had never seen before. Something akin to amusement.

"What's your plan?" Paris asked him.

"Only time will tell."

"You'll wait here, right?"

"Perhaps."

All righty, then. With the angel's cryptic nonanswer ringing in his head, Paris snapped a blade between his teeth and scaled the jagged rocks, down, down, his hands rapidly torn to ribbons. Vines slithered from cracks, stroking over him, attempting to shackle his wrists and ankles. Dangling by one hand, he stopped long enough to slice through the nearest green stalk.

Another soon came at him, and he sliced through it, too. But damn, they were everywhere. One wound around the arm he was using for balance. His heart tripped over itself with dread—and anticipation. He glanced down at the bridge. *No other way.*

Paris carved into the vine holding him, kicked the rocks with his legs and fell. When he hit bottom, he really hit bottom, jarring the air from his lungs.

Suddenly William loomed over him, scowling, snarling and bloody, his suit dirt-stained and ripped. "Do you know. How many strands. Of hair I lost. On my way down?"

Whatever. "Math was never my thing, but I'm gonna say you lost…a lot."

Electric-blues glittered with menace. "You are a cruel,

sadistic bastard. My hair needs TLC and you…you…
Damn you! I've gutted men for less."

"I know. I've watched you." Paris lumbered to his feet
and scanned the rocky bank they stood upon, the crimson ocean lapping and bubbling in every direction. The
drawbridge was only a fifty-yard dash away. "Don't kill
the messenger, but I'm thinking you should change your
dating profile to balding."

Masculine cheeks went scarlet as the big bad warrior
struggled for a comeback.

No more playing. It's D-Day. Soon, I'll rescue Sienna,
Paris thought. Maybe she would stay with him for a few
days. If so, they could make love, over and over again,
and for just a little while, he could pretend they had forever.

Or maybe she would leave him immediately. They
wouldn't make love even once, and he would be forced
to take someone else just as soon as the door shut behind
her.

Who was he kidding? She would definitely leave
him. There were too many obstacles between them. His
demon. Her demon. The fact that he'd slept with her and
then countless others. The fact that he'd inadvertently
used her body as a shield, saving himself. Her former
occupation. The fact that she'd tricked him into lowering his guard so that she could drug him and allow the
Hunters to capture him. The fact that she had watched
as he was tortured. The fact that she hated him.

And maybe, once he'd saved her, he would realize she
was not the one for him. Maybe *he* would be the one to
leave *her*. Maybe he would find that he truly couldn't
sleep with her again. That he'd made a mistake.

Maybe. But he was still doing this.

"One of these days you're going to wake up," William finally said, "and I will have shaved you. Everywhere."

"Won't make a difference. Women will still want me. But you know what else? What I did to you wasn't cruel, Willy." He offered the warrior a white-flag grin. A trick. A lie. "This, however, is."

He grabbed William by the wrist, swung the man around and around before at last releasing him and hurling his body directly onto the bridge. Frayed rope whined, and boards broke beneath his muscled weight.

William lay there, trying to catch his breath and glaring daggers at Paris. On the castle parapets, the gargoyles unleashed a chorus of battle cries.

CHAPTER EIGHT

Should she or shouldn't she? Hours had passed since Cronus's ultimatum and departure, but the same question still rolled through Sienna's mind. Should she give herself to Galen, perhaps saving her sister, perhaps succumbing to her captor's deception, or should she continue to resist, possibly causing her sister's continued torture?

Another question, one far more important: If there was a chance she could save Skye, even the most minute chance, shouldn't she take it? She'd vowed to do anything, everything, and Galen fell into the category of anything, didn't he.

Well, hell. There it was, laid bare, with no sugar-coating. The answer was a resounding *yes*. She'd spent her life searching for Skye. If necessary, she would spend her death searching, too. At least now the blinders were off, and she knew the monster she was to seduce.

In bed. With Galen. She tried not to vomit.

She wished she were stronger, more capable, the outcome assured. She wished the battle for Skye could be waged on her terms, without Cronus there to pull her puppet strings.

And maybe…maybe she could arrange that. If she escaped this hellhole before the king's return, she could go to the keeper of Hope, torture him for the information she wanted and then kill him, *without* screwing him.

In theory, that was easy. In reality, it was probably impossible. A bitter laugh—the only kind she had stored inside her lately—escaped, mimicking the sudden chill in the air. She shivered. She'd tried to escape this castle time and time again. While she could open doors and windows that led outside, she couldn't step or crawl beyond them. Her entire body would shake, pain would lance through her, a thousand needles pricking at her, and she would collapse, pass out.

The pain she didn't care about. She could endure. But the passing-out thing? There was no way to combat that.

She was curious to know whether or not someone else could pass through. And the good news was, there were three candidates upstairs who could put that question to the test. All she had to do was free them.

Time to pay them another visit, she thought with a shiver that had nothing to do with the cold. And *what* had caused such a huge drop in the temperature?

Her wings scraped the scarred marble floor as she lumbered down a hall, around a corner and into the wide, spacious ballroom. Her heart sank when the walls fell away and the memories Cronus had plucked from her mind began to play out. At her left, a young Skye began screaming for help. At her right, a horde of Gargl, as she'd heard Cronus call the gargoyles that served as sentries here, dragged a slumped-over but very much awake Paris.

Sienna stopped, a sudden lump growing in her throat. *Paris.* Her body went hot and cold at the same time, goose bumps spreading over her skin, embers igniting in her veins. Cronus certainly knew how to torment her, didn't he? He knew exactly what images would drive her mad.

And this one…whoever created him had outdone himself. How hauntingly lovely Paris was. No mortal could ever hope to compare to him. No other immortal or mythical god could ever measure up. He possessed a face designed for the luxuries of the bedroom as well as the savagery of the battlefield. Eyes of vivid blue seductively lined with kohl she'd never before seen him wear, and hair a concerto of colors. Black, brown, even a few strands of flax. A tall body, muscled in the most delicious way.

He was perfection personified, and he was nothing more than a mirage. Still, she wanted to run to him so badly, to smother him with kisses as she begged for his forgiveness.

Forgiveness she did not deserve.

At least he wasn't injured in this memory. A small comfort, but she had to take them where she could find them.

Another vision unfolded behind Paris, a second horde of Gargl carrying a second dark-haired warrior. This man was just as tall as Paris, just as muscled and, miracle of miracles, almost as lovely, but *he* was definitely injured. Bite marks covered his arms, and horn punctures created a canvas of pain on his chest. Odd. She'd never had a vision of him before. Didn't even recall meeting him.

Her gaze returned to Paris. Two of the Gargl were… humping him? Yes. Their tongues were hanging out, their lower bodies gyrating against him. Why would Cronus show her something like that? To make her jealous? Of the Gargl?

Something was…off about this, she thought.

Before she could puzzle it out, Wrath slammed against her skull, again and again, distracting her. Her temples throbbed in tune with his motions even as the heat cranked up inside her, defeating the cold, leaving her sweating and flushed. Any time a memory of Paris materialized, both the demon and her body reacted this way.

Heaven...hell... Always when they saw flashes of Paris, Wrath uttered those two words. *He can help us.*

"I know he can," she whispered, no longer surprised when she found herself talking to the beast. "And he is certainly our heaven, isn't he?" Her only ray of hope.

Well, well. Look how far she'd come. From hate to... love? Did she love him? Surely not. She hardly knew him. But if he were more than a cruel, heartless trick meant to bring her to heel, she could have learned about him, she thought wistfully.

"Sienna?" Paris's voice, deep, harsh, rasping, uniting them once again.

Another shiver raked her as her gaze locked with his. Her entire body jolted with awareness. *Enough,* she almost shouted. *You've tortured me enough. I concede.*

"Sienna!" It was a hoarse cry layered with desperation and expectation. "Sienna!"

"Enough!" There was no holding the command inside this time. Tears burned her eyes. Her chin trembled, knocking her teeth together. She fisted the edges of her shirt lest she reach out to touch him as the Gargl carried him past her.

In the beginning, she had believed the illusions to be real. She had thrown herself into them, her failure to connect destroying pieces of her—the only pieces she still liked.

Heavenhell. Help. Help!

"Sienna!" Paris fought so fervently against his captors, twisting, turning, kicking, hitting, that one of his shoulders popped from its socket. "I'm here for you. I won't leave without you. Sienna!"

HEAVENHELL. HELP!

She felt as if iron balls churned in her stomach, their swift motions tossing bile up her throat. She released her shirt to dig her nails into her thighs, cutting skin, trying to reach bone. *Steady.* Though she wanted to do something, anything to calm Paris, she knew the more she did, the more he would fight. *This isn't real. He isn't real.*

"Sienna!"

Finally the group disappeared around the corner, and if they had been real, they would have been headed for the dungeon. Paris continued to rage, and she very nearly chased after him, mirage or not.

"I'm sorry," she rasped. "So sorry."

Wrath whimpered.

Though she wanted to collapse, curl into the fetal position and sob, she forced her mind to clear and her feet to move in the opposite direction. Just like that, another memory flickered to life, playing beside her as she walked. Her long-deceased mother sat in the dark, nursing a glass of vodka.

I wish you *had been the one taken!* Great, gutwrenching sobs. *I'm sorry. I didn't mean that, honey. I'm so sorry.* Slap. *I hate you! Get away from me.* More sobs. *I'm sorry. I shouldn't have hurt you.*

Other families had suffered similar grief, similar fights, and Sienna tried not to let this recollection affect her. And anyway, it was safer than the vision of Paris. Still, she did her best to tune it out and concentrate on her task. Freeing the demon-possessed immortals upstairs, learning from them.

Cronus might have commanded the Lords to find and capture the other hosts of Pandora's evil, but the Titan king had never stopped searching himself. Now, three were chained in the bedrooms above. Obsession, Indifference and Selfishness. And not a one of them knew she was here.

Because she hadn't yet learned to fly and wasn't sure she'd ever develop the strength to do so, Sienna climbed the winding staircase. The tips of her wings caught in the frayed carpet at least a thousand times, razing her already sore muscles. Her thighs burned from the exertion necessary to propel herself upward. Twice she had to pause to hunch over and catch her breath.

When she reached the landing, she squared her shoulders, lifted her chin. The warriors up here sensed weakness of any kind, even if they couldn't see its source. And when they sensed weakness, they beat at the clear, invisible doors that contained them, tossed out the vilest of obscenities and vowed all kinds of retribution, as if she were responsible for their confinement.

Come on, come on, you can do this, you can make it. Look what you've survived already. The pep talk worked. *There you go. Good girl.* The first bedroom she passed was Cameron's. Hadn't taken Sienna long to figure out he was host to Obsession. He was a creature of habit and because it was twilight, he was stretched out on his floor, doing push-ups. Up. Down. Up. Down.

As always, seeing him caused Wrath to erupt in a frenzy of movement. Pain exploded through her head, a precursor to images the demon would next throw into her mind. Violent images from Cameron's past. Bloody battles, a woman in his arms, limp, dead, then one of himself, cursing at the heavens, screaming…screaming… vowing revenge…

Sienna hurried past, but not before the very real image of his bronzed, glistening skin, sweat dripping along the sexy ridges of his muscles, was seared into her brain. His hair was a richer, deeper shade of bronze and plastered to his head. His eyes were downcast, but she knew they were a startling lavender rimmed with silver.

In the room next to his was Púkinn. Indifference. Upon seeing him, Wrath went lethally quiet. A reaction Sienna didn't understand, and the demon wouldn't explain.

Púkinn's Egyptian heritage shone through the sharpness of his bone structure and the sensuality of his dark eyes. His hair was long, black and straight as a pen. The rest of him, however, was more beast than man. Horns stretched from his scalp. His hands were permanently clawed, his legs muscled and furred.

Cameron called him Irish, because, despite his looks and ancestry, his voice dripped with the seductive accent of the isles. Sienna thought of him that way, too.

Finally, she reached Winter's room. Selfishness. Wrath was ambivalent about her, neither tossing out images nor shooting out lances of menace, something else Sienna didn't understand.

Winter had her hip cocked against the jamb and her arms crossed over her middle. Her coral-painted nails drummed a steady song of impatience. She looked so much like Cameron they had to be blood-related. Bronzed skin, bronzed hair and lavender eyes rimmed with silver. Mile-long legs, curves that weren't just dangerous but fatal.

The lushness of her femininity would have been a perfect contrast to Paris's exquisite masculinity.

Sienna tensed, the thought alone causing thrums of jealousy to wrap around her chest and squeeze. *He's mine.*

No, he wasn't, she forced herself to think, and he would never be. She'd tried to reach him, but he'd been unable to see her. And that was probably for the best.

After everything she'd done to him, all the ways she'd hurt him, he would never be able to trust her.

"Who the hell is out there?" Cameron growled. He'd become obsessed—naturally—with ferreting her out. And perhaps she shouldn't have visited so many times, but even before today, she'd planned to free them. Somehow, some way. "I know someone's out there. Reveal yourself. Now."

"We're dealing with one of Cronus's spies, I'm sure," Winter said, her voice as smooth and sultry as a caress. Her gaze almost, but not quite, met Sienna's. "I heard him talking earlier."

"I...will...gut...you," Cameron seethed. He wasn't talking to Winter, but to Sienna. He might grouse at Winter, snap at her and sometimes even scream at her, but he never threatened her. And if anyone could find a way to slay a ghost...thing—or whatever she was—Sienna was willing to bet it was Cameron. Because, and here was a shocker, he wouldn't stop until he had what he wanted.

"Do your tirades never end?" Irish asked, that accent giving her a case of the oh-mys.

"Actually, Irish, you mythological douche," Winter fired back, "they don't, and he's going to tirade all over your ass if you don't shut your mouth."

"Someone should have spanked you a long time ago, little girl." Irish.

"Touch her and you'll soon be eating your own balls. And they'll just be the snack pack. Main course will follow." Cameron.

Sienna didn't mind their bantering. This was mild in comparison to what they'd thrown at her. Besides, they only had each other. And while they loved to snipe and snark at each other, they united the moment Cronus appeared, their mutual hatred bonding them.

She held out her hand, reaching for the clear shield that blocked her from Winter's room. Contact. She sighed when the barrier refused to yield. Yesterday she had palpated the top half, searching for any vulnerable pockets. She'd found none. Today she would tackle the bottom half.

"Sienna!" Paris's voice echoed off the walls. "Sienna! Where the hell did you go?"

Something lurched in her chest, and she was once again fighting tears. *Damn you, Cronus.* Of all his torments, this was the worst. Her hands continued to move along the shield, quaking now.

"Sienna!"

Those scalding tears flooded her eyes and splashed down her cheeks, leaving burning tracks. The memories had never followed her before. When she moved to a new room a new one would appear, one horror exchanged for another. This was the first ever to dog her.

And...she stilled, frowned. This couldn't be a memory, she realized, the answer to her earlier concern finally slipping into place. As far as she knew, Paris had never been to this castle, and she'd never seen the Gargl anywhere else. So, the two had never fought in her presence.

Could he... Was he...

Her heart skipped a beat.

"Sienna!"

Another beat.

"Who *is* that?" Winter demanded.

"Another prisoner?" Cameron.

"And who's this Sienna?" Irish.

They heard Paris's voice. They had never seen or

heard the memories before. This wasn't… This couldn't be… Her heart stopped altogether.

"Sienna! Damn it." *Grunt, bang.* "Get off me, you perverted bag of stone." *Bang.* "Sienna!"

This wasn't a memory, wasn't a vision. This was real and happening right *now.* Paris was here. He'd come for her. Was searching for her, trying to get to her. A second later, her heart kicked back into gear, slamming into a too-fast rhythm, making her pant. The Gargl might have hurt him, might be hurting him even now.

"Paris!" Panicked, she straightened and raced down the hall, down the steps. Just as before, her wings caught on the carpet. Her momentum propelled her forward, onto her face. She cringed, moaned, but two seconds after she landed, she was back on her feet and sprinting. "Paris, I'm here!"

If he continued to fight the Gargl, they would have his organs as snacks. She'd seen it happen too many times to count. And once they tasted a man's insides, nothing and no one could stop the ensuing feast.

She quickened her step and prayed she wasn't too late.

CHAPTER NINE

CRONUS FLASHED TO HIS private bedchamber in his favorite secret palace, gripping a puny, wretched Hunter by the scruff of his neck. The moment the wall murals appeared at his sides, a large bed crafted from the darkest ebony materializing in front of him, he shoved the Hunter to his knees, maintaining that hard grip. A thick crimson carpet kept the action from fracturing the human's kneecaps, the only mercy the man would receive this day.

Atop the bed, chains rattled. The naked female bound to the posts spotted him and struggled to free herself. Of course, she failed. The chains were not just reinforced steel; they were mystically enhanced. And really, she only had herself to blame for her confinement. Cronus never would have captured her if she hadn't come here with the intention of seducing and chaining *him*.

Had he not been in possession of the All-Key, she would have succeeded. Now, nothing could restrain him.

Grinning, he studied her. Dark hair tangled around bruised shoulders, evidence she had struggled long before his arrival. Skin usually the color of flawless cream was now amusingly sallow. When eyes a mix of crystal and crimson flashed absolute hatred at him, his grin widened.

"I will *massacre* you for this," she snarled. Before he had time to respond, she calmed, returned his grin with a wicked, wanton one of her own, and purred, "But only after I play with you a bit."

"Now, now, darling." Cronus *tsk*ed under his tongue. If any female were capable of harming him, it was this one, but he would *never* admit it. "Is that any way to greet your husband of countless centuries?"

Rhea, queen of the Titans, eyed him as if he were an animal—and she wanted to wear his pelt as a victory coat. "A better way to greet you would be with a sword swinging at your neck."

He waved his hand through the air as if he hadn't a care, the action so patronizing it was sure to reignite the fuse of her temper. "Careful, my dearest. You're in danger of protesting too much."

"Argh!" With her demon, Strife, flashing ruby-colored scales and gnarled bone under the surface of her skin, she intensified her struggles. "You will pay for this."

"So you've said innumerable times. Alas." He let out a mocking sigh, barely audible over her raspy panting. "How you humiliate yourself, my heart of hearts, but do go on. My favorite part comes when you realize nothing you do, nothing you say, will aid you, and you sag in defeat."

Despite his taunt, she did indeed continue to fight. And as his own wrists and ankles throbbed in protest, he lost his amusement. He was connected to this horrid creature. Connected in a way he could not escape.

When someone injured her, *he* was injured also. No matter where he was or what he was doing. Likewise, when she experienced pleasure, so did he. Yes, he always knew when she bedded another man. But then, she always knew when he bedded another woman.

Perhaps that was why they despised each other so passionately, and why they had chosen opposite sides of the war that raged between immortals and their human enemy. Cronus had aligned himself with the Lords of the Underworld, and Rhea the Hunters.

"Death is too kind for you!" she spat just before sagging against the mattress as he'd predicted, perspiration dotting every inch of her body and making her glow.

He enjoyed seeing her this way. Helpless, naked and utterly unable to protect or cover herself. She had lush breasts with lovely tawny tips. A soft belly, and even softer thighs. And once upon a time, he truly had loved her. He would have given her anything, would have given *everything,* to make her happy. Actually, he *had* given everything.

Though he'd known better, he had shared his throne with her. Had even shared his godly abilities. He'd hungered for her so absolutely, he hadn't wished to exist if she could not be by his side, ruling with equal power.

As the centuries passed, however, she began to change. From sultry to grasping, from kind to cruel, her thirst for power surpassing his own. Ultimately, she betrayed him in an attempt to usurp him. *She* was the reason he'd been incarcerated inside Tartarus. *She* was the reason the Titans had fallen to the Greeks. At least the ones she'd aided in rising up against him had betrayed her in kind.

Now, nothing would save her from his eternal wrath.

"It's that time again, my pet," he said, all hint of his softer emotions gone.

During one of their many altercations in prison, after he had killed her lover and she had killed his, they had vowed to never again harm those closest to the other, and a vow given was unbreakable. Therefore, Cronus could not touch her precious Galen or any of Galen's top advisers—though Cronus had finally found the bastard's lair, as well as his first in command, the new keeper of Distrust, Fox. In turn, Rhea could not touch any of his Lords.

They could, however, harm the minor foot soldiers. As he would soon prove.

"Your choice, Rhea. I beat you, or I kill one of your Hunters."

The human kneeling at Cronus's side jerked at the threat, mewling sounds seeping from his bloody lips, but he never spoke a word. Just a guess, but that could be because Cronus had already cut out his tongue.

Cronus wanted Rhea to choose her punishment, and he didn't care that he would, essentially, be punishing himself. Causing her to suffer overrode all other concerns. "Which is it to be?" Every day he offered her the same choice, and every day she gave the same answer.

"You think I care about a fragile, useless human?" She lifted her chin, her narrowed gaze remaining on Cronus, completely lacking in fear or mercy. "Kill him."

A whimper escaped the Hunter.

No, her answer had not changed. Cronus could have beaten her anyway, and perhaps one day he would. For the time being, he liked giving her what she asked for. Liked thinking she would be haunted by her selfishness for decades to come.

"Very well." Cronus stretched out his free arm, summoned a sword from nothing but air, and struck. The Hunter's head fell to the floor with a thump. His body quickly followed.

The scent of copper coated the air.

Rhea's thunderous expression remained the same, untouched by remorse. "Do you feel better now, my stallion? Do you feel like a big, strong male?"

Bitch. He would not allow her to gain the upper hand.

"Do you care nothing for your ever-dwindling army? The very men fighting for *your* cause."

One bare shoulder lifted in a casual shrug. "I feel the same for my army as you feel for yours, I'm sure. Nothing."

No, he did not care for his Lords, but he respected their strength and determination. Or rather, he had. Lately the warriors were too busy falling in love, too concerned with their own petty squabbles, and now too busy rescuing Kane, the keeper of Disaster, to heed Cronus's orders. Still, they were a buffer between Cronus and eternal death, so he needed them.

He frowned at the thought of all that had transpired to bring him to this moment. Long ago, the first All-Seeing Eye under his command—a being capable of seeing into heaven, hell, past and future—had prophesied that a man filled with hope would fly to him on wings of white and behead him. At the time, Galen had not yet been created. Therefore, Cronus had assumed an angel assassin would come for him, which was why he'd pitted himself against the Deity's Elite soldiers. War had broken out—among angels and gods, Greeks and Titans—and even those on earth had suffered.

Weakened from the ceaseless fighting, Cronus found himself defeated by Zeus and thrown into Tartarus. Soon afterward Zeus created the Lords, Galen among them, to serve as his personal army, ready to defend him should the Titans rise up from their moldering prison. But in a fit of foolish pique, those same warriors opened Pandora's box, unleashing the demons from within and raining down more havoc on a world still reeling from the heavenly war. When Zeus meted out their punishment, decreeing that each would house a demon inside himself, Galen was paired with the demon of Hope, wings of white sprouting from his back. *Then,* upon Cronus's escape from the immortal prison, the newest All-Seeing Eye had painted the same future that had earlier been foretold, this time *showing* Galen's victory over him.

What the first Eye had told him—and the newest did not yet know—was that there was a way for him to save himself. A woman with wings of midnight, who had lived among his enemy but craved a life with his allies, was to be his salvation.

That woman was Sienna. Everything about her fit the Eye's description, from her appearance to her circumstances.

Therefore, she had to do as the Eye had said she must do. Reign by Galen's side, despite her desire to aid the Lords. Only she could keep Galen's attention, though she didn't yet know how or why and Cronus wouldn't tell her. Only she could hold her own against Rhea, if ever his wife got free. Only she could stop the Lords from attacking Galen, for killing the keeper of Hope would not stop the prophecy from coming to pass. His demon would be given to someone else, and that someone else would then become the white-winged slayer of the Titan king.

"I will escape, you know," Rhea said, and she sounded confident.

Whether that confidence stemmed from her abilities or his capitulation, he wasn't sure. Didn't care. He rubbed a thumb over one brow, another dismissive gesture. "No, I do not know. I've never seen so weak a goddess."

Only he could unlock her chains, and he planned never to do so. Among her most recent crimes, she had convinced her sister to become his mistress and spy on him. Another reason for Cronus's insistence that Sienna do the same to Galen.

"One day…" she gritted out.

He moved to the side of the bed, away from the dead body and closer to his hated wife. "You will ruin me. You will imprison me. You will… What other threats have you issued, hmm?"

"I will peel away your skin, spit on your bones and dance in a pool of your blood."

"Sounds like a truly spectacular evening. Until then, I think I'll have a bit of fun." With a single wave of his hand, he summoned one of the countless females currently residing in his harem. A redhead with deeply tanned skin and roses in her cheeks appeared beside him. Unlike some of the others he owned, she truly enjoyed attending to his needs.

Today she wore a transparent drape of silk and lace, jewels that had once belonged to Rhea and a smile brighter than any sun. Seeing the Titan queen so helpless on the bed, and knowing she herself was a favorite of his, she puffed with pride, flipped her hair over one shoulder, and waved smugly.

Rhea hissed.

And that's why I chose her, he thought with an inward grin.

Recognizing the diamonds curling around the girl's neck, Rhea released a spew of curses.

"Majesty," the girl said with a curtsy, talking over the queen to prove how little she mattered. The fragrance of citrus wafted from her. "What can I do for you?"

"You can show the woman on the bed how much your man pleases you." He waved her in front of him, where he bent her over, her face right in front of Rhea's.

"Does *she* not please *you?*" the girl asked.

The queen gave another hiss and tried to bite her.

"Enough of that." His gaze on his wife, he lowered

the zipper to his leather pants. He despised wearing such constrictive clothing, but Rhea found this type of garment attractive, and his need for vengeance far surpassed any desire for comfort. "You know what you must say to stop this from happening," he told his wife. Rhea must only concede defeat, vowing to forever obey him.

"I'll die first."

"Very well."

He took the servant, and the pleasure was intense—and he would never admit it was so satisfying only because he kept his eyes on his wife. She, however, closed her eyes to *block* his image. No matter. She felt every sensation along with him, and that was enough. For now.

When he finished, he righted his clothing with hands trembling from the force of his release—which was humiliating; a king should recover swiftly—and sent the grinning servant away.

"Bastard," Rhea said on a panting breath. "I hate you. With all of my being, I hate you."

"As I hate you."

A smile of genuine amusement suddenly curled the corners of her mouth. "You know, Cronus, darling. You did not enjoy your whore half as much as I enjoyed mine."

The words were carefully calculated, a stinging blow to his masculine pride. But he was careful to keep his own expression equally amused. "You know, *darling,*" he said. "You might have enjoyed your men, but you only ever had them once before I found and killed them. I, on the other hand, am already looking forward to having the redhead again tomorrow."

CHAPTER TEN

FANGS IN HIS ARMS. Claws in his legs. Horns jabbing into his stomach. At least, Paris seriously hoped that it was horns jabbing into his stomach. For a while, some of the gargoyles had ground on him like dogs in heat as their friends attempted to chain him down. *Won't gag.* He would have allowed the restraints—if he hadn't seen Sienna. She was here. Alive. Unfettered.

She'd looked at him, had met his gaze, and sadness had wafted from her. Sadness and regret, and even horror. The horn-rimmed glasses she'd once worn were gone, her eyesight probably perfect in the afterlife, but her features were the same. Big hazel eyes, plump red lips. A flow of mahogany waves, now to her waist.

His woman. His *mine.* One by one his friends had fallen in love, and he'd been so jealous. Now, here was the woman who'd fascinated him as no other. He'd thought, *Must reach her...must wipe away the horror...*

Sex had thought, *Must have her.*

Now his demon retreated into the back of his mind, the coward, as Paris fought his way free of the gargoyles to run after her. In an instant, his captors swarmed him, their fervor intensified. He tossed one, then another, then another still, slamming the rigid stone bodies into walls. They recovered instantly and returned to him. More clawing, more jabbing.

They slowed him, but they didn't stop him. He was

weak and growing weaker, because he hadn't had sex all day. Didn't think he'd had sex yesterday, either. He'd already forgotten. Whatever. Sienna was here, and with one glance, he'd gotten hard for her.

He *could* have her again. No question about that now. He just had to reach her.

As the darkness rose up inside him, clouding his mind with thoughts of destruction and death, he offered no more resistance, allowing it to drive him deeper and deeper into the place where only demolishing the obstacles in his path mattered. These gargoyles wanted to keep him from his woman. They did not deserve to live.

One step, two, three, the things clawing at his thighs, his calves, hanging on to his ankles, he eked his way into the ballroom. All the while he punched at heads, kicked and stabbed at middles. Stone cracked. Pieces scattered on the floor.

"Sienna! Where—"

She flew around the far corner, her dark hair tangled behind her, her hazel eyes wild and bright. In a blink, the world slowed down and he noticed details he'd missed before. Her lips were more swollen than usual, with droplets of blood dried at the corners. A bruise colored her cheek, a blue-black testament of the pain she had been forced to endure. One of her obsidian wings was bent at an odd angle, clearly broken.

She'd been hurt. Someone had hurt her.

Red mixed with the black, both swimming so thickly in his brain they compromised his line of vision. Shimmers of rage sparked a thousand must-kill-must-protect fires, each one warring with the others. In his veins, his blood was molten, turning jerky movements into fluid, lethal arcs.

With a roar, he tossed away two other gargoyles. He

grabbed another by the neck and punched, punched, *punched,* creating a hole in the creature's cheek, the rest of the stone chipping away bit by bit. Still the creature fought Paris's hold, teeth chomping at his fist.

"Let them chain you," Sienna shouted. "Please, just let them chain you."

She wanted him bound? Hated him as much as he'd feared? No matter. Her command and plea were discarded, his determination unwavering. *Must kill...* Punch, punch. *Enemy must die.* Punch, punch, punch. Stab. *Obstacles must be eliminated.* Punch, stab. Debris flew in every direction. The gargoyles forgot about their desire for pleasure, or whatever they'd felt while writhing on him, and went on full attack, no longer going easy on him.

Sienna reached him, smelling of wildflowers and... ambrosia? He inhaled deeply. Oh, yeah. Ambrosia's sweet, sweet perfume permeated his skin, overshadowed everything else, including the need to kill, but oh, he now wanted to imbibe. Had to imbibe. His mouth watered, even as he wondered why she would smell of the immortal drug he had forced himself to stop using not too long ago, when he was hurt during a fight he would have won if he'd been clearheaded. His injuries had almost caused him to miss his appointment with a goddess to purchase his crystal blades, and he'd decided then and there to stop using. Thankfully, he had gone through the worst of the withdrawal already; he couldn't afford to go through it again. He would stop caring about anything but his next fix.

Want her. As close as she now was, Sex perked up, pouring strength straight into Paris's system and changing the direction of his own thoughts. *Must touch her... must have her...*

For once, they were in agreement.

"You have to let them chain you." When she attempted to jerk two of the gargoyles away from him, they turned on her, some biting, some clawing, some head-butting her. Her knees collapsed under their weight.

Another roar ripped from his throat. She had tried to save him? The very idea was foreign to him. Ignoring the beasts still attempting to subdue him, he concentrated on the ones climbing on top of her. He grabbed one and threw. Grabbed another, threw.

"Run!" he commanded her.

The beasts returned to him in a snap. He tried to knock them away, clearing a path for her, but she didn't run. She lay panting, her limbs unmoving, not even trying to shield herself.

Her watery gaze pleaded with him. "Please, Paris. Be still. Don't fight."

Heated breath caught in his throat, and though every instinct he possessed screamed to continue fighting, continue hurting anything and everything in his way, he planted his heels on the floor, sheathed his blades and lowered his arms. She had tried to save him; he would trust her.

He would surrender.

For a moment, the beasts took full advantage, converging on him like flies to honey. *Steady.* Like Sienna, he remained unmoving. Shockingly, the fighting frenzy soon eased. The gargoyles latched on to his arms and once again began dragging him to the prison where they'd already locked William.

Sienna lumbered to her feet and followed, never allowing eye contact to break. A good thing. If she had, he would have erupted all over again. *Can't lose even that much.*

"They'll leave you alone after they chain you." Her voice trembled, pain in the undercurrents. "They simply have to complete their task, and then you'll be free to do whatever you want."

Want her...

Despite his injuries, he hardened a second time, his demon's scent wafting from him, a rich chocolate mingled with the most expensive champagne. If he'd needed more proof that he could have this woman again, here it was. He could have her as many times as he wanted her, however many times she would allow him. He was awed. He was vindicated.

He was undone.

Finally, he was with the woman he craved above all others.

The beasts not holding his limbs leapt back on top of him, grinding, rubbing against him in that disgusting way. Harder this time, and much more determined. Even their need to complete their duty and chain him couldn't override his demon's allure, he supposed. He tuned them out, kept his focus on Sienna.

She was here—he would never tire of the thought— and she was breathtakingly lovely, the essence of all that was feminine. Even dirt-smudged and blood-caked as she was, he'd never seen a more exquisite female. His mind had not built her up during their separation. On the contrary, his mind had not done her justice. Those hazel eyes glittered with swirls of emerald and copper, hints of summer and winter combined, framed by spiky jet lashes. Her lips were bee-stung and utterly wicked. The kind women paid to have and men paid to use.

Her hair wasn't too dark or too light, but the perfect shade of russet streaked with shimmers of the purest gold. The locks were longer than before, with waves as mesmerizing as those in an ocean.

Her freckles had lightened, but they were as decadent as ever, a treasure map for his tongue. The rest of her skin, cream and rose petals, glowed as if she had swallowed the sun. Her body, so slender, so elegant, was as graceful as a ballerina's. Her breasts were small, but they would fit amazingly well in his big hands as he tongued her nipples. Her legs were long and would wrap around his waist, holding him tight.

Mine, he thought. *Mine.*

Take her. Sex had abandoned the *I wants* and *I needs,* and was now all about the commands. As if Paris would argue. One question plagued him, though. Would being with her a second time actually strengthen him?

Around the corner, William waited—and he was grinning, his electric-blues calling Paris all kinds of stupid. He had broken free of his chains, as Paris should have done to avoid the beating, and waved as Paris passed him. The beasts paid him no heed, still clinging to Paris and proving Sienna's claim. He relaxed. So close to holding her, to touching her as he'd dreamed.

Oh, the things he wanted to do to her...

She might push him away; she might not. Either way, at long last he would find out.

CHAPTER ELEVEN

PARIS WATCHED AS WILLIAM flowed into motion beside Sienna. Still she didn't look away from him and he wondered what thoughts she entertained. Was her body reacting to him, as his was reacting to her?

Blood-spattered walls framed her, and Paris cursed. He would have given anything to see her surrounded by silks and velvets. Would make it so, before he let her go. A vow, even as the thought of letting her go made him want to howl.

"Nice to see you again, Sienna," William said, as pleasantly as he was able. The frost in his eyes belied his endearing facade.

Paris tensed. If the warrior hurt her...

"We've met?" she asked.

For a moment, William radiated absolute bafflement. Then his expression cleared, and he offered a sugar-sweet smile. "It distresses me that you don't remember, but I don't mind reminding you. Allow me to paint the scene. We were in Texas, and you were crouched on the concrete like a dog, holding on to Paris like a leech." His cruel, sneering pitch was meant to intimidate her, to put her in her place for everything she'd done to Paris.

"Tone," Paris snapped. She might have done him wrong, but he would not allow her to be disrespected.

Sienna shrugged, apparently unconcerned by what the

warrior had said. "You'll have to forgive me for not noticing you back then. Next to him, you're kind of homely."

William choked on his own tongue.

For the first time in forever, Paris grinned with true amusement. The only other time he'd witnessed such spunk from her was when she had drugged him. He hadn't liked it then, but he liked it now, especially since it was directed at someone else.

William caught his breath and added, "Just so you know, I'll kill you if you harm him in any way. And I don't care how much it will upset him." So calmly stated, there was no arguing the warrior's intent. "Paris has proven to be stupid where you're concerned, and that means his friends have to pick up the mental slack."

There went his amusement. An animalistic growl left him, his lips peeling back from his teeth. Darkness rising again...rage returning... Paris struggled to free his arms, intending to wrap his fingers around William's neck and squeeze. No one threatened Sienna. No one. Ever.

You don't really want to injure him. Stop. A plea from deep inside himself, where remnants of the old Paris must still reside. William's loyalty was a nice surprise, and something he appreciated on a visceral level.

Where Sienna was concerned, however, Paris was not exactly rational, and his struggling intensified. *Must defend her...*

The gargoyles stopped dragging him, stopped humping him and returned to fighting him, shoving him to the floor and into a pile of bones. They raked at him with their claws and teeth.

"See?" William splayed his arms, his point proven. "Stupid."

Biting the inside of his cheek, Paris forced himself to chill a second—third?—time. He huffed and he puffed like the big, bad wolf he was, knowing he would be given a chance to make his point about Sienna later, when he could get to his knives. His friends could do and say anything they wanted to him, but not to her.

Once again the creatures lost interest in the battle and resumed the trek to the prison.

Sienna and William continued to follow, and soon Paris's wrists and ankles were shackled to a crumbling stone wall in a four-by-four chamber devoid of any luxuries. Claws scraped the floor as the creatures filed out, each squawking happily about what they clearly considered a job well done.

Sienna severed visual contact and collapsed at his side, her trembling fingers working at one of the metal bands. He could have freed himself. Or hell, William could have freed him, but Paris liked having those soft, elegant hands on him. They were his favorite part of her body, every movement an exotic dance.

On a raspy catch of breath, she said, "They're tasked with chaining anyone who survives the walk from drawbridge to castle, and once that's accomplished, they lose interest. You'll be free to move about the place as much or as little as you want."

He closed his eyes for a moment, letting her voice drift through his mind. Husky, low, a caress he'd missed more than he'd realized. He could listen to her forever.

Did part of him still hate her? Yeah. Definitely. Hated what she'd done to him, hated what he'd done *for* her. Hated how strongly she affected him. And beneath all the hate, he resented that she hadn't seen beyond her *own* hatred to choose him all those months ago, the way he'd chosen her.

He would have taken her home. He would have pampered her. At least, that's what he told himself now. He wouldn't contemplate what he would have done to her before the pampering commenced. Wouldn't think about the interrogation he'd planned or the chains he'd imagined buying for her.

"I'm having trouble... I can't... The fall must have hurt worse than I realized." Her voice had thinned to a mere wisp of sound, barely audible. "So...sorry..." Her hands fell away from him, and she slumped forward, her slight weight resting on his chest.

"Sienna?" he demanded, but there was no response. Anyone who could see and touch her could injure her spirit form; he knew that. And the gargoyles had certainly been able to see and touch her. But without a heartbeat or need to breathe, she should rebound quickly. Right? Except, the bloodstains around her mouth...*how* had she bled? he wondered now.

"Must have fainted from the sight of my beauty," William remarked with a sigh. "There goes the tickle fight I had planned."

Ignoring him, Paris yanked one of his arms, ripping the chain from the wall. He wrapped that arm around Sienna's waist, holding her against him, keeping her steady.

She fit him perfectly.

After he ripped the other arm free, he eased her to her back and peered down at her, his heart causing a riot of sensation in his chest.

Her head lolled to the side, and she was pale, paler than before. Another rip, followed by another, and his ankles were free. Then he jerked at the cuffs themselves until they fell away. *Then* he did what he'd wanted to do since the first moment he'd seen her. He touched her, smoothing the hair from her brow. Her skin was as soft as it appeared, and warm, so wonderfully warm. He'd craved a moment like this so desperately, had dreamed of it over and over again, and had nearly killed himself a hundred times over to have it. To his delight, reality was so much better than the dream. More than feeling her heat, he smelled her scent all around him, enveloping him. The wildflowers, the coconut sweetness of ambrosia, both creating a heady musk of arousal.

Why ambrosia? He couldn't get past that. Was she a user? If so, he'd bet someone, like, say, Cronus, had forced her to become one. She wasn't the type to willingly fall into drugs. From what little he knew about her, she liked order and craved control.

I'll protect her from further abuse, he thought next. She was his. For just a little while, she was his.

Sex jumped up and down. *Take her, take her, take her.*

Instinct demanded he obey. Still he resisted. *Not like this. Not while she's out.*

A sigh of frustration, maybe even a muttered *you're no fun* as Paris looked her over, shielding her from William's gaze as he moved her clothing out of the way to check for injuries. Every newly revealed inch of skin acted as a lick of flame to Sex, causing the demon to hiss and shake. *Or maybe you* are *fun.*

Though Paris admired the body beneath him just as fervently as his dark companion, he hissed and shook for a different reason. Another rise of darkness, another increase of boiling rage. Beneath fading bruises, his woman was as fang-and-claw-mark-ridden as he was, blood oozing from her in tiny rivers of pain.

His next mission crystallized. Finding out how to hurt the gargoyles and then making them pay for every mark.

Really making them pay, he decided when he spied a deep, angry gouge in her side. He sucked in a breath to try and calm himself down, but he inhaled so sharply his lungs felt like mini-vacuums, drawing the air in with commando force. His muscles tensed, his head fogged all over again and his mouth watered. He could actually *taste* the ambrosia in the air. Frowning, he bent down and sniffed along the line of her neck. The closer he was to her, the stronger the scent became.

"Kinky," William said.

"Can you be serious?"

"I *was* being serious. I always figured you for the in and out type. Kinda stealthy, leaving the girl wondering whether you'd even been there or not. But I didn't know you were quite *this* stealthy."

"Nice to know you've considered my sex life," he grumbled.

"Hasn't everyone?"

"Screw you."

"Again, hasn't everyone?"

"This is pointless." Another sniff. The fog thickened, Paris's brain practically swimming through it. Could the fragrance originate in Sienna's blood? Yet another sniff, another infusion of that ever-thickening fog. Yeah, it was definitely in her blood—and a lot of it. More than even an addict could handle. Her scent was as strong as if she were actually growing in an ambrosia field.

Which should be impossible. Right? Ambrosia was harvested in special meadows elsewhere in the heavens, as far from this dark realm as the moon was from the earth. Lavender petals were plucked from the foliage, the clear, intoxicating liquid squeezed out before those petals were dried and turned into powder. No one could handle the liquid, not even immortals, and humans certainly couldn't handle even the powder.

But Sienna wasn't human anymore, was she.

He was ashamed to admit he was tempted to bite her,

to drink her down and savor every drop. He'd walked the path of addiction, sprinted it, really, but he had some-how managed to skirt the edge of need during his jour-ney here, knowing his wits were required to succeed. If only that would lessen the sweet, tantalizing lure of her right now...but no.

"As interesting as this is, and honestly, I don't mean to interrupt your seductive process," William said, air-quoting the last two words, "but are you gonna get to the good stuff or what?"

"I thought I told you to shut it."

"No, you told me to screw you, and that was five min-utes ago. A lot's changed since then. Like, I'm currently bored."

Biting his tongue until he tasted copper, Paris finished his search for injuries. And shit, there was another shot of desire—his own rather than his demon's. He shouldn't notice those lovely pink nipples, shouldn't notice the soft dip of her belly or the trim length of her legs. Shouldn't be counting her freckles, already planning his tongue's attack. (He would start with the darker ones on her stom-ach, and work his way to the lighter ones on her thighs.) He was a bastard. He was sick, disgusting. He should be whipped.

When she woke up, she'd take care of that for him, he would bet.

Hate myself. "She's already dead," he gritted out. He noticed her right wrist no longer bore the tattoo of infin-ity, a symbol the Hunters used. "Why is she bleeding? Shouldn't she heal as quickly as we do?"

"Oh, now you want to talk to me?" the warrior quipped.

"Just answer the question before I cut out your tongue and nail it to the wall."

"You've really lost your sense of humor, you know that? But okay. Fine. I'll play along. She's dead, yes, but she's also possessed by a demon that is very much alive. His heart beats for her. His blood fills her veins. I shouldn't have to explain demon physiology to *you*. And what the hell is that smell? It's mouthwatering. A real party for my—"

"Stop breathing!" Paris didn't want anyone else breathing her in.

"O-kay. Possessive much?"

"Let's get back to the subject that won't get you maimed. She's possessed by a demon, yes, but she's also a dead human spirit. So..."

"So, you're still able to touch her."

To borrow the bastard's phrasing: Obvious much? "What I'm asking is, will she heal?"

"Yeah, because her demon will heal. And here's a little tip for the next person held captive by your stunning conversation. You should have started with that and saved us time and trouble."

Okay. Okay, then. Good. She would heal. Paris scooped her up in his arms—pissed all over again with the gargoyles. What they'd left on him...was now on his woman.

Sex adored the contact and purred his approval.

"I'm taking her upstairs, looking for a bedroom." Paris would clean and bandage her. If she didn't wake up and demand he leave her the hell alone first. "You're not invited."

As much as he wanted her awake, looking at him, talking to him, he hoped she slept through the cleaning. He was desperate to get his hands on her, really on her. Yeah, he was a sick, sick bastard. But that wasn't the main reason, he told himself. He didn't want her to feel any pain while he doctored her.

He studied the chains for a split second, thinking it might be a good idea to tie Sienna to a bed while he had the chance. That way, she couldn't run until after they'd discussed a few things. But he hadn't come all this way, done all those things, only to enslave her himself. His goal was, and had always been, her freedom.

And shit. She might not run from him. Earlier she had ignored him, had watched as he'd passed her, but a few minutes later, she had rushed to his rescue. Whatever the reason for the change, she hadn't sought to get rid of him.

He rubbed his cheek against the top of her head, luxuriating in the feel of her silky hair before carrying her out of the cell. The gargoyles hadn't bothered shutting the iron bars that would have kept him and William inside. At least until they'd picked the lock, that is.

"You're such a wuss," William said, pacing beside him. "I hope you know that."

"Really? I'm not the one carrying conditioner around."

"Maybe that's why your hair has so many split ends."

"Tell me about your hair one more time. You'll wake up bald."

"That's a ridiculous thing to say. We both know I'd have your guts spilled before you ever got the razor near me." William raised his chin. "By the way, only a real man can accept his feminine side."

"I don't know who fed you that line of garbage, but I can promise she's laughing at you right now."

"Surprise! It was your mom—after I boned her."

A mom joke. How original.

The gargoyles were no longer in the ballroom. Paris hadn't noticed the interior before; he'd been a little too busy getting his ass kicked. Now he had a look around. It was dark, crumbling like the rest of the place, with blood dried on the walls and bones tossed about haphazardly.

Up the stairs they climbed, the carpet threadbare in multiple places. On the new rise were statues, a lot of damn statues. Male, female, old, young. Only thing they had in common were their expressions of horror.

"I take it you're gonna be busy for a few hours, since I suspect that's how long she'll be out and you can do your thing." William brushed his fingers over a large pair of alabaster breasts. "I mean, that's the reason I'm not invited to join you, right?"

"You better shut your mouth while you still have a head." Even as irritated as he was with William's suggestion, pulses of desire shot through Paris at the thought of being alone with Sienna and touching her as easily as William had touched the statue—little flames he wasn't sure whether to douse or welcome.

"Shout if you need me. Like, if she's too much for you."

"That day will never come." Paris veered left as the warrior veered right. "By the way, if you knock on my door, you better be dying. 'Cause if you're not, you soon will be." He shouldered his way into the first room he came across. His luck was holding, because it was a furnished bedroom. All he had to do was remove the thick layers of dust and the tarp draping everything.

Or maybe he should leave the tarp. Because when Sienna woke up, this might become a war zone.

CHAPTER TWELVE

KANE, KEEPER OF THE DEMON of Disaster, could not believe his luck. Usually his life took the express train to hell, whether he'd purchased a ticket or not, with rocks falling on his head, lightbulbs shorting out and holes opening up at his feet. Stuff like that could really mess with a guy's mind, so over the years he'd developed a philosophy that had saved his life: bad shit happened, but whatever, he would deal and move on.

Now he was actually *in* hell, but he wasn't being tortured. He wasn't being questioned, and catastrophes weren't occurring. He was being worshipped. By demon minions, sure, but worship was worship, right? Their scaled, clawed hands caressed him, their horned heads rubbed against him gently, and the rest of their bodies... he wouldn't think about.

Mine, Disaster whispered inside his head, pride bubbling to the surface and washing through Kane's entire body.

Yeah, Kane knew these minions belonged solely to Disaster. Long ago, the High Lord had lived in this section of hell, had ruled here, and then had chosen to leave it all behind and escape. And even though thousands of years had passed since that time, the connection hadn't faded. The minions, or lesser demons, had sensed their leader inside of Kane and rescued him from his attackers.

Currently Kane was perched on a throne of the

freshly...excavated bones. Okay, okay. That was a nice way of saying the bones used to belong to the Hunters who'd thought to hurt Kane, and only a few days ago they'd been plucked out. And, when you considered the fact that Kane's shirt and pants were made from the tanned and leathered skins—because of the heat, the process had been swift—well, a chair of femurs? No biggie.

They were gifts, the minions had said. And like he could really say, "Thanks, but I'd rather have a toaster." In return, all they wanted was his sperm.

Yeah. That's right. His baby juice.

Seemed his demon had once possessed a jealous streak and, true to his name, had caused a disaster that wiped his male minions from existence. Only females remained and they were desperate to procreate with their favorite Evil Overlord.

Kane hadn't had sex in centuries; the act was simply too risky for his partners. So yeah, his body was primed and ready. Gnarled the demon hands might be, but they still stroked and gripped just fine. His mind, however, was *so* not on board.

"Back up, ladies," he commanded. He could have been nice about it, sure, but something he'd learned was that demons only responded to strength. Nice wouldn't get him crap.

Still, he expected a fight. Instead, moans of disappointment echoed and contact ceased. They obeyed him, inching backward. But they lingered nearby, prostrate, still reaching for him, clearly hoping he'd change his mind.

Inside his head, Disaster prowled with purpose, unhappy with the distance. The females belonged to him, they were his right, and he wanted to mate with them. *Take,* he said.

No. Kane wasn't the type of guy who could walk away from his kids, even half-demon ones, and that's what he'd have to do in this situation.

Take!

I said no. He'd rather find a way out of here. But every time he stood, and no matter what he said while he was standing, within seconds the females would swarm him, pushing his pants around his ankles. He wasn't sure whether Disaster had trained them to react so swiftly, or if Kane was just special.

Two things he *was* certain about. His friends were worried about him, and they were searching for him. He didn't want them coming down here, risking their lives when his was no longer in danger.

Take one, then. Just one.

Ah, so they were supposed to negotiate now, were they? Well, the answer was still a resounding hell no. But…maybe he could pretend, Kane thought. Maybe if he picked one of the females, got her alone, he'd have a better chance of sneaking out of the cavern.

His gaze skated over the kneeling, writhing bodies. Some had horns protruding from their spines, some had pointed wings. Some had red scales, some had green. Beyond them was the cavern, blood caked on the jagged rocks, fires blazing in every corner, and screams of the damned floating on the hot, sulfur-scented air. When he found a smaller body with no horns *or* wings, her scales on the lighter side of jade, he pointed.

"You." If for once in his eternal life, his good luck held, she would be a weak link.

Gasps of surprise. Hisses of jealousy.

"I want you," he reiterated.

His chosen stood. Her legs were twisted, facing the wrong way. Her feet were hoofed, and when she smiled, he saw a mouthful of bloodstained fangs. Disaster slammed against his skull, *bang, bang,* desperate to leave him, to touch her, to pound inside her.

Mine. She's mine!

And just how would the bastard react when—hypothetically—Kane nailed her? Murder Kane, the same way he'd once murdered his own people? Probably. Because if he managed to end Kane's life, he could remain here, a place he'd once fought to escape but now realized he missed. Sure, if that happened, Disaster would be crazed from the loss of his human host, but the demon would be free to screw whoever he desired, all by himself.

Talk about a messed-up sitch.

Demon Girl limped to the throne, and the wanton gleam in her eyes suggested she intended to climb Kane like a carnival pony the second she reached him, while everyone watched.

Bang, bang. Disaster was on board with that.

Kane shook his head and extended a hand, palm up, to stop her progress. "Nope, sorry. Don't come any closer."

A frown pulled at the corners of her mouth as she obeyed.

"Privacy," he said. *Bang, bang.* Harder, faster. "I want to…take you in a tent." He wasn't sure what verbiage these demons would understand.

"Massster?" Her forked tongue swiped over too-thin lips.

"I will not take you out here." Or anywhere. *Bang, bang.* Damn it. His demon needed to settle the hell down. "So, build me a tent." *Bang.* "All of you." *Bang.* And hell, maybe, with his present run of good luck, he wouldn't have to wait for its completion. Maybe the females would be so distracted during the building of the tent, he could stomp out of the cavern while yelling, whistling, whatever, and they wouldn't notice.

"Tent?" she asked, still so clearly confused.

"Yes. I want one. Build the tent now, and you can have babies later." *With someone else.*

Bang! Bang!

Most of the minions rushed away to gather the necessary supplies, shoving each other out of the way, but a few stragglers remained behind, staring at him. And by *a few,* he meant a little over one hundred. He sighed. So, there'd be no stomping, yelling or whistling his way out.

He wished he were more like Paris. Wished he could plow through them—in bed and out—and be stronger for it while remaining emotionally distanced and unconcerned with the consequences.

Of course, then he'd also be a drug addict obsessed with finding the woman who'd tried to kill him, but at the moment, drugs and obsession seemed like a nice change of pace. And damn. When Kane got home, he was gonna be teased mercilessly about his precious seed, his needy harem girls, and his refusal to fertilize their petunia patches.

Bring it, boys. At least he'd be home.

Home... The word echoed through his mind, a wave of foreboding slamming through him.

Something was about to happen, he realized with a twist of sickness. Something terrible was about to happen. A disaster...a tragedy of the worst sort...inside the fortress in Buda, where all the Lords and their significant others lived. *His* fortress. His demon knew it, sensed it, and in turn, so did Kane.

He was on his feet and running for the exit, not slowing even when multiple females latched on to him and held on for the ride.

CHAPTER THIRTEEN

VIOLA TRAILED AFTER the gorgeous warrior named Maddox as he carried his very pregnant wife, Ashlyn, up the stairs, past naked portraits of his friends holding rainbow-colored ribbons and stuffed teddy bears. This was the fourth time one of the Budapest residents had foisted her off on someone else, and she couldn't understand why no one wanted to spend more time with her.

From Lucien to Anya, whom she'd met in Tartarus centuries ago. They'd been cell-block-B mates. Anya had always been jealous of her, of course. Who hadn't— and wasn't? Earlier today the minor goddess had pretended not to recognize her, but Viola had taken the lie for what it was. A plea to hear all about Viola's magnificent life.

An hour later, Anya had handed her off to Reyes and his Danika. Viola was still puzzling over Anya's parting words to the couple. "Here you go. Take her. And you're welcome. You won't need to stab yourself to please your demon for at least a year, Reyes."

Just how was Viola supposed to have pleased an anguish-happy fiend like Reyes? He was possessed by the demon of Pain, yet she was perfectly...perfect, a joy to look upon and listen to, a veritable fount of shiny, priceless pearls of wisdom, with a keen sense of fashion and a knack for home decorating.

Speaking of those little life skills, she'd already decided to put them to good use. From now on she would be dressing everyone here, as well as redesigning their mansion's interior and exterior. And she wasn't even going to charge them—more than a few hundred thou.

Her eyes filled with tears as her hand fluttered to her heart. She was *such* a giver.

At one time, centuries ago, she'd done something not so giving and sent herself catapulting into a shame spiral, but she couldn't recall what that something was. She never did. Her demon stored negative memories away, hiding them from her. Anything to continue her love affair with herself. As if she would ever end it.

Anyway. An hour into *their* conversation, Reyes had handed her off to Aeron's angel, Olivia. And fifteen minutes after that, Olivia had sweetly suggested that Viola shouldn't deny Maddox the pleasure of her company. Five glorious (for him) minutes later, Maddox had stomped away, muttering something about finding his wife and Viola could join him if she insisted. So, here they were, headed to the couple's bedroom.

"I'm sure I could whip up some kind of mechanical chair that would cart your wife around," Viola told the warrior. He was shirtless, and the crimson butterfly tattoo stretching across his shoulder blades—the mark of his demon—seemed to be scowling at her. "I'm handy with tools, as you probably guessed, and your back is probably strained from her *massive* weight."

Ashlyn smothered a laugh with one hand, but she failed to smother Maddox's snarl with the other.

"She is light as a feather," he snarled. "I enjoy carrying her. I also enjoy having her all to myself."

"Okay, but it's your back's funeral. In a few years, you'll probably need a brace." Oh, yes. His tattoo was indeed scowling at her. A gnarled, skeletal face had formed between the wings, fangs extending from a tiny mouth. The edges of the wings sharpened into dagger-like points, curling toward her.

Cool, but in no way comparable to hers. The front of her butterfly stretched along her chest, stomach and legs. The back of her butterfly stretched along her shoulders, thighs and calves. A total body tat that glimmered with the radiance of crushed pink diamonds.

Ashlyn's honey-colored eyes found her over Maddox's muscled shoulder. "He's not trying to get rid of you—"

"Yes, I am," Maddox said.

"—he's just cranky," the human finished.

Viola's brow wrinkled as she attempted to figure out how the poor, addled pregnant woman could have come up with such a preposterous idea. Get rid of her? Please. Men, women and children, mortals and immortals, fought to keep her by their sides. "Don't worry your pretty little head about me," she said. Wasn't that what humans said to one another to prove they weren't offended by stupid ideas? "I'm sure he's simply overwhelmed by my magnificence."

Maddox was the one to scowl this time, tossing the dark expression at her before stopping in front of a closed door. But then Ashlyn giggled and his gaze shot to her face. His entire body softened, melting like an ice cube in the summer heat.

A pang throbbed in Viola's chest. She thought back, but couldn't remember anyone ever looking at her like that, as if she were the morning sun, the midnight moon, and every star perched in the endless sky. Even though she'd had thousands—no, bazillions!—of admirers.

"Where's your dog?" Ashlyn asked.

"Princess Fluffikans is exploring these new surroundings without any hindrance from mommy."

"That explains the screaming downstairs," Maddox muttered.

Ashlyn kissed her husband on the lips, then reached out to twist the knob. The door creaked open, and Maddox carried her inside. Fresh, clean air wafted to Viola. Out of habit, she scouted every inch in a single sweep, searching out all the mirrors and reflective surfaces. To the left was a vanity, and she made a mental note to avoid it, even as her demon urged her to close the distance…to take a teeny-tiny peek…just one, just for a second, because she would look so very beautiful….

She gritted her teeth. Dewy flowers spilled from colorful vases balanced on every piece of furniture in the room except the bed. Flowers *had* been woven in the wrought-iron bedposts, though, twining and clinging like ivy.

A portrait hung in the center of the far wall. And sweet heavens. Viola approached the thing slowly. The attention to detail was stunning. She could only take in a little at a time, studying one small section, looking away, then turning back to study another, repeating the process again and again until she'd gone over every inch.

In it, Ashlyn lounged in a lush, jewel-toned garden, flower petals in her hair, draping her body and dripping all around her. But the petals were not actually petals; they were faces. So many faces. The warriors here, their women, faces Viola didn't recognize and others she did—including her own. She quickly looked away from her own image, deciding to ponder its presence at a safer time.

One of Ashlyn's arms was bare, her skin tattooed to her elbow. Flames and snowflakes twisted together, and while the flames should have melted the flakes and the flakes should have doused the flames, the two somehow fed off each other, growing in color and intensity the higher up her arm they moved.

There was a reflective pool in front of her, and Maddox peered at her from its murky depths. Ashlyn reached for him with that tattooed arm, a silver ring winding along her index finger, glowing majestically.

Viola's nerve endings tingled. She'd seen paintings like this one before, but couldn't recall where or when. What she did know: every color, every face, every inch *meant* something. For real. This was symbolism at its finest. Only she didn't know how to decipher it.

"Who painted this?" she asked, her awe unmistakable. She straightened, turned away from the portrait before she lost hours of her life puzzling over the thing. Same as she lost hours every time she caught sight of her own image.

"Danika, Reyes's woman," Maddox muttered.

Danika. Hmm. Now that the painting was behind her, Viola allowed herself to question her inclusion in it. She'd met Danika for the first time this morning. The female appeared human, but after seeing this, she knew there had to be more to her. "It's an exquisite piece."

"Her work always is," Ashlyn said proudly.

"She sees into the future?"

"We will not discuss that," Maddox said.

So yes, she did. "She'll want to paint one of me all by myself, of course. I'll have to check my schedule and make sure I have the time to pose for her." *If not, I'll make time. Must question her. Must learn more about myself.*

Another giggle from Ashlyn. Another scowl from Maddox.

He'd placed his female on the bed and tucked the covers around her. Now he smoothed the hair from her brow, as gently as if he were caring for a fragile infant. "What do you need, sweetheart? Name it, and it's yours."

Dainty fingers rubbed at that swollen belly even as a soft smile played at her plump lips. "I would really, *really* love an orange. Just one this time, though. Last time this particular craving hit, you brought me the entire grove."

"I will bring you the best, most succulent orange you have ever tasted." He caressed her cheek for a moment, as if he couldn't bear to look away from her. Then he forced himself to do so and shot Viola a threatening glare.

"You will guard her with your life. And if you hurt her, even accidentally…" His hands fisted at his sides.

"Can't think of anything vile enough?" Viola thought for a moment. "May I suggest disembowelment? You can hang me from the ceiling with my own intestines. That would be really gruesome."

He gaped at her.

"Word of warning, though. Intestines are pink and pink is my best color. Wait. Who am I kidding? All colors are my best color. So, if you go that route, be ready to fall in love with me all over again."

His mouth snapped shut, a grimace contorting his lips. "That's it. I'm staying. Viola, you go find the orange."

"No way. Unless we go together and you carry me." All that walking had caused her feet to throb.

He looked at the door, then Viola, then the door, then Viola again.

Oh, come on. "Your resident angel already told you that I'm pure of heart, can be trusted, blah, blah, blah." That had surprised Viola, because she wasn't sure she'd ever been pure of heart. The fact that the warriors believed the dark-haired girl without a moment's hesitation had *really* surprised her. Supposedly, they were the most suspicious beings on earth. "Oh, and bring me an orange, too, but put it beside a hamburger and fries. I skipped lunch."

After issuing a few more threats to her life, he finally stalked from the room.

"Overprotective momma grisly," she muttered. "Geez."

"Have you never been in love?" Ashlyn asked.

"Hello. I'm not a fool."

"Is that a yes, then?"

"Um, yeah, that's a no."

A serene smile met her vehemence. "Why so much horror at the prospect?"

The ache in her chest returned. She rubbed and rubbed, nearly peeling off her shirt and the skin underneath, but the damn ache persisted. "I don't know." Time to change the subject. "I'm thinking about planning a singles' night here at my new home—fingers crossed it's forever—and letting the unattached warriors court me." She strolled to the bed and eased onto the edge. "Maybe a speed-dating-type thing, since I usually can't stand a man for more than a few minutes at a time. Afterward, I'll give the ones I like a rose and the others will have to pack their bags and leave the fortress permanently."

"Hmm. Well." Ashlyn tapped a finger against her chin, the corners of her lips twitching as if she were fighting another laugh. "Believe it or not, there are only a few singles left."

"Like who?"

"Well, let's see. There's Torin."

His image rose in Viola's mind. White hair, black brows, brilliant green eyes. Gorgeous face and muscled body. "He'll do. You may continue."

"Well, not that he's not wonderful, but I should warn you there's a potential drawback to dating him. He's the keeper of Disease, and he can't touch another living creature skin-to-skin without causing a plague. You wouldn't get sick from him because you're immortal, but in turn you also wouldn't be able to touch another living creature without passing on the illness. Besides him, that is."

Viola rubbed her tongue against the roof of her mouth. "You're right. I wouldn't get sick if I touched him. I'm sure you noticed how killer my immune system is. But even still, I'm not sure I want someone so flawed worshipping at my temple. Who else is there?"

"There's Kane, but he's..." Sadness dulled Ashlyn's amber eyes. "He doesn't date. Says it's not worth the hardship."

"He'd change his mind for me, of course, but that's not why you're sad, right? I believe I heard something about him being missing."

"Yes."

"Don't worry. As soon as he finds out I'm here, he'll find his way back. Even if he's dead. I don't like to brag, but that's happened a few times before. I'll just shoot out a quick little Screech, and boom. The race to reach me will begin."

Rather than cheer the girl up, her reassurances tossed worry into that storm of sadness. "Uh, you're not supposed to Screech," Ashlyn said. "Remember?"

Viola's shoulders slumped. That's right. Within five minutes of arriving here, Lucien had dragged her to the luscious Torin's bedroom and told the guy to check out her blog and website—evidently he was the resident computer guru. Afterward, both men had issued the same warning. Screech or post anything online about her location or her new BFFs and she would never be allowed back.

"Who else?" she asked.

Ashlyn nibbled on her bottom lip. "There's Cameo, but I'm pretty sure she likes men."

Viola shook her head. "I could change her mind, no problem, but I'm so over that stage of my life. Who else?"

"There's William the Ever Randy. He's not a demon keeper, but he's some kind of immortal."

William the Naughty Boy Toy. Oh, yes, she knew him. Like Anya, Viola had met him in Tartarus. "He's more than immortal, but whatever." He was also arrogant, conceited and highly annoying. "I'll put him in the maybe category."

"More than immortal? What does that mean? He's claimed to be some kind of god a few times, but I always assumed he was bragging, padding the truth. Which is—"

"Enough about him. We're talking about me. Who else can I date?"

Annnd a return of the nibbling. "There's Paris, but he's kind of obsessed with another woman right now."

"The dead one. Yeah. I know. I could still change his mind, but I don't think I want to, because…" There was a reason, wasn't there? As Viola pondered the answer, she clinked her teeth together.

Paris had asked her how to see the dead, and she had told him. Then he'd asked her something else, but Lucien arrived and ended their conversation. What had he asked? She tuned her mind's radio in to their past conversation, and her eyes widened as the answer at last slammed into place.

Consequences. He'd wanted to know if there would be consequences for tattooing himself with Sienna's ashes.

Oops. She'd let him get away without telling him that yes, there would be.

Oh, well. It wasn't her problem. It was his.

CHAPTER FOURTEEN

DAZED, SIENNA WALKED down a long hallway. Just as her past had played along the walls of the castle, Paris's past played *here,* a concerto of colors, faces, voices… limbs. On both sides of her, above and below her, women writhed, so many women. At first, she saw them smiling, heard them laughing, each one eager for what he offered, quickly falling for his charming facade.

Why wouldn't they? Whatever they wanted, he gave them. A touch, a kiss, a lick. A gentle ride. A rough pounding. He made love to all of them, knew exactly where to stroke and taste for maximum pleasure. He knew precisely the right amount of pressure to use as he kneaded their breasts, their thighs. Soft for some, firm for others.

He knew what position to place them in. On their backs, their hands and knees, right side up, upside down. Knew some wanted slow, and some wanted fast. They loved him for it, their pleasure unparalleled.

Then he left them and they cried with gut-wrenching sobs, their bodies heaving, their hearts breaking as the grief overcame them. Interspersed throughout the females were males. Paris had been with men, too, and he'd left them in the same condition as the women. They wanted him, and though they were not his preference, he took them so that he might survive. Afterward, they asked him to stay and he bailed.

One woman, Susan, was a beauty he'd truly cared for. He'd tried to make a relationship with her work, but Paris, being Paris, had hurt her in the worst way, choosing survival, as always, over her heart.

When Sienna caught an image of herself, she stopped, gasped. There, practically overshadowed by the other images, Paris was strapped to her boss's table, naked, the lights dim, and she was on top of him. She didn't need the vision to serve as a reminder. She would never forget.

She had been unable to see him, needing the darkness to relax, and he had alternated between snapping at her, hating her, hating himself, and aiding her, moving his hips to increase her pleasure. Now, however, she saw into his mind. Part of him had hoped to punish her afterward. Part of him—the deepest, most secret part—had wanted to hold on to her and never let go. To him, she had been a balm unlike any other.

Nausea rose, threatening to erupt. He had thought such beautiful things about her, and still she had condemned him.

Wrath slammed into her frontal lobe, urging her forward. To see more, to see all. She stumbled along, her feet as heavy as boulders.

Other scenes bled into the image of her and Paris, and someone must have cranked the volume control because suddenly she heard grunts, groans, moans and screams. Screams of pleasure, of pain and even of fury. Accusations were hurled, followed by pleas.

The pleas were followed by curses.

Sometimes, when Paris could find no one willing to be with him, his strength would wane, his will to live would wither and his demon would pull free of his reins. A dark, rich scent would seep from Paris's pores, intoxicating everyone nearby, luring them closer. These people would flock to him, regardless of their previous reservations about him or their disgust for casual sex. They would take him, or allow him to take them.

When this happened, Paris always battled intense guilt, because he knew the dastardly thing he was doing—but he took whatever was offered anyway.

These bedmates did not cry when he left. They watched him through narrowed eyes, detesting him, shamed by what they'd done with and to him, horrified by what they would soon lose. A loved one's respect.

He *had* broken up marriages, had committed adultery and performed sexual acts that left him cold and shaken. He then allowed those same sexual acts to be performed on him. A self-imposed punishment of sorts, she thought. All of that she could have guessed. But what astonished her? He detested himself far more powerfully than any of the humans ever had or could.

Oh, Paris, she thought. He was heaven and hell, just as Wrath had said, wrapped in the same luscious package.

Sienna wanted to cover her eyes to block the sights. She wanted to scream and scream and scream to block the sounds. *Everyone* in the crowd was crying now. Even Paris. Their tears poured from the ceiling, raining down, battering at her. But her hands remained at her sides and her mouth remained shut, her feet moving automatically. Her body was no longer connected to her brain.

Wrath wanted her to know, and so she would know.

The volume cranked up another notch, a shriek resounding at her left, spine-chilling, nauseating. All of the tears ceased. Another shriek sounded, then battle scene after battle scene came to life. Blood, a canvas of scarlet. Blades glinting with menace. Guns firing one after the other. Bombs exploding. Limbs separating from bodies, guts spilling. Death, so much death. Each delivered by Paris.

Paris, the FedEx deliveryman of Pleasure and Fatality.

There was no guilt here, however. No shame. Only cold, hard logic. Kill or be killed. No room for emotions or regrets. No hope for something better. This was it; this was the card he must constantly play. Fight for what he wanted or curl up and die.

He would not curl up and die.

Even though Sienna's own demon seemed to like Paris on some level, Wrath, being Wrath, still hoped to castigate him for all the wrongs he'd committed. The demon urged her to sleep with Paris and leave him. To break his heart. To make him sob and beg for another chance with her. Then, of course, would come the stabbing, hurting him as he had hurt so many others.

No! No, no, no. She jerked free of whatever leash the demon had used to bind her to his will and flattened her hands against her stomach, as if the puny action could settle the sickness still churning there.

"I will not punish him," she shouted, proud of her strength and conviction. Paris had done all those things, yes. And no, there was no excusing him. Though he'd been influenced by the evil creature inside him, he was responsible for his own decisions. He could have found another way.

But who was she to condemn anyone? Had *she* yet found another way? No.

Wrath offered no argument, and she frowned. That was unlike him. Usually he threw fits until she caved. But then, perhaps Aeron, Wrath's former keeper, had already fought and won this particular crusade. After all, Aeron and Paris had lived together for centuries, plenty of time for the demon to have either gotten a taste of what he desired or to have been berated into submission.

If ever she met Aeron—and if he could actually see her and didn't try to kill her—she would ask. She would do anything to return Wrath to him, too, despite the fact that such an action would kill her.

"Sienna." Warmth drifted over her cheek, sliding along the line of her jaw.

Her nerve endings perked up, firing back to life, making her skin tingle.

"Wake up for me. Come on, that's it, that's the way."

Yes. That voice...sexual and primal, blatant in its masculinity...a summoning finger she must follow. Where the voice originated, pleasure awaited her. So much pleasure.

She blinked open her eyes. Things were hazy at first, but the more she blinked, the better she could see. She was inside one of the second-floor bedrooms of the castle. The air was musty and yet chocolaty and—Paris loomed above her, peering down at her.

Breath snagged in her throat. He was just so beautiful, his face flawlessly chiseled. He could seduce anyone, anywhere. His hair was the richest shade of black, the purest shade of brown, with lighter strands woven throughout like ribbons of gold. His eyes were a wanton crystal, his lashes so thick and black they weighed down his lids, keeping them at half-mast, forever come-to-bed tempting. His lips were lush and red, and perhaps the most decadent part of an already decadent man. His skin was like crushed diamonds mixed with honey and cream. Pale, yet kissed with shimmers of the sun.

He bore a few scratches and had shadows under his eyes, but neither acted as an imperfection. They simply enhanced his appeal, adding depth. Lover, warrior...

protector of those of his choosing. And he was here. With her.

"How are you feeling?" he asked, the words scratchy now, as if there were glass shards stuck in his throat.

Was that a note of concern she detected? If so, this must be a hallucination. Paris wouldn't care for her well-being. Not after everything that had happened between them. With a shaky hand, she reached up and pressed her fingertips into the rose tinting his cheeks. Solid, warm. Real.

She gasped out a startled, "You really are here."

"Yes. I... Yes." His pupils expanded, concealing all the blue with a spiderweb of black, before snapping back into place. "How are you feeling?"

"Fine." There was a slight twinge in her stomach, a definite ache in her wings, but nothing that was un-manageable. A perk of being undead as well as Wrath's host, she supposed. No matter the severity of her inju-ries, death had no hold on her and she healed quickly.

"I cleaned you up, bandaged the worst of your wounds." Guilt layered his tone, a deeper flush bloom-ing across his cheeks. Those pupils expanded again, stay-ing that way—nope, they snapped back.

She'd never seen eyes do that. "Thank you." She moved her hand to her hair, grimaced when she encoun-tered tangles. She must look like total crap. "And you? How are you?" Her question trembled with the same in-tensity as her hand.

"Fine," he parroted, offering no more than she had.

He straightened, increasing the distance between them, though his hip remained pressed against hers. One of his arms slid forward and stopped beside her rib cage, taking the brunt of his weight.

They stayed like that for a long while, silent, looking at each other, then looking away.

This was…awkward. Really, *really* awkward. They hadn't seen each other in so long, and the last time they had, well, things had not ended well. *No one but yourself to blame,* she thought sadly.

"A lot has happened since we were last together," he began, then lapsed into silence as if contemplating all that had occurred.

"Yes," she agreed, though she had spent too much time contemplating it already.

"I know you were given a demon. What I don't know is how you're handling him," he said, staring somewhere far, far beyond her shoulder.

"We have our moments."

"He shows you the sins of others?"

"Yes."

"And forces you to punish the wrongdoers?"

"Yes."

He nodded. "Aeron, the guy who had Wrath before you, used to hate that. He would resist for as long as he could."

"And then Wrath would overtake him," she grumbled.

"Yeah."

"I have the same problem." Usually she saw the images of a person's sins while she was awake, and things would progress from there. She would fight the urges and win, or she would fight the urges and fail. She wasn't sure what to make of the fact that she'd seen Paris's transgressions while she was asleep.

Another bout of uncomfortable silence ensued. There was so much to say, but she didn't know where to begin.

"Paris," she breathed at the same time he sighed and said, "Sienna."

They stared at each other now, searching, unsure. *Annnd* once again silence reigned, so heavy she could feel the weight of it pressing her deeper into the mattress. Her heart careened against her chest in a useless attempt at escape. If the damn thing had been hooked to a battery, she would have pulled the plug. Anything for relief from this suspended, anxious sensation, fear of sending Paris fleeing preventing her from saying all the things she'd imagined saying to him.

"You go first," he said, a muscle ticking in his jaw.

Very well. She could do this. *She could.* "I just wondered how you got here and why you...why you came for me." And he had definitely come for her, and her alone. Why else would he have shouted her name like that? Did he hope to punish her for what she'd once done to him?

His eyes narrowed. "I changed my mind. I'll go first. Tell me why *you* came to *me,* that night in Texas when William saw you at my feet. William being my *homely* friend." Through those slitted lids, she saw that his irises had frosted over, the darkness still evident. His expression became granite-hard, ruthless determination cloaking him.

The man who sat before her now was not the one who'd fought the Gargl to reach her; he was not the one who'd taken such care with her wounds. And he *had* cared for her wounds. She'd been cleaned, bandaged, just as he'd said.

No, the man who sat before her was the one she'd first met in Rome. The one who had kissed her one minute and woken up strapped to a torture table the next. The one who had cursed her with one breath, and praised her with the following.

Whoever he was, she wouldn't lie to him. She would never lie to him again. "I needed help," she admitted, "and Wrath knew where you were, how to reach you. He had taken over, and I came to there at your feet."

"Do you still need help?"

"With Wrath? Yes."

He nodded, losing that knife edge of ruthlessness. "I'm sorry I couldn't see you that night."

"You have nothing to apologize for."

"Anyway," he said after clearing his throat. "I figured you would have trouble adapting, though you're doing far better than I did at this stage, so I asked Aeron if he had any tips for you. He said you'll have an easy time of things if you feed the bastard a little bit every day. Someone lies to you, you lie back. Someone cheats you, you cheat them back. Someone hits you, you hit back."

How willingly he offered the information. He didn't make her beg. Didn't taunt her because he knew and she didn't. And Aeron hadn't withheld the information, when he had to hate her for taking his companion—and they *had* been companions. Wrath had been an extension of him, still missed him to this day. But as grateful as she was for the advice...what a terrible way to live, she thought. "Thank you for that."

"Welcome," he said stiffly. Then, "Do you still think I'm evil and in need of snuffing out?"

"No! You're not evil." That she had ever placed the man in the same category as the demon... She was so very ashamed. How foolish she'd been. How gullible. "I'm sorry that I ever thought you were."

The visual perusal he next gave her peeled away her clothing, leaving her bare, trembling. "And I should believe you?"

He would never trust her, but then, why should he? "Being paired with Wrath, well, my eyes were opened. I saw the truth for the first time. The things I did...the things I'm urged to do…you've been dealing with that for thousands of years, and still you fight. Doubt me all you want, but I vow to you now." To stop herself from reaching out to him, she fisted her hands at her sides. "I will never hurt you again."

In his hooded eyes she saw flecks of anger, a blaze of arousal. Then, nothing.

He looked away from her, gaze landing on the room's only window. There was a crack in the thick, black curtains, a single ray of moonlight slipping inside. Then he offered a shrug of one strong shoulder. "You asked why I came for you."

Disappointment rocked her. A response to her vow would have been nice. But then, she didn't deserve it. "Yes."

"I— Damn it. I couldn't let you suffer."

He couldn't…let her…suffer…oh… Here was a mercy she was no longer capable of offering to others, so she knew how precious it was. Tears sprang to her eyes and tracked down her cheeks, a trickle at first, then a flood. Until her body was heaving with the same force as the women in that dream hallway. Until she couldn't see the bedroom or Paris.

What happened to growing a pair of lady balls? Breaking down now, in front of him, was humiliating, but she couldn't stop.

Her shame exploded, little pieces tossed into every corner of her body, saturating her. All her life, she'd only ever been able to rely on herself. Her mom's alcoholism, which had started right after Skye's abduction, had eaten away at any love the woman had felt for Sienna. Her dad had eventually taken off and started another family, forgetting the little girl he'd left behind.

Then in college, she'd begun dating Hugh. He'd listened to her stories about her past, offered sympathy and aid. He'd told her about himself, and his belief in the supernatural. When she expressed doubt, he promised to show her—and he had. She'd been scared yet thrilled at the same time, because then she'd had someone to blame for every single one of her troubles.

How freeing that had been. How marvelous to realize that her mother wasn't at fault. Her father wasn't at fault. *She* wasn't at fault. How soothing to think her parents would have loved her still if not for the evil the Lords had brought into the world. So, yeah, she'd jumped headfirst into the good-versus-evil game.

And yet, the Hunters had gunned her down to get to Paris.

Paris, who hadn't wanted her to suffer.

Her sobs emerged so powerfully, she was soon hiccupping, eyes and nose running freely, and that sent her embarrassment to a new level. Stalwart arms wrapped around her, careful not to brush against her fragile wings, lifting her, drawing her into a hot, muscled chest. His heartbeat hammered as swiftly as hers.

And wouldn't you know, that made her cry even harder.

"Calm down," he commanded, clearly uncomfortable. And wow. You would think a man who'd been with as many women as Paris had would know how to finesse one who was nearing hysteria, but no. He patted her back a little too roughly, then glared down at her when she failed to obey him.

How could he *not* want her to suffer? How could she ever have judged him so harshly?

"Sienna. Stop this."

"Can't…help…it. Did such…terrible things to…you. And you…you're here. And you're being so *nice*."

A pause, as if he couldn't quite digest her words. Then, very gently, he said, "But I did terrible things to you, too. Didn't I?"

CHAPTER FIFTEEN

SIENNA TOLD HERSELF TO SHUT UP, to lock down tight, but the words poured out of her of their own accord. "You were going to have sex with me and walk away. Not the most chivalrous behavior, but that hardly justifies being drugged, tortured and nearly killed. I tricked you, let them hurt you. And then I raped you. I think I raped you." She choked, but still the words kept coming. "I'm sorry, Paris. I'm so sorry. I know that's not good enough. Nothing I say will ever be good enough, but—"

"Sienna."

"I'm sorry. I am. And afterward, when I was dying, I blamed you, but it wasn't your fault. I told you I hated you, and I'm so very sorry for that, too. You didn't deserve any of it."

Another pause. His hands began to move down her back, caressing now, before sliding back up again, soothing her. "You didn't rape me," he said, and there was a surprising tinge of amusement in his tone. "I wanted you. I wanted you so damn badly, even though I didn't want to want you." Or maybe she'd imagined the amusement. His timbre was now an abrasive rasp.

"I slept with you because I was told to, because I wanted to destroy you," she said.

"I slept with you to strengthen myself."

"But I still wanted you," she added in a soft whisper.

His fingertips pressed into the muscles just under the

rise of her wings, but the pressure eased all too soon. "And I still wanted you. That's one of the reasons I took you with me when I got free, because I wanted to be with you again."

Another sob left her. "I thought you used me as a shield, and I...I..." Well, crap. The sobs became so great her voice box finally closed up.

He pressed a kiss into her temple. "I didn't use you as a shield. Not intentionally, at least. I'm sorry for how things ended, so very, very sorry. If it helps, I've punished myself a thousand times, will probably punish myself a thousand more. Had I known what would happen, I would have left you there...and come back for you later."

The last was offered hesitantly, as if he feared her reaction to such a truth. "I'm glad."

An eternity passed just like that, the two of them clutching at each other, the silence no longer prickly but calming. And, okay. Maybe she was the only one doing the clutching, but he didn't seem to mind. He continued to caress her.

She hadn't realized how much she'd craved contact with another body until just that moment. That the body belonged to Paris, well, that made it even better. He was so strong, and smelled so sweet, and if she wasn't careful, she would soon be rubbing her cheek against his chest, burying her nose in the hollow of his neck and twining herself around him like a vine.

When at last she quieted, exhaustion set in and she just kind of sagged against him, her head resting on his shoulder. Her eyes were swollen, heavy, her nose stuffed up, and her throat raw from her tears.

"Better?" he asked.

"Yes, thank you. I...I... Paris." Her lips parted, and

she inhaled through her mouth. "Despite everything, you came here to help me. You put yourself in danger."

"Danger is nothing to me." His voice had become gruff, as if he disliked the direction the conversation had gone in.

Danger might be nothing to him, but she'd seen him with his friends. *They* were everything to him, and still he'd left them to save her. A surreal—and even more shaming—realization.

What did his unwillingness to let her suffer mean? Did he, dare she hope, have feelings for her? Crave something *more* with her? Though she wasn't ready to release him, she did just that, pulling back, taking another deep breath and drawing in the dark-chocolate scent of him. If the movement hadn't disrupted the angle of her wings, lancing a sharp pain through her, she would have sat there, savoring him, drowning in a sudden burst of arousal, for hours.

Frowning, Paris maneuvered the gossamer extensions of her wings into a more comfortable position. He was infinitely careful, his every motion checked. When he finished, he eyed her warily. "Better?" he asked again.

He *had* to have feelings for her. Impossible, and yet, possible all the same. "Yes, thank you." She looked down at her hands. They were wringing her shirt, twisting and wrinkling the material, yet she hadn't realized she'd moved them. She should ask him about his feelings. She should—

"Why did you walk away from me when you first saw me?" he asked, his tone curious rather than accusatory. "When the gargoyles had me."

"I thought you were a hallucination. A memory. They're like film reels, playing around me in a never-ending stream."

His frown deepened, pulling those lush lips tight over perfect white teeth. "Even now?"

Her gaze darted around the room, and she could only gape. She saw crumbling stone, portraits draped by sheets, but no memories. "No. It's just you and me." Probably because they couldn't steal her attention away from Paris. "Paris, I want to tell you things. About the Hunters. Things that could help you and your friends. I—"

"No," he said, cutting her off.

"But—"

He gave an abrupt shake of his head. "No," he reiterated.

"I don't understand."

"I don't want you to tell me anything about them."

"But...why?" Even when she had been poised over his helpless body, moving on him, even when he had rightly blamed her for his condition, he had not peered at her with such harsh resolve. Red flickered through his eyes, those shadows once again dancing through his irises.

She didn't have to consider the problem long before the answer slithered into place, a boa ready to suffocate its prey. He thought she would mislead him, send him straight into a trap, and there would be nothing she could say to convince him otherwise. That hurt, but then she deserved that and more.

Not knowing what else to do, she shied away from the topic. "How can you see me, hear me? Touch me? You couldn't before."

The red faded, the shadows stilled. His pupils did that expanding, contracting thing, taut rubber bands ready to snap.

"I learned a few tricks about the dead," he said. "That's all."

And he wouldn't share those tricks or anything else with her; his tone made that clear. An ache ignited in her heart, dropped into her stomach and guillotined every bit of happiness his presence here had wrought.

"Did you also learn how to break a curse and bust someone out of a castle they can't leave?" she asked. Good. Back to business. *Without* another breakdown.

A terrible stillness came over him. "I knew you were trapped here, but I'm still not sure how."

"Do you know where here is?" She could guess, but the answers that came to her made her sick.

"A hidden kingdom in the Titans' section of the heavens."

Her eyes widened. "Heavens? Really? I would have bet somewhere in hell."

"What happens when you try to leave?"

"There's some kind of invisible block. I approach a door or a window and I hurt, and if I remain in front of the portal for too long, I pass out. But sometimes... sometimes Wrath takes over and the blocks fall away. I end up outside the castle's walls, not too far from here, I don't think. And I do things. Terrible things," she whispered. "Then I come back here, I can't stop myself. I step inside and the blocks immediately go back up."

He reached out as if he meant to cup her cheek, to offer comfort. Then he growled, low and guttural, and his arm dropped to his side. That made her want to erupt into a fresh round of sobbing, but she didn't allow herself the luxury. Not even when he jerked to a stand, stalked to the window and tossed the curtains aside, the distance a great chasm between them—symbolic.

Dust wafted around him. A few tugs, and he had the pane lifted. Hot, pungent air drifted inside, stinging her nostrils. He palmed a blade, extended his arm into the darkness—and met no resistance.

Others *could* leave, she realized. Only she was trapped.

He slid the glass into place and spun to face her. He didn't return to her side, but leaned back, propping himself against the wall. The bulge of his muscles stretched the black material of his T-shirt. His pants hugged his thighs—and an impressive erection.

Could he possibly...want her? The way she wanted him?

Who are you trying to fool? He's the Lord of Sex. He probably has that reaction with everyone.

"Can you let Wrath take over your body without taking over your mind?" he asked, a catch in his voice.

She forced herself to meet his eyes as heat flashed in her cheeks. "I, uh... He takes over both, but I've never just let him. I don't always win, but I always fight him."

"Stop fighting him. Let him take over your body, but try to maintain some kind of tether to your mind."

Her mouth fell open, snapped closed. Just like that, he wanted her to allow the being that thrived on punishing *everyone* to consume her, to drive her every action? "You don't understand what would happen if I did that."

He gave a bitter laugh that did nothing to mar his masculine perfection, and everything to enhance it. Maybe because with the unveiling of his bitterness came a need to kiss him better. "Oh, but I do."

Yes, she supposed he must. "Wrath hurts people. *I* hurt people. And what if I hurt *you?*"

Melted steel in his eyes, bubbling from his voice. "I can take care of myself, and I want to get you out of here."

"I want that, too." Just not enough to risk hurting

him. And really, her demon wasn't the only—or even the worst—worry. Her eyes widened. How could she have forgotten, even for a moment? "Cronus," she gasped out. "If you help me, Cronus will come after you. I'm surprised he hasn't already."

"Way I hear it, he's been too busy to concern himself with me." Paris grinned, slow and wicked. Eager. "But he and I are due a reckoning, and we'll soon have it."

Her hand fluttered to her throat. "Not on my account. I don't want you—"

"Do you have any family?" he asked, interrupting her. "Anyone I can take you to once I get you out of the heavens?"

She blinked. He'd saved her, still felt desire for her if his erection was any indication, but he didn't intend to keep her, or even be with her. He wanted to foist her off as quickly as possible. Of course. Stupid, stupid Sienna for ever hoping otherwise.

They couldn't make anything work between them, anyway. She knew more about his demon now and knew Paris couldn't sleep with her again, despite...*that*. Right? He was a one-time only joyride. *Right?*

"Sienna," he snapped. "Eyes on my face. Please."

The heat in her cheeks rose to scalding as she jerked her gaze away from his man business a second time. "I'm sorry. I didn't mean to make you feel like a piece of meat. I was just lost in thought."

"About my di—uh, junk?"

"Well, yes."

His jaw dropped with the force of his astonishment, and she had to wonder why the god of sex would find such a revelation so unbelievable.

Anyway. What had he asked her before? Oh, yeah. Her family. "No. There's no one who could take me in, no

one who could even see me." As she spoke, she looked
the rest of him over. He was still cut from the Gargl, the
wounds now scabbed. He had healed, but only slightly.
And his skin had lost a bit of its glittery sheen. Was he
weakening from lack of sex? That's what had happened
in the Hunters' prison.

"When was the last time you had a woman?" she
asked, trying to act nonchalant about a very sore subject between them.

The frost she'd seen earlier fell over his entire body.
His eyelids narrowed, the gleam in those ocean-pretty
irises flint hard.

"I don't remember," he gritted out.

The confession relieved and thrilled her, she was
ashamed to admit. He was clearly hurting. "Well, I'm…
uh, I'm, you know…available. For you. If you can, I
mean. And if you, you know, want me and can use…
that on me." How pathetic she sounded, but she wanted
to touch him again, to be with him one last time. Even if
she had to reduce the act to a simple clinical procedure.
"I owe you." Or a favor between pseudo-friends.

The ice thickened, cracked, thickened again, as if a
battle raged inside him. The ice won. "Really? You're
available to me? You owe me?" He popped his jaw.
"Thank you for that *generous* offer. How could a guy
like me ever refuse?"

A guy like him? "I didn't mean—"

"Just so you know, I didn't come all this way to enjoy
your *availability* or to collect on a debt. So, while I can,
in fact, screw you again, I hope you'll understand when
I do the unthinkable and pass. But don't worry, I'll still
help you. Screwing me isn't a requirement."

She chewed on her bottom lip to stop herself from re-
sponding. *Deserved, deserved, deserved,* she told herself

again. And maybe his refusal was a good thing. He still resented her. And as he'd already proven, he didn't trust her. Being with him, and watching him walk away afterward, would slice her into pieces so jagged she'd never be able to fit herself back together.

More than that, she had to go after Galen. The thought hit with so much force her entire body shook. She had toyed with the idea, but hadn't decided officially. Now, she saw the truth. She'd told Paris she had no family, but what if she did? And what if only she could save them? If there were the slightest possibility that Galen was torturing her sister and her child, Sienna had to act, which meant she might have to…do things with him. Necessary things. Things she wouldn't be able to bring herself to do if she forged any kind of bond with Paris. A white-hot toxin flooded her veins, stinging.

"You look disgusted and scared," Paris said, his voice as sharp as any dagger. "Why?"

"Neither emotion is for you," she said quietly. Never for him. Not anymore.

A hard knock sounded at the door, followed by the homely guy's rough timbre. "Paris. This isn't exactly life and death, my man, but things are quiet in there so I figure you haven't quite learned how to undo her bra strap. Give it a rest and come out here. You have to see this."

Paris looked like he'd just been granted a reprieve from a firing squad. He straightened. "On my way," he called. He stood there for a moment, grinding his molars, thinking about something unpleasant, judging by the expression on his face. Then he stalked to the bed and held out his hand, helping her lumber to her feet.

His calluses abraded her palm in the most delicious way, and she shivered. "Thank you."

"Whatever." He didn't lead her out, but leveled her with a fierce frown. "Don't try to leave my side. Understand?"

Was he afraid she'd run from him? Afraid she'd tell someone where he was so they could kill him?

Deserved, she reminded herself. What really sucked about the whole situation was that she couldn't ask for a second chance with him, or even an opportunity to redeem herself. As she'd just realized, they were already doomed, her path already decided.

Another realization struck. That same path could give him what he wanted more than anything. Victory against the Hunters. Not that he would ever know the part she'd played. If Cronus had his way, Paris would assume she was Galen's mistress. His sexual toy. And...and she would be, at least until she learned the truth about Skye. Then she would kill him, as *she* wanted, no matter the consequences to herself.

"Sienna," Paris snapped, drawing her back to the present.

She peered up at him. No matter how things shook out, she was going to lose him, and that was a hard fact given that she'd only just found him again. But for today, she was with him. That would have to be enough. "I won't leave your side."

CHAPTER SIXTEEN

GALEN, KEEPER OF HOPE, leader of the Hunters, leisurely explored the rooms inside his enemy's fortress. He'd only recently healed from battle wounds he'd received courtesy of the Lords of the Underworld. Now it was time for payback.

The blade he held was new and had never seen a single moment of action. Today, that would change.

"—shut that damn thing up," Cameo, keeper of Misery, was saying as she snaked around the corner and stomped past him. Draped as he was by the Cloak of Invisibility, she failed to spot him.

He studied her as she passed. In all the centuries since their creation, she hadn't changed. She had long, dark hair made for fisting, and the slim body of a dancer made for screwing. Her eyes were liquid silver—and made for dangling from his necklace. "If you don't, I will stab both of you. And let me tell you, one-point-eight people die every second. I never mind adding to the tally."

Maybe she *had* changed. The low, raspy resonance of her voice carried the heavy burden of a world's worth of sorrows. Enough to spring an ache in his chest, one that promptly seeped outward, invading more and more of him. In the heavens, her voice had brought only pleasure.

Scowling, Galen tucked the length of his wings into his sides and pressed against the wall. The action caused a white feather to loosen and drift to the floor, no longer hidden by the Cloak. He bent to pick it up, stopped.

A short, curvy blonde clutching a black dog...thing darted after Cameo. "All's I'm saying is that with a little makeup you could look like my country cousin rather than my undernourished uncle. Maybe no one's told you this, but bags are meant to be carried in your hands, not under your eyes."

The—mutant dog's?—head twisted, twisted, its beady eyes locked on Galen. A lethal growl rent the air, fangs spearing its lower lip. Evidently the Cloak's magic did not work on all creatures. (What *was* that thing?) He flipped it off, and it yipped.

"Hush, princess. Mama's teaching Beauty 101 to the clueless. Besides, we don't want the silly Lords upset with you again, do we?"

Galen didn't recognize the blonde or her ugly "princess." What he did know? The Lords welcomed only a select few into their exalted midst. That meant she was either a new addition to the Lords' army or a warrior's girlfriend. Pitiful how many of the once-stalwart men had fallen in *lurrrve* recently.

Whatever or whoever she was, she would die like the others.

The duo and their not-quite-canine companion stormed into one of the bedrooms. A door slammed. No alarm was sounded.

His scowl melted into a grin. They couldn't see him, but they could have sensed him. That they hadn't meant this would be easier than he'd thought.

Strider, the idiot, had given the Cloak of Invisibility to the Unspoken Ones, beings so vicious, so evil, even Hercules would have trembled in fear at the slightest mention of them. Cronus had enslaved them before his own imprisonment, had once thought to control them. In turn, they wanted him dead. Now they were trapped on their private island in Rome and reduced to bargaining.

A point in Galen's favor. They knew he was destined to remove the Titan king's head, and so when he visited their island, they sought his support. Their first gesture, giving him the Cloak. Their second, teaching him exactly how to use it. He'd assumed it was a shield against prying eyes, but he'd assumed wrong. The Cloak was also a weapon. A very effective one at that.

He needed every advantage he could get, even if that meant aligning himself with the worst creatures ever to roam this earth. His men were disappearing right off the streets, never to be heard from again. His queen had disappeared, as well. He'd had no contact with her for weeks.

She knew him well enough to know he looked out for Number One. He would betray anyone to get what he wanted, and if she'd decided to walk away, to betray him as he'd betrayed so many others, that was her problem. He would go after her the same way he continued to go after her husband. With everything he had.

Galen planned to rule the heavens. *And I'll succeed this time.* He knew it, but then, he always "knew" his plans would work. His demon could convince anyone to do anything—and Galen was included in that number. Hope built up everyone's dreams, then laughed when those dreams came crashing down.

But it wasn't Hope driving him this day. It was Jealousy. His other demon.

Oh, yes. His former friends might not have been bright enough to figure this out yet, but Galen was possessed by *two* of Pandora's demons.

Because he had convinced his fellow warriors to steal

her box, because he'd then betrayed them, thinking to become leader of the Elite Guard himself, taking Lucien's place, he'd committed two crimes. Therefore, he deserved two punishments. Or so Zeus had said when he'd set about pairing each Lord with their demon and restoring order to the heavens.

He *despised* having two demons. Hope built him up only to tear him down, then Jealousy would rile him back up, whispering things like, *That male has a female, yet we are far better. Why don't we take her from him?* Hope would then fill him with an urge to do just that, to take, the need becoming a living thing inside him, every ounce of his being certain he would succeed—but somehow always falling short of victory.

Well, today he would not fail.

Today he landed a stunning blow to his enemy.

He would steal away Legion, the devil-woman they'd once sent to kill him. The she-cat who had seduced him. The innocent virgin who'd been living inside a porn star's skin. She'd screwed him within an inch of his immortal life before biting him with her poisoned fangs. While he had writhed in pain, she had left him to die, only to be carted into hell thanks to a deal with her maker gone bad.

Galen had hunted her, but the Lords had found her first. They'd brought her here, and Galen wanted her back. Wanted to have her again. Wanted to punish her. To kill her and cut the tether she seemed to hold him on.

He was sick of wondering about her, sick of thinking about her.

How many warriors had she given herself to since her return?

Yeah, like that. He was sick of imagining her with

a thousand others, sick of the constant rage of jealousy concerning her.

He would discover the answer, though, and if any of the Lords had enjoyed her luscious body, they would pay a higher toll than their friends. Oh, each and every one of them would die, but some would scream for months before he took their heads.

Except…he searched the fortress from top to bottom, looked in every chamber, accounted for every warrior still in residence—and not even Torin, who monitored the place, noticed him—but there was no sign of the girl.

Very well. He'd go with Plan B. He would take a page from the Unspoken Ones' book and "bargain" before he struck.

Despising the delay, he stalked to Maddox and Ashlyn's bedroom and ghosted through the wood. He wasn't just invisible, he was insubstantial. Maddox, keeper of Violence, was no longer inside. His very pregnant female reclined on their bed, reading a book to her unborn babe. A babe Maddox would be desperate to save.

Ashlyn was a pretty thing, with hair, skin and eyes the color of a honeycomb. Truly, she was as golden as the moon on the brightest of nights, and she was delicate and fragile as only a human could be. Her voice was soft, lilting, and filled with love.

No question, Maddox would move heaven and earth to get her back.

Galen padded to the side of the bed and pushed the Cloak from one shoulder. As he materialized, another grin quirked the corners of his mouth. Ashlyn noticed him and quieted, her entire body jolting with fright.

"Galen," she gasped out.

"Scream for me, little Ashlyn," he said, reaching for her. And she did.

WILLIAM KIND OF EXPECTED to be pulverized the moment Paris emerged from the bedroom. Fists hammering at his face, teeth ripping at his jugular, something menacing like that since he'd dared to interrupt the happy reunion. After all, madness and mayhem were a Paris Lord staple. What William hadn't expected was a half grateful, half thunderous stare, but that's exactly what he got.

"What did you want to show me?" the Lord of Sex snapped.

Paris had moved mountains to get here. Had done things that made a reprobate like William look like a choirboy, all to save the girl he currently had tucked into his side. And that he was holding her hand as if she were a life raft and the flood had come, rather than swinging at the man who had just cock-blocked him…well, that was just weird.

It could mean one of two things. Paris had already had sex with her, so there'd been nothing to block. Yet only an hour had passed since their parting. So *that* would mean Paris was quick on the climax trigger and, as many ladies as he'd nailed, William would bet the guy could go all night and then some.

Option two was slightly more likely, but still improbable. Paris hadn't known what to do with the girl and had wanted to bail.

But why would he want to bail? For that matter, why, with every second that passed, did he appear more pissed than ever? Had Sienna turned him down flat?

Impossible, William thought next. She was clutching Paris's hand as desperately as he clutched hers.

William raked his gaze over her. She was pale, her freckles stark in contrast, and she was a bit shaky on her feet. Hmm. Studying her like this, he wondered what Paris saw in her.

At first glance, and hell, maybe even at second, she appeared plain. He looked deeper, though, and that's when the delicacy of her bone structure became evident. What's more, those hazel eyes were large and unbelievably lovely, the perfect blend of emerald and copper. Her hair was a waterfall of mahogany, cascading around her. And her lips…yeah, he would have committed a few crimes himself to have those fit around his shaft.

She was on the slender side, small-breasted and even underweight, but damn if she didn't call on every protective instinct a man possessed.

"Are you just going to stare at her?" Once again Paris snapped the words. This time, menace poured from him, the threat of attack very real.

Now William doubted his face would be the only thing rearranged. His favorite appendage would be on the receiving end of a nice little slice and dice. *Sooo.* The biggest he-slut ever created was possessive as hell over a woman who'd once wanted to kill him. Talk about comeuppance. But then, wasn't that what Wrath specialized in?

Paris took a step toward him, the menace intensifying. "I asked you a question."

William cut off a grin and held his hands up, palms out, questions rolling through his mind. How much did Paris really want the girl? Did he regret coming here? How much influence could she wield over his emotions? Was the plan still to get in, get out and get rid of her? Only one way to find out.

"Answer me," Paris snapped.

"Nope," William said. "I don't just plan to stare."

A growl erupted from the warrior. They both knew he'd just implied he meant to do more.

Good. Maybe William would survive what came next,

maybe he wouldn't. "I like your shirt," he said, directing the compliment to Sienna. "I *really* like your pants." She wore a plain white T-shirt, dirt-smudged and torn, and baggy cargo pants. Her tennis shoes were missing laces.

"I... Thanks?" Her brows knit with her confusion.

"May I make a wardrobe suggestion, though?"

Another growl sounded from Paris before she could reply, a hand darting out and wrapping around William's windpipe. Pinpricks of red glowed inside those ocean-blues. No, Paris's irises were no longer blue. They were black, no difference between pupils and the rest. "Are you now implying her clothes will look better on your bedroom floor?"

So. Much. Fun. "Who, me?" He couldn't breathe, so the words squeaked out. No, Paris did not regret coming here.

"Paris," Sienna said, utterly calm. "I know I have no right to ask this, but will you please not kill him? I'm not a fan of the rotting body scent."

Tighter...tighter...then the pressure eased, fell away. "Show us what you found."

Interesting. She wielded a *lot* of influence. He wondered if Paris realized how much—and exactly what the warrior thought of the development. But no matter what, William assumed the plan was still of the get-rid variety. No relationship lasted without trust, and these two had not a spark of it between them. Even as Paris eyed William like a slab of beef to carve for dinner, he kept Sienna in his crosshairs, as if afraid she'd bolt, or even do a little carving of her own.

"Come on, or you'll be ticked I didn't show you sooner." William turned on his heel and marched down the hallway and up another flight of stairs to the third floor. He didn't have to look back to know the couple followed him. Paris's booted footfalls reminded him of stampeding buffalo.

He slowed his pace and Paris came up beside him. At some point, the warrior had picked Sienna up. She was cradled in his arms, her wings tucked around her, her head resting in the hollow of his neck. Even more interesting was the fact that she hadn't uttered a complaint.

Her gaze met William's, steady as a rock. She frowned. "Wrath goes silent around you. He doesn't show me any of your perceived sins. Why is that?"

Oh, no. He wasn't veering down that conversation path. Not with a former Hunter and a dead, though brought back to life, newly possessed whatever the hell she was. "You'll have to ask him."

"I did."

He pressed his tongue to the roof of his mouth. "And?"

"And he offered no response, so I decided it's because you have to live with yourself, a punishment worse than anything Wrath could mete out."

Miracle of miracles. The demon wasn't tattling on him. "The answer will just have to remain a mystery, then. Oh, and a word of warning. Smart mouths really crank my chain. Keep talking dirty to me, baby."

She rolled her eyes.

Paris inserted himself into the conversation with a hesitant, "Did he show you mine?" That he didn't threaten William proved the depths of his uncertainty about what Wrath might have broadcast.

William had seen Paris aroused (not on purpose), playful, pissed off, blood-soaked, stubborn, drugged out, relaxed, stressed and everything in between. But he had never seen the warrior frightened. Just then, Paris was frightened, his expression haunted, his muscles knotted over bone.

"Yes," she replied so quietly he had to strain to hear.

A taut beat of silence. "Do you want me to put you down?"

"No!" Color flooded her cheeks when she realized just how loudly she'd shouted the word. "No. I like where I am."

From a mouse to a lioness. Adorable really, and William thought he might make a pass at her when Paris finished with her. Because, even as fierce as Paris was about her, he would let her go. Resolve had bled into the fear. Even though Paris had suspected she would not want to be touched by a man who had done the things he'd done, even though she had proven him wrong and that had to be a relief, he was determined to live without her.

"I just meant that, uh, my back hurts," she added. "I need your support."

"Like a good jockstrap," William said, patting his boy on the shoulder. "But then, that's Paris for you."

Even with Sienna in his arms, Paris managed to give him a two-fingered salute. Mentally, of course, but William saw it all the same.

"I should have asked him to finish you off, rather than to let you go," she muttered. Then, "Are we heading to the fifth floor?"

Ah. So she knew what was up there. "Yes."

"Why?" Paris asked.

"You'll see," William replied.

Sienna opted to ruin the surprise. "Other demon-possessed immortals are up there."

"Other demon…" Paris increased his speed, leaving William eating his dust. "Are they armed?"

"No," she said, "but they're trapped."

"Show me."

"That's what *I* was trying to do," William muttered as

he chased after them. One day it would be nice for someone to place *him* first. Not a lover, though, and not the girl who haunted his dreams. The girl he would protect with his life now and always. She wasn't meant for him.

His one true love would die—or kill him. It had already been foretold, and there was no other option.

CHAPTER SEVENTEEN

CAREFUL TO KEEP HIS MIND on the situation at hand, rather than on his aching, needy body, Paris stopped in the center of the fifth-floor hallway. He was shocked by what he found. Only Sienna's slight weight in his arms, her tropical, feminine scent in his nose, her silky hair brushing against his skin, grounded him.

Funny, that. The magnification of her drugging scent should have sent him flying straight into a round of withdrawal—or chewing at her neck. Instead, the need to protect her, even from himself, beat everything else.

There were three immortals up here, a female and two males. They stood at the back of their rooms, staring at him, making no moves toward him. He'd never met them, which meant he hadn't locked them in Tartarus before his possession. Still, they were glaring at him. Did they know who he was? *What* he was?

I want them, Sex said.

Wow. What a shock.

A whiny *I'm becoming weaker by the minute* followed.

Believe me, I know. How he longed for the days when Sex retreated into the land of silence and led him simply through urges. *Now, do me a solid and stuff it.*

That's what I'm trying to do!

Crude bastard.

Like Paris was really any better. Over the years Paris had slept with thousands of different people for thousands of different reasons, and not all of them had been about passion. He truly needed to take a woman, like, yesterday, and that's one of the reasons he was here, to be with Sienna again. But he hadn't so much as kissed her, even though he was desperate to do so, because he didn't want to be with her for any reason *but* passion.

Mutual desire mattered.

She desired him, yes. At least, he was pretty sure he'd caught the scent of her arousal while she'd offered to "service" him, but he'd treated her shabbily. She'd looked at him with those sad, watery eyes, hopeful for forgiveness, and he'd snapped at her.

Damn it, he didn't want her apology or her gratitude. Didn't want her pity, and certainly didn't want her to want him because of his demon's pheromones. Had he taken her up on her offer, gratitude and pity would have been in that bed with them, as well as anger, distrust and regret. He hadn't done the ménage thing for a long time.

Maybe he should have taken what he could get, though. Waiting was kind of stupid. Case in point—his current weakness. More than that, Sienna might not give him a second chance. She might run, as he'd feared. It was just, she wasn't like any of the other women he'd been with, and he didn't want to treat her as if she were.

What makes her different from the others?

The question sprang from deep within him, throwing him. She was gutsy, but so were others. She was witty, but so were others. She was sometimes sweet and sometimes spicy, but again, so were others.

Mmm, spicy.

Stupid Sex. Anyway. Sienna was also guarded, yet vulnerable. Determined, yet kind. She was willing to go to any lengths to see a mission through to the very end.

Just like him. She had seen visions of his past, yet had thrown no judgment his way.

Once, Paris had asked Aeron exactly what the demon revealed in regards to him. The reply had been brutal: *all the hearts you've broken, all the tears you've caused.* That's what Sienna had seen and forgiven. So, yes, she was different, and he liked those differences.

She stiffened when Paris returned to the first door from the landing. That suggested there'd been conflict between her and the man inside. So, of course, Paris studied the guy intently. He was tall, muscled and glaring more fiercely than the others, as if Paris were already tagged and under a microscope. Handsome, if you were into deeply tanned skin and freaky bicolored eyes. Not that Paris was jealous or anything.

But just how much time had the guy spent with Sienna?

"That's Cameron. He's the keeper of Obsession," she said with a tremble.

A tremble born of fear…or desire? *I won't ask. I won't.* With the way they'd left things in the room, and hell, with the things Paris had done since their first parting, the answer wasn't his business.

"Has he ever touched you?" Damn. He'd asked, and with a whole lot of force.

She looked surprised. "No. The same invisible doors that keep me inside the castle keep them imprisoned in their rooms."

Her voice. Would he ever get enough of it? His ears hummed with sensation every time she spoke. "Did you want him to touch you?" He had to stop this.

"Never!"

A beautiful reprieve. "Then he can live," Paris muttered. He repositioned her in his arms, reached out and, yep, sure enough, there was an invisible block preventing him from entering the room.

"So you're not going to murder him? That's quite generous of you," she said dryly.

Irreverent humor from her, with him, was a shocker every time. In each instance they'd been together—and granted, there weren't many—things had been serious between them, gravely so. He liked that she now felt comfortable enough to tease him.

"I try." He stopped at the second doorway.

"This is Púkinn, aka Irish. He's bonded with Indifference," she informed him.

Indifference was half man, half animal. Horned, clawed and furred. Something out of a nightmare. For real. The man beast just looked Paris up and down and turned away, as if Paris were of no importance.

At the third door, Sienna twirled the ends of her hair around her finger. "Here we have Selfishness," she said with a hint of…anger? Or the same stinging jealousy he (hadn't) felt?

"She's very pretty, isn't she?" Sienna asked.

"Yes." The female had the same bicolored eyes as the first male, the same deeply tanned skin. She was attractive, there was no denying that, but he hungered only for the woman in his arms.

"Her name is Winter."

"That's great. How long have you been here?" Paris asked, looking down at Sienna instead of the immortal. Her lids were downcast, her lashes causing shadows to tumble over her cheeks. "How long have *they* been here?"

"I've lost track." The pink tip of her tongue slid over her mouth, leaving a glistening sheen of moisture. "They were here first, though."

I want to taste her. I will taste her.

His blood heated another degree. *Get in line.*

With all of Paris's experience, he was clueless when it came to this woman. What would soften her toward him totally and completely? Not just light a fire under her sympathies, but truly seduce her? She had changed since they'd last met in Rome, but she was still just as much of a mystery to him.

That she'd cried, that she'd apologized, that she'd sounded sincere, all were far more than he'd ever un-expected from her. Try *hell had just frozen over* shock-ing. But she had, on all three counts, and she'd looked at him like she'd never looked at him before. As if he were a man worthy of affection and attention. As if he weren't some dirty, disgusting thing on the bottom of her shoe. As if *she* wanted to protect *him.*

How the hell was he supposed to deal with that? How was he supposed to react?

Was he a fool for wanting to believe her? Hell, not wanting to, but actually doing so.

Maybe he shouldn't have been so offended by her offer to service him. Maybe he should have just taken her up on it. He'd had her on a bed. He could have stripped her, spread her legs and pounded inside her. Her hands would have been all over him, her passion cries ringing in his ears.

He cut off a bitter laugh. He was all twisted up, con-fused, waffling and contradicting himself. He didn't trust her; he trusted her. He wouldn't touch her without pas-sion; he'd touch her any way he could get her. And shit. Why hadn't she run from him, despite her vow? Or was she too busy regretting her offer to service him to launch into motion?

And really, what did that mean to her? That he could

take her here, now, anytime, or that she would go down on him? *Don't think about that.* He'd just get hard again.

The bitter laugh escaped. Make that, just get harder. His erection had yet to dissipate, acting like a heat-seeking missile as the female immortal strolled to her doorway, her hips swaying in a totally feline way. Didn't matter that Paris wasn't attracted to her. His demon saw, his demon wanted.

Part of him had hoped that being in Sienna's presence would stop this kind of thing from happening. But, no. Even though he could have her again, his demon still sought other women and always would.

I'm such a prize. No wonder she'd once hoped to slay him.

As carefully as he was able, he set Sienna on her feet. When she moved to his side, he dragged her back in front of him, pressing his erection between the curves of her ass. He hissed at the beauty of the pleasure. Pure, undiluted. Yet...

She had stiffened, he realized. At least she didn't jump away, and she didn't chastise him. Eventually, she even softened against him, as if she was exactly where she wanted to be. Well, hell. She must have feared he'd set her away from him, rebuffing her, and that's why she'd gone board-rigid—and why she'd relaxed when he hadn't. Talk about an ego boost. He wanted to beat his chest King Kong–style.

"Tell me what you know about them," he said, barely stopping his hands from flattening on her stomach, burrowing under the waist of her pants and seeking the warm, wet heart of her.

"About who?" the immortal in front of him asked. "And who the hell are you?"

One question answered, at least. They didn't know him, either. "Wasn't talking to you," he said.

The female splayed her arms. "Then who? You're alone."

"Like hell I'm—"

"They can't see me," Sienna interjected. "I've listened to some of their conversations, and that's how I know who and what they are." As she spoke, her stomach growled.

The sound gave him the excuse he needed. He moved his hands to her belly and rubbed. "Hungry?"

"Yes."

Then he would feed her. He would like that, he thought. Would like knowing he was fulfilling at least one of her needs. "What do you eat?" What *could* she eat?

"I don't. And it's only recently, within the last few weeks, that I've developed an appetite." She covered his hands with her own, her skin growing clammy. "Cronus brings me a glass of something sweet once a week. He forgot this time."

A glass of something sweet. Sweet. *Sweet.* The word echoed in his mind, an answer to one of his earlier questions sliding into place. *His* stomach bottomed out as he said, "Is it transparent, with tiny purple beads floating inside?"

"Yes." Her neck craned, allowing her to look up at him, and he watched as her brow wrinkled. "How'd you know?"

That *bastard!* Paris kept the curse inside his head and his expression neutral. "Does it taste like coconut, this liquid?" he asked, ignoring her question.

"Yes. But again, how did you know? Do you know what it is? He's never told me."

Yeah, he knew what it was, and now understood why she smelled as delicious as ambrosia. Cronus had done more than enslave her. He had condemned her. And he would pay. Oh, would he pay.

For better or for worse, though, vengeance would have to wait. Cronus liked to visit Torin, keeper of Disease, and have the computer genius find things for him. Currently he wanted cell locations for the Hunters, and had given orders for the Lords not to attack. Torin was giving him the info, all right, but only a piece at a time, as per Paris's request, keeping the king busy traveling back and forth between the heavens and earth as he stalked his prey and did whatever he did to them. That way, he had little time for Sienna. But "little" had been too much.

I should have gotten here sooner. There was no way to fix the damage that had been done to Sienna. There was no cure for what ailed her. Paris would have to tell her, have to prepare her for what would happen when she was out of here and on her own. Not now, though. She would be upset, and rightly so. More than that, he wanted to first taste her blood to be sure.

"Yo. Dude. Who the hell are you talking to?" the immortal demanded. "Don't make me ask again."

"Or you'll what?" he snapped. "Flip me off? Call me names?"

Winter opened her mouth to respond, and judging by the fire in her eyes, the words would scorch, but then her gaze shifted to Paris's right and her lips pursed in disapproval.

Oh, goodie. William had just decided to throw himself into the convo.

"You again," she said, and she did not sound happy.

"I know," the warrior replied with a heartfelt sigh. "You're so lucky to see me twice in one day. You're honored by my presence, yada, yada, heard it all before. Let's just move on, shall we. I don't handle fawning very well."

She flashed a scowl full of fangs, and Paris did a double take. Fangs? She was a vampire? He knew such creatures existed, knew William liked to bed them, but he'd never met one himself.

"They're not going anywhere, and Sienna's hungry," he said. "Let's find the kitchen. I—"

Suddenly the immortal female stumbled backward, landed on her ass. Her skin leached of color, and as she crawled farther and farther from the doorway, her gaze began moving throughout her chamber. She was babbling about shadows and pain. The same babbles erupted from the other doorways.

Sienna dug her nails into Paris's arm, a great shuddering wave moving through her. "No. No, no, no."

"What?" The panic spread into him. He forced her to turn, to face him. "What's going on?"

"They're coming." Her eyes filled with horror as she peered up at him.

"Who is?"

"The shadows. The pain."

"I don't understand."

"I think I do," William said, all hint of teasing and self-praise gone. "And if I'm right, we're in trouble, Paris." Never had he sounded more solemn. "Hold on to your girl, because I'm not sure how many of us will be walking away from this."

CHAPTER EIGHTEEN

"WHERE'S MY WOMAN! My...woman...need...her..."

Viola watched as the hulking black-haired giant tore down the other half of the entertainment room. The TV, pool table and an odd assortment of other things had been destroyed already. So had everything in the room next door, and the room next to that one. She knew because Maddox had busted down the walls between them, giving her a clear view into the other side of the fortress. Only rubble remained.

The other warriors jumped on the giant, again, knocking and pinning him down. Still he fought, screaming viler curses than she'd ever heard, even from the prisoners locked in Tartarus. Last time, his friends had lost their hold on him. This time, they managed to keep him there. Still, she was kind of scared, a foreign emotion for her.

"Where is she? I have to find her!"

The last word left him, and he just sort of collapsed into the mess, sobbing so hard his ribs had to be cracking. Tears filled her own eyes, but she blinked them back. He wanted his wife back, the loss of her destroying him.

"We'll find her," someone said.

"She and the babies will be unharmed."

"Be at ease, friend."

The warriors spoke calmly, but even she heard the tension and doubt in their voices. Maddox cried harder.

Viola felt like a voyeur. She felt useless. There was too much emotion here, too much loss, and she'd never handled this kind of thing well.

"Stay calm, we all have to stay calm."

"We'll have answers soon, and we can head out."

"Just a few minutes more."

"He has her," Maddox managed to say between shudders. "That bastard has her. I don't know where to look. There's no sign…nothing… Just the feather, just the feather."

One by one the warriors released him, and inched backward. Maddox stayed down by choice, his hand moving over his face to shield his eyes from the too-bright light overhead. How deeply he must love his woman and their unborn babies. Viola had suspected when she'd watched them together earlier, but seeing *this* proved she hadn't realized the limitless depths.

"We'll go hunting," Cameo said, speaking up for the first time since they'd heard Ashlyn scream and Maddox roar.

Viola wished the female warrior hadn't spoken then, either, and had to rub her chest to ward off the ache Cameo's shattering voice always left behind.

"Tonight," the one named Reyes growled. There was a deep gouge in his neck, blood dripping from it. "No later."

"We managed to get hold of Amun, and he's on his way back to Buda." Strider, the fiercest in the room, was actually trembling. His gaze kept returning to his wife, who stood a few feet away with her sister, as if he needed to reassure himself that she was here and well. "He'll learn something. Point us in the right direction."

"And if not him, Lucien will handle this," Anya said,

ever the proud girlfriend. Lucien had taken off to track Galen's spiritual trail.

"Galen wouldn't dare hurt Ashlyn or the babies." Haidee, Amun's girlfriend, paced back and forth, back and forth, too agitated to remain in one place.

"Gideon and Scarlet are coming home with Amun. Scarlet can tell you if the babies are still...still..." Aeron scrubbed a hand over his closely shaved scalp. He was supposed to be with the others, searching for Kane, but had remained behind for some reason no one would tell her.

Viola hadn't been here long, but she'd memorized the warriors' names, faces, demons and abilities. Scarlet was the keeper of Nightmares and by entering the dream world, she could search for a specific person's mental doorway. A closed doorway meant they were asleep. An open doorway meant they were dreaming. No doorway at all meant they were dead. But Maddox and Ashlyn were bonded, one destined to die when the other died, so no one had to wonder about her. The babies, how-ever... *Don't go there.* Scarlet could also murder people while they dreamed, killing them in real life. Perhaps Galen would take his last breath tonight. Then again, perhaps not. If Scarlet could enter his dreams, she would have done so already, but Viola guessed that something blocked her.

I could take him.

Enough of that, she thought with a scowl. Once she hopped on the train to self-love, there was no turning back.

She concentrated. The warriors. Yes. They didn't trust her, and she was a little surprised they hadn't turned on her, blaming her for this catastrophe. She was the stranger, after all, and the kidnapping had happened soon after her arrival. But then Olivia, the angel who'd made them relax about her presence the first time around, had said Viola wasn't responsible in any way, and they'd all believed her without question.

Besides Olivia, Scarlet, Anya, the still-pacing Haidee and Danika, who had her arm around a girl named Gilly, there were two Harpies, half-sisters Gwen and Kaia. Gwen belonged to Sabin, and Kaia to Strider. The pair had their heads together as they whispered. Galen was Gwen's father, and, if Viola's superior hearing was on target—and it always was—Gwen planned to hunt him down herself, crack open his ribs and rip out his black, rotted heart. Just her little way of making up for the lenience she'd once shown him.

"That Torin guy didn't get any recordings of Galen?" Viola asked, recalling his wall of computers and monitors.

No one looked her way or paid her any attention.

Her demon scraped sharp, pointed horns against the inside of her temples, and she bit back a moan. Ignoring her was the fastest way to gain Narci's attention. And when Narci's attention was locked...oh, stars above. Trouble followed. Always. Viola didn't want her other half intruding on this heartbreaking event, determined to make everything about her.

"No, there are no recordings," a soft, gentle voice said from beside her.

With a gasp, she spun. She hadn't heard anyone approach, but now a tall, slender female with long, blond hair was at her side. The girl looked fragile...haunted. Pain consumed those dark eyes. More pain than any one person should ever have to bear. She watched Maddox, a tear streaking down her pale cheek.

Viola thought she'd interacted with everyone in the

house, but this girl was new. She had a blanket draped around her, the material clutched tight to her chest, her knuckles without a shred of color. "Did you talk to him? To Torin?"

The girl's chin was trembling too violently for her to speak; she shook her head.

"Then how do you know about the recordings? Better question—who are you?"

More tears tumbled. They had to burn, because whatever path they traveled, they left red welts behind. "I'm… I'm Legion." Such a soft, soft whisper.

Legion. Ah, yes. Once a demon who had made a deal with the devil. The devil that granted her a human body. A deal she'd lost, forcing her to return to hell, where she was tortured in the vilest of ways, raped, abused, passed around and tortured some more.

Viola looked at the girl. Really looked at her, the way only she could. Past skin, past bone, and into soul. Legion was dying. Actually, some part of her was already dead. Her will to live had been obliterated. She was a brittle leaf hanging on by the thinnest thread, the next cold wind all that was needed to pull her loose and finally send her tumbling away.

By nature of her birth, Viola could be that wind. All she need do was reach out, curl her fingers around Legion's wrist and draw her close. Not usually so simple, and not usually so easy; but then, willingness made all the difference. A deep breath in, and there would be nothing remaining of Legion's soul. She would cease to exist on every level.

Perhaps Viola had stared a bit too long or a bit too intently because Legion began to quake, shifting from one foot to the other, and then, when that wasn't enough, inching away.

"I won't hurt you," Viola said.

Legion stopped as if she'd shouted. Poor, broken girl. A china doll already shattered. She drew the blanket closer, trying to fold herself within and hide.

"Lucien." Anya's relief was palpable, filling the room after the keeper of Death appeared.

Viola turned, watching as the minor goddess threw herself in her man's arms. He hugged her with unyielding strength, their love a tangible thing. Once again Viola's chest ached. She wanted that. Wanted that so badly she would kill to have it. But, of course, she could never have that. She was destined to love herself, and only herself.

Everyone else in the room quieted, waiting to hear what the warrior had to say, so tense their bodies were ready to snap. The scarred warrior looked them over, opened his mouth, closed it.

"Just say it," Maddox commanded. He'd worked his way to his feet, was checking the clip on one of his guns. "Tell me what you learned."

Lips compressed, Lucien gave the room another sweep. This time he stopped on Legion, who had bravely eked her way back to Viola's side. "Legion, sweetheart," he said, his tone so gentle he could have been talking to a child locked in a closet, afraid a monster waited under her bed, "go on up to your room. This isn't for you. All right? Okay?"

After everyone turned to face her, and she had wilted under the attention, she spun and ran away. Several agonizing heartbeats passed before Maddox broke.

"Tell me. Now."

Lucien drew Anya deeper into his body. "Galen didn't try to hide. He knew I would follow his trail, and so he waited for me to catch up. Ashlyn wasn't with him," he added as Maddox opened his mouth to say something.

"He said I would no longer be able to follow him, that I'd found him only because he'd let me get that far. And he was right. Afterward, I tried. I failed. I'm sorry."

"Tell me!" Maddox had stashed his gun and now clutched two blades. One of them he held by its body rather than by its hilt, and his palm had already sliced open. He didn't seem to notice as blood dripped, dripped. "Finish it."

A stiff nod. Lucien looked as if the words were being jerked out of him, and the jerking hurt. "He said she's safe, for now, and that he'll send you a video of her to prove it. He said...he said...if we want her back alive, we'll trade Legion for her."

Viola wasn't sure anyone else heard the gasp and frantic footfalls beyond that shattered wall, but she did. And she knew. Legion hadn't gone up to her room. She'd hung back and listened. Now, though, she was at last running for her chamber, no doubt seeking sanctuary between its walls.

The warriors argued, words shooting between them with rapid-fire precision.

"Where does he want to meet? When?" Maddox.

"Rome. The Temple of the Unspoken Ones. Tomorrow. Midnight." Lucien.

"Take me there. Now." Maddox.

"Be sensible about this." Strider. "Those bastards are hard-core, and if they're on his side—"

"I don't care! Get that through your heads. I don't care about anything but my woman and my children. And you *will* take me there, and I *will* hunt him down, and when I find him I *will* kill him. Do you hear me? Take me to that island. You have five seconds to flash me or I'm catching the red-eye, and there's no one in this world or the other that can help the mortals who get in my way."

Deciding not to wait for Lucien's reply, Viola snuck out of the room. No one noticed, and that once again pricked at Narci.

Be a good girl, she told her other half, *and I'll show you how pretty you are.*

The demon bounced up and down inside her head. *When?*

Soon.

Now. A whine.

Soon.

Now. A demand.

Never.

Soon? Another whine.

Soon. You drive a hard bargain. Viola followed Legion's spiritual trail—Lucien wasn't the only one with such a talent—flashing herself into the bedroom. The girl was pacing, her hair flying wildly behind her. She hadn't abandoned the blanket, but clutched the material ever closer.

"I can't, I can't, I can't. I can't leave. I can't go to him."

"Legion," Viola said gently. Yes, she was uncomfortable with other people's feelings, but she'd peered at this broken doll's soul and wanted to help.

How odd. Once, Viola had fed on souls, on their energy. She had drained them, ended them. One day, though, she'd taken the wrong soul at the wrong time—the only terrible memory she'd managed to retain—and found herself imprisoned in Tartarus. Then, of course, she was paired with Narci and the only soul she'd been able to feed on was her own.

Like an immortal's limb, her soul kept growing back and she kept feeding on it, but it never grew back in its entirety because she never actually stopped eating. For lack of a better word. So, basically, she was half of a person, as well as a spiritual cannibal, and she never ever concerned herself with others.

Why had she come here again? She should leave.

Those dark eyes found her, tears catching in equally dark lashes, and Viola's feet rooted in place. "I can't. I can't do it. *I can't do it.* He'll want to touch me. Hurt me. I...can't."

Legion raced to her bathroom, hunched over the toilet and vomited. Viola's feet tugged free, but still she didn't leave. She walked into the bathroom and held back the girl's hair, only to realize she hadn't actually vomited. She had dry heaved. Poor thing. She probably hadn't eaten a decent meal in weeks.

Hours seemed to tick by in endless misery. Between each of her heaves, the girl sobbed. And when she wasn't sobbing, she was shaking so violently her teeth chattered. No one ever came to the door, and Viola decided the Lords had opted not to trade the girl for Ashlyn's safe return.

Finally, blessedly, Legion's outburst drained her. She slumped over the toilet, her tear ducts tapped out.

Viola stepped away, and those red, swollen eyes followed her.

I really must leave now, she thought. She'd stayed far too long, the sense of unease returning. "I'll tell the warriors you're a no-go, okay?" Maddox might try and slay her for her efforts, but Narci would dig the attention, so whatever.

"I can't go, I can't go," Legion whispered. "He was here, I smelled him, knew he was here, but I couldn't make my voice work, haven't spoken since I got here, couldn't even scream, even though I wanted to scream and scream and scream. I hid under the bed. I should have screamed, I should have screamed."

Her words were heavy on the guilt, an emotion Viola refused to tangle with. "Yeah, so, uh, good luck with that. It was nice meeting you and everything." One step, two, she backed her way out. She didn't do the friendship thing. Ever. With anyone. Especially not broken china dolls that would require way too much time and effort.

Legion's tear ducts clearly hadn't dried, because a new waterfall began. "I can't leave Ashlyn with him, either." She sniffled, gulped. "Ashlyn is so nice, and the babies, she let me feel them kick once. She's due any day. She needs to be home. Maddox needs her to be home. What should I do?"

So badly Viola wanted to reach for her phone, Screech the question and follow the ensuing flood of advice, but much as she yearned to leave this room, she wanted to stay in the fortress.

For all their faults, the Lords hadn't tried to take advantage of her. Hadn't tricked her into looking into a mirror, and they utterly adored her. And okay, maybe that last one wasn't the truth and merely came courtesy of her demon, but nothing was a lie if you believed it. Therefore, the Lords did, in fact, adore her.

"I think you should, uh, follow your heart?" Oh, ick. That sucked. Like, majorly. The girl didn't know what her heart wanted, which was why she was asking for guidance.

"What would you do?" Legion asked.

She could weave a pretty speech about always being willing to help others, Viola supposed. The guys downstairs would probably prefer that. Only problem was, lying to anyone but herself created messes. Viola hated messes.

"I would save myself, no matter the cost to those around me. But then, I've only ever cared about myself, so…" She shrugged. "It's up to you. Who do you love more? Yourself, or the ones who took you in?"

CHAPTER NINETEEN

S<small>TRIPPED AND PINNED</small> to a boulder, Kane gritted his teeth at the humiliation. Hadn't taken the minions long to catch him after he'd bolted. His *innocent little* chosen had been the worst of the lot, ripping out his Achilles tendons, hobbling him.

Now everyone in the crowd took turns attempting to steal what he'd refused to give.

He wouldn't give them what they wanted. He wouldn't. But how much longer could he survive the torment? The pressure was building, so intense it was painful.

You've survived this kind of thing before. He could survive this. *Breathe, just breathe.* His lids were squeezed together, his blood molten in his veins. All the while, his demon laughed inside his head. *Laughed.* Enjoying the disaster as it happened.

Maybe surviving wasn't the right path, he thought, the humiliation morphing into rage. Kane had never liked his demon, but now, now he hated the creature with every fiber of his being. He wanted to be free of it, and that meant dying. He wanted to punish Disaster for taking pleasure in his misery, regardless of the fate that would befall him.

And he would. Yeah. He would do some punishing. No matter what he had to do achieve the desired end, he would do.

Paris crowded Sienna into the wall, leaned down and got in her face. Her breath emerged choppily, her eyes were wild and her pupils dilated with panic. Sex enjoyed the contact, was already begging for more. Paris tuned him out and kept things as nonsexual as possible. Sienna was too upset for more.

"You have to hide," she said, the words emerging brokenly. "I'll try to draw them to me, away from everyone else. Okay? Yes? But you really, *really* have to hide."

He cupped her jaw, forcing her to peer up at him rather than scanning her surroundings for a hiding place. As if he would ever hide from an enemy and leave a female to fight for him. "What's coming? Talk to me, baby." He knew she wasn't too keen on endearments from him—at least, she hadn't been before—but then, he'd never called another woman his baby. Only sweetheart and honey, meaningless words like that, and never with such a note of affection.

Those lush lips parted on a gasp, and she blinked in bafflement. "Baby," she whispered, and he decided she liked it. There'd been a note of reverence in *her* tone. Calm suddenly smoothed out the panic. "The shadows. They dart through the walls, and they feed on us. All of us. Even the gargoyles hide. There are so many of them. They'll cover you, they'll be all you see, all you know, and they'll eat at you."

Corporal shadows with a hunger for flesh. He thought he'd traveled every corner of the heavens, but he'd never heard of such a creature.

William had, though, because he muttered, "Oh, shit on a brick. This is bad. Exactly what I feared."

Paris met his troubled gaze. "What do I need to do?"

"Just stay where you are." The grim-faced warrior reached up and unsheathed a knife from behind his shoulder blades, then sliced his arm open from elbow to palm. Instantly crimson flowed. He closed the distance, bent down to the floor, and smeared a bloody circle around Paris and Sienna. "Don't step out of this, do you hear me? Both of you, *stay there*. Disobey me, and you'll regret it."

He didn't wait for a reply, but sprinted to the entrance of the female immortal's room and dashed his wound across the clear shield separating them. The female was too busy clawing at her walls to notice. Before William reached the second room, his wound closed and he had to make another incision. He painted a line of blood over that shield, as well.

He didn't make it to the third room.

Just as Sienna had predicted, shadows burst through the walls. In a snap, it was lights-out, the black so thick oil could have been saturating the air.

The entire castle rattled and shook. Screams echoed, fervent songs of pain and anguish. The darkness inside Paris responded, practically purring with approval the way Sex always purred for physical contact, enjoying every terrible note. Wanting out, wanting loose. Wanting to cause everyone around him to hurt, too.

Paris was on the path to giving in, to stepping out of the circle William had drawn and fighting with the shadows, hell, fighting with William, when Sienna trembled against him. He pressed against her more firmly. *Must protect,* he thought. That's why he was here. For her. To be with her. To ensure her safety.

She trembled again, this one worrisome in its intensity. He wasn't sure what was happening behind him or around him or even how long this would last, but she knew, and it terrified her. And yet still she had thought to protect him, he realized. Still she had wanted to hide him. *Him,* not herself. His warrior core had been offended by that, true, but just then he could only thrill over her concern. She cared about his well-being.

I want her, Sex said. Of course, the purring started up again.

So do I. And he would have a taste of her. Finally, here and now, the circumstances be damned. She was too worried for sexual contact? Hardly. She needed a distraction, and there was nothing better than desire.

Paris felt his way to her jaw, cupping her to hold her steady while luxuriating in the silky warmth of her skin, the delicacy of her bones. "Concentrate on my voice, baby. Can you do that?"

A jerky nod.

He wished he could see her and discover whether or not color was returning to those delicate cheeks. At her ear, he whispered, "You're so soft. I've never felt anything softer. And your scent intoxicates me. I can't help but think you'll be even sweeter between your legs."

Her breath hitched, her hands finding his chest and flattening over his pectorals.

"When I drive my fingers deep inside you, you'll be so wet for me, won't you, baby? I'll eat you up, drink down every drop of your honey, and you'll scream for more."

Yesss, Sex said on a moan. *Pleassse.*

"Paris," Sienna breathed.

A needy plea for more? That's what his demon heard in her tremulous tone. Paris found himself leaning down, the rest of the world forgotten, his nose in her hair as he sniffed the heavy waves. He scented the wildflowers and the coconut, now mixed with something rare, a bloom found only at night.

Oh, hell, yes. That was her arousal.

Sex liked it, too, tossing out his own special fragrance.

The two combined, the most wondrous bouquet enveloping Paris. Wondrous—and torturous. Instantly he was revved up, more than primed, more than ready, desperate to sink inside this woman and thrust his way to orgasm. All he had to do was rip open both their pants and kick her legs apart. He'd drill her deep and sure. She would be hot, dripping and so tight around him.

Sharp little nails burrowed past his shirt and into his skin, as if to hold him in place. He could feel the heat of her, pulsing, seeping into him, blending with his own and lancing straight to his cock. He ached unbearably. Before he even registered that he'd moved, he'd edged her legs apart with his foot and arched into her, fitting his erection against her feminine core.

Hello, sweet damnation. Either he'd just made the biggest mistake of his life, or the best. They fit together like matching puzzle pieces. He rubbed against her, slowly at first, just enough to tease and tantalize them both. The pleasure built, right alongside the pressure. Yeah, he definitely should have taken her earlier. His demon was ready to burst free of his skin.

Paris couldn't gauge Sienna's reaction through sound because of the surrounding screams, so he moved one of his hands to her throat, keeping his touch gentle. Nothing could stop him from *feeling* her moans, and the vibrations were so damn gorgeous.

"Paris." Her lips pressed against his ear. Definitely not a plea this time, but not a warning, either. "You can't want me."

He circled his hips, pressing, retreating, pressing. "What is this, then?"

"A treat for the only available woman in the room."

The words were like a slap across the face, and his volatile inner darkness responded poorly, rampaging through him and demanding he hurt the one who'd harmed him. He bit back the urge and snapped, "So a guy like me can only want what's available?"

"You didn't want me before, in the room. So maybe this is punishment." Anger threaded her tone.

Punishment? His hands clenched in reflex, his own anger becoming an echo of hers.

Sadly, she wasn't done. "Believe me, I understand the concept far better than I ever did. Maybe you didn't come here to save me, after all, but to wound me the same way I once wounded you."

He hadn't trusted her, couldn't, no matter how badly he'd wanted to, and even told himself he did, and now he saw that she couldn't, wouldn't, trust him, either. Not really. He'd suspected this would happen. That hadn't bothered him (much) before, but it bothered him now. He hated that there were so many barriers between them. Clothes, reservations, doubts and worries.

"I'm nothing like the women you're used to," she went on. "I know that. I know that I'm not pretty."

"You're right. You're beyond gorgeous."

A gasp. "A-and my lips are ridiculous."

"If *ridiculous* is the new word for a wet dream."

Her little fists hammered at his chest. "Stop! Just stop. You need sex and you're trying to make a sale. I did the same to you earlier, wanting to be with you one last time. I shouldn't have thrown myself at you like that."

His back straightened. She had offered herself to him, not because she had felt guilty, but because she had wanted him. She should not have admitted that. There would be no stopping him now. He would have her, one way or another.

He licked at her lips, saying, "Baby, I've never had to try. I breathe, and the women offer."

The abuse stopped, a mewling sound leaving her. "You're—you're trying to put me in my place, then. Trying to tease me with what I can never fully have."

Oh, you can have it, all right. "You know that's not true. Not because you trust me, but because of your demon." Wrath would have been all over any deception on Paris's part.

A pause the agonizing length of three heartbeats. "You're…right. How odd," she said, both awed and hopeful. Her nails once again found purchase in his chest. "I hated the fact that a demon was placed inside me, wanted to be free of him, ranted and railed and even planned to give him back, and yet I've begun to count on his ability to read other people's intentions."

Once possessed, always possessed. For the most part, anyway. So give Wrath back to Aeron? That would be a big fat hell, no. That would kill her. Again. "You can believe me when I say that I do want you, Sienna. You're all I've thought about for months. Resisting you in that room was one of the toughest things I've ever done."

A vibration in her throat signaled her moan. "You're really attracted to me, despite everything?" Wonder saturated her voice, dripping over him like warm honey.

He had a thing for warm honey.

"Yes." Backward, forward he arched, renewing the decadent contact. He wanted to push for more still, but didn't. Not yet. He wanted her focused only on the pleasure, all her fears about ulterior motives assuaged. "Let there be no doubt on that score."

Another vibration, this one reaching a deeper part of him. "Why me?" Her nails plucked free of his chest, her hands smoothing over him. "I mean, you could have anyone."

"Exactly. I could, and I chose you. For so many reasons. You're smart."

"Debatable."

"You're witty."

"No more than a thousand others."

"You're argumentative and can't accept a compliment."

"Hey!" She reached up and tugged at his hair.

Despite the grimness of their surroundings and circumstances, he found himself grinning. "You're beautiful."

Her fingers slid to his scalp, massaging. "Not just beyond gorgeous?" she asked dryly.

"You're exquisite, and I don't want to hear you put yourself down again. Do you understand?" He had killed others for doing so. Her, he would simply spank. "You may or may not be happy with the results."

"Why? Are you thinking paddling? Because I'm getting a few images in my head."

"Well, well. There's something else to like about you. You understand me."

A snort. One he relished, because he had caused the humor behind it. "You must be blinded by horny demon-colored glasses," she said.

And she thought there were thousands of others just as stubborn as she was. He'd just issued an order alongside a threat, yet she had ignored both and continued on her merry way.

"Has your demon ever let you be with the same woman twice?" she asked, the words layered with a husky edge of arousal, as well as a note of nervousness. "I'd heard you— Never mind."

She had gotten a lot of her info from the Hunters. He

stiffened, hating the reminder of her past, but that didn't stop him from admitting, "No one but you."

The warmth of her breath trekked over his neck as she angled her head, placing them cheek to cheek. "Why me?"

"Don't know. Sex doesn't know, either. I've asked."

"Well, he should have picked someone else. I have small breasts," she whispered, as though ashamed.

He cupped the pint-size morsels in question. They. Were. Perfect. His hands were big, her nipples beading against the centers of his palms, and damn if that wasn't the most exquisite sensation in the world. He fit his lips against her ear, nibbled on the lobe.

"I want them in my mouth," he rasped.

A groan of approval. Nails in his scalp now, digging deeper and deeper.

Paris kissed and licked his way to her lips. They were parted, warm, the sweetness of her breath sawing in and out, scented with the spice of coconut. He hovered there, still not taking what he wanted. What they *both* wanted. If he started this, he was going to have a hard time stopping. A *very* hard time. He'd been without a female for too long, and his demon was too needy, but...

He didn't want to take Sienna in a hallway, in front of others, he realized. Yeah, he'd done that shit before, and it had gotten old hella fast. He wanted this one all to himself, each of her cries for his ears alone, her every reaction to his touch his personal discovery. Her scent, his. Her skin, his. His, his, *his.*

Take what's yours! Take, take, take!

Well, as alone as he could get with a demon trapped inside him.

"Paris?" she said, her tone unreadable.

"Yes."

"A word of warning. I'm really bad at this."

Confusion rocked him, his brows furrowing toward his hairline. "At what?"

"Kissing."

Before he could contradict her, she fit their mouths together and sucked the breath right out of his lungs. She wasn't bad at kissing; she was hesitant, unsure and tentative, but he craved her too viciously to teach her better. He took over, unable to stop himself. His tongue thrust forcefully, demanding she concede to his mastery.

Concede she did not. After his teeth banged into hers the third time, she bit down on his bottom lip, hard, drawing blood.

He jerked back before she cut the thing in half. "Damn it, woman."

Sex performed some sort of kickboxing move against the side of his skull. Not in complaint or to hide from the violence, but in excitement, to get *closer* to the violence. *More, more! Kiss her more!*

"I might be bad at it, but I know when someone else is, too. Do it right," Sienna demanded.

Was she frickin' kidding? "No one's ever criticized my technique before."

"That's because they didn't want to hurt your feelings," she shot back. "You and I are past that stage, so I feel okay in admitting that I got a superior kiss from Carl Knickerbocker in the third grade."

Spirit again, and damn if that didn't rev him right back up, demolishing any lingering hint of anger. He wished he could see her face. Those hazel eyes would be sparkling, her skin flushed, her lips swollen. She would be passion incarnate. "Should you be giving pointers? You're *far* worse at this than I am."

"Someone has to teach you." She patted his cheek. "Guess we'll have to learn how to do this together."

More, more, more!

His lips twitched with his amusement. Funny, that. Amusement, when his body and his demon were on fire, desperate for this woman. *I'm on it.*

CHAPTER TWENTY

"OKAY. LET'S SEE WHAT I CAN do to give little Carl a run for his money." Slowly Paris went back in, pressed his mouth gently against Sienna's, lifted, pressed again, teasing her with the contact, barely tasting. She softened against him, her nails scraping against his scalp, her hands tracing down, down, until winding around his neck to lock him against her.

He licked at the seam of her lips, sipping at her, giving her what she wanted, slow and easy, and when she opened for him he licked his way inside, deep, tasting more of her, taking more. Her tongue met his, connecting, dueling with long, languid strokes. They learned each other, learned every nuance of tongue and teeth, breath and flavor, and it was the sexiest damn thing he'd ever experienced.

During their first meeting, she had kissed him and used his distraction against him, shoving the needle in his neck. She could have done something similar now, but he wouldn't have cared. His body smoldered with passion, his blood already molten in a way it had never been. His heart was a war drum in his chest, pounding out its cry for more from this woman, this obsession. His limbs shook.

With the darkness so thick around them, his sight was still razed and his other senses picked up the slack. Sienna's floral bouquet was branded inside his nose, causing his head to swim all over again. His tattooed fingertips tingled, memorizing the satiny feel of her. His ears twitched, every sound she made a caress. And her taste…oh, hell, yeah…ambrosia in its most potent incarnation.

But then, that's what she was now, what Cronus had made her. A supplier. A walking ambrosia dispenser. Stick a straw in her vein and you could get high for eternity.

When consumed by humans, ambrosia killed. Had once nearly killed Maddox's woman. Sienna, though, was already dead and no longer human. By feeding her the nectar mixed with the bulbs necessary for the plant's growth, something that would kill even an immortal, she was, in essence, an ever-fertile breeding ground for the drug.

What ran in her veins was more addictive than what Paris used to pour into his alcohol. And if anyone immortal ever tasted her blood, they would be instantly addicted to her. They would need her, keep her, and fight to the death anyone who tried to take her.

Why in the name of all that was unholy would Cronus do that to her? Why would he make her such a target?

Something else for the two of them to hash out—with blades.

Don't think about that right now. You've got her. She's safe, and she wants you as much as you want her. He gripped her waist, lifted her off her feet, then pressed her more firmly into the wall. "Wrap your legs around me, baby."

She obeyed, and he rubbed his erection against her clitoris so hard she cried out. That was…that was… There were no words.

More.

All. Everything. There were a few words, after all. "Are you wet for me?" Usually he had a stream of lovely, meaningless praise to give. Sienna was lucky to get more than *mine, more* and *yes* out of him.

There was a beat of hesitation, then she whispered shyly, "I am."

Wanton abandon splashed with a hint of reserve...a sultry combination.

Their tongues rolled together, faster, faster still. Her kiss was like sex. Overwhelming, consuming, necessary. He couldn't get enough, didn't think he'd ever get enough. Everything he'd done to reach this point, absolutely worth it.

He'd been with so very many people, had done so very many things. Some he'd liked, some he hadn't. Ninety percent of the time he operated on autopilot, going through the motions to get what he needed while leaving his partners with a smile of satisfaction, even when he'd hated who he was with, loathed the smells, the grasping hands, the knowledge that he was inside someone he didn't know.

He wasn't on autopilot right now. Instinct drove him, a need to possess and to be possessed. A need to become one, as corny as that sounded. So he kissed her again, because he couldn't not kiss her. Because he had to know more of her taste, more of her. He slanted his head, angling for even deeper contact, moving his tongue faster, faster still, taking her mouth the way he wanted to take her body.

This time, she offered no complaint. All the while he rubbed against her. His nerve endings were so sensitized he thought they'd be raw by the time he finished.

"Yes," she moaned, and clearly, this time she liked

his fervor. "Paris…I'm going to… You have to…stop… Don't stop…please stop. Paris!"

There would be no stopping. He pressed ever harder, heard her cry out at the bliss, and hell, he was on fire. Burning for her, desperate to sink so damn deep inside her that she'd know she belonged to him.

More!

"Paris…stop…please."

There was that word again. "Stop." Her hands tugged at his hair, forcing his head to lift.

"I want you," she rasped, "but not here. Somewhere else. Somewhere private."

MORE.

He'd take her back to the bedroom, he thought, dizzy with need. Yeah. That's what he'd do, because he had to strip her, had to see her, had to get inside her now, now, *now*.

He straightened, dragging her with him. One step, though, just one step, and thousands of needle pricks shot through his lower leg. Reason returned, and he jolted back into the blood circle. He was panting, could feel the warm flow of blood down his calf, would be surprised if he had any muscle left. In the time it took to snap a finger, the shadow-things had chomped on him as if he was a steak and they were starving dogs.

That's what Sienna had endured?

Sex retreated into the back of his mind, the pain too much for him.

Darkness…rising… Paris's hand was on his blade hilt, squeezing, as he contemplated jumping into the midst and slashing.

Sienna's fingers curled around his biceps, stilling him. She, too, was panting. "Are you okay?"

"Hurt?" He patted her down, searching for injuries.

"Not me. You?"

"I'm fine." Her nipples were still beaded, her belly quivering. Need was still galloping through her, yet she'd had the strength to stop when he had not. Impressive. Irritating.

"Are you—"

Just as suddenly as the shadow creatures had arrived, they left. The castle ceased shaking, the screams died. Light swept back through the hallway. Paris had to blink against the burn in his eyes.

Sienna's cheeks were flushed a deep rose, her lips soft, swollen and parted, gleaming with his taste. He must have plowed his hands through her hair numerous times. The strands were tangled around her. She looked wanton and wicked, and so sexy his shaft throbbed against his fly.

He turned away before he fell on her, devoured her. In the center of the hallway, William crouched in his own blood circle, his head bowed. The female immortal was at her door, her eyes wide, unsure. The male William had protected was at his door, too.

The other male, the one William hadn't reached in time, was lying on the bedroom floor, a sea of crimson and…other things spilled around him. He writhed in agony, even as he fought to put himself back together.

"You know what those things were?" Paris demanded. When his world spun, he scowled and threw out an arm to catch himself on the wall. But it wasn't because of blood loss or pain.

Sex whimpered, spurting weakness straight into Paris's veins. Bastard had been primed and disappointed too many times in the past few days, and with the denial of Sienna the countdown to "meltdown" had begun. That meant, if he failed to have sex, and soon, he would rapidly fade until he was completely useless. Until he collapsed, the pheromones wafting from him, drawing people to him. Until someone simply climbed on top of him.

No way he'd let that happen. His reasons for resisting Sienna hadn't miraculously vanished, but they weren't going to stop him anymore. He'd take her however he could get her, because the alternative was taking someone else and he wasn't willing to do that.

"Yeah, I know what they are," William finally managed after catching his breath. Eyes of otherworldly blue lifted and pinned Paris in place. Tension crackled in the air between them. "A long time ago Cronus created them the same way Zeus created you, but I'd heard after Cronus's imprisonment that someone else had taken over their care. Cronus must have reclaimed them. And now I'm gonna have to have a chat with him about houseguests and manners." Utter menace poured from him.

Clearly he anticipated a chat for two, from which only one would walk away. Yeah. Paris intended the same.

"That ever happen to you?" he asked, whipping back to Sienna and jerking his thumb at the guy split open from neck to navel. Because of what had been done to Sienna's blood, the creatures would have gone crazy over her. Would have converged en masse, concentrated solely on her, not leaving until they'd drained every drop possible.

There was no reply.

"Sienna. What's—" Her eyes were glazed over, he realized, glassy and glowing a bright, vibrant red.

"Punish," she whispered.

Wrath had taken over her mind and body.

"Must punish them," she repeated in a voice she had never before used with him, all gravel, no passion. A second later, her wings burst from her back, clouds of midnight tipped with violet. They flapped up, down, stretching to their full width and scratching the wall, the floor.

"Sienna," he said. Calm, he had to remain calm. Otherwise Wrath would turn that need to punish on *him*. He snapped his fingers in front of her face. "I need you to listen to me, okay, baby?"

"Punish." Her wings glided faster, until she hovered in the air.

"Sienna."

Without another word, she darted straight at the only window, shattering the glass and disappearing into the night.

Paris made a swift dive for her but missed and ended up with half of his body ready to free-fall too many stories into that frothing lake of doom. Well, hell. He'd asked her to let the bastard take over, hadn't he? *Stupid.* No telling where Wrath would take her, or what the demon would make her do.

One way or another, he was going after her.

Never had to chase a woman this much. He pulled himself back in and studied the incline, trying to decide the best and fastest way down without drawing the notice of the gargoyles. And wouldn't you know it? There was only one way. He was gonna have to make the fifty-foot dive, after all, and pray his legs wouldn't shatter on impact.

Problem was, now that he was on the downward slide to gotta-have-sex-or-die, he *would* hurt himself and he wouldn't heal very quickly. Whatever. She was in danger; he would do what was necessary. He threw a leg over the pane.

"Stay here." He tossed the words over his shoulder. "See if you can help the immortals."

"Way ahead of you," came William's muttered reply.

When his other leg was in place, Paris counted down. Three. Two. So *stupid*. One—

And suddenly Zacharel was there, white wings spread and waving gracefully through the air. Snowflakes drifted around him, the perfect frame for his emotionless features. He arched a dark brow. "Would you like a ride?"

"Where were you when the shadows were here?" he demanded gruffly.

"I can answer, or I can help you."

So sick of his manipulations, but there's no denying I could use his help. And aren't I just the cutest damsel in distress ever? Aeron had carried Paris through the skies a time or two, so he knew there was nothing sexual about it. He only prayed Zacharel realized the erection he currently sported had nothing to do with their close proximity.

The angel wrapped his arms around Paris's waist. "You'll find good deeds are balm for the soul."

"That's just peachy." For a greater sense of being anchored, Paris wrapped his own arms around the angel's neck. Solid muscle, ice-cold skin. Even as primed and needy as Sex was, the demon stayed quiet. "But can we do this without conversation?"

"Can we? Yes. Will we? No. While you are my captive audience, I wish to discuss your unhealthy obsession with the dead girl and the fact that she will be better off without you."

O-kay. Paris brought his legs between them, pushed their bodies apart, and jumped.

CHAPTER TWENTY-ONE

BLOOD DRIPPED FROM SIENNA'S hands, caked her clothing and made her tennies squish disgustingly with every step she took. As with every other time Wrath had taken over her body and whisked her out of the castle, he had forced her to follow the shadows to their lair so that he could wage an attack and hurt the creatures far worse than they had hurt others. His crimson-bright gaze had shone through hers, cutting through their skin...or ooze...or whatever comprised their outer shell, burning them. He had laughed and laughed.

The shadows had been too sated from gorging to fight back, their helplessness an aphrodisiac to Wrath, making him crave more, more, *more,* and the moment he'd finished with the shadows, he had turned his sights on the other beings living in this hidden realm, rhapsodizing when they, too, screamed in pain.

When his hunger was finally satisfied, he tried to force her to walk back to the castle. For the first time, she had known what he was doing while he was doing it, her mind refusing to break its link with Paris, and she'd fought him—and fought hard. Ultimately, as replete as he'd been, he'd given up and retreated to the back of her mind. Now she was at the wheel and driving the (short) bus.

Sadly, her fighting wasn't yet done. There was an invisible cord connecting the castle and her neck, trying to pull her closer and closer. She wasn't sure how much longer she could resist. Her wings were shredded—not that she knew how to fly without Wrath's guidance—and though they would heal in a few hours, they were currently unable to hold her weight. Still, she dug her heels into the ground and managed to slow her momentum. Pain vibrated in her bones. She cringed as she turned… turned…and began to slip away in the opposite direction. Yes. *Yes!*

To go back, even to see Paris, to say goodbye, to kiss him one last time, to make love to him, was to imprison herself. And though she was tempted, oh, was she tempted, she had to do this. For him. For Skye. Before Cronus learned of her escape, thought to punish Paris and started pulling her strings all over again.

If she could reach Galen, interrogate and kill him before Cronus realized she was gone, she wouldn't have to seduce him, and the war between the Lords and the Hunters would at last end. Even if the keeper of Hope never told her where her sister was, he couldn't hurt the girl if he was dead. That would have to suffice.

Footsteps echoed, jerking her out of her mind. There were beings behind her, she realized, following her. She didn't have to glance back to know they were empty-eyed males with sagging, gray-tinted skin and jaws that split into rows of four, each loaded with razor-sharp fangs. They were killers without a conscience, the blood of their enemies their source of life.

A few weeks ago, Wrath had struck at their camp, leaving blood and death in his wake. Of course, that meant Sienna—the face the survivors had seen—had become Enemy One. They'd been gunning for her ever since, and would have attacked the castle if not for the Gargl.

The urge to run was nearly irresistible. From the glimpses her demon had given her of these creatures, she knew how they'd hunted in the past, knew how mercilessly they'd killed. Knew they enjoyed the chase more than they enjoyed the slaughter. So maybe if she kept a calm head, maybe if she stayed on her current path, they'd lose interest in her.

Yeah, maybe. Not.

"You took our ssslavesss, female. Now *you* become our ssslave."

That lisp came courtesy of his fangs, which sliced at the words as they emerged.

"The thingsss we'll do to you…" A calculated snicker. "The ssscreamsss you'll utter…"

Offering no reply, but remaining highly attuned to their every move, she forced herself farther and farther from the castle. Her surroundings became darker, the air thicker, scented with blood and other things. She bypassed piles of bones, crimson-colored ponds, caverns that sprang from the mouths of large, carved skulls. She had no weapons, and wasn't exactly sure where the realm's exit was—only knew it was here because Cronus had brought her through while she was semi-conscious, and besides, how else would Paris and his friend have entered?—or where in the heavens she would next find herself.

Should have questioned Paris. Hindsight sucked.

"Yesss, keep walking, female. You're headed ssstraight for our camp."

Truth or lie? Wrath was no help this time. Should she stop? Fight them? Her self-defense skills were laughable, considering she had trouble balancing her weight. No matter what she did or where she went, the men were going to attack her, and that was that. Waiting for them to strike merely delayed the inevitable.

A pain-filled grunt rent the air behind her, followed by another. Then another. The men must be fighting among themselves, she thought with a tide of relief, saving her the trouble.

A head—without a body—rolled past her. The empty-eyed stare flashed, disappeared, flashed, disappeared. She tripped over her own feet as another head rolled past. Her stomach churned, even as her relief tripled.

"Must you kill so needlessly?" a male voice asked. Emotionless, and yet there was something in the cadence, something that caressed her ears.

"Yeah. I must."

Paris! Sienna whirled around, her heart a thunderstorm inside her chest. Her gaze cut through the darkness. Where was— There! Her knees nearly buckled from the ensuing flood of happiness.

"Why?" The speaker was a dark-haired man dressed in a robe, keeping pace beside Paris. He had a sublime face, wicked in its heartless beauty. Majestic wings of white-gold stretched from his back. He looked like a fallen angel, but then, so did Galen. Still, if Paris trusted him, so would she. Snow wafted around him, but only him. The flakes seemed to absorb into his skin and crystallize.

"They were looking at her, threatening her," Paris said, but if he knew where Sienna waited, he gave no indication, "and my demon knew what they were thinking. They deserved a hell of a lot worse than they got."

"I caught you, saved you from painting the ground with your organs. You owed me a favor, and I asked for a single day without bloodshed."

"Yeah, but you didn't specify which day." With that, Paris dismissed the angel and at last focused on her.

Tall and strong, scowling, he strode toward her. He had bruises under his eyes and cuts that rode the length of his arms, but his gait, though slow, was steady. Bodies were piled up behind him. She'd thought only two of the creatures were following her, but oh, had she miscalculated. At least eleven had trailed her.

"Where the hell do you think you're going?" Paris demanded the moment he reached her.

Her gaze fell to his lips. Those lush, red lips that had kissed her and sipped at her and smashed against her own. Lips she craved all over her. "Somewhere else. I'm trying to escape, and doing an excellent job of it, thank you," she replied.

"Without saying goodbye?" He latched on to her bloodstained wrist, turned her arm left and right, searching for any damage. "Nice, Sienna. Real nice."

Was he actually mad about that? Guilt rose, followed by shame and even delight. She raised her chin, refusing to buckle under his stare. "If I had returned to the castle—and believe me, my body wants to return and even standing here is a chore—I'd be stuck there again. You said you wanted my curse broken. Well, I'm doing my best to break it."

He released her, sighed. "Fine. You did the right thing, but I hate the fact that if I hadn't come after you I never would have seen you again." He could have accused her of abandoning him, of leaving him there to suffer, or any number of other things. That he hadn't...

"I hate that, too," she admitted.

Clearing his throat as though uncomfortable with the direction of their conversation, he massaged his neck.

Those ocean-blues looked as if the sun shone behind them, glistening off the water. "Anyway, I don't want you out here by yourself. It's too dangerous."

"Well, I don't want me out here by myself, either." A wave of dizziness suddenly hit her, and she swayed.

He examined her from head to toe, some of the angel's frost setting up shop on his skin. "That's not just other people's blood you're wearing, is it? You're hurt."

Concern. For her. If she'd had any resistance left, she would have lost every bit of it in that moment. "I'll heal."

"Who hurt you?" Lethal menace in his tone.

"Wrath, when he burst through the window. The other times he took over, he made me walk to the parapet on the castle's roof. This time he was afraid you'd slow me down. So—" she shrugged "—he picked a faster route."

The long spikes of Paris's lashes fused together, barely masking the menace resting behind them. "Don't let him take over anymore."

Not the least bit intimidated by the warrior's growing anger, she rolled her eyes. "Earlier you wanted me to do just that."

"I changed my mind," he said, leaning down until they were nose-to-nose. "Don't push me on this, woman. I'm too keyed up."

They stayed like that for several seconds, breath mixing, emerging faster. She wanted him to kiss her again, to finish what they'd started.

"This area is not safe," the other man said, ruining the sensuality of the moment.

Paris jolted upright, his back going ramrod straight. "Sienna, meet Zacharel. He's a warrior angel for the One, True Deity. Zacharel, meet Sienna. She's mine."

A shiver rippled through her. Uh, had he just claimed her? Had he just warned the other male away from her, as if he were possessive of her? Pleasure warmed her up, chasing away the numbing cold the angel had brought with him.

Zacharel offered his hand to her, his fingers long and thick. "I will protect you," he said, the words somehow an invitation—and a vow.

"No touching," Paris snapped, pushing the angel away from her. "Ever."

Zacharel's neutral expression never wavered, nor did the intensity of his gaze.

She shifted uncomfortably, uncertain why he wanted to protect her. There was a note of truth in his tone, however, one she could not refute. Somehow she knew he would do everything in his power to keep her safe.

Or…maybe that was a trick. Maybe, like Galen, Zacharel built up hopes and smashed them down. Gulping, she looked to Paris for answers. "Is he…"

"Like Galen?" he asked, sensing the direction of her thoughts. "No. He's the real deal, as well as a self-righteous prig who will test every limit of your patience. He's also impotent. Now, where are you headed?" He cupped her jaw and forced her focus on him and him alone.

The heat of his touch…the rough texture of his palms…another shiver stole through her. "I'm not sure." Did she sound as breathless to him as she did to herself? "I was walking aimlessly, searching for the exit. You wouldn't happen to know where it is, would you?"

"Yeah. Two days' walk in the other direction."

"Oh." She'd have to pass the castle, then, and if she passed it, she would be drawn inside. No question. If she went inside, she wouldn't come out again.

"I'll take you," he said at the same time Zacharel said,

"I can fly you there in just a few hours. And I am not impotent. I have simply never experienced desire."

Whoa. Talk about an attention stealer. Questions immediately poured through her mind. Why not? Were angels asexual? How old was he? What kind of woman could break through that icy shell and jump-start his hormones?

Maybe when things settled down she would set the angel up with someone—not that she knew anyone—because no one should go without physical contact of some kind. It hurt.

When she'd first opened her eyes and discovered her new ghostly form, she had tried to touch someone, anyone. No one had sensed her, in any way, and her mind had threatened to snap from the lack of sensation.

"You're not flying her anywhere," Paris growled. He'd been watching her, she realized, gauging her reaction to Zacharel's offer. "I told you. No touching. Besides that, she stays with me, by my side. That's nonnegotiable."

She could have argued with him. *Should* have argued with him. They had no future together, and prolonging the inevitable would destroy her in the end. But the thought of two more days with him proved irresistible.

"I stay with him," she said with a nod.

A flare of satisfaction sparked in Paris's eyes as he, too, nodded his approval.

"After you have a woman, you quickly grow tired of her," Zacharel said. "Is that why you are so eager to be alone with this one?" He sounded genuinely curious rather than waspish, yet the words stung all the same. "If that is the case, then I will gladly allow you some time together."

She must have flinched, because Paris released her and spun for attack, two daggers in his hands.

"Do you *want* to die?"

Zacharel remained focused on her. "You have only to say my name, female, and I will come for you." He vanished.

CHAPTER TWENTY-TWO

PARIS LUNGED FOR ZACHAREL, encountered only air and let loose a dark stream of curses. The main one being, "Stupid cock block." He turned back to Sienna with narrowed eyes. "Say his name, and sign his death warrant." He didn't give her a chance to respond—not that she knew what to say—but returned to her side and swooped her into his arms. He started forward, his pace smooth, her weight seemingly insubstantial. "There's a cavern up ahead. We'll get you patched up before heading for the exit."

"How do you know there's a cavern?" She'd lived here for months, far longer than Paris had, yet *she* hadn't known about any caverns.

"I scouted out the area when I first arrived."

Such a warrior thing to do, and sexy as hell. She sighed and let her head drop onto his shoulder. The muscles bunched beneath her cheek. And now that they were heading toward the castle, the tug became less pronounced, allowing her to relax.

"You know," she said, "we've only been reunited a short time, but this is, like, the hundredth time you've had to carry me."

A snort. "Your math might be a little off, baby. Besides, I like carrying you."

Baby. She loved when he called her by the endearment, loved the way his voice dipped so huskily. Her chest constricted, and her belly quivered. He was the first to ever speak to her in such a way and, unlike the time he'd called her "sweetheart" so long ago, he clearly meant it to be something special just for her.

As she rubbed her cheek against him, his champagne-and-chocolate scent hit her, more intense than ever before, and derailed her thoughts. She pressed her nose against his hammering pulse, drinking in as much of the aroma as she could. Her nerve endings perked up, singing for his touch, his caress.

His gait slowed. A few steps later, he tripped.

Was he distracted by her, or injured? Concern overshadowed her arousal when she recalled the cuts on his arm. "Are you okay?"

"I'm fine," he replied gruffly. The reassurance was ruined a second later when he stumbled over a rock.

Definitely injured. "Put me down." She struggled against his hold. "I want to walk."

"Be still," he hissed, as though in pain. "Distract me. Tell me why you joined the Hunters. You told me before, that day I woke up in your cell, but some of the details are missing."

She struggled until the rest of her strength drained, and got nowhere. Even in a weakened state, he was stronger than she was.

Every new thing she learned about him made her want him more, and made him that much sexier.

Ultimately she relaxed back against him, conceding defeat only long enough to plan. Or not. Her thoughts derailed a second time as more and more of his scent permeated her skin. Desire for him began to overwhelm her.

"Sienna."

His question. Right. And, okay, fine. If he wanted to

carry her despite his weakness or whatever was wrong, she would let him carry her. Being close to him was a need. "I bought into their ideology. I was convinced the world would become free of hurt, disease, badness and evil if only you and your friends were destroyed."

"Killing us won't turn the world into a utopia. Humans make their own choices, bringing the bad and the evil on themselves. But let's say we *do* influence the world. Would that matter? People still have choices. They can resist, fight, and choose to act as they were meant."

"I know that." She licked her lips and imagined licking her way to his—then lower. "Now."

"Do you really?"

"If I repeat my answer, will you finally believe me?"

A moment passed in silence. A silence as thick and heavy as the air around them. "Yes."

She blinked in surprise, momentarily distracted from the subject at hand. "Why?"

"Because I *want* to believe you."

Not because he trusted her, she thought, and tried not to be disappointed. But then, asking for his trust would be like asking a human male to gift her with the moon and the stars. Impossible. And yet his faith, even given for that reason, was a promising start.

"Then, yes, I truly believe killing you would serve no purpose."

The edge of his jaw appeared chiseled from stone as he nodded. "Next question. Has Cronus ever told you why he enslaved you?"

A dangerous topic, but she said, "Yes."

He shifted his hand, his fingers brushing the underside of her breast. Just like that, the desire returned. "Well. Tell me."

Trying to seduce the information out of her? No need.

She'd lied to him once upon a time, and she'd already decided never to lie to him again. Trust was a precious thing, and she wouldn't turn her back on his, no matter the trouble she courted. "He wants me to return to the Hunters, watch their leader and steal his secrets."

Against her cheek, she felt his heart stop beating. Just stop. One second, two. Finally the organ kicked back into gear, but its strikes were too fast, too brutal.

"Will you?" he asked. They'd reached the entrance of the cavern, which just happened to be the mouth of one of the giant skulls. Paris had to hunch his shoulders to get inside without scraping his head on the teeth.

"Yes," she whispered, praying her inner torment over the fact remained hidden. "I will."

"For Cronus or for yourself?"

"For…all of us. For answers about my younger sister. She's missing, has been for years. For vengeance. I hate the Hunters. Hate what they do." *For you,* she added silently. "Though hopefully I won't have to do things Cronus's way." No reason to mention the mistress thing. Her plan to sneak in now, interrogate and kill could work.

Whether Paris believed her or not, he didn't say. He carted her to the center of the enclosure, where a natural spring rested, and set her on the ledge. He arranged her wings so that their tips wouldn't scrape the dirt floor.

A frigid breeze blasted through, filling up the entire space and making her shiver. Silent, Paris started a fire the old-fashioned way, sparking two rocks together and letting the flames catch on the twigs he'd gathered. Golden flames illuminated his face, bathing his features in a heady mix of light and shadow.

He was always beautiful, but just then he was mouth-wateringly exquisite. A mythical god of the heavens, no mere mortal worthy of him. Especially not her.

"I didn't come here to punish you," he said.

She remembered the accusation she'd launched at him while he'd had her pinned to the wall, her lips stinging from the brutal kiss he'd forced on her. A kiss she might have enjoyed under any other circumstances. But at that moment, as scared as she'd been of the shadows and of her feelings for him, she'd needed gentle.

Until gentle hadn't been enough for her riotous body.

"I'm glad," she said softly.

"You believe me? Just like that?" He snapped his fingers.

"Yes."

His gaze jerked to her, crackling with the same flickering heat as the fire. "Why?"

"Because I want to."

An angry shake of his head, dark hair whipping against his cheeks. "Or maybe because you're grateful to me."

She licked her lips, tasting him in the air, knowing they were now talking about something entirely different. "No."

"Or because you merely wish to keep me strong."

"No."

"Certainly not because you desire me," he said, his tone sharp as a whip. "Not because you hunger for me."

He wanted her to say it, wanted her to admit her desire for him while they were separated. That way, she couldn't claim passion spoke for her. More than that, he wanted her to say it without offering her the same admission. Not at first, and maybe not after. Either way, she'd be taking a risk. While a denial could save her pride, he might turn away from her, now and always. And while agreement could cause her major embarrassment, it could also bring her a pleasure unlike any she'd known before. So, no contest.

"Yes," she admitted. "Because I desire you, hunger for you."

Silence once again reigned, and she wasn't sure if he'd heard her or cared. Then his gaze shifted away from her, only to jerk back to her a second later, as if he lacked the strength to battle his own needs, the blue of his eyes mixed with glimmers of demon-red and black. Eerie and haunting, but not frightening. Not anymore.

"I wasn't sure what I would do with you when I found you," he said, his voice more gravel than anything. "Save you, yes. Definitely. Sleep with you, yes, that, too. I want you so badly I ache. All the time, I ache, but even though I want to keep you, part of me has always known that I would have to leave you afterward. I can't do permanent, even with you."

Even, he'd said, as if she were special. And the fact that he'd copped to his own feelings of desire caused her hunger for him to return in full force. Her entire body trembled, and had she been standing, she would have collapsed. "I know you'll have to leave me," she said. It wasn't something she could blame him for, because she couldn't stay with him, either."

He dragged in a breath, his fingers clenched on the rocks he still held. "I will not lie to you, and I will not cheat on you, and if we tried for something more, I would have to do both."

Like he'd done with that woman, Susan.

"Being with you may not affect my demon, may not strengthen me. I don't know, because I haven't had the same woman twice since my possession. If it doesn't work, I'll have to leave you sooner than expected and find…someone else."

There was no reason for him to know that the thought of him with another woman ate at her, leaving raw, oozing wounds. "I know."

"Because you saw..."

"Susan. Yes."

Sadness flickered in his eyes, then anger. He ran his tongue over his teeth, as though her response had somehow pricked his temper. "If that happens, I'll tell you. I'll tell you first, before I leave, and no matter what, I'll come back to you. I'll make sure you reach the exit. But after that, we have to... We say goodbye, once and for all."

The fire must have been doing its job, but the cavern seemed to warm in an instant, the cold vanquished. Perhaps her body had simply sucked that cold inside. She felt chilled to the bone. Paris wasn't going to protest her return to the Hunters. She wondered if he would object to her involvement with Galen, if it became necessary, but wasn't going to ask. As much as she wanted to know the answer, she *didn't* want to know the answer.

"Knowing all of that, do you still want to be with me?" he asked.

His tone implied he didn't give a shit about her answer. That he'd shrug and easily find someone else if she said no. But he was holding his breath, she realized, his cheeks flushing under the strain. He did want her, and he did care whether or not she wanted him back.

"I still want to be with you," she said. "Still want *you*."

He searched her face, clearly satisfied by what he saw, because he nodded. "Good. Now take off your clothes and get in the water."

CHAPTER TWENTY-THREE

PARIS WATCHED AS SIENNA dropped her shirt on the floor, where she'd already kicked her pants. Now she stood in her bra and panties. Plain, white. And yet, clinging to her perfect little body, they were the sexiest garments he'd ever seen.

His erection stretched past his navel, the base wider than his wrist. Yeah, he wanted her that badly.

More, Sex pleaded.

"The rest," he croaked. She was so beautiful...so strong. He'd come all this way, done all those terrible things, and yet she had freed herself from Cronus's hold. When Paris looked past his own masculine pride, he was glad about that. She had fought her demon and won, something he had never been able to do. Whatever happened outside this realm, she would be okay.

What happened inside of it, however...

Shouldn't do this, he thought, even as he repeated, "The rest. Now."

She unhooked the bra, dropped the garment on top of the others. Rosy nipples pearled from the lingering coolness in the air, topping off breasts he wanted in his mouth. Her thumbs slid under the waist of her panties and tugged. Down the exquisite length of her legs, until she was a whole lot of naked. His gaze was riveted on the dark triangle of curls shielding his favorite place in this realm or any other.

She shifted uncomfortably, her arms lifting and lowering as if she wanted to cover herself but kept talking herself out of doing so.

"You're perfect. So sweet and perfect." Slender, finely boned, with that deliciously freckled skin, each mark reminding him of a little drop of candy. He was going to lick her from top to bottom.

When they parted, there would be no part of her he hadn't tasted.

Frowning, she looked herself over. "How can you say that about me?"

"If you're about to insult yourself, I suggest you zip your mouth and get in the water."

His waspish tone had her blinking. "You're mad."

Hell, yeah, he was mad. "When I tell you how beautiful you are, and you express doubt, you're basically calling me a liar."

"No, I don't mean… It's just that…" She paused, reminding him of the babbling, uncertain woman he'd smacked into in Rome. The one who had fascinated him so completely, the one who'd prattled so charmingly. "Men just don't…"

Men. He cursed with enough heat to blister. "That's good, because otherwise I'd have to kill them." She was his and anyone else who looked at her, anyone else who thought to touch her— *Stop right there. Keep the possessiveness to a minimum. This is temporary. Has to be temporary.*

"Paris," she said, a hitch to her voice.

"Yes." He wanted to look away, couldn't look away.

"I think you're beautiful, too." With that, as if she hadn't just undone him, she turned toward the spring. He saw the elegant, and bruised, line of her back. Saw where those violet-and-jet wings grew in two perfect rows, saw the obsidian butterfly tattoo etched between them.

The curve of her spine made his mouth water. There were two indentions at the base, just above her ass. And speaking of her ass...had he ever seen anything more lovely? Enough to grab while he pounded deep inside her, toned, four freckles forming a starlike pattern on the right cheek.

He could worship there for hours, days.

More. Please, more. Need to touch.

A moan of bliss left her as she sank into the steaming water. She disappeared underneath the surface, saturating her hair, then came back up sputtering.

"Here." His arm shook as he withdrew a thin, wrapped bar of soap from his pocket. Embarrassment doused him when he noted he was trembling.

She accepted gratefully, her fingers brushing his palm. Beads of sweat broke out on his brow. "Thank you. You were smart to travel with one of these. I'll have to remember to do that."

Yeah. He wasn't going to explain his reason for doing so. He wasn't going there with her. Ever.

Telling her that he *always* carried a bar, that he never knew whose bed he'd end up in, or what kind of person he'd be with, or how dirty he'd feel afterward, or that he carried soap like other men carried condoms...not smart. A mood ruiner for sure.

And speaking of condoms, could he tell her the truth? He couldn't catch an STD, so he couldn't pass one on; pregnancy was rare between an immortal and a human, much less a dead human; and while he hated sleeping with strangers, hated being so intimate with them, his demon needed the skin-to-skin contact. So, no condom, even though his shaft had come into contact with thousands of people. She would be disgusted.

He shouldn't have pushed her for a sexual relationship when he had nothing more to offer her. He should have given her time to make a more informed decision, but he didn't have time. *They* didn't have time. In two days, he would lose her. And the thing was, Sex needed fulfillment now. So, yeah, if she would let him, he would take her.

He settled at the spring's ledge, need for her clawing at him. If they did this—they were so doing this—and Sex wasn't satisfied immediately afterward, Paris would... what? Do what he'd told her he would do and find someone else?

Don't think about that right now. He would lose control of his temper.

Already the darkness inside him swirled, craving a release of its own, making him feel as though he were possessed by two demons, each with separate needs. Sex, needing sex, and Violence, needing bloodshed. But Maddox carried the demon of Violence, so there went that theory.

Whatever. It doesn't matter. Only Sienna and this moment matter.

Sienna.

Soon she would leave this realm, the heavens, and hide from Cronus. No way would Paris allow her to hunt Galen. He would convince her to remain tucked away, and that was that. She would be safe, and Paris would return to his friends. To his war. To his old life.

A sick, pitiful existence, but, hell, after all the people he'd hurt throughout the centuries, he deserved it. Especially for what he'd done to Susan.

He'd truly admired and respected Susan. Had promised her fidelity even though he couldn't give it, and had slowly broken her heart. He wouldn't do that to another woman.

But… He yearned for more than random couplings. He yearned for monogamy.

He yearned for Sienna.

You can have her, Sex said.

Only to lose her.

No argument there.

Why have you allowed me to harden for her on multiple occasions, even though we've had her, yet you have never done the same with another? Over and over he'd asked this question, and always the answer was the same.

I don't know. It just happens.

A lot of things "just happened." While Paris hated the prospect of the upcoming separation from Sienna, she had easily agreed to their two-day limit. Had to be that way, yeah, but damn. Would a little fight about it have killed her?

Shit. He was being unreasonable, the darkness still driving his emotions. If he wanted this woman, he should have her. If he wanted to keep her, he should have her always. End of story.

Should, should, should. You couldn't live with shoulds, could you. Only woulds.

He shook his head, clearing his thoughts. He had a direct view of Sienna as she bathed. She lathered herself up, and damn if he wasn't transfixed as the bubbles cascaded down her breasts, caught on her nipples, then resumed their journey to her navel.

"Sienna, I have to tell you something." He ducked his head, too humiliated to face her. After this, she might walk, no chance of sex, but he had to do this or his conscience would never forgive him.

"You can tell me anything."

They'd soon find out. "After your death I had to…you know…and even on my way here, I…"

What are you doing? You know it's better if they never know what happens when we're done with them.

We. *You mean* you. *When* you *are done.*

"I know," she said, quieting both the demon and him.

No accusations, no making him unload the gory details. He liked that about her. A lot. She probably had no idea how rare that acceptance was, but he did. "The last time was a few days ago, I swear. I kept thinking I'd find you, and I wanted to be with you and only you when that happened."

"Paris, we weren't dating. We weren't committed. The last thing I said to you was that I hated you. And I'm sorry for that, I really am. So don't beat yourself up about your actions. You did nothing wrong." Water splashed as she closed the distance between them. She stood and warm, wet hands wound around his neck, twirling the ends of his hair.

He rested his forehead on the curve of her shoulder. Soft, soft skin, scented so sweetly his head did that fogging thing. Sex went crazy, too, perhaps even more desperate to touch and taste her than Paris was. "I wouldn't be so understanding with you. If you had slept with another man, even though we weren't dating, even though we weren't committed, I would…rage." He still wouldn't lie to her.

And what he would do afterward, when they split…

"At me?"

"No. Maybe. I don't know." His arms shot out and dragged her closer, needing her closer. Water soaked his shirt to his chest. Her nipples rasped at him, creating the most sizzling of frictions. "I want you all to myself."

She carried the sun under her skin, lighting him up every time he neared her. The jade and copper in her eyes were a lush, thriving valley he could lose himself in. Her mouth inspired every one of his most erotic fantasies.

Yes! This is what I've needed, what I've been craving.

What Paris had been craving.

"Since you," she told him softly, "there's been no one, and before you, years had passed."

Years. The concept baffled him as much as it pleased him.

"He was…the only man I've ever… I thought I would marry him," she said. "He was a Hunter, the one who recruited me." A pause rife with a thousand sharp edges, then, "I'm changing the subject, but only a little. I would like to express one more doubt about, um, myself, before we continue."

He stiffened, suspecting where she was headed and dreading it with every fiber of his being.

She hurried on. "I know we've been together before, and you know I'm just me. But this time it's different, because I know you better, know myself better, and I'm afraid that you'll… That I won't be… That I can't compare. To the others."

Yeah. Exactly where he'd thought she was headed. He dropped a kiss onto her collarbone, licked where his lips had been, then sucked hard enough to leave his mark. She gasped.

"I'm afraid *I* won't measure up, too," he admitted. "Here I am, the keeper of Sex. What if I can't please you? What if I can't live up to your expectations? And Sienna," he added before she had time to respond, "the others, they can't compare *to you*."

He'd been with thousands, yes, and he'd done his best to leave each one satisfied. He'd been using them, after all, so it was the least he could do. But making them come hadn't been for their benefit; it had been for his, something to ease the sting of his guilt. Had he actually cared about their pleasure? No.

"Oh, Paris." Those dainty, beautiful hands smoothed over his back. The motions were rhythmic, grace- ful, waking up parts of him he hadn't known existed. "How about this? Today you're just a man and I'm just a woman. There's no past, no future, only the present. We do what feels good. Nothing more. Nothing less."

Ah, hell. She kept that up and he would blow before he got inside her. She'd offered him the sexiest words he'd ever heard, ever hoped to hear, and it was another reason to like her. She did more than arouse him. She comforted him.

"Yeah. I'd like that," he said.

Me, too!

That's enough out of you. He settled his big hands on Sienna's tiny hips, lifted her out of the water and set her on the rocky edge beside him. The warmth of the water had flushed her skin, and now, droplets traveled all the places he wanted to go. He moved in front of her, crouching, rocking back on his heels before settling on his knees. Slowly he drew his hands along the tops of her thighs. He stopped at her knees, his thumbs dabbling underneath for several minutes before he applied pres- sure and opened her up as wide as he could get her. She was pink, wet and glistening.

He should tongue her nipples first, and he meant to. That had been the plan. Open her up, slide closer and pay proper homage to those sweet little buds. Except, now that he had a direct view of the prettiest feminine core he'd ever seen, there would be no starting up top and working his way down. He wanted *that*. Now. Wanted her dripping.

"I need you in my mouth. Down my throat. All over me. Tell me you need that, too."

"I—"

"Tell me."

"Yes. Please, Paris. Now."

CHAPTER TWENTY-FOUR

No TEASING HIM, NO TORMENTING him. His woman deserved a reward. Paris pressed a soft kiss where his thumbs had played, just behind her knees, then licked and nibbled his way up...up... A tremor moved through her, a perfect mimic of the vibrations Sex was throwing at him.

He leaned closer...closer still...breathed deeply, taking in the erotic scent of her desire. His blood fired, burning through him, scorching everything in its path and leaving only the desire. It was all he knew, all he wanted to know. Then he was there, right on her, licking his way up her center.

She cried out, the hoarse sound blending with his moan of rapture. Her arousal coated his tongue and he swallowed her, instantly addicted. His eyes closed as he savored. Wasn't just ambrosia he was tasting, either. Beneath the tropical syrupiness of the drug, there was a unique flavor all her own, something wine-rich and decadent. And for the first time in his life, he thought he could actually *taste* the aphrodisiac his demon released. Sweet as honey, rich with spice, it filled his mouth, coated his throat, seeped from his skin, blending with Sienna's succulence.

How many times had he dreamed of doing this to her, with her? Countless. He'd waited so long, and at times, he'd feared he would never know the reality. Nothing should have been able to live up to the languorous feasting he'd envisioned, but this not only lived up, it surpassed. She was everything he'd ever craved, and more.

Her fingers tangled in his hair, applying the most arousing sort of pressure. His woman wanted him back, attending to her need. There was no headier knowledge. He licked back up her core, but this time he didn't pull away. He swirled the tip of his tongue around her clitoris, teasing, taunting, driving her passion higher. Hell, driving his own higher.

He was starved for her, his cock throbbing against his fly.

"Not there," she instructed. "You're almost there. Please, just a little closer and you'll be there." The words gasped from her. Her hips undulated as she sought to place his tongue directly on that swollen clitoris.

And she thought she was bad at kissing and sex? Silly female.

He penetrated her core, sinking his tongue inside her, fast, faster, glorying as she panted his name, as her essence covered his face, as he swallowed her down, as her nails sank into his scalp, as her hips twirled and met his thrusts, as she arched into him, retreated, arched again.

"Paris! Yes, yes. There!"

When he felt her tensing, edging ever closer to release, he fit his lips over her clit and sucked, hard, at the same time driving two, then three, fingers deep, so deep. He scissored them, shifting depth and width in a constant stream of motion, and just when she reached the pinnacle of climax, he backed off a fraction, slowing his movements. Her moans tapered into incoherent mumblings, her hips following him, circling, trying to lure him back within those satiny walls.

"Paris! Finish me."

"I want to make you feel good."

"I do, promise."

"But you want more."

"Yes. Please!"

"Very well." A ruthless plunge of his fingers, scissoring over and over, his tongue flicking over that swelling bud, and she climaxed with violent force, her inner walls clenching on him. A scream tore from her, so loud and bracing it cracked her vocals. He loved it, reveled in the knowledge that he had brought her to this point.

His desperation grew critical, and he had to remove his fingers from her and clamp onto her thighs to hold himself steady, to stop himself from ripping at his zipper and slamming home.

He stayed like that until she calmed. Finally her shoulders sagged, and her head lolled forward. Those midnight wings trembled, glimmering like polished ebony. She was panting shallowly, her bottom lip cut from where she'd bitten down.

When her slumberous gaze met his, he brought his fingers to his mouth and licked at her arousal. He couldn't get enough of her, didn't think he would ever get enough.

Her pupils expanded, consuming those hazel irises and leaving only black. Black velvet, smooth and endless. He could lose himself and never care to be found.

"Take off your clothes," she whispered. "Please. Let me have you now."

He grabbed the collar of his shirt and tugged, ducking to free his head from the material's confinement. Her hands found his pecs a second later, her palms pressing into his nipples.

"Your heart is racing," she said, clearly awed by that fact. In that moment, his heart beat *for* her. Only her. He'd never craved a female this much. And that she knew what he was, what he'd done, and wanted him anyway... He moved in and fit his mouth around one of her rosy little nipples, sucking hard then easing the sting with a flick of his tongue. He turned his head and did the same to the other, leaving his mark on them both. Branding her, so that when she saw herself in a mirror she would know she belonged to someone else. To him, only him.

"Let me see the rest of you," she said.

He shook his head.

"Paris..."

Another shake. To remove his pants, he would have to stop touching her, and he didn't want to stop touching her. Couldn't conceive a good enough reason to *ever* stop.

"Please. I need to see you."

Trembling, he pressed his forehead between her breasts. He swallowed, found his voice. "You never have to beg. Not with me. Whatever you want, I will give you." Always before, he'd taken from his partners. With her, he wanted to give anything, everything. "But if I strip, I will lose control. Let me savor you, Sienna."

"Control is overrated. I want you, however I can get you."

Such beautiful words. "I wish we were at my home, and in my bed, and I had you splayed on my pillows. You deserve better than a dirty cave."

She cupped his cheeks and forced his eyes to meet hers. "After everything I've done to you, how can you say that?"

He didn't remind her that this moment had no past. He couldn't. The past flooded him, too. "Sienna, you ran to me when you were in trouble, when Cronus first enslaved you. Before *that,* you slept with me to strengthen me de-

spite the fact that you were horrified by our potential audience, despite the fact that I was your greatest enemy.
Before that, you were involved in a war and batting for
your team, same as me. You did nothing I wouldn't have
done, had the situation been reversed."

Tears filled her eyes, splashed down her cheeks.

"None of that. Not here, not now." He captured them
with his tongue, kissing them away. Now the reminder
came. "Just a man and a woman, remember?"

"I just...I always get emotional after mind-shattering
orgasms," she said with a dry undertone, and he laughed.
"Or I must, considering that was my first."

"Your other man didn't—"

Her smile was silky, wanton. "What other man?"

Good girl. He chuckled, surprising himself. Genuine
humor between lovers wasn't something he'd ever experienced before her.

"I want you anywhere I can get you." Nibbling on her
bottom lip, she reached down and pushed at his zipper.
Her fingertips brushed the weeping tip of his cock, which
stretched far past the waist of his pants. "Mmm, no underwear."

"I was...hopeful."

Now she was the one to chuckle.

He gripped her under the ass and urged her forward,
even as he leaned back on his haunches. She slid from
the rocky foundation, held up only by his hands. He positioned her core just over his erection. So hot, so wet,
but he didn't push inside. Not yet.

"Kiss me," he commanded, even as Sex got his purr
on. Guess the demon was so excited, he couldn't stay
quiet a moment longer. At least he wasn't talking. "Like
before. Own me with your mouth."

"My pleasure." A shiver rocked her as she meshed

their lips without any hesitation, thrusting her tongue into his mouth and feeding him all that she was. Owning him, just as he'd wanted.

"Can't hold back," he said. All thoughts of savoring her, this moment, fled. They had here and now, and not much else. He had to know the rest of her, had to join them. "Must be in you. Need to be in you."

"Yes. You'll own *me*."

He thrust deep and sure, filling her. They moaned in unison. Paris, Sienna, Sex. It was like coming home after a year in the desert, when you were so thirsty, so hungry, you felt as if you were drinking and eating for the first time. As if you were alive for the first time. His senses awoke, aware of her every need, attuned to her every nuance.

This was what he'd yearned for so desperately. Not just a communion with her body, but with her mind. Her soul, their every breath intertwined.

Yes. Yes, yes, yes.

She was tight, tighter than a fist, and he knew he stretched her. Knew he was too big for such a slender body, but that didn't stop him from moving her up and down, up and down from the root of his shaft to the very tip. She was so wet, the glide was smooth. Her nipples rasped at his chest, creating the most delicious friction. Friction that lanced spears of pleasure throughout his entire body.

He was utterly consumed by her. She was in his mouth, pressed against him, her weight sliding her down on him…down…all the way…her legs squeezing at his, her hands on his back, her nails scraping and clawing at him. Even the ends of her hair acted as a stimulant, dancing over his skin, tickling.

Paris kneaded his hands up her spine and stopped between her wings. Occasionally over the years, he'd had to massage his friend Aeron to work out the stiffness from battle. So he knew just how sensitive the slits in these wings could be. Keeping in mind that she had to be sore, he kneaded gently, rolling the muscles and tendons under his fingers.

A hoarse cry left her. "Paris! Oh, Paris!"

His name on her lips did it for him, totally, completely. He rarely ever told his partners his name, not wanting to hear them say it and increase his shame. But now, with Sienna, he was once again undone.

He pounded into her, harder, so damn hard their teeth banged together when she dove in for another kiss. Their tongues sparred with the same strength, the same intensity. His testicles were drawing up, the skin around them tightening. White-hot waves of pleasure and strength swam at the base of his spine, ready to burst through him, to devour him and brand her.

So badly he wanted to come, but he wouldn't, not until she'd exploded on him. Her pleasure came first, now and always.

He reached between their bodies and circled his thumb against her clitoris. And, oh, sweet heaven, that's all she'd needed. Another scream that cracked her vocals echoed around him, her inner walls milking him. He jetted inside her, pouring all of his desire, all of his need and passion straight into her core. Roaring, roaring, so caught up in the incredible sensations, uncaring about anything else.

And when, an eternity later, she collapsed against his chest, her legs lax against his, he continued to hold her, unwilling to let go. Just then, he wasn't sure he would ever be able to let go.

CHAPTER TWENTY-FIVE

HE'D BEEN ABUSED, his skin like pretty pink ribbons curling from a Christmas box.

Violated in the worst ways.

But Kane never gave the female minions what they wanted.

He was ashamed that he couldn't fight his way free, that his demon had somehow taken him over and held him down as surely as the chains shackling his wrists and ankles. He was a warrior, thousands of years old, with experience honed on the bloodiest of battlefields. This should be child's play to him. He should have escaped long ago.

More than any of that, however, he was humiliated by all kinds of other things he wasn't ready to acknowledge or face. The things they'd done to him...

Later. He would deal with it later. Maybe. Right now, all he could do was distance himself from what was happening to his body, as if it wasn't actually his body enduring the abuse. As if someone else had teeth in his thigh, hands where no others had been.

Drip, drip went his blood.

Kane had been tortured before. Many times, in fact. This was just more of the same, he told himself. Yeah. Right.

Disaster laughed, a cruel, happy sound echoing in his mind. If only that were the first time, but no. Disaster had laughed and laughed and laughed, a never-ending stream of amusement.

Hate utterly consumed Kane, kept him conscious. Every time he felt himself slipping into darkness, he thought about the demon High Lord inside him. Despite his instinct to remain distanced, he wanted to know every deed done to him. One day, he would return the favor in kind—a thousandfold. His demon would suffer this way. His demon would die this way.

Yes, one day.

His gaze pulled from the blood-spattered cavern wall above him and slipped down his body. He was a raw slab of scarlet. Dripping...dripping... Were those his ribs? Yes, he thought hazily. They were, one of them even pointing in the wrong direction.

One. Day.

Distantly he heard the pound of...horse hooves? Maybe. Whatever it was caused the minions on top of him, under him, even those around him who were awaiting their turn, to scatter in the winds, leaving him atop the boulder, naked, still bleeding...still dripping. Crimson, such a lovely yet horrifying color. Life and death, bound together.

He should be in tremendous pain, but there was nothing. Only a strange, welcome numbness.

A horse's whinny. Booted footsteps. He should care. Someone was here, looking at him, seeing him at his worst. He did care, but there was nothing he could do about it. No way to cover himself or hide what had been done to him. He wanted to kill this newcomer the same way he wanted to kill the minions and Disaster. Anything to wipe away all knowledge of this day. Forever.

A shadow fell over him, then someone was leaning down and peering into his eyes. Dark hair, eyes of the cruelest blue. "I know you. You are Kane, keeper of Disaster. Had a bad day, have you?"

Kane gathered enough strength to turn his head away. The action, small as it'd been, zapped every bit of that strength, leaving him cold, hollow. He had nothing left. Of course, the guy reached out and turned his head for him, forcing his attention to return.

"I'll take that as a yes."

Silence.

The guy grinned, and it was not nice. "Once, I could not have paid a Lord of the Underworld to visit me here. Now you guys keep popping up for free. By the way, your friend Amun called me Red while he was down here. Well, he thought it. Boy doesn't speak much, does he?" He gave a genuinely amused chuckle, and yet, there was bite to the sound. "Wish I'd picked up on that thought while he was in front of me, but then, I didn't have these, a gift from Amun before he left."

Red held up two hands—and they weren't attached to his body or any other. They were dark-skinned and held together by a strap of leather. A strap of leather he had wrapped around his neck, as if he were carrying boxing gloves. The insides of the hands had been scraped out, the flesh leathered.

They *were* gloves now. Human gloves.

Acid bubbled in Kane's stomach. Amun had come down here to rescue Legion and in the process had been infected by hundreds of demon minions, evil becoming a slick oil over his skin. The only solution had been to send him back down here to release them.

The gloves were the same mocha color as Amun's skin, possessed the same lines.

"What do you mean…gift?" Kane managed to work past his shredded throat. A throat scraped raw when the minions had stuffed things into his mouth. They hadn't cared that he'd tried to bite them, and hadn't tried to prevent him from doing so. They'd actually liked that. They had just— *You aren't thinking about this yet. You'll become as crazy as Amun was.*

"I won the mitts in a poker game," Red said, his tone casual. "You play? Wait. Don't answer that. Let me learn your secrets with my new, favorite toy." Grinning his not-nice grin, he stuffed his hands into the skin gloves and reached out.

Contact.

Those hands pressed against Kane's temples, cool and tough. Red closed his eyes, his entire body jerking as if hooked to a car with a lot of stallions under the hood. A moment passed, the only sound that of his heavy breathing.

Then another round of hoofbeats reverberated. Booted footsteps came next. A blond male with a similar toothy grin was leaning over Kane. "Whatta we got here? Another demon warrior?"

"Looks like." Red straightened, his blue gaze boring into Kane. "He's quite the mess."

"Will he heal?"

"Don't know." A shrug as if the answer wasn't important either way, then, "The man beside me is my brother. Amun called him Black. I call him Asshole. You may use whichever you prefer."

"Let me use the hands," Black said, rubbing his own with anticipation.

"Hell, no." A growl sprang from Red, an animalistic warning. "I just got them today, and this is my week to own them."

"I just want to borrow them for a minute."

"Please. You'll keep them, claim it's your turn already."

"Will not."

"Will, too."

I'm dreaming. I have to be dreaming. At the very least, hallucinating. Feral killers—and they *were* killers; they possessed the same hard edge as his friends—were not arguing like children.

"Fine. Just tell me what you learned," Black said, clearly sulking.

"He was with the Dark, and recently." Love and hate bathed Red's tone. "The Dark thinks this one will take White from us. The pair of them were captured, brought here and marked for death. A cave-in separated them. He doesn't know where the Dark is. The minions brought him here, tried to mate with him."

The Dark? Only person who thought Kane would take someone named White was William. And how did Red know—the hands, Kane realized. Those hands *had* belonged to Amun, then. Amun, the keeper of Secrets. Red had put those…gloves on, had touched Kane and dug deep into his mind, ferreting out information. A handy little weapon to have. He should be enraged, but he was still too numb.

Black popped his jaw. "White will have sensed your joy at finding a new demon, as did I. She will be here soon. We cannot allow her to meet this keeper." Emerald eyes bore into Kane. "You will not take her from us."

I don't want anything to do with her, dude.

"Shall we kill him and be done with it?" Red asked as if he were contemplating what to serve for dinner.

Black rubbed at the golden stubble on his jaw. "That would put him out of his misery. A good deed on our parts."

Kane wanted to help him with the answer. *Hell, yeah, you should kill me.* Because when this numbness wore off, when his body shrieked with the pain and his mind merged with his emotions, he was going to suffer. He was going to scream. He was going to rage.

Vengeance, he told himself. He could not have vengeance if he was dead.

"No, no killing," Black finally decided. "Not until I've had my turn inside his head."

"Agreed."

Then they would kill him a week from now, after Black had his turn. Seven days. Kane didn't know whether to laugh, thank them or just go ahead and start screaming and raging now.

The two freed him from the chains, but he didn't have the strength to move. He could only lie there, waiting, helpless to their whims.

"Green is going to rip into us for saving him," Red said. "You know how protective he is of White."

"True that." Black hefted Kane over his shoulder, unmindful of his exposed rib cage. "She's the only female he can tolerate."

The action disrupted some of the physical numbness, shooting sharp lances of pain through him. His mind began to fog, oxygen a faraway dream.

"But by then," Black continued, as Kane faded... faded... "I will have had my turn, so that is a moot point."

Kane didn't hear Red's reply. For him, it was finally, blessedly lights-out.

CHAPTER TWENTY-SIX

HIGH IN THE HEAVENS, Cronus stood at the foot of his bed, glaring down at his wife. She was still naked, still chained, but with two words, she had just changed the very foundation of their war.

"What did you say?" Surely he had misheard.

Her chin lifted haughtily, her eyes a shimmer of midnight hatred. "Beat me and let him go."

No, he had not misheard. His narrowed gaze shot to the male Hunter kneeling at his feet. Cronus had come here, as he'd come here every day for the past few weeks, and offered Rhea the choice. Watch a Hunter die or feel the hammer of his fists. Or in this case, watch two Hunters die—a male and the female who had refused to release him as Cronus dragged him from the cage. Always she preferred to watch a Hunter die. Always.

Except today.

What had changed? The Hunter in question? He was the only variable that was different. Did that mean she cared for the male? No, he assured himself after a heartbeat of bewilderment. Rhea cared only for herself. Did he mean something to her heavenly campaign? But what could a lone puny human do to aid a goddess? The answer was simple. Nothing.

That left only one option. She desired him.

Rage unfurled inside Cronus, iron fists that battered at his chest. His skin pulled tight against his bones, his marrow sharpening into dagger points and cutting at him. He gripped the human by the hair, jerking him to his feet and studying him anew. Late twenties, blond, handsome in a quiet, distinguished way only a mortal with a limited amount of time could manage. Lean, with only the barest hint of muscle.

Clearly, he wasn't a fighter. A scholar, perhaps. There could be no asking him, however. Like all the others, Cronus had already cut out his tongue. A must for these meetings. Allowing someone to speak to Rhea, to deliver a secret message Cronus could not decipher, would have been a huge tactical error.

Cronus never made tactical errors.

He looked at his wife. Her stubborn expression gave nothing away.

"Let him go," she said, chin going ever higher. "I've made my choice. I will be beaten in exchange for his life."

Let the male go? Alive and well, forgiven for his crimes against the greatest king Titania has ever known? The concept was inconceivable. Laughable. "And the female?" he snarled, tugging her hair to lift her head.

She whimpered, her obvious distress causing the male to grunt. How sweet, Cronus thought dryly. The humans cared for each other.

Eyes the color of a blood-soaked battlefield swept over the girl. "I don't care about her. Do whatever you wish with her, just let the male go."

Rhea's demon must be giving her fits. Either that, or Strife simply enjoyed the show. Well, it would be Cronus's pleasure to offer another blast of discord. "I do not approve of your choice, wife. Therefore, I think I will behead the man before I release him."

The queen sputtered for a moment, her chains rattling against the bedposts. "Are you completely lacking in honor, *husband?*"

"Of course. To win, one must do whatever is necessary. Besides that, I never promised to let your Hunters go while their hearts still beat, did I?"

"You bastard!"

"If you wish to save this one, you will tell me what's so special about him. That is our new bargain."

The male quaked with fear, his clammy sweat creating an acrid scent in the air. The female, still kneeling at Cronus's other side, reached for him, clasped his hand in a show of comfort and support. Her hair was cropped to her shoulders, and so black the tint had to have come from a bottle. Her eyes were brown, a deep chocolate, and filled with anguished tears. She was pretty in a delicate sort of way, and somehow familiar to him.

She wasn't the first female he'd brought to Rhea, nor would she be the last. There were several others waiting below in the dungeon. Now he wondered if he'd slain a sibling of hers, a sister perhaps, and that was why he thought he recognized her.

"Explaining my reasons was never part of our bargain," Rhea said in that haughty voice of hers, the one he loathed. The one guaranteed to make him see red. "Let. Him. Go."

Sure enough, Cronus's rage intensified. He returned his attention to the male. Shadows formed half circles under his eyes, his cheeks were hollowed out and there was blood dripping down his chin, all proof of his mortality.

Had Rhea once welcomed him into her bed? Was this man one of the many Cronus had felt his wife enjoying these past few months? Had this bastard climaxed inside her?

When her passions came upon her, she become wild
and wanton, and unaware of—or unconcerned by—the
damage she inflicted.

Each new deliberation tossed another smoldering
log onto the fires of his rage, until the only thing inside
his body was thick, black smoke with crimson flames
trapped throughout. He couldn't see past them, could
only choke on them. And only then did he realize that it
was not the human who was quaking with such intensity;
it was *him,* and the knowledge humiliated him.

The human had to pay.

"Look at me. Now."

Long golden-brown lashes lifted. Eyes filled with
challenge and hatred stared up at him. Resentment, too.
Did this human yearn for what he himself possessed? A
connection to Rhea?

Well, that ended now. Before Cronus realized he
had moved, he'd released the girl, palmed a blade—
and slashed. He watched as the man's throat split in
the center, blood welling and flowing. Watched as pain
took the place of the resentment…watched as even that
dulled…faded…and his body sagged.

The girl screamed, the shrill noise scraping at his ears,
annoying him. Frowning down at her, intending to reprimand her, he uncurled his fingers from the man's hair
and reached for her. *Thump.* The lifeless body hit the
floor, and she released another scream, darting out of
his way.

Not before he caught Rhea's gasp of horror.

His attention whipped to her, the girl suddenly forgotten. *His wife had just gasped.* Misery was to be her
only companion in the countless eternity that awaited
her, yes, but the fact that she'd dared to find that misery

in the demise of some frail mortal failed to fill him with any kind of satisfaction.

Such a reaction meant he'd miscalculated, that she had, indeed, cared for the man. Even as his temper flared all the hotter, he struggled with understanding. Why care for a creature so limited by time and capability? A creature so fragile, so easily killed. As he had just demonstrated.

The black-haired wench scrambled to the body of the fallen male and gathered him close. She cried, her tears a flood of emotion. Obviously, she had cared for the man, too. But…why? What had he done to draw two women's loyalty?

Cronus's lip curled up in a snarl. The answer didn't matter, not really. The bastard was gone now, never to return. "Let him go," he commanded the girl.

She looked up at him, hatred shining in her eyes. She carefully laid the body upon the floor, pressed a kiss to his forehead and stood. Her steps clipped, measured, she approached Cronus, horrible sounds of grief rising from her.

Had he not taken her tongue, curses would have been hurled at him, he was sure. But she could not blame him for her lack. He had given her a choice. Return to the cage and die another day, or stay with the man, lose her tongue and die on this one. She'd chosen to stay.

"I am not a monster," he said. "The pair of you sanctioned the wrong side of the war, and you paid for it." One thing he'd learned while whiling away the centuries inside Tartarus: a king without a firm hand was a king without a throne.

What came next was expected. She threw herself against him, her fists pummeling at him, her fury and heartache infusing every blow. He didn't try to defend himself. There was no need. Did she truly think she was hurting him? That she *could* hurt him?

A resounding *no* to both, yet her relentless effort soon aggravated him. He had better things to do. "Stop, female."

Either she didn't hear him or she didn't care to obey. He set her away from him, a concession on his part, and one he did not often offer, but she just came back, a catapult of feminine ire. He could have frozen her in place with a wave of his hand, but he refused to venture down that path. Pride dictated she obey of her own accord or suffer the consequences.

"Do you wish to die, too?" he asked.

Somehow the question reached past her mania, and she stilled, a whisper of emotion-charged air separating their bodies. Panting breaths sawed in and out of her mouth, those heart-wrenching tears continuing to flow.

What came next was *not* expected.

With a cry springing from the depths of her soul, she threw herself into his blade. Her eyes widened with her pain; blood gurgled from her mouth. His blade. Oh, yes. He still clutched the hilt, the sharp, silver tip facing her—now inside her.

She did indeed want to die.

"Very well, female. Once again, I will support your choice." A tug of his arm, and she was freed from the intrusion. A flick of his wrist, and he killed her the same way he'd killed her man. Quick, easy. A mercy slaying, he told himself.

Her eyes rolled back in her head as her body slumped beside her man's.

A long moment passed in silence. Something burned in his chest. Regret, perhaps. Though why he would feel such a strong emotion for someone he did not know and did not care about was a mystery. Violence walked hand in hand with victory. In the heavens, you could not have one without the other.

"Well, well," Rhea said, and there was no longer a hint of remorse in her tone. No anger or betrayal, either. "My compliments on a job well done, darling."

He spun to face her. He was not met with tears, recrimination or even sorrow. He was met with glee. Lips he'd once kissed with reverence lifted in a smug grin. "How did that feel, murdering two innocents?"

He schooled his expression to blankness, unwilling to reveal his confusion. "Why so haughty, wife? It is your man bleeding all over my carpet, is it not?"

"No. It's not." She arched a brow at his flinching response. "Do you think I know not our prophecies? How it will be my Galen to take your head—unless you bind him to the female with wings of midnight."

He wiped his blade on the coverlet at Rhea's feet, a stark reminder of his prowess. One she would be forced to see for the rest of her stay here. "If *your* Galen takes my head, you die, as well."

Laughter layered with ice left her, causing a chill to crawl down his spine. "I know." And she didn't sound as if she cared. "I also know how your mind works. You expect Galen to want to use the winged girl and her new demon, but you doubt he will desire the girl herself. How, then, could you force a bonding? Let me think, let me think. Oh, yes, I know. By turning her into a walking fountain of ambrosia and addicting Galen to her blood. How am I doing so far?"

Not since Zeus ambushed him and drove him to his knees had Cronus experienced such fear. "Shut your mouth. You know nothing!"

Rhea continued on, her voice a silky caress. "You

could not infect a living girl with ambrosia; you could only infect a dead one. And who better to pick than someone the Lord of Sex desired? He will convince his friends to leave her alone, and she will convince him to leave Galen alone. Finally, peace will reign and your head will be safe. Yes? That's what you believe, isn't it?"

His heart slammed against his ribs. "Wrong," he croaked. "You are so wrong."

"How you disgrace us both with your lie. Did you think I would have no idea what was predicted all those centuries ago?"

Remaining silent, he once again schooled his features, unwilling to give her any more of a reaction.

"And did you truly think I would do nothing when I learned you'd given the demon of Wrath to a dead human girl, and she was growing wings of midnight?" Another grin, devious in its joy. "Well, what I did, husband, was learn everything I could about her. About her missing sister, Skye, and Skye's mate. The two people you just killed."

A moment passed as he digested her claim. When he did, he stumbled backward, shaking his head vehemently. "No. No."

"Why do you think I allowed you to capture me, hmm? Why do you think I allowed you to capture my people? How else do you think your spies learned where they were hiding? I have been waiting for just this day. The day you brought about your own ruin, the day you realized that because you carry the All-Key inside of you, I do, as well. Think your Sienna will aid you now?"

With that, Rhea vanished from the bed, the chains that had bound her thudding onto the vacant mattress.

CHAPTER TWENTY-SEVEN

LEGION PACED HER BEDROOM floor as if her feet were on fire. The Lords had already left the fortress, destination Rome, determined to find and kill Galen, thereby saving Ashlyn and the babies. That they hadn't come for her... she knew they'd never once considered trading her.

They were *that* honorable.

How did Legion repay them? By hiding herself away. And because of her actions, Ashlyn would suffer.

Sweet, sweet Ashlyn. What was Galen doing to her? If he hurt her the way the demons had hurt Legion... Stomach rebelling, she raced to her bathroom and hunched over the toilet. As many times as she'd thrown up the past day—week?—she was surprised when her lungs remained in her chest. Surprised, and disappointed.

She wanted to die. She would rather die than go through another pawing, having hands rip at her clothing, having things...done...to... "Argh!" She cut off the venomous thoughts before they could fully form. One unbidden image and she would collapse, hysterical, useless for days to come.

With a shuddering sigh, she rested her temple on the lid of the toilet. That beautiful blonde minor goddess had asked her a question. Who did she love most? The men who had saved her, or herself? Finally she copped to the answer. The men, definitely. They could have left her in hell, but they'd come for her, rescued her. She owed them.

But…if she gave herself to Galen, he would torture her. She'd poisoned him, after all. Had tried to kill him.

He would expect her to warm his bed. She knew that. Before she had poisoned him, she had slept with him. Her first time with a man, and she had liked it, had craved more, until…

She gulped, once again forcing her mind to blank.

If she went to Galen, she would willingly place herself in another version of hell. But then, that's what sacrificing yourself meant, didn't it? Enduring pain so that someone else wouldn't have to.

That's what the warriors had done for her, time and time again. Could she really do any less for them?

A shudder of revulsion worked through her, and she closed her eyes. She was decided, then. She would go to Galen. She would trade herself for Ashlyn.

There was no other way, no other choice.

And now that the decision was made, she had only to close her eyes and think of him, and she would appear before him. The Lords had forgotten that, like Lucien, she could move from one location to another with only a thought. Only difference was, she didn't have to follow a spiritual trail. Once she knew someone, she could appear before him anytime, anyplace.

Someone knocked on her door gently, as if afraid to startle her. She sniffed the air, recognized the sky-drenched scent of Danika, Reyes's woman. She must have come to talk to her. Probably meant to reassure her that she was protected and safe, that no one thought to use her as Bait.

"Go away," she shouted.

"No, I need to— Wait. You're speaking. You're speaking to me. It's been so long—"

"I said go away!"

"Legion, let me in. Please. I need to talk to you. Need to tell you—"

"Goodbye," she whispered, knowing she had to leave now or she would lose her nerve. Knowing she would never return. After the trade, after Ashlyn was safely returned, she would kill herself. She would rather die than be touched.

She pictured Galen—blond, beautiful and wicked. A moment later, the floor beneath her fell away.

CHAPTER TWENTY-EIGHT

SIENNA RIGHTED THE CLOTHING Cronus had given her when he'd first brought her to the castle. The shirt fit around her arms while tucking under her wings without having to wrap around the tops and drape over her shoulders. No fuss, no strain, but complete coverage. She was shaking.

What she'd just done with Paris...she'd never experienced anything like it. Not even with him. Nothing could have prepared her for the total body awakening. He'd pleasured her with soul-shattering thoroughness, had known exactly where to touch her, how to kiss her, what to say to ramp her desire up, up, oh, sweet heaven, up. She'd been completely into him, her mind focused on him, the rest of the world forgotten.

And yet, as beautiful as the loving had been, they were now, half an hour later, steeped in all kinds of awkward. For her, that had been way more emotional and meaningful than she'd been equipped to handle, and she had to wonder. Was it always like that for him, with everyone?

"So, uh, did being with me work?" she asked, then wished she could swallow her tongue, both dreading and excited about the answer. "For your demon?"

He nodded as he sat at the edge of the spring. "Yes. I'm strong now."

Despite the affirmation, her dread increased. He'd

closed off his expression, hiding his feelings behind a blank mask.

"Do you know how to use a weapon?" he asked abruptly. And clearly, that was the end of the demon conversation.

O-kay. So they weren't going to talk about what had happened. Which meant they wouldn't be talking about what came next in their relationship.

Two days does not a relationship make, idiot.

"What kind of weapon?" Dumb question. Whatever he said, the answer was the same.

"Any."

"Not really. When Wrath overtakes me, he kills using my body or whatever's available. I'm never aware when he does it—it's only after the fact that the memories flood me—so the skills aren't something I've retained."

"What about before your possession?"

"I was always a behind-the-scenes girl." Oh, damn. Why'd she have to go and mention the one thing sure to turn him into Mr. Distant? Or rather, Mr. Way More Distant.

But he surprised her. He showed her a small handgun thingy, then how to flip the safety. He released the clip, revealed the bullets and taught her how to put everything back together. "All you do is point and tap the trigger," he said. "Hollow points will do enough damage to whatever you're aiming at, no matter where you hit."

And what about when she missed, which was a very real possibility? Because just thinking about holding the gun made her hands shake. "So, you want me to buy one and carry it, like, all the time?" She'd never, in all her life or death, fired one.

"No." He leaned over and stuffed the metal in the waist of her pants. Cold, heavier than she would have guessed. "I want you to carry this one. The safety's on, so you won't hurt yourself."

"You're not afraid I'll shoot you in the back?" The joke fell flat, their relationship—or whatever—too new, and she blushed

Of course, he surprised her yet again. "No. I'm not." Utter confidence coated the words.

Relief swept through her. "I'm glad."

He cleared his throat. "Do I have your full attention?"

"Yes. Of course." And right then she knew, reality crashing into her hard enough to hurt. This was his way of saying goodbye. His way of preparing her to live without him. Her knees threatened to buckle, but she managed to remain upright. "Yes," she reiterated.

"Good. Now listen up, and listen well." His gaze drilled into hers. "I've done a lot of research about the living dead. If anyone threatens you, that means the person can see you. And if he can see you, he and his weapons will be solid to you. I won't remind you about the men out there, how they saw you and would have been able to touch you. If they can touch you, that means you can touch them. So you need to act first, and think about it later. That means you shoot the culprits without hesitation. Got it?"

"Y-yes."

"All right, then. Moving on." Next he withdrew a crystal blade. He stretched out his free hand and motioned her closer.

One step, two, until she was at his knee. Apparently, though, that wasn't good enough. He latched on to her hip and dragged her between the deep vee of his legs. Though he wasn't in a sexual mood, the touch excited her all over again.

He forced her to curl her fingers around the hilt, those

ocean-blues grave. "If someone gets in your grille, they deserve what they get. Go for vitals, where they're soft and you don't have to worry about cutting through bone. Like here." He moved her hand to his side, laying the blade flat a few inches above his hip. "And here." He moved her hand to the ropes of his stomach.

Touching him there reminded her of just how hungry she was, and not just for his body, causing her own stomach to growl. Her cheeks heated all over again. Was she cursed to always embarrass herself in front of this man?

His beautiful lips curled into the semblance of a smile. "Still haven't eaten, huh?"

Though a mere shadow of what it could be, that half smile lit up his entire face, dialing "beautiful" to "exquisite." She, too, lit up, her nerve endings pulsating. Gulping back her always increasing desire, she nodded. "I'm starving."

A moment passed. He cursed. "This goes against what few morals I have left." Frowning, he released her to dig around in his pockets. He withdrew a plastic baggie filled with dark purple powder.

"What does?" Holding her? Giving her weapons? Now that she was aware of her hunger, the pains started up, her blood heating to the point of boiling, her skin shrinking over her bones.

Don't think about it, and you'll be fine.

He set the baggie aside, stared at it for several minutes, and released a ragged breath.

Wanting to give him time to come to grips with whatever was bothering him, she studied the knife he'd given her. The crystal blade was jagged, rainbow shards trapped under the clear exterior. The handle was a dull copper, solid, and warm with his body heat.

"I've never seen anything like this," she said.

"And you never will again. There are only two in the world, and I've got the other one. That baby will kill anything, even a god of this world, and do whatever you command, as long as it's in your hand. Like, if you need to hide it, grip it and think *invisible*."

Her eyes widened, and her jaw dropped. "I can't accept this. The two are obviously a matched set and—"

"Don't argue with me." His tone was hard, uncompromising. He withdrew a small flask from his other pocket, picked up the plastic baggie and dumped half of its contents inside.

She'd told him where she was going when they parted, and who she would be with. He had clearly forgotten, or he would be insisting she give the crystal back and pretend she'd never seen it.

"Paris, listen to me. I'm going after the leader of the Hunters. Do you understand what I'm telling you? You can't risk something like this falling into enemy—"

"Don't. Don't say another word right now. I've decided you're not going near that psycho, and that's that, so just take the knife and say thank you." He swirled the liquid in the flask before lifting the small round rim to her lips. "Now drink."

"*You've* decided? You can't—"

"Drink."

She had no choice but to obey; he'd already begun pouring the contents down her throat. And sweet heaven, she loved the taste. A diluted version of what Cronus gave her, but delicious all the same. She gulped back one mouthful, then another and another, the warmth sliding into her, dancing through her, easing her pain faster than a blink.

"Enough." He removed the flask before she could start licking at any stray droplets.

She moaned her disappointment, then closed her eyes for a moment and savored. Her skin plumped back up, and wow, she could have floated away on a cloud of bliss, forever lost.

"What is that stuff, anyway?" Cronus had never told her.

"Ambrosia."

Huh. A substance consumed by the immortals, she recalled reading, used for pleasure and the reaffirmation of power. As she now knew, myths often misled, straight-up lied or barely touched upon the truth. "Why do I—"

"Nope. No questions about this particular subject right now." He hooked the flask to one of her belt loops and tucked the baggie carefully in her pocket. "When you feel yourself going into withdra—I mean, when you feel yourself getting weak, take a few swigs. You'll perk right up."

"Clearly."

He met her gaze, the blue of his eyes frosting over in seconds, turning the ocean into a river of glass. "You said you could go a week with what Cronus brought you, right?"

So. She couldn't question him, but he could question her? She could have refused to answer, or demanded they trade answers. She didn't. "Yes." The change in him upset her, and she wouldn't add to his obvious stress.

"What you just drank should last a few days." He gripped her forearms and shook her. "I need you to listen to my next words. If you retain nothing else I say, retain this."

"Okay," she repeated, tensing as his anxiety bled into her.

"Never, under any circumstances, are you to allow

someone to taste your blood. Do you understand? They do, and you are to kill them before they can escape you."

"Who would want to taste my blood?" Humans? Impossible. They couldn't see her or even sense her. Vampires? Maybe. The nocturnal creatures existed, but they wanted *everyone's* blood. Why target a ghost of a woman?

A muscle ticked in Paris's jaw, a sign of his growing anger. "You'd be surprised. Now promise me. Promise me you'll kill anyone who does."

"I promise." Her hands fluttered to his shoulders, an offering of comfort. He was trying to tell her something without freaking her out. She knew it, sensed it. Trying to protect her, even though they were destined to part.

He released her to shove his hair off his brow. There were dark smudges on his fingers, she saw. Wanting to help him, even in so small a way, she took one of his hands and rubbed at the inklike spots. They remained. She frowned.

"They won't come off. They're tattoos," he explained, no inflection in his voice. He'd gone very still, had even stopped breathing at her first touch.

Why would he tattoo smudges on his fingertips? Her eyes met his, a tangle of confusion and an ever-present desire. She ignored the first and concentrated on the latter, lifting the tip of his finger to her mouth and sucking.

His pupils did their pulsing thing, stretching, snapping back into place, stretching again. The scent of dark chocolate and expensive champagne drifted from him, enveloping her, fogging her thoughts, electrifying her already sensitized nerves. She bit his pad lightly, and a hoarse groan left him.

"Do you have any children?" she asked, then had to

fight a wave of sadness. *I can't. Never again.* To distract herself, she sucked his finger deeper than before, swirling her tongue at the root and sliding the appendage out with a *pop.*

The sudden topic switch didn't faze him. "No. I always know when a woman is…I mean, Sex knows, and he wants her that much more, but impregnating a stranger is one of two things I've never let him force me to do."

Her head tilted to the side. "What's the other?"

"Lie with someone under the age of consent."

How vigilantly he must have to fight for such concessions. She knew firsthand how powerful a demon's compulsions could be. "Do you want them? Children, I mean. One day, with a woman you love?" *Stop this. It's too painful.*

He offered a casual shrug, or tried to. The lifting of his shoulder was stiff, jerky. "I want *you,* here and now," he said. "Let me have you. One more time before we head out."

One more time, a thought as arousing as it was depressing. Refusal, however, was not an option. She hadn't lied earlier. She would take him however she could get him. "Yes."

A slight whistling behind her, a cold splash through her, and then Paris's entire body jerked. His eyes widened, and his hands fell from her. He frowned, looked down. A blade hilt protruded from his chest.

Sienna screamed and whipped around, using her own body as a shield for his. Except, one blade had already gone through her, as if she were nothing more substantial than mist. For whoever had thrown the weapon, she wasn't. He could not see the dead, nor touch the dead, so neither could his blade.

The culprit was a large—really large—guy with pink hair and tattooed teardrops of blood under one of his eyes. He stood in the entrance of the cavern.

His punked-out features blazed with hatred. "How's that for not fighting fair?" he snarled.

Paris shoved her behind him, and she stumbled from the force he used, falling into the water and sputtering. Her heart raced out of control as the two men slashed each other with their eyes. A physical slashing would follow, no question. Both were familiar with the dance of death, an undeniable truth as they got into position.

"How'd you find me? You know what, never mind. I don't care. You tossed that dagger at my woman. For that I'm taking your throwing hand." With a tug and a grimace, Paris removed the blade from his chest. His eyes glowed bright red, casting a crimson spotlight on the man he clearly wanted splayed on the chopping block.

"Your woman?" A snort, a sneer. The newcomer reached up and slid two serrated blades from a crisscross at his back. "What woman? It's just you and me, demon."

"I don't give a flying flip that you can't see her." The words emerged on a growl, more animal than human. "She's mine, and you brought violence to her door. For that, you're losing your balls."

"Is that so? Well, I say you hurt me over my woman, so now I'll hurt you over yours." He grinned without humor, metal glistening and whistling as he twirled the hilts.

"Doubtful." Paris clasped the other crystal blade.

Another snort. "If you want to walk out of here alive, you'll tell me where my goddess is."

"You're the one who likes more pain and less talking, right?" Paris said. "Come on, then. Come get your pain."

Just like that, they were on each other. They fought faster than she could track. What she caught, like clicks of a camera: the pause as Paris pinned the punk, his boot coming down on a throat. The horrible suspension as a blade arched toward Paris's midsection. The heart-stopper of hope as Paris swung for a knee, connected. The terrifying beat of time as Paris hit the ground, his opponent snarling on top of him.

And what followed *that* was a ballet of hammering fists and kicks with enough vigor to snap bones. Knees going for sensitive places. Teeth ripping. Claws tearing. Metal clanging. They slammed into walls, rolled around on the floor, hacked at each other. Blood splattered in every direction. Never had she seen anything more brutal.

They wielded their blades beautifully, horrifically. *Annnd* yes, as promised, there went the newcomer's throwing hand. Blood sprayed anew. That didn't stop him from launching at Paris and going for Beat Each Other Senseless, round two.

So badly Sienna wanted to take out her new gun and fire, but the two were tangled together, and she was afraid she would shoot Paris. Having joked about nailing him in the back, she was now faced with the very real possibility and couldn't risk it. More than that, the bullet probably wouldn't hurt the punk, would probably soar right through him the way his blade had soared through her.

So…what could she do? Unsure, but knowing her current position helped no one, she slogged her way out of the water and stood. A cold blast of air hit her, making her shiver so vehemently her teeth rattled and ice crystals formed on her skin. A second later, the angel Zacharel towered in front of her.

"Stop them," she pleaded.

His green eyes were hard, unflinching and totally focused on her. "Come. We will leave them to their battle."

Her impromptu swim must have waterlogged her ears. She could not have heard him correctly. "Come with you, as in *leave* Paris behind?" Weren't the two men friends?

"Yes." He waved his fingers with definite impatience. "You grasped my meaning correctly. Paris would prefer you not be around such violence, I'm sure."

"Don't care. I'm staying." Warriors like him and Paris were unfamiliar with denial, and took every measure of resistance as a challenge, she was learning. Before this one could leap at her, she held her hands up, palms out, and backed away from him.

Cowardly, perhaps, but effective. He frowned at her.

"I'm staying, and that's final," she added.

Paris sensed the new threat and unleashed an unholy roar. He dove on Zacharel, knocking the robed warrior down. The angel didn't shove him off. Didn't touch him in any way, in fact, and yet Paris propelled across the cavern and slammed into the opposite wall.

The pink-haired punk was on him a second later, the fight speeding into a new level of ferocity. But through it all, Paris never dropped the blade that had done a meet and greet with his heart. He cozied the tip, and then the hilt, up to those extra-special soft spots in the guy's side and stomach, just as he'd showed her.

A pain-filled grunt, a black curse. Then the guy was slumping over and Paris was whipping back around, his crimson sights once again on Zacharel—who was now standing beside Sienna.

With a gasp, she skirted around the spring, creating as much distance between them as possible. "Back off, angel boy."

Black brows winged into his hairline. "Hardly, demon girl. I do this to save you, to save thousands of others."

Uh, what now?

"Walk to me, Sienna." Paris was panting, bleeding, shaking, and the crazy, animalistic glaze hadn't left him. "Now."

With every fiber of her being, she wanted to run rather than walk to him. And she would have, if the angel hadn't said, "I cannot let her do that, demon," and appeared at her side in the next blink, taking hold of her wrist and locking down.

CHAPTER TWENTY-NINE

OH, HELL, NO, PARIS THOUGHT. Two pansy wingers—one of them practicing, one of them fallen—were not gonna get the drop on him. He hadn't killed the fallen, not yet, he'd just hurt the guy a little. Or a lot. Whatever. Now he wanted the bastard to suffer for a long damn time.

His need to protect Sienna burned hot. The fact that the fallen had interrupted their sexual play, the fact that someone other than himself had seen her delicate features overcome with desire, were reasons to kill. Savagely.

Zacharel he actually kind of liked, but that didn't mean he'd tolerate interference in this matter. Only thing going for him right now was the fact that Sex was either asleep or hiding, and thankfully had no opinion.

"Let her go," he snarled. He was losing blood fast, his chest like a waterspout that had sprung a leak. Hurt like a son of a bitch, and he knew he'd go down sooner or later. He was determined to make it later, when Sienna was safe.

The angel gave a single shake of his head. "Your temper is too fierce."

So the hell what? "I've got myself under control."

"Do you really?"

No. "I said I did, didn't I? So let her go before I make you."

"By taking my hand? My balls, as you told the fallen?"

A pregnant pause, anger fighting to be freed from a man who clearly denied his emotions—but couldn't fully suppress them. One day he would erupt, no question. "What will you do to yourself when you accidentally hurt your female?"

One stomping step, two. "Back off. Now." The darkness inside him was so deeply rooted, he knew the stuff had moved in and set up shop and he'd never get rid of it, even when he and Sienna parted. Especially when they parted. Already he was going to sink into despair when he lost her, and if he allowed himself to relax with her, to like her that much more, he would only drag her down with him. That's why he'd fought his emotions so hard after having sex with her.

Now he was glad for that. If he had to murder the angel, he would, and the darkness would be shooting out happies over the deed rather than remorse.

"Your darkness," Zacharel said.

"You reading my mind?" The invasion would cost him.

"No," the angel replied, saving his life. "Your eyes. The darkness is there. Do you know what it is, warrior? Do you know what you play with? No? Well, allow me to explain. As a human body can grow a child, a demonic one can grow evil. That is what you have done. You have allowed your demon to birth another demon, for lack of a better word. This one is all yours, your baby, and like the other possessing you, he will never leave you."

Should have surprised him, didn't. Shouldn't have angered him further, did. Sienna had heard those damning words. "Unless you want a personal introduction, you better step away from my woman."

"Paris," she said, sadness dripping from her tone.

Sadness rather than anger, leaving him confused.

Whatever. If she tried to tell him that she wasn't his woman, that this second demon—or whatever it was—was a deal breaker, he'd lose it. When he had to let her go, fine, whatever, he'd reevaluate and dial back the possessiveness. But here? Now? There'd be no dialing back. He'd just pounded inside her, had just come inside her, branded her, and he still had her decadent taste in his mouth. She'd cried his name, had wanted more, and would have given him more.

"I still have your present," she reminded him. "Should I… Do you want me to…use it? I thought he was your friend, but…"

He blinked. She would stab the angel? For him? The thought probably shouldn't have cranked up his desire for her, but it did. And that she would do this after hearing Zacharel's condemnation of him was heartwarming.

"Not yet." Behind him, he heard the punk lumber to his feet. His hand tightened on his weapon.

"No," Zacharel said, stopping him. At last he released Sienna. "The red is receding from your eyes. That is good. You will not hurt the girl now. Therefore I will take the fallen elsewhere and return later. As for you, you will head for the doorway leading out of this realm." He vanished a moment later, the fallen going with him though Zacharel had never touched him.

As if his presence had been the only thing keeping Paris upright, he collapsed, toppling to his knees. Sienna rushed to his side and eased him the rest of the way down. Thick black spiderwebs wove through his line of vision. Any moment, and he'd sink into unconsciousness.

"I've got you," she said. "I'll take care of you. I won't let anything happen to you."

He didn't want to say what he now needed to say, didn't want to spoil what had happened before with what had to happen now. He'd been here, in this very situation, a thousand times before. Injured and fading—with only one way to heal.

"I have to… You have to… Sex, I need sex."

His demon was all over that, torpedoing out of hiding to shoot blood into his cock. Happened so fast, Paris suspected the demon would battle whiplash for days. This was uncharted territory, though. Until Sienna, he'd never been with the same woman twice. Now that he had, he knew it would keep him level, strong, but would being with her more than once actually mend his body?

"Sex? But you're in no condition for that. You should rest."

"No resting. I hate that it has to be this way, but I can't change it." When he was injured like this, he needed full-on, hard-core sex with as many different partners as possible. But even if a hundred beauties had surrounded him, he'd still only have wanted the one looming over him, silent, her hands gentle as they explored his wounds. A woman he shouldn't trust, especially while he was like this, but one he couldn't, wouldn't, turn away from.

No matter what happened next.

"Please, Sienna. Ride me."

Only the slightest pause. "You don't have to beg me for anything, Paris," she said, using his own words to comfort him. "I told you I'd take care of you, and I will."

CHAPTER THIRTY

IF I EVER GET PARIS completely naked, Sienna thought wistfully as she unbuttoned and unzipped the black, flowing material of his pants, *I'll probably spontaneously combust.*

Not wanting to jar him, she stretched the fabric apart rather than tugging it down his legs, allowing the massive length of his shaft to spring free, just as he'd done earlier. No man should be so beautiful all over, a study of hard strength and dark sexuality no matter where you looked.

He threw an arm over his face, hiding his features from view. "I hate this."

She'd been reaching for him, but now reared back. "I'm sorry. I can find you someone else if you'd rather—"

"No," he rushed out. He must have heard the horror and distress in her voice. "I don't hate being with you, and I don't want anyone else."

Good, because she wasn't sure she could have followed through. Becoming his pimp would be a special kind of hell.

"What I hate is that we're chasing something meaningful and organic with something clinical and mechanical. Something forced."

Her first thought: he'd enjoyed the sex, too, and considered it meaningful. Joy careened through her, bright starbursts that warmed each of her cells. Her second thought: he was ashamed right now. The joy withered, cooled. They had so much working against them already, she couldn't allow him to add such an awful emotion to the mix.

"You're not forcing me to do this, Paris. Before we were interrupted, I was wet. I'm still wet." And she didn't mean from the water. "Why does this time have to be any less meaningful than the other when we were headed in this direction, anyway?"

He'd groaned at *wet*. Now his arm fell away, and he peered up at her with those amazing eyes of searing azure. "You're so lovely."

When he looked at her like that, all heavy-lidded and dreamy, she *felt* lovely. "Let me show you the rest of me." She pushed to her feet and disrobed, his gaze tracking her every movement.

Throughout the centuries, he had seen countless others naked. She knew that; she had seen them. He had been with tall women, short women, skinny, heavy, black, white and everything in between.

Sienna was nothing special, and yet, when he said, "Beyond gorgeous," with a fine sheen of sweat dotting his brow, she believed him this time. He was right. Her demon would sense a lie. The joy returned.

"I think the same about you," she admitted. Naked, emboldened by his praise, she straddled his hips and eased down. But she didn't impale herself on his thick length. Not yet. He needed the sex, and time was imperative, but he needed stroking more. Needed assurance that she was here, in this moment with him, all the way.

His arousal jutted out between her legs, her warmth all over it. She traced her fingers over the tip, and he sucked in a breath.

"Climb up here and straddle my face," he croaked. His

palms found her breasts and kneaded, rolling her beaded nipples through his fingers. "I want to taste you again."

The desire to do just that nearly slayed her. Blood rushed through her veins at an alarming rate and heated dangerously, chasing away any lingering chill. "I'll hurt you. My weight... Your chest is injured."

"How about this? I *need* to taste you again, and I don't care if my chest hurts."

She licked her lips. "How about this? *I'll* taste *you*."

He stilled, even seemed to stop breathing.

"Unless you don't want me to," she hurried to assure him.

"It's not that." The words sawed from him, hoarse and throaty, more grit than substance. "I haven't let anyone do that to me in more than a thousand years." He sucked in a breath. "No, that's not actually true. I let a slave perform the act on me on the journey here, and I hated every moment of it."

"Oh." Bafflement widened her eyes. All men loved receiving oral sex. Right? So why had he stopped the women from sucking on him? And he'd stopped them, she knew that he had. Every woman he'd welcomed to his bed had probably wanted to fit her lips over that cock and drink him down.

"But you," he went on, still on edge. "I will let you. If you want to."

She flattened her hands on his stomach, felt the cords of the muscles clench. "I don't want to make you uncomfortable or do something you don't like—"

"No. You misunderstand." His shook his head, all that astounding hair performing a ballet around his temples. Strands of black and brown and gold she longed to fist. "I didn't let the others do it because I was already using them and didn't want them doing me any more favors.

And the only reason I let the slave was because I needed answers, and that was the fastest way to get them."

Answers about me.

"And Sienna? The slave was...he was a male."

And that was not his preference. Sympathy washed through her. To have no control over your body and its reactions, to be forced to submit to a desire you yourself did not feel, had to be torture. "Just so you know, there's nothing wrong with that. And I won't be doing you a favor, Paris. You are a beautiful, charming, intelligent, sexy as hell man, and I'm dying to have you. Just as you are. With all the others you were simply practicing for this moment," she said, hoping to tease him into seeing the truth of her claim. "In doing this, I'll be pleasuring us both. I hope. I mean, I have about as much experience with blow jobs as I do with sex."

"If that's the case, I'm about to come my brains out. You'll be perfect."

"Quiet. Sienna's not done putting you in your place."

A smile bloomed. "Yes, ma'am. But, uh, what's my place?"

"The pedestal for the most admirable man I know. I don't care what you've done, or who you've done it with. You could have rampaged the entire world, could have raped viciously, constantly, but you don't. As for the sex of the slave, well, I hope you respect me in the morning, because I think you're even sexier now and I'm going to be very upset if I don't get my turn."

He licked his lips. "You want a turn?"

"More than anything."

Already his hips were writhing underneath her, as if he were imagining her mouth on him, working him over. "Please, Sienna. Please, do it."

"Yes. But only if you'll like it." She shimmied down

until her lips were poised over that beautiful erection. *This is mine,* she thought, dazed.

"I'll like it. I swear I'll like it."

"Let's find out for sure." Her tongue emerged, licking up and down his shaft, treating his length like a lollipop. Groan after groan left him, and she took that for approval. On her third upward glide, she fit her fingers around his base and her lips around the head. As she gloried in his flavor, her hand continued the erotic journey on his shaft.

Her wings arced down and around, the tips stroking his sides. For the first time, she understood the joy of having them. Surrounding him like this, she forgot about the rest of the world. Only they existed. Only the pleasure.

A curse roared from him as his hips jerked, thrusting him deeper. Immediately he apologized and backed off. "More. Please, more." He pounded his fists against the floor. "I have to have more."

She sucked harder, tasting him deeper, savoring, then swallowed him down as far as she could go. He was too big and stretched her jaw, but she didn't care. His entire body shook with the force of his enjoyment. She never stopped working him with her hands, either, one doing the stroking, the other tugging at his testicles.

But then she started wondering what those tasted like and released his cock with a *pop* to run her tongue over the tightness of his sac. He enjoyed that, too, especially when she drew one, and then the other, into her mouth.

Would she ever get enough of this man?

When he was shouting her name, she returned to the main event, taking him in, taking him down, his wild reaction spurring her on and on and on, her body lighting up, desperate for him, for all of him.

"I'm close, baby, I'm so close. If you don't want to taste me, you need to—"

In answer, she sucked him so hard her cheeks hollowed.

"Oh, yeah!" His hips jerked up, his muscles knotting on his bones, and a roar far louder than any that had come before ripped out of him. He jetted down her throat and she swallowed every drop, holding on until the very end, when he sank onto the ground, his panting breaths filling the entire enclosure.

"Ride me," he commanded in that voice full of gravel. "I need to be in you. Now."

"Yes. Now." She knew she had just repeated what he'd said, again, but that rich scent was seeping from him, surrounding her, blinding her to everything but him. And this. Oh, sweet heaven, *this*.

She lifted, surprised to find that she was shaking. A quick glance, and she saw that his wounds were no longer bleeding, and the skin had even sewed itself back together. And despite his recent climax, he was still rock-hard and ready for her.

Once again she straddled him, and this time she took him in, all the way, until she was sitting on him, her ass resting on the backs of his thighs. Now she was the one to cry out. Like before, he stretched her, but it was such a good, burning stretch and she was so damn wet, so damn eager.

He clamped his fingers on the rise of her hips and moved her, up and down, his strength a shock. Because when he moved her down, he slammed her, forcing himself as deep as he could go, lifting himself up to meet her halfway.

"Kiss me," he growled. "Lean down and kiss me."

Even as she rocked on him, she obeyed, her chest

smashing into his as she slanted her head and meshed their lips together. His tongue immediately shot inside her mouth, claiming her as his, owning her. His hands went to her back, sliding under those slits that housed her wings. It was as though he'd put his fingers and his mouth on her clitoris at the same time, using his nose and his chin and his beard stubble, anything and everything to stimulate her to the fullest.

Release slammed through her with the same force Paris used. Wild exhilaration pumped through her, the pleasure so intense her nerve endings were electrified. Pinpricks of white behind her lids, fire in her veins. A storm of satisfaction through every inch of her.

She didn't mean to, but she bit his lip until she tasted blood, and even that was a stimulant. Her nails dug into his scalp, holding him still for her abuse as she rode out the thunder and the lightning. But he didn't seem to mind, seemed to like it. One of his hands fell to her ass and pressed her down as he rose up, and then he was roaring, spurting inside her, sending her over the edge a second time.

When at last they calmed, they collapsed on the ground in a tangled heap of arms and legs, shaking together, gasping, desperate for air but not caring that they couldn't find it.

"Thank you," he panted.

"You liked?" she replied when she found her voice.

"Woman, you nearly killed me. I should be manning back up, putting us back on track, but I'm completely blissed out."

So was she. Each time together was better than the last. "I hope we do that a thousand times today."

"I hope that's an accurate guesstimate and not hyperbole."

"If anything, I *under*estimated. You're very good with my wings."

She felt the warm stroke of a chuckle against her skin. "I'm not too rough?"

"You're perfect." A kiss at the cord that bound his shoulder to his neck, a scrape of her teeth. "Ever been with a winged woman before?"

"Uh...I..." He hesitated, even as his skin prickled with heat beneath her mouth.

His shame had returned, and once again she experienced sympathy for all he'd endured. "I'll take that as a yes. Was she an angel, like your friend?" He needed to purge the memories and the feelings that accompanied them.

"Uh..."

"Another yes. A demon, too?"

Only the slightest pause. "Yeah." He ducked his head in the opposite direction, as bashful as a schoolboy.

Adorable. Just adorable. As strong as he was, as fierce as he was, he cared about her opinion. "Paris, it's okay. I know you have a past, and I wasn't pressing for details to embarrass you or to make you uncomfortable. I just wanted you to know there's nothing you could have done to disgust me."

Slowly he relaxed and turned toward her. Those dark shadows swirled in his irises, but as she watched, they thinned and misted away. Zacharel had said those shadows were another demon, an evil inside of Paris that he could never get rid of. She wasn't sure why he'd welcomed that evil, or "birthed" it, and she didn't care. To her, he was Paris, only Paris, and she would never again make the mistake of hating someone for a perceived malevolence.

"Thank you," he said again, tightening his hold on her.

"Listen, you. If I can't put myself down, you can't thank me for my stunning common sense."

One of his hands slid to her face, cupped her jaw. She'd meant to make him smile, but his expression had never been fiercer. "It's a deal."

Emotion clogged her throat, and she forced a cough. "How about I tell you something embarrassing about me, so that we're even?"

A rough, ragged, "Please."

"When I was little, I played beauty shop with my younger sister. I was the stylist and put her gorgeous honey-blond hair in a ponytail—then I hacked off the entire thing. She was the makeup artist, and painted my face with permanent markers. Our parents were horrified." A bombardment of nostalgia had her choking back a sudden sob.

Enna, Tommy from class says I have too many freckles, and that they make me ugly. Tears rolled down cheeks still baby-round.

Well, Tommy from class is stupid. You don't have half as many as me, and I'm the prettiest girl in the world. You said so.

A girlish giggle. *And I never lie!*

I miss you so much, Skye, she thought now. *I'll find you. I'll save you.*

Paris's thumb caressed the rise of her cheek. "I lost you there for a moment."

"I'm sorry."

"Don't be. I was just saying your story isn't embarrassing. It's cute. By the way, I think your wings are hot, and I'm curious to know why I never wanted to lick them when Aeron had them."

She placed her hand over his and forced herself to smile. Soon she would lose him, so she had to enjoy him while she had the chance. "Don't take this the wrong way, but I hope you get stabbed again. Like, real soon. I loved kissing you all better."

Finally, a surprised laugh barked from him. He pulled her down until her body covered his. "Baby, I'd willingly stab myself for that kind of kissing. But thankfully there's no need. I already have another owie and it needs your special doctoring skills."

CHAPTER THIRTY-ONE

BY THE TIME THEY WERE DRESSED and stepping out of their private cave into the big, bad realm where Zacharel the Chastity Belt waited, Paris had regained every bit of his strength and then some. His muscles were jacked with adrenaline, his bones fortified with steel. His steps were heavier from his increased weight, surer with his superior balance.

All because of Sienna.

"I used my energy escorting the fallen…someplace else. We'll have to walk to the doorway," Zacharel said to Sienna. His cheeks *were* a little gaunt, his bronzed skin now lacking any shine. "That is what you still prefer, yes? Before, you told me you would rather walk with Paris than fly with me, anyway, and though you will soon discover why that is unwise, it is the best I can offer at the moment."

"Yes, thank you," she replied, ever polite.

"If you're going to hang with us, make yourself useful." Paris took the lead, urged Sienna to follow him and forced the angel to take up the rear. "Guard her with your life."

A gust of wind danced around the angel, and only the angel, more chilling with every second that passed. "I plan to do so. No matter the threat against her."

An easy tone, but his expression implied Paris himself was a threat, and Zach would take him down if necessary.

Good to know.

During the trek to find Sienna, hardly any creatures had been out and about, and there'd been a small measure of light, a crimson glow from the moon. Now, there were a lot of those hungry, oozing shadows slithering in every direction, and the only light came from the occasional fiend—like the ones who'd followed Sienna, with every intention of harming her. They were staked to poles and burning alive.

Paris reached back and hooked her fingers around the waist of his pants. "Don't let go of me unless you have to fight." *I don't want her to have to fight.*

"I won't." Confident, unafraid.

That's my girl. Their little train crept through the wilderness, and, like now, some sort of campground. Tents stretched on either side of him. Sex kept his big mouth closed, and this time Paris knew beyond any doubt that the demon was sleeping off the pleasure rather than hiding.

A hiss. A snap of teeth.

Enemy.

Paris searched through the darkness, found the source just up ahead at the top of the closest tent, and leapt into action. He went low, sliding on his knees, running his blade along the trunks of the same vinelike creatures he'd encountered on the climb down that cliff. He was back on his feet a second later, watching as the remains slithered along the sides of the fabric.

No time to relax. Three more rained down. He kept his pimp hand moving, arcing, slicing, and from the grunting he heard behind him, he knew Sienna and Zacharel were doing the same.

A quick look to check on his woman—she had her gaze on his back, swiping at anything that made a play for him—proved she had no wounds, hadn't been hurt. One of the vines snapped in her direction, dripping fangs protruding from a pair of razored leaves. She was too busy protecting him to protect herself.

Paris swiped out his arm, and got a hunk of skin and muscle torn away. He sucked back a howl of pain. Okay, so now he knew what dribbled from those teeth. Acid.

"Fly her out of here," he commanded Zacharel, even as he spun, hands crisscrossing and chopping, pieces of vine flung away. He'd rather lose her that way than another, more permanent way.

"Told you. I expended the rest of my energy removing the fallen."

From the beginning, Paris had known he should off the punked-out bastard, but *noooo*. He'd sympathized with the guy's plight. Lesson learned, though. Show a softer side, and boom, you'd be punished later.

"I'm not leaving you," Sienna said while grabbing on to a stalk and hacking off the head with the crystal blade he'd given her. She was fast, but not fast enough, and soon they would be all over her. "Must have dropped the gun in the water. Sorry."

Darkness...rising... Paris dropped his daggers and went for his own crystal blade. A single mental command, and the metal elongated...becoming a torch crackling with flames. He pressed those flames against the leather walls, the material soon engulfed...and the sparks jumped to the next tent.

Shrieks blended with the blaze's crackle as he, Sienna and Zacharel raced away.

After a mile or so they slowed down and Zacharel said, "I thought you wished to remain inconspicuous."

"We needed to send a message." Thankfully, the shadow creatures got the message, too. Mess with Paris's ragtag group, and fry. They kept their distance. Only Sienna's presence prevented Paris from stomping over and doing some damage.

He wanted to hurt them, but he wanted her safe more. *You can always return for them.* True. When Sienna left him, he'd need a good fight to level him out.

Great. Now, at the thought of her leaving him, he was ticked all over again. He only began to calm a few hours later. Nothing and no one dared approach, and more than once his thoughts skipped back to what Zacharel had said.

Paris's darkness…his temper. Zacharel had implied that Paris would one day hurt Sienna. Yet, when they had been inside the cave and he'd been worked into a dark, consuming rage, he had remained totally aware of her. He hadn't let the action near her.

With the vines, same deal. He'd remained aware of her. Had sought to protect her, placing that need above the one to maim.

Good news, right? Except, what if *she* ever pricked his temper? What if all his darkness focused on her?

Oh, hell, no. That wasn't happening. Zacharel had made him paranoid, that was all. But doubts, once planted, could take on a life of their own, and Paris found himself sweating over the possibility.

Sienna affected him in a way no one else ever had. She accepted him as he was, good, bad and ugly. But if she ever betrayed him, if she ever lied to him, if she ever fought him or turned against him, he couldn't predict how he would react. Especially now that he knew the thrill of her complete surrender.

What are you doing, pondering the worst? He'd given

her a small measure of his trust. By succumbing to these fears, he would dishonor them both. He'd never minded dishonoring himself, but the thought of dishonoring *her* weighed heavily on his shoulders.

She'd taken him in her mouth, tasted all that he was, and loved his body with such shattering sweetness he would never be the same. She'd seen him at his worst. She knew his past, his future, and yet she still watched him with awe in her eyes, as if he meant something to her. He would not diminish that gift. And it *was* a gift.

A stumble over a rock propelled her into the side of his body and jerked him out of his head. He caught her with his free hand before she fell.

"Sorry, I didn't mean to space out," she muttered as she straightened. While the sex had strengthened him, it had clearly tired her.

He shouldn't have felt such pride about that, but he did. "You don't hear me complaining about having you in my arms."

Her lush, lovely grin flashed up at him. "True."

Zacharel might have rolled his eyes.

Paris gave him a mental bird before scanning the stretch of land ahead. There were miles of dark yet to travel, filled with lots of little landmines. Like the puddle he next had to jump over, then help Sienna do the same. His nose wrinkled. The water smelled like rotting corpses. Probably because...yep, he saw a pair of dull, dead eyes floating underneath.

A fly as big as his fist darted past, then another. One landed on his arm and immediately bit his biceps. He slapped the insect, meaning to fling it away from him, but he ended up smashing it, the damn thing splattering all over him.

The entire realm was a cocktail of creepy from some

of his favorite worst horror movies ever. Yeah. He dug the cheese. He also enjoyed romance novels, bench pressing buses and baking chocolate chip cookies.

He hadn't had time for that stuff in a while, and now... now he realized just how much he'd missed it. How cool would it be to throw in a DVD, kick back with Sienna beside him and watch the bloody good times roll. After that, they could curl up together and maybe read a few scenes from a romance novel.

None of that would happen, though. He and Sienna were parting as soon as they reached the exit. And what do you know. Now he wanted to kill something— simply hurting was no longer good enough—with his bare hands. Was actually praying some feral, foaming-at-the-mouth male would jump out and attack him.

This wasn't good. Meant his obsession with Sienna had reached the next level.

Paris maybe could have forced himself to let her go without much of a fuss before their time in that cavern. Now? Not likely. She was everything he'd ever wanted for himself and everything he hadn't known he needed, all rolled into one sexy little package. A warrior when she needed to be, a siren when *he* needed her to be, yet always soft and sweet and giving. And brave, so brave.

When that pink-haired punk had invaded their private space, she hadn't run. She'd stayed put. In case Paris needed her, and to keep Zacharel out of his face when things got dicey. He admired that about her. Hell, he was beginning to admire *everything* about her.

Suddenly Paris understood his man Amun in a way he never had before. Amun's woman was a former Hunter, too, and once upon a time she had helped murder their bestie Baden. Because of that, every single Lord of the Underworld had despised her and had wanted to see her guts spilled all over their fortress, Paris included, but Amun had stood his ground and defended what was his, and everyone eventually—reluctantly—climbed on board the welcome train.

Maybe, after he'd taken care of Cronus, he would do the same for Sienna—take her home and play house. Things would be difficult at first, sure. She hadn't killed anyone, but the Lords still didn't and wouldn't like her. They'd seen his cut and bruised body after her comrades had finished torturing him. They'd watched him suffer over her loss—and heard him curse himself for caring about her when she had never felt the same for him.

Until now. She'd changed her mind about him, and he'd changed his mind about her. He wasn't sure *what* had done the changing on his end, though he suspected it had more to do with simply wanting to believe in her, as he'd claimed. He wasn't even sure when the change had happened. All he knew was that she wasn't out to get him.

Accepting that once again drove home the point that his earlier fears, planted by Zacharel, were foolish.

Paris knew women, and he knew sex, and he thought he was pretty good at reading the former's emotion while engaged in the latter. More than that, he'd been with Sienna before. She might have wanted him back then, but that want had nothing on what she felt for him now. Total, all-encompassing and *real*.

He wasn't sure what had changed her mind, either, but he was glad that something had. He loved being with her. She eased him. In so many ways, she eased him. So what the hell was he supposed to do without her, while he hunted Cronus?

Who would he take to bed when the first wave of weakness hit him?

Oh…damn. The thought of being with someone else made him sick. Like, vomit blood sick. He wanted Sienna and only Sienna, and when they parted, and they would because he couldn't take her with him to hunt Cronus—too dangerous for her, considering the ambrosia in her system—he would have to take *someone*.

If he continued on this thought path, he would break down.

Maybe she sensed his turmoil. She twined her fingers with his, brought his hand to her mouth, and kissed the pulse hammering in his wrist. The world came back into focus with a whoosh.

"—did you do with that other guy, the fallen you called him?" she was saying to Zacharel. "Did he, uh, survive?"

"He lives, yes," the angel said, but offered no more.

"He'll come back for me." That kind of blame and hatred wouldn't fade. But by the time the fallen healed, Paris and Sienna would have already parted. She would be safe.

"Yes," Zacharel said. "He will."

A spike of fear added a layer of spice to the sweetness of Sienna's scent. Paris traced his thumb over her knuckles, reveling in the softness of her skin as much as in her worry for him. "He won't get the drop on me."

Suddenly a shadow at his left surged into motion, darting at Sienna with the speed of an arrow. The only color in the six-foot slash of darkness was the flash of bloodstained fangs inside its mouth.

Without missing a beat, Paris stepped in front of her, whipping out of Sienna's clasp to grasp the creature by the neck. He was surprised by the solid feel of flesh and heat. He commanded his crystal dagger to become whatever was needed to destroy a living shadow and stabbed, going deep into that mouth and feeling those fangs cut into his skin.

The dagger began to pulse with the light of the sun, bright enough to cause his eyes to tear. There was a howl of pain, a gurgle, before the writhing mass exploded into particles of mist and scattered on the breeze.

"Thank you," Sienna said on a wispy catch of breath. The roses had faded from her cheeks, making her freckles stark.

"We don't thank each other for this kind of thing, remember?" Protecting her would never be about the accolades.

Those exquisitely plump lips curled into a radiant smile he would see in his fantasies for the rest of eternity. Desire for her spun to new life.

She reached up, perhaps planning to trace a fingertip along the seam of his now aching mouth. Then Zacharel said, "May the Deity save me from such nonsense," and she dropped her arm to her side.

"I don't think your deity will have to worry about saving you," Paris snapped. "I'm pretty sure females will recognize the fact that you're not worth the effort from glance one."

The angel seemed pleased by that.

Polar opposites, Paris thought; that's what he and the angel were. Zacharel had never experienced a spark of arousal, so he had no idea what he was missing. Paris pitied the poor girl who finally gained his notice. She'd have to have balls of steel. Zach would fight her every step of the way to the bedroom, and probably even blame her for his introduction to passion.

Now that might be fun to watch.

If the circumstances had been any different, Paris might have unleashed Sex's special scent upon the angel.

More than likely even Zach would fall prey to the lush, candlelight-and-silk-sheets imagery that always consumed everyone else, and his horror at wanting Paris would amuse for centuries to come.

Sienna stiffened. As attuned to her every nuance as he was, Paris's attention whipped to her. The roses had returned to her cheeks, but they were too bright, as if she were suffering with a fever. Her eyes, now more emerald than gold, were glued ahead—on the castle that had just crested into view.

Her bond to the structure must be growing stronger, he thought.

Paris wrapped his arm around her and tugged her as close as he could get her, remaining careful of her wings. She didn't protest. In fact, she nuzzled her cheek against his neck, warm and soft and his.

He kissed her temple. "Don't worry. I won't let you go."

A sigh of relief and unmistakable gratitude. "Than— I mean, whatever."

"Good girl," he said with a grin.

Zacharel frowned at them. "Do you still mean to part?"

Paris lost his good humor, and shot the angel an I-hope-you-die-painfully glare. Now was so not the time to get into that.

"Yes," Sienna said in a tone as cold and biting as the wind buffeting against Zacharel. Then, contradicting the harsh affirmation, she rubbed a fist against her chest as though a hot poker burned there. "We're still going to part."

Indignation rose up, but Paris swallowed it back. That was the way it had to be. He knew it, had agreed to it. Shit, he'd even been the one to suggest it.

"This is good." The angel nodded his approval, the action allowing several snowflakes to catch in the satin of his hair.

"Why do you care?" Paris demanded. He still hadn't figured out the reason for Zacharel's continued presence.

A shrug of one strong shoulder. "I would not say I care. I simply know that the two of you cannot successfully sustain a relationship."

With that note of truth in his voice, it was clear the angel wholeheartedly believed what he'd said. "Our relationship isn't your business, so your opinions aren't welcome."

"Actually, the two of you were made my business."

Paris saw red. Demon-red. A volatile reaction when one was not needed, but he was helpless against it. Sheer will alone kept his hands at his sides rather than hammering into Zacharel's face. "By who?"

Wings of white and gold spread, the angel beside him one moment, then in front of him the next. Zacharel's feet floated above the ground, those wings flapping slowly, holding him steady. Paris had to grind to an abrupt stop to avoid slamming into him. Around them, snowflakes tumbled and swirled only to land and melt.

In case things got ugly, he shoved Sienna behind him. "What happened to being too weak to fly?"

"I have regained my strength."

"How?"

"The answer will not change what is about to happen."

He arched a brow, weapon at the ready. "Are you sure you want to go this route?"

"Some part of you hopes to keep her. Otherwise, you would not have reacted so violently to my observation." Before Paris could respond, he added, "Do you recall when I told you that if you continued on your current path, you would lose everything you'd come to love?"

He popped his jaw. Only the gentle caress of Sienna's hands on his back prevented him from hurling obscenities.

"I did not lie, demon. I never do. And now I think it's time I proved just how terrible an enemy I can be."

Paris blinked. Suddenly he hovered in the air, high above the castle's drawbridge, Zacharel cradling him against a hard chest honed on the battlefield. His heart pounded an unsteady beat.

"How the hell did you do that?" And where the hell was Sienna?

"With powers you cannot begin to imagine. But this is not what I wished to show you." One finger at a time, the angel loosened his grip. "I hope that you will soon learn I can help you…or destroy you."

"You better not do what I think you're going to do, you dirty piece of—"

His anchor vanished, and Paris free-fell toward the dilapidated slats of wood. He landed on the creaking boards with a hard slam and good loss of oxygen. Behind him, he heard the gargoyles screaming out their war cries, the flap of their wings, the scrape of their claws.

Zacharel had. He really had. "Son of a bitch!"

CHAPTER THIRTY-TWO

"COME. I WILL ESCORT YOU to the exit."

Sienna gaped at Zacharel, who had just appeared in front of her. Paris and the angel had been standing in front of her, bucking up against each other, ready to throw down as testosterone charged the air, only to disappear without warning. The angel had returned the very next second. Without Paris.

"Where is he?" she demanded, though she wasn't too worried about the answer. Paris and Zacharel were friends despite their differences, and Wrath had yet to make a peep.

"I took him to the castle and dropped him on the bridge."

Reevaluation time. Paris and Zacharel were not friends on any level. Wrath, on the other hand, must think angels could do no wrong. "Why would you do that?" Sure, Paris would be carried inside and locked up. Sure, he would escape, and he would be fine. But none of that mattered to her just then. Fury rose, dark and hot and dangerous.

Calm down. Before she whipped out that crystal blade Paris had given her and went to town on angel flesh. She'd so had enough of males and their abuse of supernatural abilities.

Zacharel blinked as if the answer should be obvious

to one and all. "That, as you called it, is what one male does to another when they are arguing."

"No. No, it's not."

His lips edged down in the slightest of frowns. "That is what your Paris did to William of the Dark only this morn."

Well, she had no comeback for that, did she?

Zacharel shook out his wings, the white-and-gold feathers lifting slowly, elegantly. Snow glistened between the down. Her anger did nothing to lessen the impact of his beauty, the murky landscape somehow providing a suitable backdrop for him, dark where he was light.

No, not light, she mused. An aura of dawn radiated from him, causing him to glow.

"Well?" she prompted. "Will you take me to him?"

"Your eyes…" he said, his frown deepening.

"What about them?"

"I can see that Paris's darkness has taken root inside you already."

He spoke the words and somehow she knew they were true, the knowledge simply becoming a part of her. Paris's darkness, the one his demon had given birth to, was indeed inside her. A small twinge of worry was quickly followed by a shrug of unconcern. Wrath lived inside her. What was one more entity?

"You've ignored my first question long enough. Now I'm taking over. Listen up, and listen good. I want you to take me back to the castle."

The demand was unwise, unnecessary and counter-productive to her screw-Cronus plan, followed by her bagging and tagging of Galen, as well as her search for her sister, but that wasn't going to stop her. Paris would fight to reach her, that protective side of his demanding he witness her escape from the realm, she knew that now. If that happened, he would be harmed.

"You intended to part company in two days," he said, unwavering. "I merely sped things along."

She'd been looking forward to those two days with Paris, had wanted to make love to him again and again and brand him inside her mind, her body, until her every cell smelled like him.

"You keep reminding us that we can't be together." Suspicions tangoed with her thoughts as she crossed her arms over her chest. "Why is that?"

"Because you both need reminding." Simply stated, as if she should be ashamed for asking.

"Why?" she insisted.

"Why would you *want* to be with him?" Zacharel's dark head tilted to the side, his study of her intensifying. "Do you love him?"

Did she, when doing so would cause their break to hurt that much more? "I like him." A lot. Like, really, *really* a lot. And she respected him. Admired him. Craved him like a drug. He was witty and kind and protective and loyal, and even though he had every reason to despise her, he hadn't once treated her as if she were the enemy.

"We need you in the heavens, Sienna."

Did they, now? "Well, get in line. Lately, everyone needs me." And no one would explain the reason. She fisted her hands and propped them on her hips. "What is it you think I can do for you? Because right now, I'm having trouble taking care of myself."

"All I know is that you will herald our victory in the most gruesome war this world has ever seen."

Forget sputtering. She gaped. Her, responsible for winning a war. No pressure, though, right? She so couldn't deal with this right now.

Zacharel stiffened, glanced over one strong shoulder. "Cronus comes," he said. "He has the answers you seek, though I would not trust him were I you."

Stomach cramp. Not Cronus, not now, and not outside the castle. He would flip. Although, keeping him out of the castle would keep him away from Paris, so... "Get lost, angel boy."

At that, he quirked a brow. "I will allow you to leave with him. I don't think you will thank me afterward, however. Until we meet again, *demon girl.*"

He was gone a moment later, and what do you know, Cronus appeared a moment after that. No longer dressed as a Goth reject from hell, he now wore a gray silk suit tailor-made for his frame, all elegant lines and overflowing bank account.

Wrath stopped prowling and started slamming at her skull, very much wanting a go at him, but unable to figure out why. What he didn't do was fill her mind with images of the king's sins. Weird.

Cronus glanced left, right, and frowned. "Why are you outside the castle? For that matter, how did you *get* outside the castle?"

"Wrath took over," she said, lest he puzzle out that she had been aided by other immortals.

"Ah." Smiling, revealing his dazzling pearly whites, he extended a crimson rose in her direction. "For you."

"I, uh..." Not just stunned but completely flummoxed, she accepted the dewy bloom. "Thank you."

He inclined his head ever so slightly as he accepted her appreciation. "And that's not the only gift I come bearing. I have what you need." A clear vial filled with glittering violet liquid followed the same path as the rose. "My apologies for the tardiness in its delivery."

His apologies? Seriously? "Don't worry about it?" A question when it should have been a statement.

Cronus cleared his throat, clearly uncomfortable. "Drink."

Because she had no desire to confess that she'd already been fed, she took a small sip of what she now knew was ambrosia. What she didn't know was why she needed ambrosia, or why Paris had looked ill when he'd handed her that flask.

Cool coconut flowed down her throat, sprouted wings and flew through her entire body. And wow, it packed a powerful punch. Both strength and weakness blazed through her, cannibalizing off each other and leaving her in a fog.

"That's a good slave girl," he mumbled.

I love being patronized, I really do. "Why are you being so nice to me?" she asked, swaying as she returned the vial to him.

He waved his hand and the glass disappeared. "I must show you something," he said, and with another wave of his hand, her surroundings fell away. From warm to cold, dark to light.

From salvation to damnation.

CHAPTER THIRTY-THREE

SUDDENLY SIENNA WAS STANDING inside an unfamiliar chamber with white walls that stretched so high she could barely discern the domed ceiling above. Portraits hung everywhere. There was no furniture, just marble columns that boasted the occasional string of ivy, and stands that held sculptures and other crafted artifacts.

To stop herself from screaming from the mental calamity of the location switch, she bit her tongue until she tasted blood.

"This," Cronus said, splaying his arms and slowly pivoting, "is the Chamber of Futures." There was a reverent quality to his voice, one she'd never before heard from him. "Here, destiny takes shape and endless possibilities await, for this is where my All-Seeing Eye records her visions."

"All-Seeing Eye?" She was still so disoriented that it was nearly impossible to get the words out.

"A female who sees into heaven and hell, time and space, present, past and future." Every syllable held a new layer of urgency. "When one dies, another takes her place. Over the centuries, many have served me. There are no limits to how far back or how far forward these women can view. No limits to how high or low their scope."

To have such a power would be both a blessing and a curse, she thought.

"Everything you see here was created by my Eyes."

Sienna tucked the rose behind her ear, forgetting about his weird mood as she tripped her way to the nearest portrait. In it, an older, frailer version of Cronus stared back at her. He had gray hair, wrinkled skin, and wore a long white robe. This was the god she'd first met. Only this one was dirty, bruised and trapped in a cage.

"I have learned that everyone has several different futures, and the choices they make ultimately decide which road they will travel. Come," he added without a breath, taking her by the forearm and ushering her through the long, seemingly endless expanse of the room. "There is something you must see."

With every step she took, the portraits rearranged themselves, gliding over the wall, changing places with fluid grace. She didn't try to pull away from him. Dizziness held her in thrall, and she needed the anchor of his hand to keep her upright.

"These Eyes, they do not always understand what they see, for they cannot determine the context of the actions they record. They do not know if they see past or future, how to stop something or how to make it come to pass."

"And so you have to guess," she finished for him.

"Correct." He stopped, and so did the movement of the portraits.

In the frame now in front of her, warriors fought to the death in every direction. Not just any warriors, but familiar faces. There was Galen, his white wings outstretched, his long, bloody sword raised. Before him was Cronus, with a thin line of blood connecting one ear to another—his head about to slide from his neck.

Sienna's heartbeat quickened as she took in the rest. There was Paris, off to the side, watching what happened to Cronus with wide, shocked eyes. Blood caked him. His mouth was open, as if he were shouting something.

"This is one of the futures that await me," the king said. "Long ago, my first Eye warned me that a warrior with wings of white would someday slay me. I assumed it would be an angel, only to later realize there were other warriors, like the Lords of the Underworld, who were equally capable of doing so. And then my newest Eye painted this."

"Why didn't you kill all the Lords, then?" Sienna asked. She knew he'd already considered that route. A being like him wouldn't have been able to help himself. "Just to be safe."

He moved two steps forward. Again the pictures danced into new locations. "The reason is here." He stopped, as did the pictures. "Look."

Frowning, Sienna obeyed. In this one, a young Cronus sat on a throne of solid gold, the Lords of the Underworld lined up behind him, expressions reverent and stances determined. They were clearly protecting him, guarding him with their very lives. So badly she wanted to reach out and trace her fingertips over Paris's lips. How beautiful he was. How strong.

"This is my real future," Cronus said. "Or rather, the one possibility I must ensure comes to pass."

"How?"

"The answer lies in the two warriors missing from this army."

She gulped, studied every face. "Galen is missing. And…no one else."

"Do you see the keeper of Wrath?"

"Of course. Aeron is right—"

"I do not speak of Aeron. He is no longer the demon's keeper."

"Me?" she squeaked.

"Yes. You are the key to this future, Sienna."

Disbelief thrummed through her. "I don't understand." The angel had mentioned she would get her answers— and that she shouldn't trust what she heard. Seemed like an eternity had passed since he'd issued the warning. She wasn't sure what to believe, what to discard. "How am I the key?"

"Look closely at the bottom."

She leaned over, gaze homing in on the portrait's lower edge. Surrounded by a crowd of onlookers was a woman. Her profile was to Sienna, her skin freckled, her nose and cheeks and chin— Her eyes widened. Hers. Those features were hers. The woman's hair was brown and wavy, just like hers, and black wings stretched from her robe. She stood beside a kneeling man who had his arms wrapped around her calves, holding on as if she were precious to him.

Galen, Sienna realized. He wasn't missing from the painting after all.

"All those centuries ago, when my Eye spoke of my death, she also told me there was a way to save myself… or, to be precise, a woman who could help me do so. I looked for this woman around every corner. She never appeared, and I despaired."

What came next was going to hurt, Sienna thought, straightening. Didn't take a genius to figure that out.

"Eons passed, and I was imprisoned when the worth-less Greeks conspired with my wife, whom they later betrayed. I knew I would escape, for that, too, had been foretold, though the Greeks were too foolish to believe. When I at last reclaimed my rightful place on the heav-enly throne, I sought out the Lords, thinking to destroy them before they could destroy me."

He paused, sighed. "But newly returned to power as I was, I did not like the idea of killing the Lords and free-ing their demons, thereby having more enemies knocking at my door. More than that, I *liked* the idea of control-ling Zeus's warriors, of using the beings he created as my own personal errand boys as I searched for the one among them with the power to kill me.

"And oh, has that decision paid off. I have kept a close eye on their comings and goings and indeed, the Lords have proven surprisingly useful to me. That is why I know that the future you see before you in this painting, of me reigning in harmony with these warriors as my stalwart army, is already coming to pass.

"But still there is the matter of my predicted execution—and my predicted rescuer. Just when I had given up hope, you at last appeared, a woman who be-longed to neither side of the war and yet also belonged to both sides. A woman who pledged her allegiance to Galen but whose interest had unmistakably been cap-tured by Paris. A woman who had the power even in death to influence a warrior's every thought and action."

She could only shake her head.

"Oh, yes. He's thought of you, only you, and that's what brought you to my attention. I had never before noticed a human soul, but I had to know why he craved yours so very much. That's when I discovered you were the one the Eye had foreseen. You look like the woman in the painting, and you have the same past as the woman I was told would save me. Both of those revelations can mean only one thing. You are to be my salvation."

"I don't care about your salvation," she whispered.

"I know. But you care about Paris's, and if Galen dies, so does he." He waved his hand and another portrait ap-peared. In this one, Galen, Paris and a few other Lords lay in pieces on a blood-soaked floor. Her heart sank at the sight.

"And so we are back to your role as savior—mine, Paris's, in the end it makes no difference, as either path leads you to Galen. You should thank me," he went on. "I gave you Wrath. Made you strong enough to survive whatever the keeper of Hope chooses to do with you." His gaze pierced her, a swirling black that increased the intensity of her dizziness. "Galen adores power, and you are to be his mate."

"No." A gasp, a plea.

Merciless, he continued. "Because of your demon, you will know those who lie to him, who befriend him when they truly hate him, and you will stop them before they are able to harm him."

First sleep with him, and now protect him? "No! I hate him."

"I did not say you had to love him to carry out your task. Merely think of the alternative if you do not carry it out. Paris dies."

No. No, no, no. "What happened to learning Galen's secrets and betraying him?" Fury sparked to life. "What happened to finding my sister? And why would you want me to stop others from harming him if he's the man destined to kill you?"

Red flashed within the black of his eyes, scarlet pools of his own fury. "Let us say that I have my reasons, and my plans. So listen and listen well. There are but a few possible futures for me and thus, the world. The first is that I reign as king for eternity. The second, I am killed, which means my wife is killed. If we are both lost, *chaos* will become king and the Lords will die." He twirled his finger and the portraits began their dance anew.

A new frame stopped beside her and she looked it

over, her mouth going dry. Angels, so many angels, bloody tears raining down wings of white and gold. Men and women wearing togas fought each angelic warrior savagely.

And there on the ground at their feet were the Lords, bloody, broken…lifeless. She wanted to cry, to collapse.

"To answer your other question," Cronus continued, "I do wish to know Galen's secrets. I do wish for you to betray him. For this to occur, I need you to protect him, as well. As I said, I have my reasons and my plans, and by rights I should punish you for daring to question their logic."

All she could think about was Paris's death. Paris, dying. Paris, dead. Paris, gone forever.

Cronus added, "Before you think that my faithless wife had the right idea when she conspired to lock me away, before you think to put in place any plot that would result in finding a way for my wife alone to reign—" his voice went low, harsh "—know that if Rhea rules, your sister's killer will control the fate of your world."

Her head spun with even more disbelief, fury and dread. Cronus had just said…had just claimed… "But you told me she was alive," Sienna croaked.

"She was."

Was. Not "is." *Was.* "And now?" Another croak.

Wrath chose that moment to get his slam on, and this time, he snarled. *Something is wrong. I don't like this.*

His voice jolted her. He'd spoken to her before, of course, but usually he limited himself to words like *punish, kill, heaven* and *hell.*

Is he lying? As Zacharel had implied. *Please, tell me he's lying.*

I don't know. I don't know anything right now.

A whimper slipped from her.

"I have done my research. Skye became a Hunter," Cronus said. "Perhaps for the same reason you did—to right the wrong of her abduction. You could have met her, talked to her, and never have known it, for she was a child when you saw her last. Nor would she have known you. She eventually got out, but she was married to a Hunter. She was trying to get him out, as well. She... died with him."

"No." This was too much to take in. She couldn't process it all.

"And when Rhea learned that you, my winged savior, were searching for the girl, she had her..." His gaze skittered away. "Rhea had her killed."

Wrath released another snarl. *Something is wrong.*

"You're lying. You have to be lying." Sienna's knees shook and she barely managed to remain upright. That she could have been so close to Skye and not even realized it...that now she would never have another chance... "Prove it. Prove she's...that she's...gone." A lump of grief congealed in her throat. Her eyes burned, tears bubbling at the backs.

"Very well."

The air in front of her shimmered, crystallized, and then, as if she were looking through a magical peephole, she saw a bedroom, a black-haired girl sprawled on the floor, her throat slit, her body resting beside a man who'd clearly met a similar fate. A lake of crimson pooled around them, thick and black at the edges.

Sienna fought down her instinctive revulsion—how many gruesome images of those she cared for would she be forced to endure this day?—and pushed herself to think back. To the best of her recollection, she had not interacted with this girl during her time with the Hunters, but then, there were hundreds, if not thousands, of

Hunter compounds and cells, and she'd never had access to the database of members.

"That's not her," she said with a violent shake of her head. "My Skye had blond hair."

"So does this girl. You know the black is not her natural color. Her lashes prove this."

Sienna made herself look closer. Long brown lashes framed dulled brown eyes.

Enna, when you grow up and get married, will you still love me? Brown lashes fluttering innocently as Skye awaited her answer.

I'll always love you more than anything or anyone.

"No." Plump lips, soft and pink, and as big as Sienna's. A delicate bone structure, a stubborn chin. "No." Acid created a toxin of rage and sorrow in her stomach.

"Yes. When I…found her like this, I scoured her mind, her memories. This is your Skye."

"No!"

Her sister…lying on the floor. Ruined. Dead. Gone forever, like Paris would be. No longer a little girl, but a woman. Gone…forever… The words echoed in her mind, horrifying and shocking and sickening. Gone…

Is that truly her? she asked Wrath.

Yes. I can see her life, and you in it, but I cannot see her death. Why can't I see her death?

Sienna locked on the affirmation, nothing else registering. Skye was…was…dead. Dead. Her precious Skye was dead. "Bring her back." She pushed through the shimmering air and fisted Cronus's lapels, shaking him. "Bring her back the same way you brought me back."

"It is not always so simple, even for me." Guilt, so much guilt in his tone, all over his features, radiating from him.

Wrong, so wrong.

THE DARKEST SEDUCTION

Enough with the babbling! "You're the self-proclaimed king of the gods." She shook Cronus all the harder. "Ruler of the Titans. Jailer of the Greeks. Leader of the Lords of the Underworld. What's one little soul compared to all that? Bring. Her. Back."

"There are laws of life and death even I must obey."

"Her soul—"

"Is no longer savable."

"I don't believe you."

"That doesn't change the circumstances."

"Bastard!" Her palm darted out of its own volition, slapping his cheek so sharply she would not have been surprised to find she'd peeled away his skin. "You lied to me. Said she was Galen's prisoner."

When he failed to retaliate, or block himself from further abuse, she struck again.

"You lied!"

"To ensure you obeyed me and kept Galen under control, I did what I felt I had to do," he at last admitted. "I knew you would not kill him if you thought only he knew where your sister was. And as I said, I have my reasons for wanting him protected for now. But no, Galen never imprisoned her. She never had a child with him."

Another slap, this one so hard she thought she fractured her own bones. Still he accepted the abuse without comment. "Her death could be another of your lies. Anything to jerk my chains, right?"

Wrong, so wrong, but she is dead. She is dead.

A blink and Sienna was standing in the very room Cronus had shown her. The woman's body, motionless at her feet. She could smell the coppery tang of blood and death. And here, in this chamber of fatality, there was no missing the resemblance to her mother.

To *their* mother.

Wrath released another snarl, another and another, something "wrong" continuing to prod at him. But he didn't know what the problem was, and Sienna didn't have the strength to reason things out with him. Grief slammed through her hard, knocking the breath out of her lungs. Breath she couldn't steal back, no matter how hard she tried. The fog thickened in her mind. Razors dipped in flames razed her chest, burning her up.

Her surroundings faded as she waded in and gathered the girl to her chest, clutching her close, letting her heart beat for both of them. The tears finally cascaded, falling, falling, a never-ending river of pain.

"I will return you to the castle," Cronus said, voice as gentle as if he were speaking to a babe, "and I will give you time to come to terms with what has happened. Your memories will no longer haunt you, and you will be able to leave the realm, should you wish it. In this, you have my word. But I will come back for you, Sienna, wherever you are, and I will expect you to aid my cause. And now…now that you've seen what my wife, Galen's ruler, is capable of, I think you'll want to, yes?"

CHAPTER THIRTY-FOUR

THE LORDS OF THE UNDERWORLD were here, on the island in Rome, and nearing the Temple of the Unspoken Ones at that very moment.

They would have a plan of attack, Galen thought. The most likely: all but one warrior would surround him, staying hidden in the shadows, and that one would approach him to speak to him. Unless, of course, they *all* thought to hide, shooting him full of arrows and bullets now and asking their questions later.

Wouldn't matter either way. The warriors must know they were walking into a trap. That Galen would not have set the meeting here if he could not use the Unspoken Ones to his benefit.

Once the Lords reached the threshold of the temple, the Unspoken Ones would have them, would whisk them here into their inner sanctum, as one, right in front of Galen, and lock them in place with invisible bindings, allowing him to do his thing.

However, Galen didn't want to go that route. It was too time-consuming, with too much risk. Not to his life, but to theirs. If he killed one of the Lords, none would ever complete the trade he'd demanded. All he wanted right now was Legion.

His hands fisted. If the warriors had failed to bring her, he would honor his word for once in his life. As he had told Lucien, he would take another loved one from the Lords, and another and another—until they broke down. He would not kill, but he would harm.

Every day Galen's need for Legion worsened. Hope had built up dreams of having her, of punishing her, of taming her...of *owning* her. Jealousy had tossed fuel on an already smoldering fire of resentment as he wondered where she was and what she was doing.

A rustle behind him had him tensing.

He whipped around. Standing between fat white pillars were all five of the Unspoken Ones. The furred one with a headful of hissing snakes in place of hair. The scarred one, with more muscles than three roided-up boxers fused together. The female, with the face of an ugly bird and horns lining the length of her spine. Lastly, the tallest two—one with shadows seeping from his skullet, and the other with blades that dripped poison spiking from the crown of his head.

Each creature was bound by chains they couldn't break. And yet, the tenuous bonds mattered only as long as Cronus lived. The moment he kicked it, these beings would be loosed upon an unsuspecting world. No one, not even Galen, would be able to stop the destruction they would undoubtedly mete out.

On an altar in front of them lay Ashlyn, pale and panting, sweating, like a virginal sacrifice of old. Only this virgin was heavily pregnant and about to give birth. The fright he'd given her had caused her to go into labor.

Oddly enough, Galen didn't like that she was in pain. She wasn't a bad sort, and hurting the fairer sex had never been a particular favorite of his. He'd do it, *had* done it—he'd do anything—but he never enjoyed it.

"Cut the babes from her belly," the horned, beaked she-devil commanded him. "I would have them for my own."

Babes? As in more than one?

"They must die," the scarred male snapped.

"No. We will use them as barter," one of the mountains of muscle said.

Ashlyn moaned in pain, in supplication, her glassy gaze pleading as she looked to Galen. "Please. Don't do this."

Begging the enemy. To do so, she must love those babies with her whole heart, even though she had yet to meet them. He thought he understood that. Nearly twenty-nine years ago, he'd inadvertently fathered a daughter; he had not learned of her existence until she was fully grown. Knowing she was of his blood had been all that was needed for him to…not love her, he didn't think he'd ever experienced that emotion, but to feel a sort of kinship with her despite the fact that she was as different from him as he was from the Lords.

His Gwendolyn. A Harpy. A female he could not bring himself to hurt. A female who would cut him down without a moment's hesitation. He liked that about her, felt pride in her ruthlessness.

Galen had done terrible things throughout his life. Betrayed his friends, killed for power, razed cities, purposely addicted his own people to drugs so that they would need him, follow him. He had destroyed their families when they dared to disobey him—or even so much as *thought* to betray him. He'd slept with females he shouldn't have, in ways he shouldn't have.

There was no line he hadn't crossed. No line he *wouldn't* cross. He had done all of that—and would do a thousand times worse—yet he had never cared about the consequences. Still didn't. Unlike the warriors he'd been created with, he hadn't come with a sense of honor, a bond of brotherhood or a need to help anyone but himself.

Baden, the first to be created, had gotten most of the goodness and the rest a mere trickle. Galen, the very last to be created, had gotten what remained—nothing but the cold and the dark.

Perhaps that was why he had gone after Baden first.

None of the Lords knew he had spoken with Baden before he'd sent his Bait to lure the man to his death. A private meeting Baden himself had arranged. None of them knew Galen had vowed to leave the immortal army alone, to stop the war, if Baden sacrificed himself.

Possessed by the demon of Distrust, Baden had not believed Galen's vow, but he'd made the bargain anyway, just in case. Galen knew it was because he'd blamed his demon for his instinct to mistrust, and hoped for the best—because of Galen's demon.

The Bait—Haidee, one of the keepers of Hate—had gone to the warrior, unaware that her victim knew where she would lead him. Baden had not wanted his friends to know he willingly rushed to his grave. He had not wanted them to witness the event, either, but of course they had followed him. There had been no stopping the war after that, even if Galen had wanted to. Which, of course, he hadn't.

"Gaaaaaleeeen." A low, pained moan echoed as Ashlyn writhed atop the stone. Her face was red, swelling, her breaths coming in shorter puffs.

"Don't look to me for aid, female." The next half hour was mission critical, and he could not allow her to distract him. "I told your man what he must do to save you."

"Please. Pleeeease."

A pang in his chest. If he told her the only way to ensure he would give the babies to their father was for her to crawl to him, she would find the strength to do so. She'd even kiss and lick his boots. She would do anything and everything he asked, no matter how vile.

Oh, yes, she loved her children. They were flesh of her flesh, blood of her blood, and they would love her in return.

Nothing and no one had ever belonged to him and only him—except Legion. Not that she would do anything necessary to save him, nor would he do anything necessary to save her. But. Yeah, there was always a but with him. He had been her first lover—and he wanted to be her last.

He wasn't sure what had happened to her during her forced stay in hell. Didn't know what she had welcomed, and what she hadn't. But she would no longer be his alone, that much he knew. Something else to punish her—to punish all of them—for.

"The babes," the female Unspoken said again. Was that...yearning he detected in her voice? Did she actually crave a chance at motherhood? "Give. Me."

The males turned on her, scowling, tossing obscenities, arguing over what should be done versus foolish desires. Whatever happened to the mother, Galen decided in that moment, he would not allow the Unspoken Ones to have or hurt those children.

Finally, a decent act on his part. One of goodness, without guile or selfishness. Never let it be said he was all bad all the time.

"G-Galen. I am h-here, as requested."

Every muscle in his body went taut, his blood instantly firing, blistering through him. A hallucination? He sniffed, taking in the earth, a hint of hellfire and the subtlest trace of sea salt. No hallucination.

Legion was here.

The wealth and variance of emotion he felt nearly overwhelmed him as he spun to search her out. And there she was, a few feet away. She stood at the edge of the temple grounds, trees stretched out behind her. She was lovely, though not exactly as he remembered. Tall, buxom, with a fall of pale hair and eyes of the smoothest brown. Her lips were chapped, as if she'd been chewing them, and she'd lost so much weight her T-shirt and sweatpants bagged on her.

The Lords hadn't taken proper care of her. For that, they would suffer more than he'd originally planned. She was to be punished, yes, but by his hand and only his hand. Anger became the front-runner inside him.

"Are you armed?" he asked, not expecting the truth.

"I—" Her hand fluttered to her throat, and her gaze skittered past him, widened. "Ashlyn." She raced forward, only to jolt backward when he stepped in her path, her desperation to avoid him palpable.

"You will stay where you are."

"L-let her g-go." The stutter told him more than her words. She was afraid of him. "You said y-you would."

"Legion, gooooo!" Ashlyn screamed, speaking through a contraction. "Tell Maddox—"

"Silence!" Galen snarled. He would accept no interference in this matter.

Legion grabbed her stomach, her skin taking on a greenish tint. Her chin trembled.

This fear of hers scraped at his nerves. Before, she had been brave and full of the fire she had been raised in.

"The warriors are almost upon us," one of the Unspoken said. "We will whisk them here the very moment we can. Now, give the females into our care, so that you may fight without distraction."

That had been their plan, and one he'd pretended

to agree with. Then and now, the thought of allowing anyone to touch his woman grated. And when he noticed Legion's reaction to the idea—a cold wash of horror in eyes glassy with unshed tears—he was decided.

"Back away," he told her. "Stand in the rubble at the edge of the trees. And if you so much as think about flashing away or running, I'll hurt the human."

The tears finally fell, but she did as commanded. He hated the increased distance between them, and blamed the Unspoken Ones.

"What are you doing?" one growled.

"Give them to us," another shrieked.

They had only one weakness that he knew of. They could not take what they wanted; it had to be given to them. Usually they used trickery to ascertain free will, as they had done to obtain the Cloak of Invisibility from Strider. When trickery failed, they resorted to scaring their victims into submission.

They would learn. Galen feared nothing.

"Don't move from that spot, no matter what happens," he told Legion, peering at her until she nodded to acknowledge she had heard him.

Then she gulped, raised her chin. "But only if...only if you give Ashlyn and the babies back to Maddox. Alive."

Of course, the Unspoken Ones reacted first.

"No!"

"Never!"

"She will leave you the moment you comply!"

"Do not be a fool!"

Legion glanced behind him. The greenish tint returned to her skin, and damn if she didn't look ready to scream.

"Eyes on me," he snapped, and she immediately submitted. Such lovely eyes. Rich and dark and boundless, even with their cascade of tears. "Do not look away from me."

A tremor in response.

He backed up until he stood beside Ashlyn, then twisted and bent, sliding his arms underneath her, picking her up. She was heavy, her muscles knotted from strain. Legion maintained the connection between them.

The Unspoken Ones demanded to know what he thought he was doing. He ignored them, carrying the girl to Legion's side.

"We gave you the Cloak, Hope. You owe us the females."

Had they meant to keep the humans as their due, then? He laughed with just a bit of humor. Probably. Something he would have done, as well, so he couldn't really blame them.

Wait. Yes, he decided. He could.

"Should you betray us now, we will hunt you. We will destroy you in the old way." The female let loose a cackling laugh. "Do you have any idea of the awfulness that entails?"

He ignored her, saying to Legion, "Vow to me here and now that you will not try to escape me, that you will go with me willingly and do everything I tell you, when I tell you to do it. A blood vow." One she would not be able to break, even if she wanted to.

For immortals, keeping blood vows became a compulsion.

Another tremor shook her. Those liquid eyes with their spiky lashes roved over him, causing his cock to fill and harden. He would have her. Tonight. "I w-will, but only if you vow to give Ashlyn and the babies back to Maddox, without hurting her. Or them. Today. And without fighting the Lords."

The girl had learned to bargain, to cover all the bases. A complication, but not anything that would stand in his way.

Galen placed the still panting, pregnant female on the ground as gently as he was able. She was in too much pain to notice or speak. As he straightened, he removed one of his daggers.

Legion shrank away.

That fear would have to be dealt with. He wanted his firecracker back. The one who had seduced him at the bar, screwed him in the bathroom. Bitten and poisoned him before he could finish.

Speaking of, she owed him an orgasm. And so many weeks had passed, she now owed him more than one. Interest was a bitch. But first, ensuring her cooperation. "In exchange for what I have asked you to promise, I vow to you here and now, this day, that I will give the female Ashlyn and her offspring back to her male Maddox, and I will hurt none of them. I will fight not with his friends, but give her and the babes over, unharmed by my hand or any other, and go on my way." He pressed the tip of the blade into his palm and cut so deeply he hit bone.

Blood welled. He smeared crimson on both sides of the blade, making sure to saturate the tip. Then he offered the weapon to Legion, hilt first. Part of him expected her to take it and slash at him, but no. She knew she was beaten, merely watched him, undecided about her next move. Cooperation was her only option. Unlike Lucien, she did not have the power to flash others alongside her, so she couldn't spirit Ashlyn to safety.

"Hurry." Any moment now, the Lords would arrive and it would be too late to walk away with what he wanted. He couldn't fight the Lords *and* watch Legion. And he couldn't run with her, avoiding battle, because she could flash away from him any time she wished. He needed her vow. "Before I change my mind." As if he would ever change his mind.

With a trembling hand, she accepted the blade. Nervously she licked her lips.

He waited, on edge.

Finally, he heard the words he craved. "In exchange for what you have already promised, I vow to you here and now, this day, to willingly accompany you to wherever you wish." Those glitter-ripe tears continued to rain down her cheeks. "I will do w-whatever you ask. And stay as l-long as you demand my presence."

She pressed the blade's tip into her palm and cut. Not as deeply as he had, but enough to ensure a successful exchange. Her blood welled, mingling with the droplets he'd left behind. He liked that, liked knowing some part of him was now inside her.

He reached out, clasped her hand against his, her wound against his. At the moment of contact, he felt a *pop* inside him, a tear on his soul, and though he'd never done anything like this before, he knew the vow had just made a place for itself inside him. Judging by her grimace, hers had just done the same.

At last, she belonged to him.

Legion flinched.

Had he said the words aloud? Or perhaps she, too, had snapped back to reality as the Unspoken Ones hissed and cursed and threatened behind him. Galen cupped her cheek with his uninjured hand, his thumb caressing the rise of satin-covered bone. She trembled, but didn't pull away.

He rattled off the coordinates to his home. "Leave now, make no other stops, talk to no one, and I will give the girl and her babies to her man as promised." And the Unspoken Ones could not stop her as they could the Lords. Well, all the Lords save the ever-annoying Lucien. "Hurry, I am almost too late."

She gulped, jerked from his clasp. He mourned the loss. Wanted to roar as she vanished before his eyes. *She goes to your home. You will be with her again.*

He had only to take care of two tasks. Ashlyn, and the Unspoken. They could lure anyone, him included, with their gazes, cast illusions and hypnotize. And they liked to do so; they also liked to play with their prey. Something they didn't need a willing spirit to do.

He knew, because he'd fed them some of his own men. The ones he'd disliked, the ones who hurt the innocent. Ironic, yes, considering all the things he himself had done, but also another of his very good deeds. He did them upon occasion, if for no other reason than to amuse himself.

Soon the Lords would be too close for him to divert. As promised, he couldn't, wouldn't, fight them, but the Unspoken Ones *could.* If he allowed that to happen, the Unspoken would forgive him for his unwillingness to share the females. Except, Ashlyn could be hurt during the battle, which meant Galen could not allow it. Soooo, he couldn't take care of the Lords or the Unspoken this day. Both would have to be dealt with later.

Keeping his gaze trained on the ground, he approached the pillars. Heard chains rattle. Stealthily he dug the Cloak from his back pocket and unfolded the material. The creatures tracked him, even as they hissed at him; he felt the heat of their gazes.

Acting quickly, he flared his wings and the Cloak at the same time. His feet lifted off the ground, and he spun...spun...letting invisibility overtake him as the razor-sharp edges of his wings sliced into the Unspoken closest to him while the Cloak extended like a tentacle and wrapped around the neck of the farthest, crushing his windpipe.

The first lost his insides, and hunched over with a howl of pain. The second couldn't breathe and collapsed, unconscious.

Galen was on the next two a split second later, a tsunami of movement, twisting, diving, cutting and doing a little more of that crushing. They couldn't see him, couldn't fight him, and oh, he had fun.

Less than a minute after his initial attack, all five were on the ground. The Cloak sagged in Galen's grip as he planted his feet on the ground, his body coming back into view.

"Shouldn't have taught me how to use the Cloak properly," he *tsk*ed.

He bent down and scooped Ashlyn into his arms. Sweat soaked her, her cheeks were puffed from the strain, and she clutched her stomach as she wheezed. Without the Cloak, he couldn't flash her, and with it, her man would not sense her. That left Galen with only one option. He stalked away from the temple without any explanation. Tree branches reached out, slapping at him. Twigs snapped under his boots.

"You. Will. Die," he heard one of the injured choke.

"That is *our* vow to you," another panted.

"Your screams will echo into eternity."

Ignoring them, again, he picked up his pace. After this, they might opt to aid the Lords. No matter, though. They were stuck here, so what could they really do to him, even with immortal help?

"Cry out for your man, Ashlyn."

That fall of honey hair remained plastered to her scalp as she shook her head wildly. A moment passed. She cringed and covered her ears with her hands, an action he understood. Wherever she stood, she could hear every conversation that had taken place there.

Using the arm wrapped under her shoulders, he angled his wrist to tug one of her hands away. "You heard my vow to Legion. I cannot hurt you or your man today. Call for him. Bring him to you."

Perhaps she meant to deny him a second time, but she opened her mouth and a scream of pain was unleashed. Birds flew from the tops of trees. Insects ceased mid-song. Animals of the four-legged variety raced for cover.

He could have set her down and left her there, but he didn't. Whatever the Lords had planned to do to him, they changed their minds when they heard that scream and came running. He heard the thunder of their foot-steps and ground to a halt, waiting. A few seconds later, they ruptured the thick green foliage, becoming a half circle of menace around him.

They were closer than I realized, he thought. Interesting. They might have won this round, after all.

Maddox cared not for his own safety. "Give her to me." He sprinted the rest of the distance, and with a tenderness belying his savage expression, he took his woman into his arms. "Oh, my love. I am so sorry. So sorry."

Another pang ripped through Galen's chest.

She moaned. "Hurts."

"I know, darling, I know. Lucien," the warrior growled as his narrowed gaze landed on Galen. "Flash her out of here. Now. She's in labor."

"Maddox," she panted. "Don't want...to leave...you."

"Shh, love. Shh. We'll get you help. Let Lucien take you. Then he'll come back for me. He can't take the two of us at once, but I'll only be moments behind you."

"Promise?"

"Promise."

"If something happens and I can't get back to you—" Lucien began.

"What?" Ashlyn screeched. "Why wouldn't you be able to get back?"

Maddox gave the scarred warrior a hard look.

"Remember what Danika said to us." Lucien gently took the still protesting Ashlyn from Maddox's arms. "We won't be at the fortress."

Maddox maintained contact for as long as possible. When the keeper of Death and the pregnant female disappeared, he straightened to his full height and once again met Galen's stare.

Galen wasn't sure why he stayed, even then. Each warrior had weapons, and all of those weapons were trained on him. Guns, blades, a crossbow. His own daughter, Gwen, was the holder of the bow, an arrow notched and at the ready.

Ah, now he knew why he'd stayed. Deep down he'd known she would come, and he'd wanted her to see what he'd done. See one of his rare good deeds. And maybe... maybe even decide to like him.

"Why did you give her back?" Maddox demanded. Despite the fact that his woman had been returned healthy and whole, he reeked of rage.

"Why else? I now have what I wanted from you."

The warrior's brows lowered, surprise a slash of crimson in his eyes. "You have Legion?"

So. They hadn't brought her. She had come to him on her own. Another interesting tidbit—and enough to ripen every thread of possessiveness inside him. "She is mine, yes."

"How?"

He grinned slowly with glee. "How do you think?"

A flash of bone and scales under Maddox's face, his demon rising to the surface. "There's something you should know about Legion."

"And that is?" He knew what would happen next, knew exactly what the warriors planned to do. Knew it would hurt like a son of a bitch. He could have covered himself with the Cloak, could have flashed away. Instead, he stood there, his grin widening.

"You're not going back to her." Maddox raised a Glock, as Galen had known he would, and fired, nailing Galen in the chest.

On the heels of the bullet, blades sliced into his stomach, an arrow right into his heart. He met his daughter's gaze as he fell to his knees, reached back and at last grabbed the Cloak. "Now we're even," he told her, voice faint as he shielded himself from view.

CHAPTER THIRTY-FIVE

WILLIAM WATCHED AS PARIS was carted closer and closer to him by those horny, humping gargoyle fiends, amused as ever-loving hell. In fact, he nearly busted a gut laughing. Yeah, he knew taunting the new and improved Paris 2.0 was borderline idiotic, and that the warrior would come gunning for him in the next few minutes, but like William could really pretend to be sad about this, so, *bring it.*

"Dude," he said. "You've already got several money shots wetting your chest. Classic!"

Sex didn't say a word. Just gave William the finger and held steady, emotion seething in his eyes. Emotion in the form of badass shadows, yeah, but that failed to lessen William's amusement.

Paris was clearly planning to murder someone other than William before the day finished ticking out, because, also clearly, more was going on here than simple humiliation. And William suspected that someone would be…the suspiciously missing Sienna? Nah. She was already dead. Zacharel? Had that pisser come back for more? William really hoped so. Hoped Paris gave it to the winger but good.

William didn't have a good history with the sky-bound, and though they didn't seem to recognize his too lovely mask of a face, they'd jump him like a pack of rabid dogs if he revealed his *true* form.

Not that he ever would. Anyways. It was best not to go there, even mentally. Mind readers abounded in this realm.

Just as Paris disappeared around the corner, a grave and desperate Lucien materialized right in front of William, a screaming, panting Ashlyn clutched in his arms.

The words exiting her bleeding lips were things only back-alley whores and junkies in need of a fix would say. And maybe Lucifer, the self-proclaimed king of the underworld.

"Bad day?" Never had William heard the gentle beauty utter such filthy, vile things. And really, she'd never looked prettier to him. Rock on.

"Danika told us she needed to have the babies wherever you were shacking up," the keeper of Death said without preamble. Lines of tension branched from his eyes like little rivers of poison. "Following your spirit trail was not easy or fun, especially since my warriors have need of me. Show me to a bed now."

"Are you sure she said where *I* am?" William thumped his chest just to be sure.

"Bed. Now."

"Now!" Ashlyn yelled. "They're coming now. Please, please. Or I'm going to tell Maddox you tried to feel me up!"

"*So* cruel. He vowed to remove the best part of my anatomy if I so much as breathed in your direction." Despite his cavalier tone, William moved quickly as he led the pair up the stairs, down the hall and into the bedroom he'd cleaned for himself, intending to free the trapped female immortal and spend a few days getting to know her body in every twisted position he favored. So far, no luck.

Lucien laid Ashlyn down, careful, so careful. "I'll get Maddox now."

"Thank you. *Ohhhhhhh, Gooooood.*" She squeezed Lucien's hand, and William heard the bones crack. When she came down from the pain an eternity later, she released the now-pale warrior. "Maddox. Now. Or I'm going to rip your face off and…and… *Ohhhhhh!*" The last was an evil screech better suited to a banshee from hell's darkest corridors.

"And tell Maddox he felt you up with it?" William said, always willing to help out.

"I'll be back in just a few. Take care of her." Lucien disappeared, his "or else" unsaid but no less evident.

"Well, hell," William breathed, scrubbing a hand down his face. Alone with the pregnant Bride of Chucky, as well as the Seed of Chucky. And he was supposed to do some good? Yeah. That was so not happening. Best he could do was stay right where he was and not vomit blood.

One by one, Lucien flashed the other warriors inside. Maddox first, then the others, then the women, then the two godly artifacts they had in their possession. Was the Budapest fortress under attack or something? Because damn.

Since no one touched the drawbridge, the gargoyles never came for them, so they were free to mill about— aka run like hell away from DEFCON Five.

And still, hours later, Ashlyn was in labor. The worst kind, at that. The babies wanted out, needed out, but they were stuck, and no one here was a stupid doctor, so no one knew what the hell to do to help her.

Maddox was barely holding himself together as he paced, shouting, punching walls. The others had stopped exploring and now congregated in the hall outside Ashlyn's room, pacing alongside him. Except for Danika, the brave soul who'd taken over as labor coach. She was inside the belly of the beast. Wait. She was peeking out the door.

"Get over here," the blonde screeched at William.

He was surprised he heard her. After Ashlyn's last round of curses, his ears were still leaking blood and brain matter. He'd taken up residence against the far wall, arms crossed over his chest, and was all about warding away intruders into his personal space. "Who, me?" Again he found himself thumping his chest.

"Yes. You. Standing around wasn't part of your job description when I told the guys Ashlyn would need you for this."

Smart-ass. "News flash, little Dani. I know nothing about human births." Still, he entered the room and approached the bed. Sweat soaked both women from head to toe, and both were pale, trembling. Scared, too, judging from the size of their pupils.

"But you do know about demon births, don't you?"

Sometimes he forgot that Danika was the current All-Seeing Eye, that she could peer into heaven and hell, past and present. And he'd also forgotten Maddox was half human, half demon, and one quarter asshole, capable of spawning demonic offspring with special needs.

"Okay, yeah. I'll take over." And he knew what to do now, which was a relief. For him. Ashlyn was about to experience the worst pain of her life. Pain she would beg to escape—even at the hilt of a sword.

"He isn't touching her," Maddox growled, stomping over to get in William's face. Bastard must have entered the room behind him.

William merely cocked a brow. "You want your woman to survive?"

"Of course." A hiss.

"Then get the hell out of the room! You, too, Dani, and tell your man to stand guard and keep everyone else out, too. And I do mean everyone. No matter what they hear." If they got a whiff of what he planned, they'd remove his hands with a rusty butter knife.

On the bed, Ashlyn was no longer writhing, no longer screaming. She was just a lump of flesh and covers. Getting weaker by the second…almost too late…

"Now!" William shouted. "I'm the only chance the three of them have of surviving."

The petite Danika put her arm around the hulking Maddox and somehow managed to drag him into the hall. William strode over and shut the door, closing himself inside with Ashlyn. Then he moved the dresser in front of it, knowing he'd need a few minutes' head start if anyone busted past Reyes.

Deep breath in, deep breath out. He was trembling as he unsheathed a dagger. "Sorry about this," he said, and got to work.

CHAPTER THIRTY-SIX

AFTER A SHORT STINT in the dungeon below the castle, Paris freed himself from the tunnel-visioned gargoyles' newest restraints and found his friends. As glad as he was to see them, he was also upset by what had gone down while he was away. Ashlyn kidnapped by Galen. Legion trading herself to save the pregnant female. Kane, still missing. No contact. A dead-end trail even Amun now had trouble picking up.

He plopped on a bench someone had dragged into the hallway outside Ashlyn's room. He was trying to keep himself distracted and calm. Zacharel had Sienna. Had probably shown her to the realm's exit. She was probably on her way...wherever, her bond to this place at last broken, her will her own.

This was for the best.

The best sucked.

I want her, Sex said with a pout.

Me, too.

"This castle is lacking something," Viola said as she eased next to him.

She was the first to speak to him in a conversational tone. His friends had been too preoccupied with Ashlyn to do more than bark orders for water, towels and a muzzle for...someone. William probably.

The goddess had given up her I'm-on-the-prowl dress and had changed into a glittery T-shirt and some kind of gray silk pants, the material so sheer he could see her underwear. Okay, so maybe she hadn't given up the gotta-get-me-some attitude altogether. She'd pulled her pale, silvery hair into a high ponytail, the length swinging with her every movement.

"Hello? Are you listening to me? Of course you're listening to me! I need permission to redecorate or I'm afraid I'll have to leave."

I want her! In just a few seconds, Sex was foaming at the mouth, bouncing around in Paris's head, desperate for the goddess rather than Sienna. Far more desperate than the demon had ever been, in fact. *I need her. I have to have her. Now, now, now.*

What was *that* about? They'd had Sienna earlier this very day. Sex should be shiny new until tomorrow.

Want, I want! Want, want, want!

Paris frowned. When Kaia strode past him a heartbeat later, her hips swaying with her every step, his cock following her like a heat-seeking missile, he really frowned.

Usually when he thought about taking a woman he'd already been with, his erection deflated like a balloon. Or, if he didn't remember being with a particular woman, he simply couldn't get hard while he was around her. Surely this didn't mean…surely he couldn't…

Want her, need her! Want all of them!

Yeah. He could. He could take Viola (who he hadn't already had) and Kaia (who he had), Paris realized, his cock twitching with need for both of them. Rather than exciting him, the knowledge filled him with dread.

How was this possible?

Your commitment to Sienna…I don't know…but I can have them all and I want them all.

But…but…Paris had dreamed of this, of finding a woman and being with her multiple times. Any woman.

All women. Sienna, as well as all the others. After his first encounter with Sienna, he'd thought she was his only hope for getting it. He hadn't understood, but then, he hadn't cared to understand. He'd accepted and he'd rolled. Yet now that he could have the same with some-one else—anyone else, apparently—he still…wanted only Sienna, he realized.

He'd never been with a woman like her. Someone who knew about him, but accepted him anyway. Someone who gave more than she took, even when he wanted her to take more than she gave. Someone with grit and fire who wasn't afraid to tell him off or apologize when she made a mistake. Someone who fought for what she be-lieved in, did what it took to win, *whatever* it took. A hated quality once. Admired now.

Suddenly Strider was in his face, navy eyes glittering as he pressed the back of Paris's head into the wall. "That baton in your pants better be for the goddess next to you and not for the redhead who just walked past you."

Liked him better when he was preoccupied. Rather than engage the guy further and risk a fight Strider would have to win to stay upright, Paris nodded. "Right. The goddess." Finally he understood Strider's annoying possessive streak. How the warrior would kill another man for even looking at what was his. Paris would kill male or female, god or goddess, good or evil, for making a play for Sienna.

There'd been enough truth in his tone to mollify the warrior. "Okay." As Strider straightened, he cracked the bones in his neck. "Okay, then. We're good."

Paris watched him walk away, and caught Gideon's amused gaze. The keeper of Lies must have sensed the layer of deception. No one smelled a steaming pile faster than Gideon. No matter how small that pile was.

Guilty, Paris looked away. This shouldn't be happening.

His demon cackled with glee, still wanting, still needing.

He felt dirty and disgusting and ashamed, was suddenly glad Sienna had chosen not to chase after him. If she saw him like this, he would lose it. He needed a shower. Needed to scrub his skin off, layer by layer, until the last drop of blood drained from him.

When the scent of chocolate and champagne began to waft from him, he cursed under his breath. *I'm not sleeping with Kaia or Viola or any other woman here.* He didn't give a shit what his body or his demon demanded from him. He wasn't allowing it. Wasn't putting up with it. *And you can't make me, can't lure them. Do you understand? You stop that right now, or I'll cut off my cock and laugh as we wither away.*

But...but...

No! No excuses, no pleading. He wasn't sleeping with anyone today, tomorrow or the next day. Or even the next. No way. *No one but Sienna,* he thought with a determination that shocked him. And he didn't care how weak it made him. His hands still tingled from touching all that soft, warm skin. He still had her sweet, tropical scent in his nose. He wasn't giving that up, wasn't welcoming someone else.

"Hello. I'm still here," Viola said, pouting like a child. "Don't you care that I might leave if you don't give me what I want?"

He so didn't have the patience to deal with her right now. "You can't leave the castle, okay? This is the safest place for all of you, safer than the Budapest fortress. Galen and his Hunters can't enter without serious injury, and if they try, we'll all be alerted."

Plus, he'd seen the crimson streaks over each of the

windows and doors, and knew William had smeared his blood there. That meant the shadow monsters couldn't come inside again.

"Who said anything about caring for our safety? We need portraits of me there, there and there." As she spoke, she pointed.

"I'll be sure and alert the decorator," he said darkly.

"And there."

Sex hadn't yet given up the quest to get inside her, and Paris's cock did that twitching thing. He gnashed his molars. The goddess was gorgeous, no question about that. Naturally feminine and sensual in a way most could never be, even with centuries of training. And once upon a time, Paris would have been all over her. Cancel out her personality, and she was just the type he used to go for. Lushly curved.

Now, having basked in a satisfaction so complete he would never be the same, settling for anything less held no appeal. Sienna's lean body did it for him. Made him hunger. Blinded him to others. Her scent, her taste, both had been specifically designed to ramp him so high up no one else could ever hope to reach him.

"You're beyond maddening," Viola said.

He was maddening? Right. "You can decorate all you want. Happy?" If he didn't change the subject, she'd keep that shit up all day and he'd end up introing her tongue to his blade. "So where's your dog?"

"My little princess is resting in my new room. Travel is so hard on his delicate constitution."

"Of course." Because all vampire Tasmanian devils possessed delicate constitutions. And what was up with calling a male "princess?" Paris scrubbed a hand down his face, tired, hungry and torn up inside. Screw this. As soon as he knew Ashlyn and the babies were okay, he was taking off, finding Sienna and making sure she was okay. *Then* he'd let her go once and for all so that, when he slept with someone else, he wouldn't be cheating, wouldn't destroy her sense of trust.

But maybe…maybe he'd be with her one more time first. Sex with her was a revelation, not just because she'd strengthened him, healed him and made him come harder than he ever had in his life, but also because sex with her wasn't about him. It was about *them*. Their needs. Their desires.

There was nothing dirty about it. Nothing tainted, one-sided or detached. They touched each other, kissed each other and pleasured each other because it felt good, because passion burned bright and inexorable.

"—listening to me?" Viola threw up her arms in exasperation.

He shook his head, almost told her the truth, and then stopped himself. He did, and her demon would give her fits. She'd probably follow him around like a lost little puppy. "Yeah, uh. I'm fascinated. Interesting stuff."

Maddox paced back and forth, back and forth in front of him. Reyes tried to stop him with a pat on the shoulder, but the warrior shrugged him off and kept going. Lucien tried next, but Maddox shrugged him aside, too. A mistake. In punishment, Anya tripped him as he passed her.

"Why do I always try to befriend the hopeless causes?" Viola said. "Could you be any more selfish, tuning me out when I have such riveting things to say? Then again, I guess I shouldn't be surprised. I mean, you're married because of me, and you haven't ever even thanked me."

"Mmm-hmm. Like I said, fascinating," Paris said absently. And then her words penetrated. "What's that now?" He twisted on the bench, pinning her in place with his narrowed stare. "Did you just say the word *married* in reference to me?"

"That's right. And I never repeat myself. Except for those times that I do, in fact, repeat myself. But that's usually only when I'm mentioning how silky my hair is, how sparkly my eyes are and how sexy my body is. Hey, do you think someone has a bag of peanuts? The spicy kind?"

I will not choke the life out of her. "Exactly who am I married to, and when did the supposed ceremony happen?"

"Oh, did I forget to tell you again? You're married to your ghostly girlfriend, the one you tattooed yourself for. That's how undead marriages are forged. Ashes to ashes, dust to dust, and all that. Well, that's how one-sided marriages are forged, anyway. She's not married to you, so she can tap whoever else she wants without violating any ancient laws and having to endure horrible punishment."

His jaw creaked open and closed as Viola continued to talk. And talk. "Shut up for a minute. How am I married to Sienna?"

Silence.

But then, Viola's glare said enough.

"Sorry," he muttered. "I'm just in shock. I can't be… What you're saying isn't… There's just no way…"

"You are, it is and there is. That's part of the reason you're able to interact with her now. You bonded yourself to her."

Bonded. His mind had short-circuited. He was bonded. He was married to Sienna. She was his. His woman. For real. His wife. Forever.

His.

Wife.

And apparently, despite the fact that his body could now breach any feminine core of his choosing, he couldn't do so without violating a law he'd never heard of, thereby sentencing himself to some kind of punishment. A punishment he wasn't sure who would mete out.

His demon's reaction to the other women now made sense. Sex had been on the right track. With Paris's commitment to Sienna, his infidelity would now feed the demon. Making love with Sienna would, too, though. He'd married her before finding her, and they'd since made love three times.

"You're sure?" he croaked when there was a lag in Viola's monologue. He wanted this, he realized. He wanted this to be true so badly he could taste his own anticipation. Could feel the hum in his blood, the song in his ears. He wanted to be bound to Sienna in the most irrevocable of ways.

Viola patted him on top of his head. "As if I'm ever wrong. But Paris, listen to me. We've *got* to get serious for a minute."

They weren't serious already? "So you weren't serious about the marriage thing?" He would kill her. Just press on her carotid and snuff her out.

"Of course I was serious." She cupped his cheeks, her expression sad. Then she sniffed, and licked her lips. "Hmm, you smell good." Closer…closer…she leaned in. Sniffed at his neck. "Really, *really* good."

Stupid demon.

"Now tell me the truth," she said, her voice lowering, going husky. "Do you think I'm the most beautiful woman you've ever met? And more important, do I look fat in this outfit?"

"I'm so going to give you to the fallen angel," he muttered, putting a little distance between them. Her hold on him tightened, her eyes already glazed with want. "That'll be his punishment for chasing me."

A slow, confused blink. "The fallen who?"

She didn't remember her own ardent suitor. Nice.

"What's wrong with me? Why do I feel this way?" she asked, just before a low moan left her. "I don't find you attractive, don't want to rock your world, and yet, I'm ready to climb on board."

A scream ripped through the entire enclosure, saving Paris from having to form a response. Everyone in the hall stilled, not even daring to breathe.

"Ashlyn." Maddox rushed toward the bedroom door, but Reyes tackled him.

The keeper of Violence fought for all he was worth, and several other warriors had to dive into the pile to shut him down. Paris was about to join the fray when he caught sight of familiar black wings at the entrance of the hallway.

His gaze shot up, and he met gorgeous hazels that were wider than usual. Sienna's face was flushed, her eyes red and puffed as if she'd been crying, and her mouth swollen. He was running at her a second later, leaping over the pile of his friends, tripping, getting up, and running some more.

SIENNA WASN'T MAD. What she felt was so beyond mad no single word could describe it. A mix of rage, guilt, sorrow and more rage, maybe. And then some more rage with a splash of heartbreak. And a lot more rage. Her sister was dead, and the queen of the Titans had killed her. Just slit her throat and left her on the floor as if she were garbage.

When Cronus had dropped Sienna here, all she'd wanted was to find Paris and throw herself in his arms.

Not to cry, she doubted she'd ever cry again, but to forget, if only for a little while. Instead, she discovered some strange beauty had beaten her to the finish line.

A beauty his friends probably liked. The group had apparently taken over *Sienna's* castle, and they were likely to tackle Sienna as they'd just tackled each other if she took a single step in Paris's direction.

The big, hulking giants were heavily armed, an army of menace, each soldier possessing a feral red gaze that spoke volumes. The main chorus being *I'll smile when I kill you,* but they never went for kill strikes. They were simply trying to subdue the one on the bottom of the pile.

What seemed an eternity ago, she had studied these men for nefarious purposes. Seeing them live and in person should have freaked her out. And maybe it would have, if Wrath hadn't just whipped up a party in her brain, tossing out image after image, all of them involving the handsy blonde.

With her smile, her laugh, her *everything,* she enticed men to fall in love with her. Their adulation was her nourishment. And then, when she had them at her feet, she left them, just moved on to the next one, and forgot all about them.

That's what she would do to Paris. And why wouldn't he fall for her? Sienna wondered. She was the most beautiful woman Sienna had ever seen. Hell, even *she* was tempted.

Paris appeared in front of her, gathering her in his arms, rubbing his cheek against hers. He smelled of desire she recognized, such heady desire. "I'm so happy to see you."

"You…you…"

"What's wrong, baby? What happened?"

Glaring up at him, she tugged from his hold. "I'm

gone a few hours—" and in that time had decided to be with Galen to save Paris's life, she thought but didn't add "—and already you've moved on." She gave a bitter laugh. Even knowing this would happen couldn't have prepared her for the flood of pain actually seeing it wrought. "You tried to warn me, didn't you, and I told you I understood." *Well, I don't!*

"Moved on? With Viola?" He grimaced. "Hell, no. We were just talking."

"Yeah, I know. Your body language said plenty." Before, she'd only seen his hard-on—and it had been pointed at the blonde. Now she felt it, hard and long and thick, and sweet heaven, she still wanted it. Still wanted him.

"Are you jealous?"

"Of course not!"

"You are. You're jealous." He laughed, awe and delight bubbling in the undertones. "Can I just tell you how much that turns me on?"

"Everything turns you on," she snarled, struggling to dampen her anger. He was just so damned pleased with himself. And her! "And I'm not jealous."

"You are, and I love it. Anyway, something's going on with my demon, that's all. I swear to you, I haven't been with the goddess and I won't be. Ever."

"She's a *goddess?*"

"Who holds no appeal for me."

He could be lying. He could be telling the truth. Actually, he was telling the truth, she decided in an instant, not needing Wrath's help. Paris wasn't the type to lie. Consequences weren't something he feared.

"It doesn't matter." Her shoulders sagged with defeat. "I shouldn't have come back."

"Doesn't matter? Are you giving up on me? On us?"

He gripped her forearms and shook her. "I know we said we'd part when you could leave the realm, but I want to revisit that decision. It's no longer an option for me. And I know you're going to have a difficult time believing this, but no matter how my body reacts to others, no matter what my demon wants, you are it for me. Do you understand?" Another shake, harder than before.

"Uh, Paris," Strider called. "Who you talking to, buddy?"

He twisted, and she peeked around him. The warriors had stopped fighting each other, and everyone but the scarred one and the blonde goddess were eyeing Paris as if he'd just flipped his ever-loving lid.

"They can't see me," she said.

He was saved from having to reply to her or his friends when the door in the center of the hall swung open and the dark-haired William stepped into the hall. He was pale, clearly shaken to his soul and bathed in blood.

She gasped. "What happened to him?"

William clapped to gain everyone's attention. "All right, listen up. I've got good news and bad news. Because I'm such a positive person, we'll start with the good. Ashlyn survived the birthing, and so did her personal horde."

The hallway echoed with breathy sighs of relief…none louder than Maddox's own.

"So what's the bad?" someone demanded.

After a dramatic pause, the warrior said, "I'm out of conditioner. I need someone to flash out of here and get me some. Hint, I'm looking at you, Lucien. And, yeah, you're welcome for my amazing contrib to your happy family. Little terrors clawed me up but good."

"William!" someone else snapped. "Stay on track, and

keep the unnecessary details to a minimum. We're dying here."

"That's gratitude for you. So anyway, come on, come in, and meet your nephew and niece, Murder and Mayhem. Or, if you want to call them by their nicknames, and I'm sure you will the moment they get their mitts on you, Pistol and Shank."

CHAPTER THIRTY-SEVEN

AS HAPPY AS PARIS WAS with the births, as much as he wanted to meet the babies, he had to take care of his woman first. He tossed Sienna over his shoulder with the finesse of a bulldozer, shouted, "No one enter my bedroom, no matter what you hear," and stalked to the room he'd used before, passing through the hall of statues. Each of his friends cast him weird looks before he rounded the corner. Mainly because they were all laid out flat and hadn't recovered from Maddox kicking and shoving them out of his way, so they were dazed, but also because they assumed Paris had just spent a good five minutes talking to himself.

I want her still, Sex said with no small measure of surprise.

Don't worry. We'll get her.

Sienna had been stunned silent and remained still at first, but with his every step she worked herself into more of a lather. Soon she was slapping at his back, jerking at his hair and attempting to knee him in the face and balls. Up the stairs he went, down another hall, barely able to prevent his emasculation. He shouldered his way inside the chamber and slammed the door with a backward kick.

He'd been torpedoing his way into a black rage, but seeing Sienna had calmed him. Just like that. Zacharel could blow him, because clearly he would never hurt this woman.

She'd come back for him. That deserved a reward.

He set her on her feet, and she immediately launched herself into full-blown attack. To be honest, he was glad as hell. Anything was better than that moment of defeat. Her little fists pummeled at him, and he accepted the abuse. Until he realized she'd made an improper fist and was actually hurting herself. He wound an arm around her waist, spun her and slammed her into the hard line of his body to still her.

"Let me go!"

"In a minute." As she struggled, he pulled her thumb out from beneath her fingers and rearranged her fist. "Hit like this." Done, he released her.

She swung back around to beat at him some more, and this time the blows stung. "You aren't walking out of this room until I've killed you!"

That'd be a nice little trick, and maybe something to try later. "I'll let you do anything you want to me, but I'd like an explanation first. What's this about?"

"Argh!" She leapt away from him, paced like a caged lion. Energy radiated from her, practically lifting her hair off her head. "It's about the fact that all men suck! And in case you didn't realize, you're included in their numbers."

"I would hope so. Otherwise our romance would be missing something."

Her eyes glittered with jade fire, the gold lost. "Was that a crack about your penis? Because if so, you can do better." She stalked to the dresser and shoved with all her might, knocking the thing to the ground. Wood splintered. The granite surface shattered. The drawers spilled from their holders. Scowling, panting, she grabbed one and lobbed it at him.

He ducked, and the empty container smacked into the door. Both fractured. Another quickly followed, and he barely managed to dodge it.

"Why are your friends here? Aren't you afraid I'll spy on them and learn their secrets?"

"No." And he wasn't. Not anymore. He'd judged her harshly before, but he wasn't going to make that mistake again. "Just like you aren't afraid I'll sleep with anyone else while we're together."

Another drawer. "That's what you told Susan!"

"I know, and I've lived with the guilt ever since. I will *never* do that to you. Tell me you know that."

"Yes, I know that, but we weren't together a few minutes ago. Which means you went after the first tail to twitch in your direction the second we were separated. But I'm not your girlfriend, and I will never be your girlfriend, so I can't complain, can I?"

"No," he said quietly. "You won't ever be my girlfriend." *Because you're already my wife.* Those words. He'd never thought to use them in regard to himself. But now that he had, yeah, his possessive instincts flared, insisting on their due. Didn't help that Sienna was the sexiest female he'd ever seen. A live wire, sizzling, crackling, the essence of passion. Yeah, he was hard as a steel pipe.

Another drawer was flung his way. Only four more were left. He'd let her have them, and then he was going in.

"I'm so sick of this world, the lying and the tricking and the killing." One. "That woman is going to pay. Oh, she's going to pay so bad." Two. "I'm going to join in and do a little killing of my own. Not through Wrath, but with my own hands." Three. "That bastard Cronus thinks he can manipulate me, but he can't. I'm done with all of you!" Four. "And I'm not going to save you, so there! You can go to—"

Paris barreled forward, snagging her around the waist and tossing her on the bed. As she bounced on the mattress, her wings shot out to slow her momentum. He dove for her before she could catch herself and hover in the air, and for once he didn't try to be careful. He pinned her, trapping her legs beneath the muscled weight of his own and her arms over her head. She tried to buck him off, but all she succeeded in doing was rubbing his hard-on against her clit.

A cry of need parted those pretty lips.

More!

"You wet for me, baby?" He didn't ask for permission, but transferred the shackling of her wrists to one hand and shoved up her shirt and bra with the other, baring her breasts. Her nipples were red and swollen, begging for him.

"No," she said, and he knew she lied. "Not wet, not wet, soooo not wet." Yeah, she knew it, too.

He dipped down and sucked. She released another of those beautiful cries, her hips undulating against him. He kept sucking and she kept bucking against him, until he couldn't stand the pressure anymore and shoved his hand down her pants, past those panties and straight into the heat of her. She practically bowed off the mattress.

Yes, please, yes.

One finger, two, three. He thrust them home, as deep as he could get them.

"Paris... I... Oh, yes, yes!"

"There's my girl." She drenched his hand, just the way he liked, so hot and silky, fitting him so damn perfectly, even this way. "When you used your mouth on me, I wanted to have my face buried between your legs. I still do. And next time, I will. I'm going to have all this honey down my throat."

"Paris…I'm going to… I'm so close already." Her eyes were squeezed shut, those long lashes fused together. "Let go of my hands. I want to touch you, too. *Need* to touch you."

"You think those little taps you gave me weren't fore-play? And hell, baby, I was hard for you long before that."

"Yeah?"

"Oh, yeah. You still mad at me?"

"Yes, but don't stop."

"Got to. Gotta give you something more." He removed his fingers just before she climaxed, and she screeched in frustration. "Gotta give you something better."

Her inhalations rasped in, her exhalations stormed out, both quick and heavy. Need truly was riding her hard—but not as hard as he was going to. He was *drunk* with his passion for her, his head swimming with it, his veins burning with it.

He jerked her zipper down, but didn't bother with shoving her pants away. Couldn't. He was too busy undo-ing his own. He didn't shove those down, either, and once his cock was free, he poised himself at her entrance. She couldn't open her legs very wide, the material wouldn't let her, so when he pushed in, he had to bear down some of his weight. But when he was in, he was really *in,* her inner walls locked around him, tighter than any fist he'd ever made.

She screamed at the contact, and he loved the sound.

Every thrust was a slow grind against her, and yeah, his body rubbed her clit with every downward glide. No longer did her words make any sense. She was panting and incoherent and lost to an all-consuming fervor. Sex, too. Hell, Paris, too. His balls were drawing up tighter and tighter, yet still sliding against the tops of her thighs.

Her arms fought his hold—oh, baby, he hadn't let her go, had he?—but he kept a steady grip, her breasts thrust up, her nipples rubbing his chest, the friction sparking all different kinds of flames. Satisfaction, lust, clawing need, contentment. With his free hand, he cupped her chin.

"Look at me." He slowed his thrusts.

Took a moment, but ultimately she obeyed. Those hazel eyes were fever-bright, glazed, her pupils utterly blown.

"You're not done with me. Do you hear me? You are not done. You are mine."

"I'm…" Another scream, her inner walls milking him, her hips lifting…lifting…even lifting his weight, sinking him deeper than should have been possible.

Sex shouted at the amazing pleasure.

And like that, Paris erupted, the orgasm churning in his spine, shooting through his sac, up his erection and into her, pumping his seed straight into her body. A white-hot jet, again and again. He came so hard he saw stars.

When he was at last emptied out, he opened his eyes to find Sienna had collapsed on the mattress and he had collapsed on top of her, was probably smashing her. He rolled to his side, but they were still connected so he took her with him. Her head just kind of lolled into the hollow of his neck.

There was a long period of silence as they caught their breath and their heartbeats slowed, but all the while he knew one fact to be true: he'd never experienced sex like that with anyone else and he never would again. Hell, he didn't want to.

"I never had a temper before," she murmured groggily.

He ran a hand up and down the ridges of her spine. "Well, you've got one now, that's for sure."

She bit his collarbone, a playful nip. He expected Sex to respond, but the demon had gone to sleep. "We shouldn't have done that."

"I wanted to calm you down, and I did. Missionary accomplished."

Another nip. "I meant, we shouldn't have had angry sex."

He said, "Couldn't help myself. I liked your temper."

"I could tell. Is there a position you don't excel at, though? You're giving me a complex."

"If there is, will you help me practice until I do?"

"So many times you'll lose respect for yourself."

He laughed. He just couldn't help himself. He was… happy. She was teasing him, as if they were friends. They *were* friends. "I wasn't going to sleep with the goddess," he said. "I swear to you. Never will I sleep with that female."

She placed a kiss just above his heart. "Don't do that. Don't promise things like that. Because even as jealous as I was, and yes, I'm freely admitting to a stalkerlike rage, I would rather you slept with a thousand like her than weaken and die."

His chest got tight. Gently he pulled out of her sweet, sweet body, and they both moaned at the loss. He stripped her, stripped himself, then placed his gun on the nightstand beside the bed, and his blade under his pillow. Safety taken care of, he went right back to cuddling Sienna into his side. First, though, he gave her nipples a *Daddy's back* kiss.

"We're going to talk about that, and about what you were so upset about, because I know there's more to it than the goddess," he said. "In a few minutes. Right now, I want to say a few things, and then I want you to tell me something about you. I want to know you better." In all ways.

They weren't leaving this bed until he'd seen her brain naked, too, and that was that.

"O-kay."

"Susan Dille," he said. "I cared for her. I wanted something to work with her, but I was growing weak. Finally I caved and slept with someone else. I was miserable, she found out, and things only got worse from there. I don't want that with you."

"What makes me so different?" she whispered. "I mean, how can you be with me more than once?"

"I've wondered about that myself, and I think it's because my desire for you is more powerful than my demon."

"That's... Oh, Paris. That's the sweetest thing I've ever heard."

"Good. Now it's your turn for a confession. Start talking."

CHAPTER THIRTY-EIGHT

"I, WELL… HMM," Sienna said.

"Come on, baby." Paris combed his fingers through her hair. "Look past my terrible personality and hideous looks and throw me a bone. Teach me how to woo you properly."

She snorted. "I'd argue the hideous looks part."

"But not the terrible personality? Ouch. That hurts, baby."

Her next snort was half-bathed in laughter. "Well, this won't teach you anything but my stupidity. Once I tried to spray tan my freckles away and ended up looking like a diseased carrot."

"I adore your freckles, and my favorite fantasy involves licking every single one of them. More secrets, though. I want more." Was so hungry for them.

A heavy pause, and when she next spoke, she'd lost her air of playfulness. "The guy I was going to marry, well, I was going to have his baby, but halfway through—" a shudder rocked her "—well, I lost her. My baby girl. Afterward I just sort of broke down and my fiancée left. I was moved to a different division of the Hunters' enterprise."

"Oh, Sienna, oh, baby, I'm so sorry."

Tears filled her eyes, quickly masked. "I recovered."

No one ever recovered fully from that kind of loss.

"I never allow myself to think of her. That's probably unhealthy, but…"

"But it's how you survive. What did you name her?" He knew she'd given the little girl a name.

Another pause, then a hesitant, "Rebecca Skye."

He remembered when she asked him if he even wanted to have kids. Had she ever wanted to have another? Probably. The loss would have left a wound inside her, one that would never fully heal. He knew that kind of loss well. But pregnancy wasn't a possibility for the undead. Still, he wondered if adoption was. Perhaps she could take in one of the kids with unexplained abilities Anya had hidden around the world to save them from Hunters. Sienna would make an amazing mother, protective, loving, fierce.

"She's in heaven, I think. Not Cronus's heaven, or this heaven, or wherever we are, and not Zacharel's heaven, either. I've never told anyone this, but when I died, I knew there was someplace wonderful to spend eternity, as well as someplace terrible. Maybe Cronus is my personal hell, my something terrible, but Rebecca is in that other place, that far better place, where someone far better than Cronus or Zacharel's Deity rules. And now I want to talk about something else. Something light."

Light. He could give her light, even though he had a thousand questions about this "better place" and this "better" ruler, and her suffering and her dreams. "I enjoy watching romantic comedies, action adventures, horror, whatever. Anything but subtitles. That artsy crap is lame." He cupped the sweetest ass on the planet and found himself hard all over again.

"Tell me more." With a voice full of rasp, she said, "I want to know about you, too."

"I'll tell you anything you want to know." And he meant that.

"You and your friends…you're really close."

Those same friends would have told him she had a hankering for information so that she could use it against him. Paris knew better. "We were created together. We're family."

"Created?"

"Yeah. Zeus made us from the blood of his best warriors, steel, baser instincts, things like that."

"So you have no mother or father?"

"Nope."

"I'm sorry. Blood family isn't always hearts and flowers, but there's comfort there. I'm sorry you didn't have that."

"Just made me that much closer to my boys, but I did sometimes wonder what it would have been like. Then I'd think about what I did have, men who would die for me, and I would realize I've got everything I need."

"Having someone who is willing to die for you is rare. And several someones? Awesome."

"Yes. It is."

"I'm glad you have that. It's better than family."

How wistful she sounded. "You don't?"

"No. Never."

And didn't that just break his heart. *I might die for her,* he thought. *Might throw myself in front of a sword for her.* "Now I'm the one who's sorry. I mean, you died for me, but I haven't—" Oh, damn. Wrong words. He expected her to tense, waited for the mood to shatter.

She didn't, it didn't. "Yeah, I did, didn't I? You *are* lucky."

No animosity, just a kind amusement, a contemplative dreaming. There went his heart again, breaking into a few more pieces.

"When we met," he said, "you claimed to be writing a romance novel. You even had pages. I remember how they scattered at your feet when I slammed into you. Was that true? Were they yours? Since waking up in that cell, I figured they were a lie, but now that I know you better, I'm thinking differently."

"They were mine, yes. I love romance novels, and I did want to write one. Maybe I will one day. Not that there's a publisher for the dead."

"Well, you've already got a built-in audience of one. I want to read what you wrote, and what you will one day write. Promise?"

She licked her lips, her tongue caressing his skin, too, and oh, did he like that. "Have you, uh, ever fallen in love?" she asked, ignoring his demand.

Okay, all right. He'd let her lack of an answer about the novel slide. For now. "Once I thought I was, but it didn't work out. And there were a few times, after I was with a woman, that I would wish for more and hang around. A few times I even dated a woman without sleeping with her, hoping for some type of relationship, but all along I'd have to sleep with others, so I'd feel guilty and then I'd just stop seeing her so that the guilt would fade."

"I'm sorry."

"Don't be. Not your fault."

"Doesn't help that Hunters threaten everyone you love."

"Yeah."

"How do you deal, having a group of people hunting you, hating you?"

"It's not easy, I won't lie. Sometimes we push ourselves over the edge. Drugs, alcohol, sex, whatever our particular vice is, but we go on and we look out for each other." The warmth of her breath stroked over him, tantalizing him. "And lately we are Addams Family normal— you know, doing the hearts and flowers thing while navigating everything our enemies throw at us."

Her nails dug into his chest. "The Hunters…more than half of the organization is brainwashed. We're told over and over how evil you are, how you are responsible for everything bad that has ever happened to us, to everyone. How perfect our lives could be if you were gone. They show us pictures, horrible pictures of torture, disease and death, and they prey on our weaknesses. Like with my sister, telling me that little girls wouldn't be kidnapped if there were no demons in the world."

First she'd lost her sister, then her baby. He squeezed her tight. "I'm sorry for her loss." For all the crap she'd endured throughout her too-short life. Crap he'd only added to. "I should have told you that when you first mentioned her, but…"

"But we had only just reconnected and didn't trust each other."

He kissed her temple. "We've always known the Hunters were studying us. Is that how you knew I was in Rome that day? How you knew the romance novel would distract me, and what drug to use on me?"

"I knew through Dean Stefano, my boss, and he knew through Galen. Galen, I'm sure, knew through Rhea, Cronus's wife. Funny, but I never understood the chain of command until after my death."

Paris couldn't help himself and gave her temple another kiss. They were getting heavy again, and he didn't mind that, wanted to travel that road with her, all roads with her, but she didn't and he would honor her wishes.

"I'm going to switch gears for a minute, okay?"

Her relief was palpable as she said, "Please do." One at a time, she plucked her nails from his skin.

"I know you've never been married, but other than the douche who left you have you ever…wanted to be?" He tried to ask it casually, as if the answer was no biggie, but he couldn't keep the yearning from his tone.

Her reaction, when it came, was one of shock, and he wasn't sure whether that was surprise-party good or you-just-hit-my-car bad. She jerked upright, that dark flood of hair draping one bare shoulder. Her eyes were still more green than brown and they dominated her pixie face. The lips he'd kissed until they were puffed and red were parted.

"I…I…"

Balls to the wall. He would finish this. "I want you to marry me," he said. He wanted her tethered to him the same way he was tethered to her. Mentally, emotionally and physically.

"Paris…"

He threaded his fingers through her hair. "Don't say anything right now. Just think about it." Because, bottom line? No more talk of separating. They were staying together, and that was that. He wasn't letting her go, and he sure as hell wasn't cheating on her. No matter the cost to himself.

From now on, there was only one sheath for his sword. Would there be problems? Complications? Oh, yeah. Probably more than he was aware of, and he was aware of plenty. But he'd rather deal with those problems *with her* than be without her and have smooth sailing.

"I have to tell you something," she whispered, the defeat returning in an instant. "I lied. I won't kill her, and he can manipulate me. Otherwise, the rest of you are dead, too, and I can't allow that to happen."

"Won't kill who? Who can't manipulate you? Tell me, and I'll fix it." *I will slay her dragons.*

"You can't. Rhea, she…she… When my sister Skye was taken, we were swimming in the neighborhood pool. Mom told us never to go there alone, but I was fourteen and thought I could handle things, and Skye wanted to swim so badly. We were just supposed to walk to the park, but we went to the pool instead. It was so crowded that day, and I had to go to the bathroom, and when I came back out, she was being dragged away by a stranger. Everyone must have thought she was throwing a fit, because no one stopped them, and I couldn't get to them."

He opened his mouth to offer comfort, to tell her it wasn't her fault, that even though she'd gone against her mother's orders, she wasn't the one who had abducted the little girl, but she wasn't finished.

"Today I learned that all these years Skye has been alive. Until recently. She was murdered. Rhea murdered her. If I'd only found her earlier, but I didn't, and now I have to live with the knowledge that she…that I…" She was rambling, the words spewing out as if they'd been trapped for a long time and were now tangling on her tongue as they fought for freedom.

He ached for her. As he'd never ached for anything, he ached for her, and he didn't take the decision to slay her dragons lightly. He'd do what needed doing. "Go on, baby. Tell me the rest."

A shudder moved through her. She inhaled forcefully. "Cronus told me that Skye was Galen's prisoner, then he told me that he didn't actually know where she was, *then* he showed me her lifeless, bloody body."

Paris had known the bastard was low, but this…he had no words. His reckoning with Cronus needed to happen soon—with knives. No wonder Sienna had been so upset when she'd returned to the castle. "I'm so sorry, baby. If I could take away your pain, I would." Finally he told her what he'd wanted to tell her. "This isn't your fault. It was never your fault. You aren't responsible for the things other people do. Never have been, never will be. This is their shame, not yours. But I know it hurts, I do, and however you want to handle it, I will help you."

"He showed me because he expects me to spy on Galen and to…to be with him."

Spots of black flashed over his eyes. "When you say *be with Galen,* do you mean be with him sexually?"

A shameful nod, and maybe even a bit resolved, as if she deserved nothing better.

"That you'd even consider it tells me that you want to punish yourself," he said, comprehension a slap in the face. "For what you did to me, and what you think you allowed to happen to your sister."

Her chin jutted stubbornly. "Maybe."

"So, what else is it you did exactly, that some part of you thinks you need to be punished? Fought for a cause you believed in? Check. Slept with a man you were attracted to, despite everything else? Check. Saved him when you could have left him to a slow, torturous death? Check."

Her hand balled into a (proper) fist. "I told you that I hated you as I lay dying."

"Every couple says things they don't mean when they're fighting."

"Well, I meant it at the time! And before that, I drugged you."

"Yeah, and I planned to screw you and leave you like

I'd done to a thousand others." She flinched at his crudeness, but he kept going. "And guess what? At the time I was blithe about it. I loved women, and I protected them, but I still used them. In my mind, it was my right. I needed a wake-up call, and you gave it to me."

"No, you—"

"Don't make excuses for me. You've seen my past, and you know I've spoken true."

She snapped her teeth at him. "So you're saying you bear me no ill will? None at all?" A snort lacking any hint of amusement.

He fisted her hair a lot harder than he'd intended, but he didn't loosen his grip. "Baby, I'm saying I *adore* you."

Once again, she floundered for a response. The anger drained from her, and utter longing peered down at him. "Adore?" she squeaked.

"Your ears are working just fine."

The harshness of his reply had her sighing dreamily, something that puzzled and aroused him. "I was wrong earlier. *This* is the sweetest thing anyone has ever said to me."

And so I'll be stepping up my game now. If that made her happy, his A-Game was gonna make her blissful. "Nothing to say in return?"

"Well, yeah. Cronus says that my being with Galen is the only way to keep you and your friends safe."

Hell, no. When they'd lived in the heavens, Galen had been one of Paris's go-to guys. They'd hung together, fought together. Paris had admired the guy's emotional distance, his ability to do whatever was necessary to finish a job successfully. And okay, fine, they'd shared women, sometimes even at the same time.

He hadn't cared then. He cared now. Not just because

Galen was Enemy One, but because Sienna was his and his alone. She was staying with him.

"You're not going back to Galen." No way, not ever. Actually, Paris would die first. "And just a quick FYI. Apparently my friends plugged the keeper of Hope full of bullets earlier today. He's no good to anyone right now."

"But he'll recover, I know he will, and then...then..." The rest of the story flooded from her. The Chamber of Futures, the portraits, the three possible outcomes for the world. For Cronus. *For him.*

Too much to digest at once, but still, nothing changed his mind about Sienna staying put.

"We have time," he said. "We have time to figure this out, and we will. But you're not going to him. You're mine. Only mine. And I'm yours. I will never sleep with anyone else. Do you understand what I'm saying? Never. When I said you were it for me, I meant it. No one else, whether you're with me or not. And Sienna, you will be with me."

As he spoke, her mouth fell open, snapped closed. "Do *not* say things like that."

"Baby, I will do more than say it. I will blood oath it." He reached for the daggers under the pillow, but she threw herself over his body and batted the weapon to the floor. Then, clearly suspecting he'd just reach for another weapon, she swiped her arm over the nightstand and sent the gun flying.

Now, there was the shocker of a lifetime. He wasn't offended by her resistance, though. She wanted him safe, alive, thriving. Was even willing to sacrifice her happiness for his.

"Did you just challenge me?" he asked. They were flesh to flesh, male to female. Her wings spread, blocking out the rest of the room. She was all that he saw, all that he felt. Her breasts pressed into his chest, her nipples already beaded for him. Her core rubbed against his swollen length, and her legs splayed over his. "I think you just challenged me."

"No. I did not."

"You did. Quick fact—you mess with a man's weapons, and you might as well knee him in the balls. You'll get the same results. So I accept." Moving so quickly she couldn't possibly resist, he flipped her over, onto her back, spread her legs and shoved inside.

No preliminaries. Just straight-up, hard-core sex in the most basic fashion. She was wet, so very wet, so they had no problems.

"Paris!"

"Yeah, baby, that's it. Take me all the way in."

"Is this how you reward all challengers?" she asked between panting breaths.

"Only you."

Her moan of pleasure filled the room, blending with his hiss of inexorable bliss. By the time he finished with her, she would know the man she belonged with—because there would be no part of her that he left untouched.

CHAPTER THIRTY-NINE

GALEN APPEARED IN THE CENTER of the bedroom, and Legion shrank deeper into her shadowed corner. She'd been here for over an hour, having whisked herself to the coordinates he'd given her. She had no idea what the rest of the place looked like. Coward that she was, she hadn't left the relative safety of the room. To her immense relief, no one had entered, either.

Though she'd been tempted, she hadn't even explored the rest of the chamber. Gorgeous pile after gorgeous pile of shiny gold coins, glittering jewels and odd, ancient weapons abounded. Weapons she couldn't use against her captor, so what was the point of studying them?

While Galen had worn white at the temple, he'd since donned a red robe. A *drip, drip, dripping* red robe. She frowned. A copper tang coated the air. That's when she realized. Not a red robe, but a blood-soaked one.

His knees gave out and he fell, barely catching himself before a face-plant. His wings were tattered, and there were blade hilts and arrows protruding from his chest.

All that blood…

—hands grasping at her breasts, her thighs—

—teeth scraping over her skin—

—claws in her eyes, plucking them out—

—something hard between her legs—

—laughter, so much laughter—

—shackles on her wrists, her ankles—

Bile burned holes in her stomach and escaped, quickly spreading through the rest of her. She covered her mouth with a trembling hand, fighting tears. The memories of her time in hell never left her, but sometimes they completely overtook her, dragging her into a different sort of hell. One of humiliation, degradation, helplessness and horror.

"Fox!" Galen's ragged shout rang out. "I need you."

Legion must have whimpered at the sound of that shout, because Galen's head whipped in her direction. His sky-blue eyes were rimmed with red, his cheeks streaked with dirt. Was he going to watch as "Fox" did things to her?

His expression softened. Only a little, but enough to stave off the encroaching hysteria. "You think I'm in bad condition, you should see the other guy."

Tendrils of hope reached out, tried to wrap around her. Hope for something better. Hope for a future with the man in front of her. Panic infused her, after all, and she fought them with all of her mental strength. Finally the tendrils thinned, vanished.

"Please don't hurt me," she croaked.

He frowned at her.

Rushed footsteps beyond, and the door swung open. A tall, slender woman with jet-black hair and angular features flowed inside. She was attractive, in a regal way, with eyes like the differing temperatures of flames, an odd mix of blue and gold.

But there was a gray cast to her skin, bruises under her eyes, and though she gripped a gun in both hands, she was trembling. A quick scan, and she found Legion. Lifted one of the guns.

Yes, Legion thought, strangely comforted all of a sudden. *Yes. An end. Finally.*

"No!" Despite his injuries, Galen dove in front of her.

The girl—Fox?—had her finger off the trigger in a heartbeat, the weapon lowered.

Disappointment settled on Legion's shoulders. Perhaps she should have ended herself long before now. Why hadn't she? Suddenly she didn't know, couldn't remember.

"You don't hurt her," Galen said, menace a strong undercurrent. "Ever."

Confusion joined the disappointment. He'd just... defended her.

Fox ran her tongue over her teeth. "She do this to you?"

"No. Now help me to the bed."

As Fox sheathed her weapons, her gaze remained locked on Legion, narrowed and hate-filled. Even as she approached Galen, wound her arm around the warrior and eased him to his feet, she kept Legion in her sights. He leaned his weight into her, and they inched their way to the bed. Slowly, carefully, he sat at the edge of the mattress.

Were they lovers? Legion wondered.

Visibly weakening, now wheezing, Galen said, "Get your tools and get this shit out of me."

With one last warning glare in Legion's direction, Fox flew out the door.

"Will she obey you?" Legion asked softly. "About me?"

Sky-blue eyes found her, the lids heavy, casting his face into the come-to-bed sexy realm, and she hated herself for noticing. "Yes. The only person you need to worry about is me."

So. He planned to save her torturing all for himself. And he would torture her. She had no doubt about that.

—something slicing between each of her ribs—

—rotted breath fanning her ear, trailing down her chest—

She wrapped her arms around her middle. *Distract yourself.* "Did the Lords do that to you?"

"Yes," he repeated. "As promised, I let them go without hurting them back."

"Th-thank you." Worry for them was another constant in her life.

A long moment passed in silence, allowing her thoughts to once again careen out of control. Soon she was imagining what would happen to her once Galen healed. "Why do you hate them so much?" she asked, just to fill the void.

"I don't hate them." He balanced his elbows on his knees and his weight on his elbows. "I'm simply looking out for myself."

"Why?"

"Who else will?" Then, "Enough about me. What happened to you in hell?"

The blood drained from her face, then the rest of her, leaving her cold and empty. "I can't...talk about it, please don't make me talk about it."

He stared at her, different emotions washing over his face. Fury, regret, hope, jealousy, fury again.

Fox rushed back in, the black bag she held slamming into her thigh with a loud *thump.* Legion curled her knees into her chest, doing her best to become a smaller target, but Fox was through intimidating, her focus on Galen.

She crouched in front of him, set down the bag, and dug inside. After cutting away his robe, she whistled as she looked him over. "This is going to hurt like a son of a bitch."

"Don't care. Do what's needed."

As she worked, Legion kept her attention on the back of her head. Maybe because Galen kept his on *her,* still staring at her, trying to see past her skin and into her soul.

Fox was demon-possessed, she realized. Having grown up among the dark lords of hell, Legion sensed the evil inside her, could feel the ooze of her…distrust. Yes. That's what she felt rubbing her nerve endings raw.

Distrust. A High Lord. The strongest of the strong, a leader of many minions. Legion was a minion of Strife, and the two demons had warred constantly, pitting their armies against each other. Distrust was no longer…right, though. The malice seeping from the girl's pores was warped, almost frantic. No wonder her skin was grayish and her face bruised. She must have to fight the demon every hour of every day to remain sane herself.

"So, you want to tell me what happened?" Fox asked. "What's going on?"

"No," Galen replied tartly. "I don't."

"Do it anyway. You take off for Rome to deal with the Unspoken Ones and get the Cloak, and I don't hear from you for weeks. I thought you were dead. Then suddenly you're back, and you practically are dead."

She'd removed everything that didn't belong, and was now cleaning the blood from his chest. As the crimson was wiped away, she began to piece together the tattoos on his chest, stitching his skin in place. A butterfly over his left pectoral, and one over his right.

Two butterflies?

Legion's gaze jolted up and clashed with his. He was still eyeing her through those narrowed lids, daring her to say something. She gulped, kept quiet.

"I got the Cloak, stole Maddox's woman and traded her for this one." He motioned to Legion with a tilt of his chin. "Hey! Can you at least pretend to be a woman and try for gentle?"

"Wuss. Why her?" Fox demanded, spreading some kind of paste over each of the wounds.

"Don't worry about her. She's mine, and she's not going to hurt me. Are you, Legion?"

If only. She shook her head.

"Say it. Say the words."

A tremor moved through her. "I'm not going to hurt you." She couldn't. Even if he chained her up and did… and did… *Bile, spreading faster and faster…*

"Because I'm commanding you to take care of me, and you have to obey me, don't you." Not a question.

"Yes," she whispered.

"Calm down, Gay Man," Fox told him. "Your heartbeat is jacked up, and it's causing you to bleed more heavily."

"You know I hate when you call me that."

He'd grumbled the admonishment, but he hadn't struck at her, and that shocked Legion to the bone. He must really like the woman, she thought. And was that… could that be…jealousy swimming through her?

No way. Legion wanted nothing to do with Galen. Nothing! *Hate him.* For what he'd done to Aeron, to Ashlyn.

A short while later, Fox had him bandaged up and lying flat on the mattress. She tucked the covers around him and stood there, brushing his hair from his face until he fell asleep with a last shuddering command. "Don't hurt her."

That's when Fox turned and leveled Legion with the evilest stare she'd ever seen—and she'd been chained to the devil himself a few times.

"Galen might think of you as his, little girl, but *he* is

mine. And I protect, and avenge, what's mine. You harm him in any way, and not even he will be able to stop me from harming you in kind."

CHAPTER FORTY

CRONUS SEETHED WHEN he discovered his Lords had found his hiding place, the Realm of Blood and Shadows, where he kept Sienna and the three demon-possessed warriors he'd locked there. They'd invaded his private castle. All except for Torin, the keeper of Disease, who was back at the fortress in Budapest, having refused to let Lucien flash him. Too much risk, he'd said, even if he was draped from head to toe with protective gear.

One touch of Torin's skin against his, and Lucien would be infected with the very disease running rampant in the other warrior's veins. Torin put his friends before himself, always, an attitude Cronus did not understand or respect. But the thought reminded Cronus there was a way to work this situation to his favor.

Torin would do anything to touch a female human without hurting her. Even accept a gift that wasn't a gift. A gift that was a curse. A gift that was a death sentence. A gift that would ruin Rhea's own plans. Not that he would know it. Cronus grinned.

Unlike Lucien, Cronus did not have to touch an individual to move him. Cronus simply spoke, and Torin appeared in front of him.

The warrior palmed two blades in his gloved hands and spun, searching for the culprit, even as he oriented himself to his new surroundings. He stilled when he noticed Cronus, though his gaze continued to rove, memorizing the details, the exits.

A field of ambrosia stretched for miles, scenting the air oh, so sweetly, the violet petals glistening under the gleam of a sun that offered the perfect amount of light and heat.

"Cronus," Torin said with a nod of his head. If he was upset or even thrilled about being pulled from his Budapest fortress for the first time in centuries, he didn't show it. No bowing, either, so of course, no scraping.

All of his current problems stemmed from his leniency with the Lords, Cronus mused. They issued commands and expected him to obey. Then, when he issued commands, they refused him, sometimes openly, sometimes by more stealthy means. His mistake was trying to connect with them, to become one of them. He should have proven his strength and demonstrated the consequences of defying him from the beginning. He wasn't their friend, would never be their friend. He was their king, their master.

And now he would prove it.

"You rang?"

Oh, yes. He would prove it. Cronus studied him, this warrior he was about to use. Torin had white hair that shagged around a wicked face humans craved for the rest of their lives if they were unlucky enough to catch a single glimpse of it. Emerald eyes, more sinful than anything. Lips that had never known a female's taste.

"Walk with me," he commanded, expecting absolute compliance.

And getting it. When the warrior reached his side, he pivoted and strode through the field, the lush leaves caressing his suit-clad legs. He ran scenarios through his mind, gauging the pros and cons of his decision.

"So…what's up?"

The impudent tone irritated him, but he made no comment. For now. "I have a new task for you."

A groan. "You and your tasks. Torture so-and-so. Kill so-and-so. Rally my boys and send them into the danger zone. So, fine. Let's hear this new one. I'm sure it will delight me as much as the others."

"Tone," he snapped.

"Yes. I have one."

Calm. "And you'll lose your tongue if you use it again."

Silence.

Excellent. "Today, Disease, I give you a gift. The greatest treasure in my possession. *Despite* your disappointing, offensive attitude."

Those green eyes rolled. "All right. I'll bite. What's this gift?"

"My…All-Key." He needed to give it away, but doing so irked considering the lengths he'd gone through to get it.

"Great, but I have no flippin' idea what that is."

Of course not. Save for four others, Cronus had murdered everyone who knew about it. The four? Anya, the minor goddess of Anarchy and its former possessor; her father, Tartarus, who had given it to her; Lucien, who knew every one of Anya's secrets; and Reyes, who had once dared to shackle Cronus and barter for his woman's freedom. And the quartet lived only because Cronus had a use for them. Had they ever spoken of the key, he would have stopped caring about their usefulness, and they knew it.

"This key unlocks any door, any prison, any curse. Anything. Nothing can bind you. And if anyone tries to take it from you, they will die." That did not mean Torin would be free of his demon. The two were bonded, two halves of a whole. One could not live successfully without the other.

"Sounds cool, but why me?"

Because Torin was solitary, spending more time alone than with his friends. Because he would never fall in love, nor betray his secrets to a female while they whiled away too much time in bed. Something that happened far too much for Cronus's liking. Something he himself had once been guilty of doing.

"Should you tell anyone about this gift," he continued, not deigning to reply aloud, "I will kill you as well as the one you told. Should you try and give it away, I will kill you and all those you love. And, when I ask you to return it to me, you will do so without hesitation. One moment of resistance, just one, and I will do more than kill your loved ones. I will hurt them in ways you cannot imagine."

Torin's purposeful stride never faltered. "Yeah, well, thanks for thinking of me, but I'd rather eat dirt."

Cronus sent a wave of power slamming into the man's temples, knocking him off his feet. He hit the ground, writhing from the pain of it, blood soon spurting from his ears.

Looming over him, Cronus said, "You were saying?" A wave of his hand, and the pain eased.

Torin lay there, panting, dripping with sweat. "I was saying dirt is delicious, thanks for the mouthful."

His lips pursed. Breaking the Lords would clearly take more than his usual strong-arm tactics. They smiled when he hurt them, laughed when he threatened. As much as that frustrated and angered him, it also fascinated him. Despite everything, they were honorable. When they gave their word, they stood by it. A foolish practice, really, but one he'd come to rely on where they were concerned.

Only when he threatened those they loved did they fall in line with him. But Torin could not simply coop-erate because of fear. Not this time. Not with something as important as the All-Key.

"Do this, keep the key safe for me, and I will grant you a boon," Cronus said. "Anything you wish. Anything that is in my power to give, of course."

Suspicion danced in the warrior's eyes, and Cronus knew he was weighing his options. Refuse the king, and face punishment. Accept, and face potential trickery. Be-trayal. But for the prospect of such a reward, he would not say no.

"I think we both know what you want," Cronus pressed. "A chance to touch a woman without sickening her and starting a plague."

Breath caught in Torin's throat, and Cronus knew that he had him. "Can you give me that chance?"

"In a way. What happened to the vial of water the angel Lysander gave you?" If there was but a single drop left, Torin could touch a woman, then feed her the drop-let and save her, for the water healed any wound on any creature. Would he be able to touch her after that? No, but his condition would have been met.

"Gone. And the angels won't give us any more."

Unfortunate, but understandable. The angels had to endure terrible, terrible things to even approach the River of Life from whence the water came. Cronus himself had never dared go near it. "There is a woman...I will force her to meet with you. You can touch her all you desire, and she will never sicken."

"Yeah, uh, no thanks. I want to pick my own woman."

"That, I cannot give you, and that was not the bargain. You wanted a woman to touch. I can give you one."

A long while passed in silence while Torin considered the offer. "Is she dead?"

"No. She lives."

"Old? A child?"

"No. She is neither too old nor too young."

"How will I be able to—"

"Answers were not part of the bargain, either. Decide!"

Finally Torin nodded, as Cronus had known he would. "Very well. You have a deal."

He did not allow himself to smile. When the All-Key left him, its powers would leave Rhea. He could imprison her. Have her at his mercy—or lack thereof.

What he did not mention to Torin: the All-Key wiped the memory of the one who gave it away. Except Cronus's, and probably, because of their connection, Rhea's. Cronus had created the key, and so had ensured it would never adversely affect him. However, no one else, Torin included, was extended the same courtesy.

When Torin bent his knees, as if to push himself into a stand, Cronus shook his head and reached down. "Stay there. This might hurt a bit."

ON THE OTHER SIDE of the heavens, Lysander stepped from the cloud he shared with his Harpy mate, Bianka, his wings spread and gliding just enough to leave him hovering in place.

"I am failing you," Zacharel said, the words gritted. The snowstorm that followed him constantly increased in ferocity, the flakes catching in his eyelashes, between the feathers of his wings, weighing them down.

"You have not failed me, and you *will not* fail me. I

have complete faith in you. Now, what report do you have of the girl?"

He rallied and said, "While she thinks she will be able to walk away from Paris in a few days, the pair has grown closer. Worse, she now carries his darkness." He'd seen the shadows swirling in her eyes after he'd carted Paris away from her.

"The war grows ever closer," Lysander replied. "She will still be of great use to us."

"Are you sure? Cronus has tricked her, convinced her to aid him. I expected him to lie to her, but I also expected her demon to catch on. He hasn't. And now that Paris has learned of his marriage to her, he will fight for her to the death." He'd thought Paris would never learn of the connection, which was the only reason Zacharel had helped tattoo him. Had he refused, Paris would have done it anyway and begun resisting him ahead of schedule.

"Cronus is a greedy fool, but Paris has surprised me. He might have shared his darkness with her, but she has shared some of her light with him." Lysander thought for a moment. "If he wants her as I want my Bianka, he will not part from her easily."

Too true. Passion, desire, lust, whatever you wanted to call that wild craze to mate, still remained completely out of Zacharel's realm of understanding, yet he could not deny *something* took hold of the pair whenever they so much as looked at each other.

Like magnets, Paris and Sienna were drawn to each other. They fought for each other, and parting would destroy them on some fundamental level. That he'd once thought to convince Paris to willingly walk away from her had been foolish. Force would be needed.

"Whatever you wish me to do," he said, bowing his head, "I will do."

Lysander expelled a weary sigh. "We need her. No matter what, we need her. Do whatever you must to convince her to side with us. If that's not enough, simply take her."

IN THE DEPTHS OF HELL, Kane sank in and out of consciousness. As vulnerable as he was when he slept, he much preferred it to the crippling pain of having his guts tucked back inside his body and his flesh stapled back together. Then, when the staples failed, having that battered flesh cauterized with liquid fire. He felt like someone had parked a bus on his chest, done some donuts, then let the passengers stampede off.

And the laughter...oh, the laughter from his demon. Disaster loved this. Loved the pain, and the degradation, and the helplessness. Kane imagined this was exactly how Legion had felt when she'd been stuck down here.

He should have supported her better. Should have tried to help her. Not that Kane wanted help himself. Part of him still wanted to die.

The horsemen—Black and Red—were saviors as well as tyrants. When he'd screamed as they "doctored" him, they'd next taped a ball gag in his mouth. When he'd thrashed, they had chained him down. They weren't cruel about it, though; they were matter-of-fact, as if they were doing him a favor. A reason he wouldn't take them with him when he kicked it.

Red stood over him now, blowing cigar smoke in his direction. "You up for a little poker yet?"

Whenever the pair realized he was awake, they always asked the same question. That one. He shook his head, unsure why a game of cards was so important to them.

"Bummer." Genuine disappointment shone in his features. "Soon, though."

Kane nodded in agreement because he didn't know what else to do, and closed his eyes. Without any resistance on his part, he drifted back to his favorite place, a black void of nothingness.

CHAPTER FORTY-ONE

THE NEXT MORNING, AFTER spending the entire night making love to Sienna, Paris showered, threw on clothes someone had brought him from home, weaponed up and ensured Sienna's crystal dagger rested on the nightstand, ready for her use if it proved necessary. Though he hated leaving her, he exited the bedroom and entered a whole new world.

Apparently Danika, the current All-Seeing Eye, had foreseen that terrible things would take place at the fortress in Budapest, and she'd sensed staying close to William was the only way to survive. So here they all were, one happy family—though how his friends had so quickly installed a weight room, a wet bar and a media room in the castle, Paris might never know.

He concentrated on the changes as he stalked the halls, so he wouldn't think about his woman sleeping peacefully in his bed. Naked, sated, rosy from his mouth and his hands and his body. Wouldn't think about the breathy sounds she'd made, the way she'd cried his name and begged for more. Wouldn't think about the way she'd made *him* beg for more. The way they fit, so damn perfectly.

Maybe at first he'd been obsessed with her without really knowing her. But he was learning her. Underneath her prim and proper exterior, and even underneath that iron spine of stubbornness, she was soft and gentle. Delicate. She loved with her whole heart, and she fought to protect what she considered hers. Hell, she sacrificed her body, her time and her life for what she considered hers.

She was dedicated. That temper of hers was a huge turn-on. Every time she'd tossed a drawer at him, he'd gotten harder. How many females were brave enough to challenge him in a contest of strength? Not many. But she had, because when she looked at him, she saw past the face and the hair and the stained, corrupt past. She saw a man. Just a man.

He almost turned around and strode back to his room. He wanted her arousal on his face, and her nails going down his back. He wanted to be branded by her in every way. Then, anyone who looked at him would know. *He* belonged to *her.* And—

What the hell was that hanging on the wall? He skidded to a stop. Just like at the fortress in Buda, there were portraits lining the corridor walls. Only, every single portrait was of Viola.

Viola in a gown. Viola in leather. Viola lying down. Viola standing up. Viola looking over her shoulder. An endless stream of poses.

"Breathtaking, aren't I." A statement, not a question, coming from directly behind him. Viola moved to his side, a vision of loveliness in a pink tank and hip-huggers. "I fetched them from one of my homes."

"Uh, yeah. Sure. Breathtaking."

"Which one is your fave?" She tapped a fingertip against her chin, studying them. "I'm having a hard time picking between that one and—all the others."

"Uh...let me think about it."

While he pretended to look them over, Sex purred, wanting to be closer to her. A second later, Paris was sporting massive wood. Shit. He raked a hand through his hair, shamed. Even this was like a betrayal to Sienna.

Why are you doing this to me? he demanded of his demon. *I thought we talked about this.*

Cheating feels good. I want to feel good.

Well, cheating's not gonna happen. And I want you to think about this for a moment. Every time we're with Sienna, it's a two-for-one deal. Or hell, maybe more than that. She's a human, a ghost, an ambrosia supply, a former Hunter and a demon, all wrapped into one tasty package. And if we are untrue to her, we lose her. And you will never get a quintupping again.

Why, she's an orgy waiting to happen.

Exactly.

A layered pause. *Oh...well...hmm.*

"Well?" Viola insisted.

Right. What would pacify her? "I can't actually pick. They're all equally amazing."

"I know, right. I'll have one delivered to your room. You and your hand can spend countless hours studying the details. I had a few surprises painted throughout. You're welcome." She whistled as she skipped away.

He stood there a moment, thinking about the fallen angel who desired her. He really should help throw the two together. Because really, was there a worse punishment for the guy than ending up with *that* for eternity? Food for thought.

He beat feet to the next hallway, and wasn't surprised to find Anya taking down the pictures of Viola and replacing them with pictures of herself. The decorator wars were on, he supposed.

"Gwen, Kaia, seriously," the (minor) goddess snapped, having trouble hanging on to a frame and a hammer at the same time as she balanced on a ladder. "This is the most important mission of your lives and you're riding pine on the sidelines? Get in here, you lazy bitches!"

Not wanting to be recruited, Paris ducked his head and kept walking, hands shoved in his pockets. From the corner of his eye, he caught a glimpse of the Harpy sisters in one of the bedrooms, studying a life-size—and warped—drawing of Galen. Guy had horns, crooked teeth and three fingers on each hand. His clown feet were too big for his body, and rather then genitals, he had an X. A really small X.

Gwen was pretending to pull back a crossbow, aiming for his heart, and Kaia was shaking her head no and pointing to the man's groin.

Sex started in with his purring. Out of habit, maybe, because a few seconds later, those purrs faded. Best part? Paris never got hard.

A wary sigh echoed inside his head. *If we do this relationship thing, I'll need her often.*

The demon was willing to try. Paris couldn't help himself. He gave a fist pump toward the ceiling. *Believe me, I know. And we'll have her a lot more than just "often."*

What an amazing damn day this was turning out to be. A megawatt smile bloomed. Yeah, he had a whole lot of shit to do. Talk to Cronus, spank the guy's wife, kill Galen while he was at his weakest and find Kane, but first, he wanted to catch up with his friends and visit the newest additions to the family.

Down on the next floor, there was a table piled high with snacks. Without slowing, he snagged an apple and a box of Strider's Red Hots. A bite of apple followed by a few of the cinnamon candies, and you had a mouthful of delicious.

A lot of his boys were congregated in the hallway outside of Ashlyn's room, eating, talking, laughing and more relaxed than he'd seen them in a long time. This was what their lives should always be like, he mused.

William was in the corner, a dark-haired girl tucked into his side, the pair of them locked in earnest conversation. Gilly was a teenager on the cusp of womanhood who'd suffered unimaginable abuse as a child. Danika had taken her in, and the girl had been leery around everyone but William. For some reason she'd adored the bastard from day one.

Maybe because she didn't yet know that William had recently slaughtered her entire family. Paris wondered how she'd react when the truth came out. And it would; it always did.

Gilly had hated her mother, stepfather and brothers, but deep down she'd probably loved them, too, and it was hard to forget that kind of feeling. Most likely scenario: she would leave, and William would follow her, protect her. He wouldn't be able to help himself. The need to protect ingrained itself in a man's very soul, and once he felt it, it was hard to forget, too.

Now that William had shed blood for her, that need would be even stronger, as Paris well knew. Every time he'd taken a life, his desperation to reach Sienna had increased. But he had her now. They were together, and he wasn't letting her go.

When Paris reached the pair, he tapped the girl on the shoulder to gain her attention. She yelped in surprise, slapped him out of reflex and sank deeper into William's side. Not wanting her to assume he was angry or that he would retaliate, he kept his gaze on the warrior. "What's the word on the three immortals?"

He could have stopped by their rooms, they were just down the hall, but he'd rather find out through the gossip train that was William's mouth and save time.

Willy frowned at him. "For frick's sake. Apologize."

Frick? "She doesn't need to apologize to me." He gave her a reassuring grin. "I was recently informed that I have a very slappable face."

"I wasn't talking to her, I was talking to you. Apologize for startling her."

Oh. "Sorry, Gilly."

She offered him a soft smile in return. She was a pretty little thing, with dark hair and dark eyes, a sun-kissed complexion and the kind of curves no father ever wanted his daughter to have. "No worries. My bad. I lost track of my surroundings."

"Well, I can see why you'd want to tune things out rather than pay attention to Willy's ugly mug."

She chuckled and Paris faced William, saying, "So, the immortals?"

William shrugged. "No change. I've tried everything I can think of, and believe me, it was very impressive sh—uh, crap, but a no-go all the same. They're locked tight in those bedrooms."

"Any word on Kane?"

"Uh, yeah, about that." With his free hand, William massaged the back of his neck. "He's alive and he's in hell, but he's out of enemy hands. You guys want him back, though, you'll have to go down there and get him."

Something was off in the guy's tone. "How do you know this?" Not even Amun had been able to get to the truth.

"Just do. Group's leaving tomorrow, and by the way, you weren't invited. My guess is they think you're a crazy psycho who makes out with himself, but that's just a guess."

Whatever. "Who's going?"

"Amun, Haidee, Cameo, Strider and Kaia."

Mostly girls. Were their taskforces changing or what? "You're not going down there with 'em?"

"As if. I mean, sure, the captors kind of made it a condition to Kane's release, but…nah. I don't think I will. Got stuff to do, you know. Me and my Aussie have an intimate evening planned."

Intimate with his conditioner. Figured. "Who are *the captors?* And why are they insisting you go?" He didn't bother touching on William's refusal, because honestly? That didn't mean shit. If his appearance was a condition for obtaining Kane's freedom, he'd make an appearance. End of story.

William looked down at Gilly, his expression all gentleness and reverence, and gave her a little push. "Be a darling and find me some gummy bears."

Her eyelids, usually at half-mast and always halfway to the bedroom when she gazed at the warrior, narrowed. "So patronizing." Still, she stomped away, just as he'd wanted, affording them a bit of privacy.

"Be sure to watch your mouth while you're searching for my sweets," William called after her. That's when Paris caught sight of his T-shirt. It read, Save a Virgin, Do Me Instead. "Talking back isn't attractive."

"You're right. I should respect my elders." She didn't turn back, but she did extend a hand and flip him off.

Paris chuckled. "What are you teaching that girl?"

Suddenly serious, William gritted, "How to survive. Now, returning to our convo. Kane's captors happen to be some serious badasses I used to know down there."

Badasses tripped a memory. "You're talking about the Horsemen of the Apocalypse, right? Because yeah, Amun might have mentioned you're their baby daddy."

"That damned Amun." Electric eyes gleamed with the promise of retribution. "What a sissy gossip!"

Back to cussing were they, all the darns and fricks out of the equation?

"Oh, and speaking of gossip," William continued, his expression now anticipatory. "Have you seen Blood and Gore yet?"

"Who?"

"Pistol and Shank. I rename them every hour or so. Keeps things fresh."

Yeah, but what were their real names? "That's why I'm here. I want to meet them."

"Well, why didn't you say so?" William threw an arm around his shoulders and ushered him through the sea of familiar bodies. "Out of the way, mutants. My boy P is going in next."

"But it's my turn," Cameo said, and damn if that wasn't a whine in her voice, mixing with all the world's misery. She stepped in front of them to block their path to the door, her arms crossed over her chest. "Did you know that seven thousand babies die every year of—"

"*That's* why you're getting skipped." William offered her a sugar-sweet smile. "Besides, I delivered those hellions and almost had to take an eternal dirt nap because of it. I pick the order, and I say Paris is next."

Cameo frowned. She was one of the most beautiful women Paris had ever seen. More beautiful, even, than Viola, with long black hair and liquid silver eyes. Lips as plump and dewy as a rose.

"Did you know that about one percent of all births are stillborn?" she asked. The whine was gone, leaving only the misery.

She was also a major downer.

Stab me in the heart already, Paris thought. Because she played hostess to the demon of Misery, the sound of her voice was always enough to tear a guy up. Throw in her death statistics, which she'd been offering unsolicited more and more, and watch a party deflate like a balloon.

"Someone get this girl a lollipop and shove it deep in her mouth, stat," William shouted, urging Paris past her to the door. He didn't knock, but barreled inside. "All right, ladies. Our turn."

Reyes was sitting beside the bed, dark and menacing, with Strider the blond giant at his left. Both warriors were cooing at the thickly blanketed bundle of joy Reyes held.

Ashlyn was propped up on the bed, pale, shaky and clearly weak. Maddox sat beside her, holding the other bundle.

"Out," William added. "Paris wants to see Smith and Wesson."

"Don't call them that," Maddox said. Paris had never heard the keeper of Violence use such a gentle tone. It was more startling than being punched in the face.

"What do you want me to call them? Shits and Giggles? Fists and Kneecap? Nah, I don't like that one. Hammer and Nails? Dude, these kids are hard-core gangster. They need kick-A names, not that blah, blah sh— crap you gave them."

Slowly Reyes stood, waited for William to close the distance and gently placed the bundle in his arms. The dark warrior patted Paris on the shoulder as he left, and Strider did the same. Only, he stopped and said, "Meet me in the gym when you're done," before leaving.

Battling a wave of foreboding, Paris nodded. Then the two were gone, the door closed behind them, and he pushed the upcoming chat from his mind. He made his way to William, who seemed perfectly at ease holding such a fragile being. Only in secret had Paris ever allowed himself to contemplate having a family, because no way had he wanted to father a kid with a one-night stand. Now, with Sienna, who had been denied the chance to be a mother...

He wanted to give her this.

At William's side, he peered down at the first demon-human hybrid infant to join their crew—and what he saw nearly shocked the piss out of him.

"Gorgeous little fiend, isn't she?" William said, beaming down. He tickled her belly. "Oh, yes, she is. Yes, she really is."

Gurgling happily, the baby waved her little fists. Her eyes were open and clear, a vibrant, crackling orange-gold, and so freaking intelligent, despite the fact that she peered up at William with total, absolute adoration. And yeah, she was gorgeous. Already had a cap of honey-colored hair, the corkscrew curls spiking up from her head. But the real shocker? She had a mouthful of teeth. Really, really sharp teeth. And those cute little fists? Topped off by curling claws.

"Will she ever be able to pass as human?" he asked quietly, not wanting the probably sensitive mother to hear.

"Maybe, maybe not," Ashlyn answered anyway. "Time will tell. Either way, they are both beautiful beyond imagining."

Figured that she'd heard him. She herself might be human, but she could hear any conversation anywhere, no matter how many years had passed. That was her curse. And weren't the twins in for a real treat, never able to hide anything from mom.

"What's her name?" he asked.

"Ever," William said with no small amount of disgust.

Ever did a fist pump in the air. With pride? Or anger?

"The name is perfect, just like her," Ashlyn said. Her

eyelids were fluttering closed, as if she were having trouble staying awake.

"Go on to sleep, sweetheart," Maddox told her. "I'll take care of everything."

"Thank you," she said as she sighed, head already lolling to the side.

"Want to hold her?" William asked Paris.

"Ashlyn? No, thanks." Maddox would brain him, same as Paris would brain any warrior who tried to hold Sienna. Not that any besides William and maybe Lucien could even see her at the moment.

William rolled his eyes. "You know what I meant. The *baby*. Ever."

"Oh, uh, yeah. I totally knew what you meant."

"Do you have to be so loud?" Maddox snapped in that quiet, gentle voice so at odds with the roughness of his features.

Paris held up his hands, palms out, whispering, "No way on the holding of the kidlet." He was too big, and too hard to do anything but bruise the little girl. Besides, Ever growled in his direction, her lips peeling back from her fangs, and it was very clear she was happy where she was.

He moved around to the other side of the bed, where Maddox held the boy. Of course, the warrior beamed with pride as he smoothed the blanket from the kid's face. Like Ever, the baby looked months old. He had a cap of black hair and his eyes were the same shade of violet as his daddy's and diamond-hard. Two little horns peeked from his skull, and there were patches of scales on his hands. Those scales were black and as smooth as glass.

With focused intensity, the boy studied Paris. And Paris had no doubt the kid had sized him up in a single heartbeat, learning his weaknesses, his flaws, and his bad habits, and was preparing for attack.

"What's his name?"

"Urban," William answered before Maddox could, and again he was all about the disgust.

Ever and Urban. Cute, in a Hollyweird sort of way. "What made you pick those particular names?"

"We didn't," Maddox said. "They did."

His eyes widened. "They can speak?"

"No, but they are very good at communicating."

And that would be…how? "So, I hear the birth was troublesome. How'd William save the day?"

Maddox stiffened, even as William shook his head and placed Ever in the bassinet beside the bed. When he straightened, William rocked his hand over his neck in a slicing motion. A kill-that-line-of-convo-*now* gesture.

"That goshdarn mothertrucking a-hole cut my woman up, ripped the babies out and sewed her back together." Maddox's nostrils flared, so heavily did he breathe. "Without anesthesia."

William popped his jaw. "There wasn't time. They were clawing their way out, and waiting any longer would have killed your Ashlyn for sure. And better a dagger slice, which is smooth, than the savage tearing that comes with claws. And by the way, you're welcome. They're all alive."

Well, all right, then. Like a coward, Paris abandoned ship, leaving William to endure Maddox's wrath on his own. He made his way to the gym on the bottom floor. Strider was there, as promised, running the treadmill like a man possessed. Which he was.

Blond hair was plastered to his scalp, and rivers of sweat ran down his deeply tanned skin.

The white-haired Torin was at the far side of the room,

bench-pressing enough weight to have fractured the marble floor. Shock rooted him in place for a moment. Torin never approached the masses, too afraid of someone accidentally touching him.

How'd he get here, anyway? Last Paris had heard, Disease had turned down Lucien's offer for air travel. And when the hell had Torin gotten so ripped? He usually holed up in his room, covered from neck to foot in black. Now, without a shirt, Paris saw the guy had the chiseled body of someone who could kick his ass.

Both men stopped what they were doing when they realized he'd entered. Paris whipped off his shirt, his gun holster and his blades, stored them on a bench and moved to the treadmill beside Strider.

"What'd you want to talk to me about?" He hit a few buttons, and then the thing was lifting and moving, giving him a grueling incline and a sprinting pace that felt unbelievably good. He hadn't exercised like this in a long time.

"What's this I hear about you having an invisible Hunter on the premises?" Strider asked, catching a towel Torin had thrown at him. He wiped his face, his gaze remaining on Paris. "The Hunter possessed by Wrath, I might add."

Shoulda known. "She's not a Hunter, not anymore, and she's not up for discussion."

"Like hell she isn't. My woman is here."

"Yeah, and your woman can take care of herself."

Pride flickered in Strider's navy eyes. "True enough. Fact remains, though, that an unseen enemy is the most dangerous. Your girl can do all kinds of damage to everyone here."

He cranked the speed up another thousand notches,

until his boots were hammering into the base and rattling the entire machine. "She's not out to hurt us."

"Yeah, so, I've got some wiring to do," Torin said from behind them. "You boys have at each other." Footsteps, and then it was just the two of them.

"You're telling me the girl who drugged you, who watched your torture, is no longer a threat to you or anyone?" Strider asked skeptically. "Please."

"We worked it out." Sweat beaded on his skin, too, dripping, dripping. His muscles burned just right, soaking up the strain, loving it.

"In the sheets, no doubt, but all that means is that you're thinking with something other than your brain. You gotta know that."

Don't challenge him, don't challenge him, don't you dare challenge him. You had to be careful around Strider. His demon took exception to any hint of confrontation, and then Strider had to battle it out, doing everything in his power to knock you senseless, or he'd suffer for days as punishment.

"Everyone accepted Haidee," Paris reminded him, "and she was a Hunter."

"Now she's the living embodiment of Love. It's kinda hard *not* to like and trust her. Your girl, we can't see or hear her. Can't judge her actions and her words for ourselves. Can't see how she is with you. And do you really need another *you're thinking with your man junk* speech?"

Darkness...rising... "I'm asking you to step off," Paris said, "before things get nasty and we have to work this out the hard way." If he had to go the challenge route to stop his friend from verbally slamming his woman, he would.

Silence. Then, a grisly, "I feel—"

"A burning sensation when you pee?" *Now you're just being mean.*

"Real mature," Strider said, but he calmed down a notch. "Me and you, we got history. More than the others know, more than the two of us ever want to acknowledge. But we both know it's one of the reasons we went our separate ways when the two groups split for while, me with Sabin and you with Lucien."

Heat seared Paris's cheeks, and it had nothing to do with physical strain. "We said we'd never talk or think about it." And he'd always kept up his end of that agreement.

"Apparently, times change. You were weak, dying. There were no humans around, and you refused to let any of us help you."

"Shut up." His happy day was going down the drain fast. "Just shut up."

"So, my demon took up the challenge, and I took care of you. Now I'm asking you to take care of your friends in turn. Get rid of the girl," Strider went on, ignoring the demand. "We lack one artifact, just one, and once we get it back we can start searching for Pandora's box. We can finally save ourselves. Not only can she spy on us, steal from us and hurt our more vulnerable members, she could ruin our future. Just think about it. For me."

Strider threw his towel in the hamper and stomped from the room.

CHAPTER FORTY-TWO

FOR SIENNA, THE NEXT few days passed in a blissful haze punctuated by moments of mourning. Except for two things, all was right in her world. But she wasn't going to think about those two things. She would erupt into one of her rare and shocking rages, and rip the entire castle apart.

Instead, she would think about the fact that Paris *adored* her. She would think about all the times she and Paris had made love, and how each time he had been more frantic to get inside her than the last. He'd taken her in ways that scandalized, delighted and thrilled, and in the quiet afterglow, they had talked.

No subject had been off-limits. They discussed the Hunters—where certain facilities were, the names of some of the higher officers, the location of the cavern where Galen supposedly met with Rhea and the pair performed rituals for "the greater good." Then they'd talked about themselves, about where they would travel and what they'd do if there hadn't been a war to fight.

Paris picked the mountains, with the cold and the snow and a soft rug in front of a fireplace. She picked the beach, wanting to watch him rise from the water, glittering droplets sliding along the ropes of his stomach and catching in her new favorite place on his body—because the waves would have stolen his swimsuit.

Of course, earlier this morning he'd strode out of the

shower, dripping wet, no towel in sight, with a wicked smile on his face, and she'd laughed at his antics (after she caught her breath). She was desperately trying to guard her heart against him despite his demand that they stay together, because she knew she still had to leave him for Galen, that she had to stop Rhea from taking the Titan throne, that she couldn't kill her greatest enemy because doing so would kill Cronus, and as he'd said, if he died, chaos would reign and *Paris* would die.

The only way to save him was to control Galen, and thereby Rhea. Not the best revenge, but it was all she could allow herself.

She wished Skye could have met Paris, wished the girl could have seen the good in him, that man and demon were not truly one and the same, that the demon was dark and dangerous, destructive, but the man was fun and caring, worthy of respect. Just like Sienna was not the sum total of Wrath's deeds, but a woman who fought for what was right.

Once upon a time, Sienna had considered giving the demon back to Aeron. But if she did, she would die—for real and forever—and she would be unable to avenge her sister, even in the smallest way. Plus, she needed him. He still hadn't figured out what was "wrong" with Skye's death.

Don't cry, Enna. Boys are stupid, Mama said so, and if that fathead Todd doesn't want to go to the dance with you, he's the stupidest ever!

I miss you so much, Skye. Sienna turned the corner—and barreled into a speeding golf cart. After crash-landing on her butt, she saw the cart was blue with orange flames painted on the sides, and the minor goddess of the Afterlife/keeper of Narcissism was at the wheel.

"Sorry, I'm sorry." Most times Sienna didn't bother watching where she was going, because only Paris, Viola and Lucien could see and touch her. Everyone and everything else she ghosted through and no one ever even knew. But because the cart belonged to Viola, Sienna could feel the metal that had just flattened her lungs.

"I'm late," Viola said, waving a piece of paper in the air. "You, too? Do you need a ride?"

As always, Wrath shot Sienna's mind full of images. Viola, breaking hearts. Viola, double-crossing others to save herself. Viola, unconcerned by the pain she left in her wake.

Punish...

A whisper rather than an urge. For some reason, Wrath had been on his best behavior lately, never trying to overtake her, his hunger under control though she'd done nothing to feed him.

"Sienna. Female...ghost person. Do you need a ride? Time is a serious issue right now."

"I would love a ride." She needed a few minutes alone with the woman, so this was actually perfect. "I've been looking for you." No longer did she bear any ill will toward the woman. After all, Sienna had watched Paris interact with her, and the guy could barely mask his impatience to escape.

But having done all of that watching, Sienna now knew how to deal with the goddess. She also knew Viola was one of the few people who wouldn't curse her outright, who would hear her out.

"Well, hop on and stop standing there all lost in your thoughts. I don't want to miss the good part."

Sienna didn't ask what "the good part" was, because the woman would have explained in minute detail about how everything pertained to her. She simply unfolded from the floor and slid into the plush leather seat, careful of her wings.

"Well?" the goddess prompted, stomping on the pedal. They jolted into motion, cutting corners, honking at nothing, flashing their lights. "What did you want to talk to me about?"

To begin: flattery. "As intelligent and powerful as you are, you're the only one capable of helping me."

"Well, of course I am. Here's a well-known fact. I'm more than made of awesome. I am the original awesome." From behind the wheel, Viola flicked her pale hair over her shoulder. She wore a gown of shimmery gold, the material cinched just under her breasts and flaring at her hips. Red-carpet worthy, for sure. "Soooo?"

"I'm trying to figure out how best to ask for what I need."

"Try opening your mouth and forming words. That's what I do, and I can assure you my methods are always stellar."

Sienna ran her tongue over her teeth, not allowing herself to issue a snappy retort. She didn't think Viola meant to be so haughty, but hello, a girl could only take so much. "Well, I'm running out of time."

And there was the main reason for her recent string of temper tantrums. Her time here was ticking, ticking away. Soon she would have to leave. Not just because she had heard some of Paris's friends plotting her downfall, and not just because those same friends hated her guts and would never trust or forgive her, but because she really was going to Galen, keeping him away from Cronus, so that Cronus could keep Rhea away from his throne, no matter how sickening the tasks she had to perform.

"Do you want me to buy you more time?" Viola asked,

as if such a thing were possible. They reached the stairs. Without pause, she took them. Bounce, bounce, bounce. "You'd have to pay me back. I mean, with two-hundred-percent interest, but—"

"No, I...well, when I leave, Paris will weaken." Her head slammed into the roof of the vehicle. *Oh, please, please don't let my next death be in a tragic golf cart accident.* "I don't know if you know this, but he has to have sex every day or his body shuts down. His demon is...needy, you know."

"Yada, yada, boring." Landing smoothly, the cart erupted into full speed. (Twenty-five miles per hour.)

She bit her tongue to hold in her retort. "When I leave I want you to make sure Paris sleeps with the women Lucien brings him, and that he *keeps* sleeping with them."

And there was the second reason for her temper tantrums. Due to pressure from Sienna's staunchest haters, Lucien kept disappearing and reappearing with a new woman in the hope that one would entice Paris away from her.

While Paris could easily ignore his friends, the persistent and determined Viola would find a way to get her way. Otherwise, she would be a failure, and the goddess would never allow herself to be a failure.

"What I'm hearing is, I'm the only thing standing between your man and his certain death," Viola said. "So what's in it for me if I save him?"

For a moment, Sienna couldn't reply; there was a giant lump in her throat. This was killing her. She wanted Paris all to herself, now and always, and oh, she really did love the man, didn't she? Body, heart and soul, she loved him. She'd been falling slow and steady, but now she was flat on her face, nothing but a puddle of love.

He was everything to her. Her light when things became too dark. When she cried, he comforted her. When she laughed, he laughed with her. He treated her as if she were a special treasure. He protected her, cared about every ache and pain she might experience.

She would tear the world apart to keep him safe. She would willingly suffer without him, as long as she knew he was out there, alive.

"What would you like from me?" Sienna wasn't going to quibble. What the goddess wanted, she would give. It was as simple as that.

"You're Wrath, right? Well, when I call on you to slay one of my enemies, you have to slay him. No questions, no hesitation."

"As long as the enemy in question isn't someone Paris or his friends know and like. Or want alive."

The goddess thought for a moment, nodded. "We have ourselves a deal."

"Good. Now, I have one other request for you." She outlined what she wanted.

Viola shot her a sly smile. "Wicked, and quite shocking coming from you. I had no idea you were into that. You look so mousy. But it's always the quiet ones, isn't it?"

"Will you do it?"

"You'll owe me two slayings, same conditions."

"Done." It was done.

"Now, hold on tight because I'm cranking this baby up. I'm just certain they won't start without me, but these Lords sometimes defy logic, so you never know."

"Oh, good." A woman with curly dark hair, a face as innocent as a cherub's and wings of the purest white appeared just in front of them. "I found you."

Viola slammed on the breaks, and the cart skidded to

a stop mere inches from crushing the newcomer under the tires. "What's with all the ladies jumping in front of me and keeping me from where I want to go? Jealous much?"

"I seek Sienna."

"Me?" Sienna's heart suddenly felt as if it had been injected with adrenaline. That had been a close call, sure, but that wasn't why she was palpitating. "Heaven," she whispered, the reverent yearning in her voice flowing straight from her demon.

"Yes, you. I'm Olivia," the angel said with a sweet smile. A white robe draped her from shoulders to ankles, making her look as if she'd just stepped from a dream.

Viola jumped out of the cart and hurried past Olivia. "Have fun girls, I'm needed elsewhere." Pale hair streaming behind her, she disappeared into the ballroom about a yard ahead.

"I recognize you," Sienna said, even though the two of them had never met. She stood on shaky legs, closed the distance—*heaven, my heaven*—and reached out, pinching a strand of those curls between her fingers. Soft, silky. "Wrath loves you, I think."

Olivia's smile went full-on sunshine as she scratched Sienna behind her ear. "How's my darling boy doing?"

Wrath purred like a kitten.

"He's, uh, good."

"I'm glad. He really is a sweetheart, isn't he?"

Wrath?

The demon rolled to his back, kicked up his legs and shook as great tides of rapture swept over him.

"Let's you and me chat later, all right?" Olivia said, arm dropping to her side. While Wrath pouted like a toddler, the angel added, "Aeron sent me to find you. He wanted to speak to you himself, but he can't see you and conversing with the woman who has his Wrath through a third party would be a little too painful. Maybe one day. But I digress. He's ready to leave this castle and hunt for Legion, but won't because Paris is about to have an aneurism. At least, that's what Aeron said, and he thinks you're the only one who can calm his boy down."

Paris. Worry instantly flooded her, her demon's preoccupation with the angel overshadowed. "Where is he?"

"Just follow the trail Viola blazed." Stepping to the side, Olivia motioned toward the ballroom.

Sienna darted into motion, flying through the open doorway and once again stopping dead in her tracks. A group of the warriors and their mates stood under a banner that said only INTERVENTION in big block letters. They each held a piece of paper. Viola had taken her place in the center, shifting eagerly, ready to say her piece.

Sienna's gaze locked on the warrior named Aeron, the man who'd once hosted Wrath. He had closely cropped dark hair, beautiful violet eyes, and his body, which had once been covered in the tattooed images of the victims of his blood rages, was now slowly being covered with tattoos of his angel.

Seeing him, Wrath went crazy inside Sienna's head, wanting to reach out, to touch the warrior. *Friend. My friend.*

I know, but now's not the time to catch up with him. Honestly? She wasn't sure any time would be right. The guy scared her. He looked like he ate kittens for breakfast and thumb tacks for lunch. His dinner wasn't something she dared contemplate. Organs might be involved.

Wrath pouted. The demon had wanted back inside of Aeron as much as Sienna had wanted to get rid of him. But she had changed her mind, and she hoped Wrath had, too. He wasn't begging to escape her. For all she knew, he was as addicted to Paris as she was.

Friend. Talk to friend.

Soon, she promised. Wrath whimpered, and she had to force herself to look away. Paris stood in front of the group, his back to Sienna. His sun-bronzed skin was bare from the waist up, and his muscles were knotted. At his sides, his hands were fisted.

Anya was reading her letter out loud. "—you're okay, I guess. I mean, if Lucien says you're good people, you're good people. I think you've got a really hot body with a lot of delicious brawn and sinew, and even though I wouldn't do you without having an emergency medical exam afterward, a lot of women with low self-esteem would totally hit that."

"Anya," Lucien said with a truckload of exasperation.

She glanced up at him, all innocence. "What? You said start the letter with praise before going into the root of the problem. Now zip it so I can finish. You already got to read yours." She cleared her throat, glanced back down at the paper. "Making out with an invisible woman is a disease. And really creepy. If I see you with your hands squeezing air one more time, I'm going to sandpaper my corneas."

"Enough," Paris said with quiet menace.

"My turn," Viola said.

Ignoring both of them, the lithe goddess of Anarchy continued. "Add in the fact that Inviso-babe is a Hunter, and you've got a recipe for *oh, shit.* Which isn't good for your health. Or ours. Mainly ours. That is why we humbly request that you enter some sort of treatment program before that woman enters you in a death program with guns, knives and a rack. And by *rack* I don't mean boobs."

Wow, that hurt. It shouldn't. Sienna had brought this on herself, deserved it one hundred percent, and had done nothing to earn their trust. *Still.* Ouch. Her lover's friends had hosted an intervention to get Sienna out of his life.

One of Paris's hands slid back, around his waist, his fingers curling around the hilt of a knife.

He was going to blow a fuse, she thought, and she didn't want him at war with his friends because of her. Not now, not ever. So, yeah, she was leaving. Sooner rather than later.

Her chest constricted, heralding the sharp lances of pain from a breaking heart. Didn't matter, though. She would take one more day with him. Just one. Then, bye-bye forever. "Paris," she said, doing her best to mask her hurt.

He spun, those electric-blues she loved so much crackling with fury, the malicious shadows dancing through their depths.

Gently she said, "Come up to the roof with me," and waved him over. "I need to practice my flying." Truth, and the reason she wasn't leaving the fortress right this second, was instead allowing herself this extra day with him. She had to be prepared for anything. And, yeah, she wanted to say goodbye properly—in bed. "No need to worry about the vines there. The gargoyles eat the walls clean, and William's blood is on the outer rail, I checked, so the shadows won't bother us, either."

"My friends are… They need…" He was dragging oxygen through his nose so intensely his nostrils were flaring.

"No, they don't. You are not going to be mad at them over this." A command she had no power to enforce, but one she would see through.

"Yes, I am."

Behind him, Viola relayed the conversation only she and Lucien could hear, clearly thrilled to be the center of attention. Sienna tuned her out. Only Paris mattered right now.

More forcefully, she said, "Paris, I'm not offended by this." She was destroyed. "Now come here. I need a cheerleader, and I'm thinking you'll look great in a skirt, holding poms."

He didn't crack a smile. That unholy, malevolent rage still held him in a tight grip. So, really, there was only one other thing do to.

"Catch me," she said, sprinting to him. He would never forgive himself if he fought his loved ones.

"No, don't come near me while I'm like...*this*. Humph."

She'd launched herself at him. Those strong arms did indeed catch her, winding around her and clamping on like shackles. Tremors vibrated from him and into her.

Acting fast, she nipped at his ear. "If you hurt them, you'll get blood on my castle walls—well, more blood, and I'll be very upset." Only once before had she ever tried to use feminine wiles, and that had been the first time they met. Now she lifted her head just enough for him to see her face, and batted her lashes. "Please come to the roof with me. Please."

He peered at her for a long while, silent, before finally relaxing. He pressed a kiss straight into her mouth, daring the quickest of tastes, the tease, before striding out with her still clutched in his arms.

"My eyes," Anya whined. "Oh, my eyes."

"I think we just made a huge mistake," Lucien said gravely.

Paris never looked back and neither did Sienna.

CHAPTER FORTY-THREE

THE MOMENT PARIS STEPPED onto the roof, he sensed the evil waiting to attack. Thanks to William's blood, the shadows couldn't get inside the castle or pass the rail, just as Sienna had said, but what waited for him wasn't exactly a shadow.

Wanting no part of the coming action, Sex retreated faster than ever.

Palming his crystal blades—nope, make that *blade,* he had just the one now—Paris maneuvered Sienna to her feet and behind him. The sky was a strip of black velvet with no pinprick of stars, the moon a crimson hook in the corner, just as before. Moisture clung to the air, hot in spots, cold in others.

Either Sienna sensed the menace, too, or she knew not to distract him. She remained quiet. His gaze arrowed over, lit on a darker patch of onyx, and shit, another dark patch, then another, gliding together, coalescing, elongating...until a man stood before him, shrouded by the black, the mist like a veil in front of him.

Sienna gasped. In fascination or horror, he wasn't sure.

Guy was handsome, if you liked serial killers, with cold black eyes, more muscles than even Paris sported, and shoulders wide enough to take down the entire first line of defense in a game of touch football.

Paris crouched, a coiled snake ready to dart and bite.

Dude had made a mistake, approaching now. Since Paris had walked into that intervention and realized his friends were still gunning for him to ditch Sienna, fury had been a seething tide inside him.

He understood their reasons. He did. And he couldn't blame them. But doing what they'd done out in the open, just to hurt her, was taking things too far.

He commanded his crystal to become a weapon capable of killing such a creature, and the thing instantly morphed into—a klieg? Someone play whaa whaa whaa for Debbie Downer, because seriously. Kinda felt like he was going to a shootout with, well, a freaking klieg.

Shadow Man laughed, the sound all creepiness and no joy. "I know what you wonder. I can bypass the blood, yes. And I will if I must. My phantoms feed from the immortals, and that is payment rendered for their stay. Yet now you house the Lord of the Dark, their enemy, and keep my boys from their due. That is unacceptable."

"Your phantoms aren't feeding on my friends." He recalled the warrior lying in a pool of his own blood, what was left of his insides spilled on the floor. The prisoner's pain had been unbearable to witness, so Paris could just imagine what the guy had felt.

"Other arrangements must be made, or I will force you out of my realm. You will not like my methods, I assure you."

There was a time for physical confrontation, and a time for bargaining. "What else would they like to eat?"

"Immortals." Clipped, angry. "Only immortals."

"Then we've got a problem." He inched backward, edging Sienna to the door.

Shadow Man lurched forward, that dark mist stretching and gliding like wings. Paris swung the flashlight, his thumb flipping the on switch. White light cut through the darkness, but just before reaching his opponent, the man rolled through the air and out of the way.

When he stilled, they faced off. Paris twirled the thin flashlight in his palm. "That all you got? Huh?" A taunt meant to buy Sienna enough time to blast inside. He hoped she understood that, but he couldn't hear footsteps, couldn't hear the door slam.

"If I showed you what I've got, it would be the last thing you *ever* saw."

"Prove it."

Like that, they were on each other, a choreographed dance straight from *Star Wars*. Funny that they both knew the moves. Paris used the klieg like a light saber, twirling the golden stream as he contorted his body left and right to dodge the sashay of those misty wings.

Finally, contact. When the light sliced through one of Shadow Man's legs, there was a sizzle, a rise of steam, and the big guy released a firing-squad shout, his anger like little bullets that pelted against Paris's mind, causing him to stumble.

That stumble cost him.

One of those dark wings whipped out and hit his arm with so much force the flashlight flew from his grip. Not mist, after all. Then that big body engulfed him, closing around him. Screams, thousands upon thousands of screams, echoed around him. So loud his eardrums burst and warm blood poured down his lobes.

Releasing a scream of his own, he covered his ears and fell to his knees. Ants were crawling all over him, surely eating at his flesh, ripping it away, consuming him bite by tasty bite.

Another firing-squad shout sounded, and the darkness instantly lifted from him. Took him a moment to orient himself, and what he saw made him want to vomit. Shadow Man was a few feet away, and Sienna was holding him off with the flashlight. Their mouths were moving, but Paris couldn't hear what they were saying.

Until...*boom,* his eardrums healed and the volume came back on in an explosion of noise.

"—how many would you be willing to settle for... consuming?" Sienna was saying, trying not to reveal her disgust.

"Five. A day."

"They never got five before! One," she snapped. "A week."

"Three. A day."

"Three. A week."

A moment of silence before Shadow Man nodded. "Agreed. First payment must be given *today.*"

"Yes, but only if all of us—the Lords, their loved ones, the babies, the immortals, me—are safe, no matter where we go in this realm or what we do."

Another moment of silence, another nod. "And so the deal is made. But best you hurry, female. I might change my mind before the first payment is delivered." With that, the black mist thinned, broke apart and disappeared altogether.

Sienna rushed to Paris's side and sank to her knees, patting him down, checking for injuries.

"Are you okay?"

He hung his head. He hadn't saved her, hadn't helped her. She'd had to save him. She'd had to help him. He'd let her down in so many ways. What kind of warrior *was* he?

"I'm sorry, baby."

"What? Why?" She handed him the flashlight.

A quick mental command, and the crystal blade returned. He stashed the thing at his waist. "I let you down.

You could have been hurt." And Zacharel had warned him about that, hadn't he? That Paris's temper would get the better of him and he would hurt his woman. He'd thought that meant he would strike at her, which he knew would never happen. But, no. The angel had known better. His temper would cause him to lose focus, to allow *others* to hurt her.

Yeah. Well. That was so not happening again. He'd keep himself level no matter what the hell he had to do.

"Paris, you've never let me down," she said with feeling.

Yeah, he had, but that stopped now. His thigh muscles burned like a son of a bitch as he stood. He helped her do the same. Inside the castle, he tucked her into a corner, checked the only window in the small alcove to make sure William's blood was still smeared over the top—it was—then cupped her cheeks.

"Stay here for me, okay? I've got to tell Lucien to find us three acceptable, uh, meals."

"They don't have to be immortal," she said. "He finally admitted that immortals taste better, but anyone will do."

Then Paris knew exactly who to use. Last he'd looked, there were Hunters stashed in their Budapest dungeon.

"Who are—"

"Don't you worry about that." If she knew the men, well, he wasn't sure how she'd react. "In fact, why don't you go to our room instead of staying here? I'll join you in a bit. Okay?" He kissed her before she could reply, and left her there.

Didn't take him long to locate Lucien. The warrior was still in the ballroom, and when he caught sight of Paris he apologized all over himself, his mismatched eyes filled with regret.

"We'll talk about the intervention later. Right now I need you to do something."

He explained what he needed, and the warrior was Johnny-on-the-spot, disappearing and returning a few minutes later with a Hunter clutched in each hand. Humans were easier to transport than immortals.

The men, both in their late thirties by the looks of them, were grimy, weak and had no fight left. Paris claimed them, and Lucien went back for a third.

Maybe this should have settled heavily on his shoulders, but these men had been captured while trying to slaughter his friends and their lovers. They would have cut the throats of the females without a moment's hesitation.

They deserved what they got.

When Lucien returned, they muscled their loads up the stairs and back into that small alcove. Sienna hadn't moved an inch, and Paris cursed under his breath. But she didn't say anything when she spotted his burdens, even though her mouth opened as if she had plenty to unleash. She just watched with wide eyes as he and Lucien stepped onto the roof.

"Stay," he commanded, shutting the door in her face. He didn't want her to see what happened next.

He and Lucien approached the edge and looked down. A whole lot of airtime before reaching the rocky, blood-soaked ground. Whatever. He still wasn't gonna feel bad. But he did wonder, again, if Sienna knew these guys. If she'd understand why he'd picked them. If she'd understand that he would use the information she'd given him to find more Hunters, to bring them here and use them in the same way, for as long as necessary.

Drop them, a disembodied voice he now recognized said on a sudden wind.

Only then did the Hunters begin to struggle. Paris and Lucien shared a moment of oh, shit before shoving them over. Shadows immediately darted from the sky, surrounding the men, catching them, and then devouring them. Screams, more pain-filled than the ones he'd heard while inside Shadow Man, rent the night. Then, silence.

And so the deal is sealed, another wind proclaimed. *You are safe. For now.*

He wasn't sure he could trust the Shadow Man, but Sienna would have caught a lie, so there you go. "Thanks," he said to Lucien.

"Of course." A pause, a sigh. "Listen. I *am* sorry about what happened, and I will talk to the others. I've never liked what we were doing to you, how we were pushing you, and I'll make sure your woman is respected. She's who you want, she's who you'll get."

His throat tightened up. "Thanks," he repeated.

Lucien drilled a hand on his shoulder, a love pat with more strength than he probably realized, before taking off. As he exited, Sienna entered.

"Hey," she said, expression blank.

"Hey," he replied. Trepidation, foreboding, yeah, he felt them.

"So the toll's been paid?"

He nodded mutely.

"Good. I saw their sins. Those men were awful, had done terrible things. Wrath wanted a go at them."

That was it? That was her response? She wasn't going to question him, castigate him? Was just going to accept? "I love you," he said. He couldn't hold the words back. There was no hiding the truth any longer, not even from himself.

Her jaw dropped. Those beautiful hazels were once

again all about the emerald, the chocolate completely overshadowed. He was more into this woman than he'd ever been into another. So into her that he would die for her. Willingly, happily.

She just fit him. Made him happy. Relaxed him, excited him, challenged him.

"I—I…" Twin pink circles appeared on her cheeks. Arousal, maybe. At least, he hoped.

"No, don't say anything." He motioned her over, said huskily, "Just come here."

She stumbled over to him, and he drew her close for a hug. Breathing deeply, he drank in her tropical scent, letting it brand him, remake him. There wasn't anyone or anything that could keep him from this woman. She was his. Now and always.

He placed the sweetest of kisses against the wildly hammering pulse at the base of her neck. "Let's practice your flying, okay?"

"O-okay."

She loved him back; she had to love him back. If she didn't, he would seduce her, romance her and woo her until she did. *Most important battle of my life.*

He set her away from him, and they spent the next few hours working on extending her wings properly and quickly enough, as well as getting her feet off the ground. Having never flown himself, he repeated the things Aeron had told him, the things he'd learned simply from watching the warrior, and he was happy to note Sienna made progress. But shit, he knew there was a lot he didn't know.

Eventually Sex came out of hiding, enjoying the contact, pushing Paris to take things to the next level.

Not yet. This is too important.

You told me "often."

And you've been getting often, you stupid shit.

"She'll never learn to sustain flight like that." Familiar male voice. Behind him.

Paris didn't bother turning around. "What do you suggest?" He was willing to take suggestions in this, and only this.

Zacharel sidled up to him, his fingers stroking his stubble-free chin. "I can only teach her the way I was taught. She must stand at the edge of the roof and spread her wings as far as she can get them."

"What if I fall?" she gasped. "I won't be able to catch myself in the air."

"You will not fall," the angel said, and the layer of truth in his voice was as convincing as ever.

Sienna met Paris's eyes, and he nodded. Flying was important. Flying could one day save her soul. Because yes, as the shadows had proven, even souls could be ravaged.

Gulping, she brushed past him. The moment her fingers trailed over his, he grabbed on to them, linked their hands and decided to walk with her. Her trembling increased with every step.

"Afraid of heights, baby?" he asked, when they reached the flat edge.

"I shouldn't be, but that's a long way down."

"S'all good. We won't let anything happen to you. Promise."

"Step back," Zacharel commanded, and though reluctant to sever contact, Paris obeyed. "Now stretch your wings," the angel said to Sienna.

Those black gossamer wings extended to their full length, lovely in a way he'd never before noticed. A deep, rich purple veined the black, swirled in the center and stretched to the tips.

"Excellent. Now, try not to let this next part frighten you." Without any further warning, Zacharel pushed her off the ledge.

She gave a horrified gasp as she tumbled from the roof, heading down...down...

"Noooo!" Paris's stomach bottomed out as he launched forward, meaning to dive off after her.

The angel stopped him with a right uppercut to the jaw, sending him propelling backward. Sex whimpered at the pain exploding through his head, but refused to retreat, refused to hide.

"You said she wouldn't fall!" Paris shouted as he stood, intending to try again. He was going after her, and that was that.

"She didn't fall. I pushed her."

"If she's hurt—"

Zacharel vanished, reappearing a second later with Sienna at his side. There was a green tint to her skin, and when she realized solid ground held her up, she hunched over, gagging, trembling uncontrollably.

"You...bastard..." she got out.

"This is the only way to learn." No emotion layered Zacharel's voice. Just a whole lot of *what'd-I-do-wrong*. "This is how we are taught. Besides, you are a soul. Had you made contact with the ground, I doubt you would have burst open like a melon."

"You doubt!"

"Find your brave core, demon girl. Step back up and we will try again."

Paris delivered an uppercut of his own. The angel's head whipped to the side, blood leaking from the gash in his bottom lip, but he merely straightened and blinked in confusion.

"You do anything like that again, and I will end you." Paris didn't wait for a reply, but gathered Sienna in his arms and carried her to their room.

CHAPTER FORTY-FOUR

"WHY DON'T you take a shower and relax, baby?" Paris said as he set Sienna down on their bed. "I'll be back in a few."

She had no idea what he was planning or where he was going, but she nodded. She could use a little alone time. Her heartbeat was currently engaged in a world-record race.

He kissed her forehead and was off, shutting her inside. Shower, yes, that's what she needed. After all, she had just plunged toward certain death, unable to force her wings to work, and the only reason she had survived was that the angel who'd tried to off her had caught her seconds before the splat.

Punish, Wrath said.

The first time he'd ever wanted to hurt an angel. Either he'd taken the shove personally or his hunger had returned.

On her stumble into the bathroom, she noticed that Viola had come through for her. A ring rested on the nightstand, its only stone a huge amethyst in the center. Good. Yeah. Good. Not heartbreaking.

The warm water relaxed her somewhat, but she had no desire to linger. Just shampooed, soaped up, rinsed off and towel-dried. About five minutes had elapsed. What a day. And yet, despite the near-death experience, she had a feeling that, when she looked back, this would be her favorite day of all time. Paris had said he loved her.

Not saying it back had nearly destroyed her, especially as he'd worked her over, his hands sliding along her wings, caressing yet firm, as he taught her what he knew about flying. But she was leaving him tomorrow, never to return, never to see him again, and well, yeah. Not going there.

When she emerged from the bathroom, she saw him sitting on the edge of the bed, facing her, his elbows resting on his knees. He wore an expression she'd never seen on him before, one of such glowing tenderness her knees almost buckled.

"Come here," he said.

Dropping the towel, naked and glistening, she obeyed without hesitation, stopping between his spread legs. His big hands settled on her hips, his thumbs lightly rasping over the flare of her waist. She shivered.

"Where did you go?" She tunneled her fingers through his hair, adoring the soft strands as they lifted and fell.

"Just out in the hall. I was going to lose it, and I didn't want you to see. Punched a few holes in the wall. Now I just want to hold you for a minute. Okay?"

Always. "Yes."

He tugged her closer, his arms tightening around her, and then he laid his head just over her breast, his warm breath trekking over her skin, his ear pressed into her heartbeat. They stayed like that for a long while, until she was shaking with the need to touch him, to be with him fully.

He must have sensed her desire because he urged her forward, taking more of her weight, more, until he lay flat and she was on top of him. Then he turned both their bodies sideways, rolled her and settled her in front of him, so that he cradled her. His chest to her spine, his erection pressing between her cheeks.

"Let me love you," he whispered. "I want to fill you and move in you and come in you. I want to be so deep in you, baby. So damn deep." His hand moved between her breasts, angled, and kneaded the upper, rubbing against her nipple, creating the most delicious friction.

"Yes," she repeated. Her brain was fogging, her every thought belonging to him, to what he was doing.

His other hand moved between her legs and found the center of her desire. "All this honey. All mine." One finger burrowed into the gap her legs created and penetrated her, then another.

She rocked with his inward strokes, arching into him. "I love the way you work me."

He nibbled on her ear. Slid a third finger home. Moan after moan cut through her throat, booming through the room.

"Get me all wet, baby. I want you all over me, coating me, drenching me."

She continued to rock…rock against him, losing herself, happy to lose herself, never wanting to be found, desperate to remain here, with him, always, lost, so lost.

"So perfect. More."

She squeezed her eyelids shut, her ears picking up sounds she'd previously missed. The hard rasp of his breath, coming faster and faster. The shift of his hips against the sheets, the slow grind of flesh against flesh. "Paris."

"I'm going to do you so good." His voice was guttural, almost totally animal. "I'm going to be in you, and I'm going to have you down my throat, your taste in my mouth. You're going to welcome me inside, aren't you."

"Oh, yes. Please, yes."

He removed his fingers, and she cried out, her desperation for him cranking out of control. How he'd get everything he wanted, she didn't know, but at least she wasn't empty for long. He clutched her upper knee and parted her legs, and without a pause in the glide of his hips, he slid as deep as he'd promised. She cried out again, this time in relief, stretched and filled and nearly insane with her need for more.

He moved in her, even as he traced her lips with his wet fingers—wet with *her*—and slid two digits inside her mouth. "Suck them."

She did, oh, she did, tasting herself, the erotic act new for her, but so damn arousing. She rolled those fingers around, sucked on them as commanded, bit down on them. Then his fingers were gone and he was angling her face, and his mouth was pressing against hers, his tongue darting inside, taking the taste of her into himself. All the while he moved in her, so, so deep, then almost all the way out, then so, *sooooo* deep.

This was more than sex, some distant instinct told her; this was a bonding, a mating. He was all over her, in her, and she was all over him, in him. This man...oh, this man. She couldn't get enough, would never get enough.

"Where am I?" he suddenly demanded. His thrusts were becoming jerkier, slamming inside harder, harsher.

"Here." A moan of passion. "With me."

"Where am I?"

"All over me. In me."

"Yeah. That's right. All over you. In you. I'm yours, and you are mine." He dove back in for another soul-stealing kiss, shattering her, claiming her. "You like this."

Not a question, but she answered anyway. "Love. This." As many times as they'd been together, he'd never been this intense, this focused on ownership. And hell, she wanted to own him, too. She reached up and back and fisted his hair, holding on tight, not caring when the strands pulled.

He hissed in a breath.

Her hips arched back, with force this time, slamming into him. Both of them groaned at the bliss. She edged ever closer to release, and he was right there with her.

"Take me, baby. Take all of me. Yeah. That's it. You know the way."

Pressure, building and building, consuming. Just a little more... "Paris!" One more hard slam and she was shooting into the stars, pleasure flooding her in a rush, a storm. Her inner walls clutched at him, grabbing on to him, letting him know he was where he belonged, that this was right, that they were right.

He rolled her all the way to her stomach, pressing her face into the pillows, and hammered harder, faster. A roar ripped out of him, as rough as his thrusts, and he filled her up, coming and coming and coming some more. She was right there with him, launching into a second orgasm, one that snuck up on her, but took her ever higher.

When she came back to earth, she blinked open her eyes. Had she passed out? She must have, because Paris was on his side, and she was on her side, and they were facing each other, but she didn't recall moving. His breathing was a little off, so she didn't think very much time had passed. He'd drawn the sheet over their bodies and was peering over at her, as if memorizing her features.

"I want to leave with you," he said. "Go somewhere Cronus can't find you. Where no one can hurt you."

Her heart lurched. No one—meaning his friends. "I

told you. I don't want you to be mad at anyone on my behalf."

"They disrespected you."

"And I deserved it."

"No!" He threw a punch, his fist going through the headboard, wood shards raining. "*I* told *you* not to talk like that. And the next time you do, I'm putting you over my knee. They aren't perfect, not a single one of them. We've all done things. Things that would shame hardened criminals."

"Well, they're reformed."

"So are you. I'm not saying I want to leave them forever. I love them. Need them. I just want to give them time to accept you. And just so you know, if I ever treated their women the way they've treated you, they would retaliate."

She had to change the subject. *Had. To.* He was melting her resolve. Being what she needed, saying such wonderful things. And he meant them. His tone was all about the serious.

"Hiding from Cronus," she said. "I don't think that's possible."

Gradually he relaxed. "There are medallions. Whoever wears them is hidden from him and all his followers. He gave them to us once, then took them away. I can steal one."

And enrage the beast, placing himself in eternal danger? "No. I have to do this, Paris. I have to go to Galen, and Cronus is going to take me. I just have to," she finished lamely. *For you, for me.*

"That's it?" Anger returned to those electric eyes. "You're not even going to think about it? When the very idea of my enemy breathing the same air as you drives me to commit murder?"

Her own anger sparked. "When it comes to putting you in danger? When it comes to making sure you survive? There isn't anything to think about."

He softened, but only slightly. "Same with me. I don't want you in danger. Ever. And you think about this. I will waste away without you. Yeah, I know I'm the king of manipulation, playing on your emotions, but I will do *anything* to keep you. I will kill. I will lie. I will betray and cheat and steal. I will topple mountains."

"Paris, I—"

He wasn't done. "All my life I have fought and I have fucked, and I thought I was happy until you pissed me off and woke me up and I realized I'd simply existed and accepted. And you might have gotten my attention through my demon, but you kept it because of *you*. I could have anyone right now, and no, that isn't ego or a front, it's just me telling you that now that Sex knows I'm committed, he's making me hard for every damn female in the place, or he was, and he can again, but I don't want them and I won't take them."

Careful, girl. This man, *this man she loved,* could talk her into anything. There could be no spending the rest of the night with him. She had to leave. And she had to leave now.

The knowledge shattered her.

"Sienna, baby. I know I'm coming on strong. I know I'm pushing for a lot. Just…give me some time, okay? We'll figure this out. There's a solution, there has to be. Trust me."

So many pieces of her, scattered and broken, never to be fitted back together. "I do," she croaked. "I trust you." The truth, but it wouldn't stop her.

"Good." He must have assumed she'd agreed to give him time.

She didn't correct the mistake.

"Now, I want you to listen to me. Do you remember when I told you not to let anyone smell your blood, to always clean yourself up if you are injured?" He waited for her nod before he went on. "That's because Cronus has made you into an ambrosia spout. Your blood is a drug for immortals and highly addictive."

"That's not—" Yeah, no reason to finish that sentence. Anything was possible. She was living—er, undead— proof of that. Bitterness rose, joining the anger and the hopelessness. "How did he do it? *Why* would he?" Even as she spoke, she knew the answer to the latter.

Why—so that she could more easily "seduce" and control Galen. That's how she would keep his interest. How dare he do this! she seethed. How dare he turn her into a...a...walking narcotic!

Punish...PUNISH.

Yes. She would punish. Would that stop her from doing what needed doing? No. Not when Paris's life was at stake. But, oh, she and Cronus would have a reckoning one day.

Wrath grunted his approval.

Gruff, Paris said, "I'm sorry about what happened, baby. I wish I could go back, stop him."

Melting... "Is there a way to fix me?"

"Not to my knowledge."

She leaned into Paris, pressing her lips into his. He wanted to continue the conversation, she could tell, but he was into the kiss and accepted her tongue, taking it as his right—and it was. While he was distracted, she reached for the ring Viola had left her. Slid the metal onto her middle finger.

Tears burned the backs of her eyes. *Do it.*

"Sienna," Paris said. He cupped her jaw as he liked

to do, as gentle as if she were a precious treasure he couldn't bear to bruise. "Talk to me. Tell me what you're thinking. Please."

Do it. Do it! First, one more kiss, just one more. She dove back in, filling her mouth with his special taste. All that heat and chocolate. What lay ahead of her was an eternity of misery, but then, that was her punishment, wasn't it. For what she'd done to him before. Part of her even thought Wrath approved, for the demon was now purring in the back of her mind, as he'd done for Olivia, feeding off Sienna's sorrow.

Do. It. Still she hesitated. Was she going to talk herself out of this? No, oh, no. She was talking herself into it, she realized when her next thought hit. Paris had to fall out of love with her. He just had to. He had to forget the vow he'd made her, and live. Live happily.

And so she did it. She did the one thing guaranteed to make him hate her.

She positioned her ringed finger at his throat, just as she'd done once before, that day they'd first met. His pulse was erratic, a drunken drumbeat.

DO IT. A tragic "I'm sorry" left her as she struck. She shouldn't have said that. Should have been cold, heartless.

His eyes flared wide. "What the—" Comprehension bled into his irises, even as they glazed. The liquid had broken the blood/brain barrier instantly. Rather than shout at her, curse at her, he slurred out, "Don't leave me. Don't…leave… Stay…mine…please…"

Though he fought the effects, he couldn't stop them, and his eyelids drifted shut. His arms plopped to his sides. He was very still, his chest rising and falling evenly. Took everything she had to climb out of the bed. To dress in clothing Cronus had provided for her, choosing a long-sleeved T-shirt that fit around her wings, black leather pants and combat boots. She quaked the entire time, tears pouring down her cheeks.

She claimed two daggers, and neither of them were crystal. Those she left on the nightstand, resting next to each other. They were his. He would need them. She strapped the weapons on her wrists, hilts down. A shake of her arms, and those blades would slide right into her palms.

For a moment, she closed her eyes. *Had to be done, had to be done,* she chanted. Didn't make her ache any less, or feel any better. Or any less guilty. Why couldn't Paris have looked at her with anger there at the end? Why'd he have to be so understanding?

She refused to delude herself. He would come after her.

She had to stop him.

Though she almost broke down and sobbed when she exited the bedroom, she somehow managed to pick herself up and scour the castle. She found Lucien down the hall, in the room he'd claimed for his own. He sat in a velvet-lined chair, a glass of something amber in one hand, the other wrapped around Anya, who perched in his lap.

He sensed the intrusion immediately, his gaze arrowing straight for Sienna. He set his glass on the floor.

"What's wrong?" Anya demanded. "You tensed."

When he registered Sienna's identity, he relaxed, his scarred face easing off the *someone's-gonna-die* throttle. "Anya, sweetheart, will do you something for me?" he asked, tenderly running his fingers through her fall of pale hair.

"Anything, Flowers." She licked up his neck, humming ecstatically. "You know that."

He fisted a thick lock and lifted her head, forcing the pleasuring to end. "Will you go to the kitchen and make me some hot chocolate? With whipped cream *and* marsh-mallows?"

"Wait. What?" Her red lips pulled into a frown. "I thought you wanted me to do something totally, absolutely freaky to your body, and I was one-hundred-percent racer ready for that. Hot chocolate—"

"Anya. Please. I have a craving."

Her eyes narrowed. "Are you pregnant?"

"Anya."

"What? It's a legit question right now, considering what you're willing to give up, but fine. My man has a craving." Off Anya went, grumbling, leaving Lucien alone with Sienna and not realizing it.

"I drugged Paris," she admitted. And wow, what a way to kick things off poorly.

Scowling, Lucien jumped to his feet. "Did you hurt him?"

"No, no. Of course not." She leaned against the door, no longer able to hold herself up. "Cronus wants me to go…to Galen…to spy for him, to control him." Why was this so difficult? She'd drugged the man she loved; this should be as easy as breathing. "It's the only way to save Paris, and you guys, from certain death. The longer I stay here, the more likely the chance Galen will get to Cronus, and Rhea will take the throne." And the harder it would be to leave Paris.

His blue eye swirled, hypnotizing her, while his brown one seemed to lock her in place. "I could accuse you of lying, of saying this so that we won't suspect you of re-joining your flock and sharing our secrets."

Her tongue thickened with the need to curse, but she plowed ahead anyway. "Yeah. You could. And that's fine, more of the same, but Paris, he trusts me and he wants me to stay. He wouldn't let me go."

In the ensuing silence, she noticed something. Wrath was quiet now; he'd truly fed from her pain and her actions, and wasn't concerned by Lucien in any way. And also, maybe she'd gotten it right before and Aeron had already won this battle. Maybe the Lords were exempt from the demon's brand of justice. Whatever. Didn't matter. She wasn't going to be around them anymore, was she? Wrath could feed off her sorrow for eternity.

"Paris will want to come after me," she said. "You know he will."

A dark brow knitted into Lucien's hairline. "So he can retaliate for being drugged?"

"No. To save me from Galen."

His lips pursed as he considered her words. "What do you want me to do?"

"Stop him." The words were shards of glass in her throat. "I have to stay with Galen, have to somehow find a way to control him."

"Here's a tip. Kill him," Lucien suggested.

If only. "Cronus says I can't, that if Galen dies you guys die, too. This is the way. The only way." As she spoke, she straightened her shoulders. Her determination grew, turned her into a rock.

Sienna wasn't weak, and she wasn't a coward. Not any longer. She was doing this, even at the expense of her own happiness. "Don't let him come for me. Keep him here, and keep him strong. So. Yeah. That's all I came to say."

A long, torturous pause as he considered his reply. "You know what you're asking, right?"

"Yes." To mask the newest flood of tears, she looked down at her booted feet. "You're a good friend to him, and I'm glad." *Getting choked up again.* "I'm glad he has you. Take care of him, Lucien. If ever there's information I obtain that can help you, I will somehow send it on. Trust it or not, but it will be there if you want it."

"Sienna—"

"Just...take care of him, like I said." No need to open the door. She simply stepped through it and pounded her way to the roof.

There was only one thing left to do.

CHAPTER FORTY-FIVE

Sienna's wings lifted properly and were no longer drag-ging against the floor. Her shoulders ached, but the shooting pains were nothing she couldn't handle. She was determined. Still rock-solid. Unbendable.

She would do this. Wouldn't waver.

She pushed her way onto the roof, the cloying dark-ness of the realm once more enveloping her. No sign of that shadow guy…thing, but of course, his blood toll had been paid and he'd vowed to leave everyone alone. Whether or not he'd keep his word, she couldn't be sure. Wrath had sensed the menace in him, yet the images the demon had shot through her head had been grainy and, well, shadowed, confusing them both.

Nothing had been clear, so she had no idea what the shadow guy was capable of doing. She trusted him be-cause she had no other choice.

In the center of the parapet, she stopped and spread her arms. There was no hesitating to take a breath. No re-flecting on what could have, should have, been. "Cronus! Cronus! I summon you!"

A flash of white at her left. Heart thumping, she spun. The angel Zacharel had taken shape, lovely in his heav-enly glory, glowing with an aura that pulsed with energy, yet seeing him caused a tremor of fear to crawl down her spine. His expression was devoid of emotion, those white-and-gold wings spread regally, his robe pristine.

Wrath reacted as if he'd just spotted Olivia. *Heaven!*

"My people need you, Sienna," Zacharel said. "I told you this."

She raised her chin. "And I told you to get in line."

"Why do that when I can simply take what I want?"

"If you could settle for my unwillingness, you would have taken me already."

He inclined his head at her logic. "Then come with me of your own accord. You are the key to our victory."

So sick of those words. "Why am I the key? *How* am I the key?"

"I do not know."

So sick of nonanswers. "Well, then, you don't get the key. Besides, I didn't think angels and demons ever worked together."

The slightest softening around his emerald eyes. "High Lord demons, like the one inside you, were angels once. I know—knew—your Wrath. Once upon a time, his justice was not perverted or warped, but fair and right."

"That doesn't change my mind." Where the hell was Cronus? "Paris comes first, and this is my way to save him." And if Paris himself hadn't changed her mind about her current path, Zacharel had no chance.

His brow furrowed as he tossed her words through his mind. "Why do you love him?" He sounded genuinely baffled. "Why do you sacrifice yourself and your happiness for him?"

"He is strong."

A snort. "Others are strong."

She remembered doing the same thing to Paris, contradicting everything he said. Had *she* been this annoying? "He's smart, and giving, and caring, and kind, and—"

"He is a killer."

Though her eyes narrowed, she continued as if he hadn't spoken. "He is protective of me, and he makes me feel special. He takes care of me. And he sacrifices for me, too."

"You wish a sacrifice to be made? Done. Name your price and I will see to it immediately."

Hope ignited. "Can you save Paris from the fate Cronus showed me? In two of the potential futures, he dies. Can you save him and his friends?"

"No," Zacharel replied honestly, and that shouldn't have surprised her but it did. "The roadways have already been paved, the vehicles placed upon them and in motion. There are no breaks."

As vivid as the metaphor was, the reality was inescapable. Hope burned to ash and floated away. "Very well, then. Cronus!" she shouted. "Cronus!"

Zacharel skimmed a fingertip along his brow. "The Titan king has lied to you, you know. Lied about so many things."

Breath caught, froze in her lungs. "About Paris?"

"No."

Then nothing else mattered. "Cronus!"

He heaved a ragged sigh of frustration. "Help us, Sienna. A war brews in the heavens. Good versus evil. You want to be on the side of good."

Been there, ruined lives because of that, she thought. "Cronus!"

"We will never lie to you," he said, floating closer, "and you will have a chance to avenge the wrongs committed against you and those you love."

Wrath really liked that idea, and slammed against her temples to gain her undivided attention.

Don't need to sell that any harder. The thought of

working on the side of the angels—for real this time—
was hard-core awesome, and yeah, part of her wanted to
be all over it. But. Yeah, always a but. "I'm sorry, I really
am, but I drugged a good man to do this, and you can't
guarantee his safety, so I can't help you."

Zacharel studied her for a long while, silent. Then,
"Very well. I will allow you to leave with the Titan.
When you need me, and you will, simply speak my name
and I will come for you."

And take her straight into the heavens. "Find a way
to save Paris and his friends, and I'm yours. See, I've
learned something in this new, immortal world. Everything has a price, a toll. The Lords are mine. Their lives
for mine, or no deal."

"Very well," he repeated just before he disappeared.

A split second later, Cronus materialized in front of
her, and oh, was he pissed. His scowl broke up the clean
lines of his face, turning regal features sinister. At least
he'd given up the goth mesh and tailored suits in favor
of his white robe.

"You summoned me, and then you blocked me?" Eyes
a shimmering mix of ebony and scarlet, he snarled, "How
did you block me?"

Just as before, Wrath went silent, unable to see into
Cronus's past. Frustrated them both. Much as she raged
about the sick things the demon had made her do, she'd
come to rely on his keen insight into the people around
her.

"I didn't block you," she replied honestly, the words
laced with venom. *I hate this man,* she realized. For
everything he'd done to her, and everything he was doing
to Paris. "I summoned you to tell you I'm ready. I want
to go to Galen. But first…"

Steps unhurried, she approached him. Her arms were

lowered at her sides, and she gave a little shake. The blades slid into her hands, as planned, and the moment she reached Cronus, she whipped into a frenzy of motion, shoving him back, into the castle wall, the tip of her weapon poised at his jugular.

He could have thrown her off, but the threat happened so quickly, he could only widen his eyes in astonishment.

"You fed me ambrosia, *made* me ambrosia."

Finally he shoved, propelling her backward. Only by frantically flapping her wings did she prevent herself from flying over the rail.

"And the problem?" He brushed a piece of lint from his shoulder. "I did what was required to make this work. You were right, you aren't pretty enough to capture Galen's attention, and we need his attention."

No apologies, the bastard.

One day...

He went on silkily, "Now, allow me to capture yours."

She blinked and her surroundings changed, from dark to light, bleak to ostentatious. Befuddled, she sheathed her weapons.

Above, a teardrop chandelier hung from the center of intricately carved woodwork. At her sides, thick red-velvet curtains spilled over the windows, with chairs and lounges made of the same material scattered throughout. A rosewood desk, candelabra, tables with swirling bars of gold at their bases. Below, a plush wool carpet with the loveliest blooms woven in jewel tones. The scent of jasmine and honeysuckle saturated the air.

"What is this place?" she asked.

"This," he replied, "is your new home."

She wouldn't cry. She *wouldn't*. "Galen lives here?"

"In Rhea's realm of the heavens? Yes. Usually his men occupy every room, but many of them are currently missing." Steps light, Cronus closed the distance between them. He gripped her forearms, forcing her to peer up at him. "In exactly sixty seconds, you are going to enter that room." His gaze shifted to a closed doorway behind her.

Why the wait? Then again, who cared? "All right."

"Galen will not accept you as you are, not any longer. You stink of Paris, his enemy."

And she was supposed to convince the horrible man otherwise? Fabulous.

"There's only one way to avoid that," Cronus added.

Sickness in her stomach, ice in her veins. "And what's that?"

"This."

She never saw him move. One moment Cronus was holding her, the next he was stabbing her in the stomach. Sharp pains tore through her, and she glanced down through widening eyes. His hand was wrapped around a blade hilt he had slammed into her belly.

Wrath roared at the injustice, and in that moment, the demon had no need to see into Cronus's past to experience a desire to strike. *Punish!*

"Why would you... Why...?" Blood trickled from her mouth. *One day, I really will kill him.*

PUNISH. PUNISH. PUNISH.

"I told you. Galen would not have wanted you otherwise." Cronus stepped back, taking the weapon with him. Again he offered no apologies for his actions.

Hate him. Blood wet her shirt, poured down her skin. Her knees shook, collapsed.

PUNISHPUNISHPUNISH.

Eyes narrowing, she inched toward him, once again palming her blades.

He grinned. "Unwise to waste your remaining energy

on me. I suggest you crawl to the doorway I showed you and find Galen. Otherwise, I'll return to Paris and kill him myself."

With that, he abandoned her, leaving her alone and slowly bleeding to death.

Spiderwebs wove around her vision. Zacharel had been right, she thought dazedly. Cronus had lied and betrayed her time and time again, and like a fool she'd let him. Had come to regret her decisions. But she couldn't cry out for the angel.

Her desire merged with Wrath's. Somehow, some way, she would finish Cronus, Rhea *and* Galen, and save Paris, and tell the rest of the world to screw itself.

CHAPTER FORTY-SIX

PARIS JOLTED UPRIGHT. Fog enveloped his mind, and a great sense of doom had taken up residence in his chest. He patted the spot beside him. Cold, empty.

"Sienna," he called, thinking she might be in the bathroom. He needed to hold her, to know she was okay. A sense of foreboding was overtaking him.

Silence.

"Sienna." He shouted her name this time, and with the reverberation of his voice, the fog thinned and memories flooded him.

Sienna had left him. Left him to go to Galen. He threw his legs over the side of the bed, ignoring a wave of dizziness.

Need her, Sex said.

I know. I'll find her.

"Don't get up," a familiar voice intoned. Lucien had just flashed inside the room.

Paris tensed, did his best to focus. His friend had pulled a chair beside the bed, stretched out his long legs and locked his fingers over his stomach. Though the position was relaxed, his dark hair shagged and tangled around strained features and grave eyes.

"Have to." Paris performed a quick scan of the room, checking off things he'd need. Clothes. Boots. Weapons. His gaze landed on the nightstand where both of his crystal blades rested. He gritted his teeth. She was out there, unprotected.

Fear momentarily overwhelmed him, and he dropped his head in his hands.

Need her!

I know, damn it! You think I don't know?

"She came to me, you know," Lucien said. "Asked me to keep you here."

He lifted his head and met his friend's multihued stare, his fury rising on a swift tide. "Did you hurt her?"

Lucien blanched, the scars on the side of his face seeming to rise up. "No."

Okay, then. Okay. "What did you say to her?"

"We'll get to that. Apparently she also went to Viola and asked the goddess to make sure your demon was properly fed."

He popped his jaw. Sienna wanted him to have sex with another woman. The knowledge might have undone a lesser man, and yeah, it angered and upset him, but he understood her motive. His well-being above hers. It was the same for him, which was exactly why he was going after her. Then he would find a way to bind her to him permanently, through fair means or foul.

She's ours. Sex might have been reluctant at first, but he was totally on board now.

No argument from me.

Once Paris had thought he would be able to let her go. He'd thought he could never ask anyone to spend 24/7 with him. Had thought the complications would be too great to overcome. Well, he'd thought wrong. When it came to Sienna, there was nothing he wouldn't do, nothing he wouldn't endure—or demand she endure.

Paris stood, swayed.

Lucien followed him up.

He rolled his shoulders, gearing for battle. "You gonna try to keep me from her?" *Nothing and no one keeps me from her.*

"Hell, no." The warrior whipped out his Glock and checked the clip. "I'm going with you to get your girl."

SIENNA CRAWLED toward the doorway. She left a trail of blood behind her, but finally reached her destination. She expected to ghost through. Instead, she met resistance. A solid wall. *Damn it!* Lifting up to curl her fingers around the knob was a production. Already she was light-headed and weak, but with every second that passed she grew more so.

Two things drove her. Hatred for Cronus, Rhea and Galen, and love for Paris. She could do this. She would do this. She'd come so far, wouldn't stop now. Fat white stars winked through the spiderwebs. Breathing proved difficult, the air seeming to thicken each time she inhaled.

Knob, twisted. Door, butted with her shoulder. Hinges squeaked. Yes! Success.

One hand in front of the other, knees dragging in behind her. Past the threshold. One hand in front of the other, knees still dragging. Stars, stars, so many stars, outshining the webs completely.

Rustling a few feet away. A female's whimper.

A male's curse.

Galen? "Help…me…" Sienna managed.

Feet hit the floor. Footsteps echoed. The slide of feathers over wood planks. Then a handsome blond male was crouching in front of her. Hello, Galen, the man from the portrait. He was bare-chested and covered in blood-stained bandages. He had a blade poised overhead, as if he meant to strike at her, but then he hesitated, his nostrils flaring, his eyes instantly glazing over.

"Who are you?" he croaked.

Her heartbeat sped up, which in turn caused her to bleed out faster. Her thoughts were like mist, impossible to grasp. "I'm...Wrath. Hunter." And why wasn't her demon flashing images of Galen's crimes through her head? Was he as weak as she was? His strength reliant on hers, as hers was sometimes reliant on his?

Across the way, she saw a pale-haired female peek from the shadows of a corner. Her features were tight with strain, her skin colorless. Was this Legion, the girl the Lords were searching for? The girl who had traded herself to save Ashlyn?

The girl Galen had risked his life to obtain?

Hell, Wrath said with a whimper.

"Why are you here?" Galen demanded. "How did you get here?"

Sienna wished she'd come up with a story beforehand, wished Cronus had given her one. Now she had nothing. No words to soothe him and convince Galen of her trustworthiness. At least until she could defend herself.

"Help," was all she said.

Legion crawled forward. "Wr-Wrath? I can't see you, but I feel you."

My hell.

"Stay back, Legion," Galen barked, and the girl instantly scampered back to her post. He never removed his attention from Sienna.

What had he done to Legion to create so much fear in her? What did he *plan* to do to her? No matter what, Sienna couldn't let him hurt the girl. Had to find a way to get her to safety.

As if he read her mind, he said savagely, "She's mine. You touch her, and you die—after I play with you a bit."

Sienna glared at him. So many threats had been tossed her way lately, his was just white noise.

He licked his lips, bent down and sniffed. "You smell so good." His words were beginning to slur. "*So* good."

She remained motionless, part of her wanting him to taste her blood, the rest of her repulsed by the idea. But this was it, the way she would control him, and as much as she despised Cronus for it, she was suddenly a little grateful. When Galen was under the ambrosia's spell, Paris would be safe.

And then she would rewrite the predicted future, creating a fourth road. As she'd promised herself, she would kill both the king and queen of the Titans. There would be no locking them up, no mercy.

Another sniff, a shudder of pleasure and then Galen jolted back, stumbling to his ass. "Fox," he shouted, crabwalking the rest of the way from her. "Fox!"

Damn him. Sienna drew on what modest strength she had left and edged toward him. Had to get him to taste. Had to… She reached out a bloody hand.

"Fox!" His eyes widened with horror when he hit the wall, unable to move as she inched…inched…

Footsteps behind her, a hard hand fisting in her hair, jerking her backward. So she was visible to more than just the master of the house, she thought dimly as her strength ebbed. Evidently Cronus had worked his magic on Galen's henchmen, as well.

"Kill her," Galen croaked. "*Kill* her."

KANE KNEW HE WAS DREAMING. Why else would he see Amun and Haidee facing off with the two horsemen, daggers clanging together, grunts and groans filling the air? Why else would Haidee's skin be changing to straight-up blue ice, her hair into icicles? Why else would William be buffing his nails as he leaned against a wall?

Why else would a beautiful female with long silver-blond hair cascading over one shoulder and eyes of the purest lavender be looking down at him, frowning, tugging at the shackles on his wrists and ankles?

Hell. Maybe he *wasn't* dreaming. Maybe she was an angel. "Dead?" he rasped. After all, he'd willed himself to die, and maybe, finally, blessedly, his soul had left his body. Maybe he was free of his demon. Maybe he was being sent to that secret realm in the heavens where the deceased Baden and Pandora lived. A realm where the demon-possessed were to spend the entirety of their afterlife.

Baden, once his best friend. Once the keeper of Distrust. Aeron had spent a little time in that secret realm, had spoken to Baden, and even to Pandora, who hated them all with a passion that hadn't dimmed through the centuries.

Aeron had escaped with his Olivia. Kane, however, did not want to escape.

"Dead?" he asked again. Even as he spoke, his brain flashed a neon sign into his awareness. *Mine.*

The female, surely the loveliest creature he'd ever beheld, said only one word. "No." But he felt the force of her voice in every single one of his cells. Pure, enchanting, intoxicating.

Mine. A roar now.

Angels couldn't lie, so he knew she had told the truth. Even though there was no actual layer of truth in her voice. So, if he wasn't dead, he was alive. The thought didn't please him. He hated that such a beauty was seeing him like this. At his worst, violated, injured, weak.

"Kill me, then," he commanded.

Mine. Louder than before. He didn't understand the possessive instinct, and didn't want to understand it. He might veer from his current path.

Silence, such heavy silence. The calm before the storm. Because, in the next heartbeat, Disaster protested. Loudly. Screaming and screaming and screaming inside of Kane's head.

No, he wasn't dead.

Kane reached up to cover his ears, and succeeded. His arms had been freed from the chains, he realized distantly. That's what the woman had done. Unchained him.

"No," she repeated. "I won't be killing you."

Mine.

Shut up. He returned to his dream theory. This was a dream, only a dream, which meant she had to do whatever he wanted her to do. Right? "Kill. Me."

Her hands slid underneath his shoulders and pushed him up, up. He felt her heat, the smoothness of her palms. Smelled the fragrance of patchouli, deep, rich and musky, erotic and earthy. Deep in his nose, clinging to his sinuses, spreading into his stomach, his bloodstream.

MINE.

A growl was rising up his throat, threatening to spill out of his mouth. His arms went limp and fell uselessly to his sides, and yet he still had to fight the urge to reach up and grab on to her. He wanted his mouth on her, wanted his body in hers.

He wanted…and so he would have.

MINE, SHE IS MINE.

The blonde—who was suddenly no longer a blonde, but a lovely black woman—no, a sultry Latina—got all up in his face, dark eyes piercing him. "I am not here to end your life, but to save it," she said. "I will take you to the human world—and in return, *you* will kill *me*. I'll have your vow first."

Disaster stopped screaming and started laughing again.

CRONUS WALKED THE CHAMBER of Futures alone, his emotions balanced on the razor's edge of destruction. He'd searched everywhere, yet he hadn't found Rhea. The Hunters he'd captured and locked away were now missing. Rhea had somehow freed them, he knew. And Sienna had not yet done her job with Galen.

If he had to raze the entire world to save himself, he would.

One way or another, he would obtain what he wanted. Dominion over the human world. Control of his wife. And life. *Eternal* life. He was an immortal, a king, the most powerful of his people—even if a few out there left him trembling.

He stopped in front of a vase one of his Eyes had sculpted and painted so long ago. In it, Rhea's hated daughter Scarlet, the keeper of Nightmares, was in the process of removing his head. So, yes, there were two predictions about his death. Two supposed murderers. Two different places, in two different times.

Why?

He had never been able to figure out this particular mystery. Only one person could kill him, true? Unless Galen and Scarlet worked together? But the pair despised each other, fought for opposite sides. Proof: Scarlet had recently invaded Galen's dreams and convinced the man of his own impending downfall. Those dreams had driven the keeper of Hope to attack her man, Gideon, which had enraged her further.

Cronus blinked as an idea took root. Could the answer be that simple? Had Scarlet somehow invaded his Eye's dreams? Had she shown her a false reality? He and Scarlet had been enemies since her birth, and hurting each other had become something of a game.

Perhaps, he thought. Yes, perhaps. Which meant he was most likely on the right path. Galen was the biggest threat, and so Galen had to be corralled.

Sienna now knew exactly how ruthless Cronus could be to ensure his goals were met, and she would come through for him. If she failed, he would make good on his threat. Paris would die. And he would make her watch.

CHAPTER FORTY-SEVEN

A STAY OF EXECUTION, Sienna thought, but only because Galen's bodyguard, Fox, had done what he had not and tasted her blood. As the woman had dragged Sienna out of the bedroom and into a cellar room boasting only a long table with a drain underneath it, she'd gotten blood on her hands. Sienna had made certain of that. She'd promised Paris she would kill whoever tasted her blood, and she would do her best to see that through.

And as the woman lifted her onto the table, she'd caught the sweet coconut scent of ambrosia. She'd licked, closed her eyes and moaned in bliss. Then, of course, had come the feasting. Fox had fallen on her, lapping at her, biting her. And when she'd finished, she hadn't rendered the death-blow but had carted Sienna to her bedroom and tied her up in a corner.

That had been…how many days ago? Sienna had lost track. Time passed too slowly for her—and yet too quickly—measured only by the number of visits Fox paid her. Her initial injury had healed, but Fox kept making new incisions, taking more blood, keeping her weak.

What was Paris doing right now? Resenting her? Hating her? Had Lucien managed to keep him inside the castle? Yeah. Probably. The Lords had made their feelings about her clear, and they would jump on this chance to deepen his negative emotions.

Don't go there. It's bad for your mental health. Besides, she needed to plan. First up? Getting Legion out of here. Second, returning and force-feeding Galen her blood. 'Cause no way he'd trust her after she absconded with his woman, and she really needed his trust. She couldn't kill him if she couldn't get close to him.

Legion's frightened face flashed through her mind. Not Galen's woman. Galen's *perceived* woman.

Wrath stretched inside her head. Like her, he was growing weaker. He needed to feed himself, was desperate to punish someone, and Galen was the perfect candidate.

She wiggled on the floor, rubbing her bound wrists against the wall behind her. Unfortunately, her wings kept getting in the way. And there was a gag in her mouth, so she couldn't call for help. Not that she would have. Zacharel would sweep her straight into the heavens and expect her to march to his Do What I Say band. So not happening.

The bedroom door swung open, and Fox stomped inside. She wore combat boots, black leather pants and a bustier. Her hair was pulled back in a ponytail, and she was licking her lips. She'd come to toke up.

She fell to her knees in front of Sienna, removed her gag, said "Miss me?" and palmed a blade.

Come on, fight her. Do something. "You're pathetic, you know that? Galen had the strength to resist me, but not you. Are you embarrassed?"

Fox was too enraptured by the pulse in her neck to reply, and never even bothered to check her restraints, something she'd done every time before. The addiction was getting worse, then. Good.

"I bet you're not. You're too stupid to—"

With a growl, Fox lunged, lowering her head. Sienna jerked her knees up, knocking the female in the temple and sending her flying to the side. Sienna lumbered to a stand, which was difficult to do with her arms shackled behind her and her ankles held together. Not to mention the Tilt-a-Whirl inside her head.

Scowling, Fox jumped to her feet. "You're going to pay for that."

What she would do next, she didn't know, but then, it didn't matter. Suddenly Legion was there, behind Fox, unnoticed—and swinging a frying pan. The cast iron slammed into Fox's skull, a loud *clang* echoing. Fox's eyes went wide, rolled back, and her knees collapsed.

Legion dropped the pan as if the handle was on fire and stood there, panting, staring down in horror.

"Grab her knife and cut me loose," Sienna commanded, taking over. "Hurry, we don't have a lot of time."

Shaking, crying now, Legion remained exactly as she was. "I—I know you're here, but I can't—I can't see you, can't hear you."

No. No, no, no. If Legion couldn't see her, Legion couldn't touch her. Sienna tried everything she could think of to make herself known. All the while Wrath slammed against her temples, desperate to escape. Finally, not knowing what else to do, she allowed him to take over.

For the first time after ceding control to the demon, Sienna was aware of her surroundings, of her body and her mind. She wasn't sure if it happened because she was stronger or Wrath was weaker, but she felt her skin change, from smooth to scaled. Felt her teeth sharpen and her nails elongate.

A second later, Legion gasped. "Wrath."

"Hell." Sienna's voice was lower, gruffer than ever before.

The girl worked up the courage to bend down and pick up the knife, then close the distance between them. Delicate hands cut the rope away, freeing Sienna's arms.

Through the demon she commandeered the knife. Bending down proved to be a huge mistake, though. The dizziness cranked out of control, and she ended up sprawled on her stomach. She drew up her knees and sawed at the rope, cringing as every inch of her throbbed.

"I knew she hadn't killed you," Legion's soft voice proclaimed. "I could feel my Wrath. I would have come sooner, but Galen commanded me to stay in his room for however long he had to stay inside it. Turned out to be three days. He left this morning, nullifying the order, and I followed Fox to the kitchen and then to her room."

Sienna's mind caught on only one fact. Three days. Paris would have had to sleep with at least one woman to maintain his strength. More likely two. *Don't think about that, either.* A breakdown would stop her from doing what needed doing.

Completely free now, she anchored the blade at the waist of her pants, pushed to a stand, and held out a hand to Legion. The girl hadn't moved, was frozen in place, her expression one of great misery.

"Where is Galen now?" Sienna asked, still using that gruff voice.

"I don't know. He hasn't returned."

Good. That was good. "We're leaving." She waved her claw-tipped fingers. "Me and you, right now."

Blond hair fluttered around slender shoulders as she shook her head. "I can't."

"Can. Come on."

"No, I can't. I took a vow." The misery increased. "I have to stay with him."

We'll see about that. Vow or not, Sienna was taking

this girl to safety. *Now.* Arguing would waste time. Fighting would be ineffective. As weak as Sienna's body was, Legion would escape her in seconds. *Sneaky route, here we come.*

"All right. We go without you," she lied. "Need another weapon first." Though she almost fell a thousand times, she managed to pick up the pan, straighten—and brain the girl the same way she'd brained Fox. *Clang.*

Legion crumpled, landing on top of Fox. Yeah. That was gonna leave a mark.

Getting the girl, who was no lightweight, positioned properly on her shoulder was a nearly impossible task. At the last moment, Sienna found the strength to pull through and level out. But the burst cost her. Wrath lost his hold on her, her image returning to normal and her body now moving under her own steam. She stumbled her way into the hall.

A long hallway. Papered walls, freshly polished furniture. Only the best. A spiral staircase loomed ahead. Miles away, as far as she was concerned.

Then, at the far end of the hall, Galen took a corner as if he were wearing skates, all speed and furious grace. He was armed like a tanker, and menace rippled off him. Had she spotted him on the street, she would have run like hell and prayed for a quick death. Now, she could only watch as he barreled toward her, intent on taking Legion back.

No, he would never trust her now. Her only hope was to engage him, and force her blood down his throat. Then he'd want her alive. *Right? Please be right.*

She was about to set Legion down when she caught sight of Zacharel on one side of her and the shadow guy from Cronus's realm on the other. Dang it, how many people were after her? These two were closing in. Galen noticed them, too, and shouted a black curse. They would reach her before he did.

And then it happened. *Contact.* The black mist enveloped her first. She and Legion were swept up into a world of dizzying screams. Beneath those, she thought she heard Zacharel's roar of frustration and anger. A mistake on her part, surely. The angel was emotionless.

Wrath retreated to the back of her mind, and just as Sienna opened her mouth to release a scream of her own, the noise quieted. Wrath caught those grainy images again, and had no idea how to react. She tried to fight her way free, but the black mist held tight around her, blocking the view of her surroundings.

"Female." Shadow Guy's voice was raspy and coaxing. "I have a bargain to propose to you."

Legion slipped from her grip. Sienna reached for her, but couldn't quite get to her, the girl remaining inside the mist, floating, spinning. Eyes closed, she slept on.

"Do you have a name?" she asked.

"Yes."

When he offered no more, she snapped, "Well, what is it?"

"Some call me Hades."

The king of the dead? High Lord of the Underworld? Greek god? The one Hunters feared above all others? *That* Hades? *I am not intimidated.* "I'm listening," she said, because she had no idea what else to say.

"Your man needs you."

Her stomach bottomed out. "What do you mean?"

"He refuses all women and grows weaker by the moment. I will take you to him. *After* we reach an agreeable end to our negotiations."

Paris, weak and growing weaker. The news that he'd remained faithful to her shouldn't have relieved and delighted her, but it did. It so did. "How do I know you're telling the truth? What would you want in return?" More bodies to feed his shadows?

"Unlike that fool Cronus, I have no need to lie. And part of me hopes you turn me down so that I *can* force you. Your screams will join my others, and the symphony will thrill me for centuries to come. I'm feeling magnanimous, however, and we will try your way first."

This can only end badly.

He continued, "I heard what the angel said to you. I heard what Cronus said to you. You are a key to victory, and I want you to play for my team."

Argh! Once, no one had wanted her. Now everyone did. "Nope. Sorry. I've already picked my side."

"I thought you would say such a thing. But I heard you bargain with the goddess. She asked for a boon, and you agreed. I will accept the same arrangement."

"You want me to slay one of your enemy?" Shocking. He should have no problem doing that on his own.

"No. I simply wish for a boon, to be named later. Anything I desire, as long as it does not hurt your man or his friends. Do you agree?"

"I can't go back to Paris. You'll have to do something else to save him."

"I cannot, but you can. All you must do is allow me to take you to him. So simple, so easy."

Hardly. "Leaving him nearly killed me."

"Staying away from him *will* kill him." His voice became a caress. "Let me take you to him. You may be with him, strengthen and save him, and then you can convince him to give you up, for no one else has been able. No one else *will be* able."

I'm so weak. Can't leave him in danger. "The girl goes with me, and that's nonnegotiable."

"Of course. For a second boon."

Sweet heaven, how many would she owe when this was over? "Very well, but only if the same conditions apply."

"They do. And so the new bargain is struck." Though she could make out no faces in the dark, the shadows thinned in one area, light seeping through to reveal a hint of a grin. "I take you to your man, who is searching for you, and the girl to Aeron, the one searching for her."

Sienna blinked, and next found herself inside a tent located somewhere outside the Realm of Blood and Shadow. Too much light seeped in from the tent's cracks. But then she spotted the fur rug and her location ceased to matter. Paris was sprawled on top of it. He was still. *Too* still. Fear nearly drilled her to her knees. Until she inhaled. Warm air, scented with champagne and chocolate, fogging her up in the most succulent of ways. His demon's special scent. Her mouth watered, and her blood quickened. Her own injuries were forgotten as warmth pooled between her legs.

"Paris," she whispered. His skin was fever-bright, flushed and beaded with sweat. He was gloriously naked, and thickly aroused. His eyes were calm behind his lids, his chest barely rising with his breaths. "Oh, Paris." *I can't let him get like this again. Have to do something.*

"Sienna?"

She rushed over to him and kissed him, knowing even so small a gesture would help revive him. The more their tongues dueled, the more aggressive he became. When his lids flipped open, eyes of brilliant red pinned her. With a growl, he grabbed her by the waist and tossed her to her back. Her heart sped into a superbeat as her wings flared to avoid being crushed.

He ripped at her clothes, shredding them. The very

moment she was naked, he had her legs spread and was inside her, thrusting hard and deep.

As he worked her, he threw back his head and roared. She arched up and took him even deeper. Brutally, wondrously.

She'd missed this, missed him. Needed this, needed him. Her nails went to his ass and guided him into a faster rhythm. The passion swept her up, overwhelmed her, consumed her, broke her heart and fit the pieces back together. Her love for him knew no bounds, had no limits.

Just as climax loomed, he stopped. Just stopped, and peered down at her, panting breaths bursting over her. The flush had drained from his cheeks, and realization now flooded his eyes, followed by concern and horror.

"Oh, baby. Did I hurt you?" His thumbs dusted over her lips with exquisite care.

"Talk later. Make love now." So close. Any second now, she would hurtle into satisfaction.

His cock jerked inside her, as if the command had sparked all kinds of naughty desires. "How are you here?"

"Later!" She squeezed at his massive length.

"Yesss." His hips pistoned once, pistoned again, and then he was slamming in and out, and they were both moaning. Then his lips were on hers, and their tongues were intertwining, and she was swallowing his taste, and it was better than ever, and she couldn't get enough, never wanted this to end, and…and…and… Oh!

Little pleasure bombs exploded through every inch of her. His name left her mouth over and over again, the chorus joined by his shouting of *her* name as he came. He jetted white-hot, giving her every drop of his passion.

She relished the moment, savoring him, thrilled by all that he was.

When he fell on top of her, she cradled his weight, exactly where she wanted to be. Where she wanted to stay, forever. She'd left him once. She didn't think she could leave him again.

"I love you," she whispered. "I love you so much."

"You better," he murmured against her ear.

That's my man. Such a Paris thing to say, and she grinned.

He disengaged and rolled to his side, but kept her close, his arm wrapped around her. "And now that I'm not dying," he announced, expression growing somber, "we talk."

CHAPTER FORTY-EIGHT

PARIS KEPT HIS BODY LAX, not wanting to make Sienna un-comfortable, or aware of the fact that he basically had her in a choke hold. A gentle choke hold, one that did nothing to impair her ability to breathe, but a choke hold all the same.

She wasn't going anywhere, and that was that.

Thankfully, Sex was out for the count and unable to comment.

"All right," she said. "Let's talk. I'll start. Do you hate me now?"

"Hate you? Baby, that might be the stupidest thing you've ever said. No offense."

"None taken. I'm too relieved. After what I did to you…"

"All you did was remind me that I need to up my game where you're concerned." And honestly? Her actions had given him hope that she felt as deeply for him as he felt for her.

"You're not mad at me for going to Galen?"

When he would have done the same thing? "Only at myself. I should have sated you so sublimely, you were never again able to walk."

"A little more practice on your end," she teased, "and that'll be a possibility."

"Witch."

When she reached up to brush her hair off her face, he

saw that she was cut up and bruised. He swallowed back a bark of fury. Having been restrained a time or twelve throughout his life, he recognized the markings for what they were. Rope burns. "Did Galen do this to you?"

Dread shuttered her features. "No, and I don't want to talk about it."

Very well. He wanted to reassure her about a few things first, anyway. But he *would* find out who had harmed her afterward, and as soon as he did, he was going on a rampage for revenge.

"That means you're ready for talk, part two," he said, all hint of his amusement gone.

"I—I don't know about that."

"Too bad. You need to know that I didn't sleep with anyone while we were apart." No matter how weak he'd gotten, no matter how many females his friends had shoved at him. Finally, all but Lucien had continued on their quest to find Sienna.

Mental note: tell Death to call off the search party.

Speaking of, he was pretty sure Lucien had popped in while they were having sex, thinking to protect him from whatever had come to kill him, then had popped back out when he realized what was going on.

"I know." The tips of her fingers traced languid circles around his nipples. "I trust you. But Paris, you were so near death." She kissed his chest, just above his heart. "I don't like that you allowed yourself to get in that condition."

"Don't care. And just so you know, Sex missed you, too. You wear a lot of hats, and he wants to do them all."

She chuckled, a warm, rich sound that acted as manna for his ears. "Right now I've got my stern taskmaster hat on, so you two better listen. I have to leave. I just have to, but I need to know you're taking care of yourself and—"

"No."

"Don't be that way."

"Try to leave. Just try it. See what happens."

"Paris—"

"You stay or I let myself fade. End of story. Promise me."

Such heavy silence. "I have a plan I have to see through."

"Plans change. Deal."

She banged her fist against his chest. "You are so frustrating."

"Tell me what I want to hear, Sienna."

A sigh slipped from her, seeming to drain the fight out of her. "Fine. I'm staying with you, but we're going to have to brainstorm a solution to our Cronus and Rhea problem, our Galen problem, and our you're-gonna-die-prophecy problem. Because, did I tell you? Cronus told me that if Galen dies, you and your friends die. If Cronus dies, you and your friends die."

"I'm not saying I doubt what you've heard, but I do doubt the source. But even if what he said is true, there will be a way around this prophecy. There always is. I'm not worried in the least." In fact, he was overjoyed. And were those *tears* in his eyes? Yeah. Yeah, they were. If that made him a wuss, that made him a wuss. He didn't care. She was here, she was staying. She was his.

He glided his arm from around her neck to her lower back, splaying his fingers over her curves. "Thank you," he said, but the words weren't enough. They didn't convey enough. "And now that we're officially together, I want to tell you some things about me. I want everything out in the open, nothing hidden. I want to share all that I am."

She must have sensed the direction he headed. "You don't have to. What happened in the past is the past."

"Full disclosure. I want you to know what you're getting with me. That way, if Wrath ever shows you something, or my friends ever say anything, we'll already have dealt with it."

"Whatever you say won't change the way I feel about you."

"I'm glad, but I'm doing it anyway."

Her sigh caressed his skin oh, so deliciously. "All right."

She loved him. She'd copped to the feeling. This would be okay. "I'm an ambrosia addict. But I haven't touched the stuff since before reaching you," he rushed to add. "And if something ever happens and I'm exposed to your blood, you don't have to worry. I will *not* hurt you."

Her silky hair tickled his chest as she nodded. "I know you won't hurt me, but Paris, I drugged you. I didn't know about your addiction, or I would have found another way to knock you out. I am so, *so* sorry, and I will never forgive myself."

He hated the implication that she would have left him still, but he drank up her concern for him. "Forgive yourself right now. That's an order. But I will, of course, be spanking you before *I* forgive you."

The most adorable noise escaped her, a snort and a laugh combined. "I accept the spanking. Deserve it."

His lips twitched with the sweetest kind of humor. "You can't accept your own punishment, baby. You'll have to fight me."

She purred, actually purred, and the vibrations had him rock-hard again.

Tell her the rest, so you can move on to the good stuff.

He lost his half grin. "Okay, here's part three. I know you told me you've seen my past, but I'm not sure if Wrath showed you everything. I told you about that one slave, but he wasn't the only one. I've...been with men."

Not even a pause. "Oh, yeah? Well, in college I kissed a girl. She was my roommate, it was raining outside, dark with the occasional flashes of lightning, romantic yet scary. You know how it goes."

That she wasn't going to make a big deal about it, that she again just accepted each facet of him...no wonder he loved this woman. "Did you like it?"

"I kinda did," Sienna said in a scandalized whisper.

Mmm, but he liked her scandalized. Wondered what he could do to ramp that up, what would make her nervous but too excited to say no. Finding out, well, he'd never looked forward to a bedding more.

"Later, after your spanking, we're gonna do a little role playing. I'm going to be your sweet, innocent roommate, Parette, and you're going to demonstrate that kiss on me." *And then I'm going to talk you into doing things you've only ever dreamed about.*

"Incorrigible beast."

"But you love me anyway."

"I love you *always.*"

Before he could respond, there was an explosion of white light at the front of the tent. In a flurry of movement and frothing rage, Paris grabbed both the crystal blades, pressing one into Sienna's hand. He was standing a moment later, unconcerned by his nakedness.

Cronus had arrived, and if his fearsome scowl was any indication, he was ticked. First instinct: attack. Paris tamped it down. Barely. Second: recon. Answers, he needed answers.

The king's narrowed gaze slid past Paris and onto

Sienna, who had just finished righting her clothing. "You ruined everything," he growled.

Paris moved in front of her, blocking the king's view. Cronus merely pointed to the side of the tent, and Paris was propelled there on a powerful gust of wind, his arms spread, his legs spread, invisible ropes tying him in place. Though he fought, he couldn't free himself.

Helpless. Just like that. Panic was like bitter pills in his mouth, and he swallowed so many he might just overdose.

Darkness...so much darkness...I will hurt him. I will kill him. He struggled so viciously his muscles began to tear from his bones. That didn't slow him.

A scowling Sienna popped to her feet. *Use the crystal,* he projected with the last vestiges of his control. She didn't; she stood her ground, her chin held high.

"I'm not going back to Galen," she announced.

"Even if he were addicted to you, Galen will not trust or follow you now. He hates you. You took his prisoner, damaged his soldier, and he is not the type to forgive or forget. To him, every offense is to be returned a thousandfold."

Those gossamer black wings extended. "There's another way. We'll find it. Just give us time."

"Time? *Time.*" Menace pulsed from Cronus. "You once asked me why I wanted you willing. The answer was simple. Eventually you would have turned on me. Now you have and that's no longer a concern. So, no, I'm afraid you're out of time. Now I will destroy everything you hold dear."

Paris snarled as Cronus vanished and reappeared in front of Sienna in a single blink. He snagged her by the hair. At last Paris managed to free himself, both shoulders popping out of joint. He was running for them. Nearly upon them.

Just before he reached her, Sienna shouted, "Zacharel! I summon you."

Cronus reached out and stabbed Paris just before Paris reached them. Sienna gasped. The pair vanished, her gaze locked on Paris as he fell to his knees, a searing pain consuming him.

CHAPTER FORTY-NINE

"WE ARE *NOT* DOING THIS again," Sienna shouted, worried for Paris, desperate to return to him. "I'm sick of everyone flinging me where they want me to be." Black, all around her. In her nose, in her lungs, pouring through her bloodstream. No color, no life, just an endless void. "That ends *now*."

"You failed to take the easiest route, and now you'll have to live with Plan B," Cronus said, his voice slithering from the nothingness.

I won't ask. His plans mean nothing to me.

"Zacharel!" she called again. Work with the angels? Why not? She would learn to fly properly, and finally, once and for all, control her own destiny.

A flicker of light. A return of the dark. Another flicker, lasting just a bit longer. She caught a glimpse of big, puffy clouds, glued to an endless expanse of night sky. A star here, a star there, twinkling from their perches like eyes trained on her, watching her every move. She must be in another realm. One without a single living creature in residence.

She turned a full circle, and found Cronus standing a few yards away. His arms were crossed over his chest, his legs braced apart. She was suddenly very grateful she'd maintained her grip on the crystal blade Paris had given her.

"Another reason I wanted your willingness," Cronus

said. "If you had turned on me, you would have become Rhea's soldier and therefore been under her protection."

Now he wanted to talk? Well, he could take his confessions and shove them. "I'm warning you. Return me to Paris. *Now.*"

He arched a mocking brow at her. "Or what?"

"Or I will fight you." *Planned to, anyway. You just sped things along.*

A booming laugh, sharp and bitter, even anticipatory. "You could try."

"Return me to Paris," she repeated. "This is your last chance."

He continued on as if she hadn't spoken. "Rhea did not kill your sister. I did."

Her heart skipped a beat as denial rushed through her. "No." A lie, surely. One meant to punish her. Because, if he were telling the truth, she would have helped the very man who'd destroyed her precious Skye, leaving her bloody and broken, her last memory of a knife slicking through her skin. She would have bled for the man who had destroyed an innocent. She would very nearly have sacrificed her own life and happiness for *her sister's killer...*

No!

And yet, Wrath's earlier insistence that something had been wrong suddenly made sense. The moisture evaporated from her mouth. A knot grew in her throat, and she had trouble drawing in the necessary oxygen. Dizziness took center stage in her head.

"I held her in my hands, and I slit her throat. I watched the life drain out of her. I killed her husband first. Made her watch. I can prove it." He reached up and jerked a chain from around his neck. A butterfly carved from a black diamond dangled from the center.

In the next moment, the shield that had prevented Wrath from seeing his sins crumpled to nothing. She clutched her temples, squeezed her eyes closed as the scene unfolded inside her head. Cronus, holding Skye and a human male at his sides. Making them kneel. Stabbing the male. Skye, fighting, shoving herself into his blade. Skye, bleeding. Cronus, finishing her off. Skye, dying.

Nausea rolled through Sienna's stomach, a churning acid threatening to boil up and out. A fury drenched in seething flames and sharpened by jagged bits of glass.

"I have lived for millennia," Cronus said. "Think you I have not learned a few tricks along the way?"

We will punish him. A whisper. *WE WILL PUNISH HIM.* A scream.

I will, she replied. A vow. *Oh, I will.* For Skye. For Paris. For herself.

"You ruined my plan, and now I will ruin yours," he seethed. "I will bargain with Galen. For his eternal allegiance, I will hand you over, his to punish as he sees fit. If you run from him, I will bring you back to him. And if you think to flee to your demon lover, I will make Paris suffer before I kill him. And have no doubt, I will kill him. He thinks to take revenge on me for everything I've done to you."

The king had made that kind of threat one too many times.

Hatred joined the sickness, as did a dollop of darkness. Violence waltzed between those shadows, the urge to maim and destroy so strong she felt as if she were drowning in them. She didn't fight them; she embraced them.

He *would* be punished. Here. Today.

Hold, Wrath said. *Not yet...not quite yet...*

She didn't know what Wrath planned; she only knew she trusted him to lead her in vengeance.

Cronus added blithely, "Did you know four artifacts are needed to find Pandora's box? Galen has one, and the Lords have three. That will change. I will take the All-Seeing Eye, the Cage of Compulsion and the Paring Rod, and I will bestow them on Galen. All four artifacts will be his. He will be so grateful for my gifts, he will vow never to harm me. He will find the box, and your precious Lords will die."

Hold...

"You trust Galen that much, do you? You actually think he'll keep his word? That he won't try and take *your* demon, too?" She flashed a patronizing smile. "I bet he's as trustworthy as you are. So, after you do all of that for him and he goes in for the kill shot, what will you do, hmm? Are you going to fight him? Or finally accept your death sentence as your due?"

Cronus stalked to her, but stopped midway, his ears twitching. A smug, eerie laugh bubbled from him. "Speak of the devil. Or in this case, the man who masquerades as angel. Galen approaches, woman. And never has a warrior been angrier. He wants what you stole from him, and he will extract his pound of flesh from your body."

Hold...

"Bring it," she said. Because, yeah, she was going to punish Galen, too. Punish him for every crime he'd ever committed against Paris. For everything he'd done to Legion. Everything he'd ever *thought* to do. At long last.

The king's nostrils flared. He clearly wasn't fond of her lack of fear.

Well, too bad.

Hold...

"No worries, baby. We've already brought it," Paris said from behind Cronus.

The darkness fell away, as if a curtain had been jerked to the floor. Bright light exploded, the sun shining so vividly. Her eyes stung, but she kept them open. Paris was pale and bloody but steady on his feet. He stood with the rest of the Lords behind Cronus, who spun to face them. They were armed for war. Unlike in the painting, they weren't here to protect him.

Even better, an army of warriors whose white wings proclaimed them angels stood behind them, and *they* were armed for war. Zacharel claimed the helm. Every time she'd encountered him, his lack of emotion had amazed and even disturbed her. Now, she was grateful for it. He was determination itself, as cold and cruel as the snow falling from him, clearly willing to do *anything* to meet his goals.

"You broke the rules, Cronus," the warrior angel said flatly, "and now you will pay."

What rules?

"Mind if we join the party?" another voice—a female voice—said from behind Sienna. "I've been waiting for this moment for far too long."

Sienna whipped around to see a beautiful brunette who could only be Rhea. The regal Titan queen stood beside Galen, who was glaring at Sienna as if he would come for her first. An army of Hunters flanked them, and she recognized a few faces.

I've picked my side. Beware, she projected through her narrowed eyes.

"What is this?" Cronus demanded.

"The first battle of the new war," Zacharel replied gravely.

"Well, then. It begins. I'll need my own army, won't

I?" He waved his hand and a great throng of his people appeared, Titan gods and goddesses enveloping him, hiding him in a sea of stunning, flawless faces and immaculate, jewel-studded gowns and togas. They were obviously confused by the sudden change of scenery and none were armed.

When they spotted the unrest surrounding them, they wised up fast. Weapons of every kind appeared out of thin air.

"To the death!" Cronus shouted.

As if his voice was the starting bell, the armies rushed each other.

Now! Wrath shouted at her.

Sienna opened her mind to her demon, allowing him to take over, and threw herself into the thick of the action.

CHAPTER FIFTY

PRIORITY ONE: SIENNA.

For once, Sex didn't hide deep in a corner of Paris's mind. The demon, on a high from their woman's body, pumped strength straight into his veins as he rushed toward her, the wound from his stabbing having already healed. The darkness inside him frothed and writhed, guiding him but not consuming him. The three of them were one.

When he saw a man, a Hunter, coming up behind Sienna with a Glock raised and aimed, he roared, quickened his pace. Met the guy with an arcing blade to the throat before a single shot was fired, even as he spun his woman behind him.

Zacharel had warned him that up here, in this realm between realms just above the heart of the heavens, *everyone* could see her. And if they could see her, they could touch her. If they could touch her they could hurt her. And like him, she could be killed, her body too injured for Wrath to repair it, especially considering the damage done to her during their separation—which she still hadn't told him about.

Paris's first casualty of the battle crumpled. One down. Only about a thousand more to go. "Can you fly to safety?" he asked, nailing another Hunter. There went number two.

She offered no reply. Fearing the worst, he swung his

sword to take down any threat in front of her. Only, she had worked her way back in front of him. He spotted the back of her head, her wings tucked safely out of the way, and realized she was engaged in her own battle. Either she had allowed Wrath to overtake her or she had learned some new skills in the hour they'd been parted. He was betting on the former. Good.

Clasping only the crystal dagger, she danced through the crowd with lethal menace, her focus on Cronus and the men and women surrounding him. Hunters fell all around her. She spun, she ducked, she darted left and right. Her wings flared suddenly, and she lifted high, higher, cutting someone down below her.

A true angel of death. Paris had never seen anything so beautiful. He trailed behind her, and anyone who turned their sights on her, he killed savagely. No hesitation. No regrets.

A throwing star sliced his forearm. There was a sharp sting, a warm trickle of blood. Neither slowed him, and he didn't bother checking for the culprit. There were so many people, so many bodies, so many wings and weapons.

The gods and goddesses wore bejeweled robes and hummed with electrical energy that lifted his hair. Some could shoot fire from their fingertips, some could shoot ice. Besides Cronus and Rhea, he'd never really had a beef with the Titans, but the angels, who were, miracle of miracles, on his side, *did* have a beef, so…*the enemy of my friend is my enemy.* Anytime Paris spotted a Titan, he slew first and decided to ask questions later.

Why Titans versus angels, though? A turf thing, maybe? Like, the heavens belonged to the wingers and they weren't going to tolerate encroachers anymore? Made sense, but even if the reason had been something as lame as "We don't like the Titans, whaa, whaa, boo-hoo, they're mean," he'd be in this at full throttle.

A group of Hunters surged toward Sienna, claiming his complete focus and rage. They seemed to recognize her as one of their own. Or rather, a traitor to their kind. Their abhorrence was evident, as was their spotlighting of her, as though Rhea and Galen had placed her at the top of the must-kill list.

Moving faster than human eyes could track, Paris twisted and turned, arms always crossing, swinging, cutting. Grunts and groans sounded. Screams, too. Ahead, a Hunter aimed a .40. Even as he continued forward, Paris threw his crystal blade as if it were a deadly boomerang. And actually, it was. It changed shape midflight and sliced through the Hunter's wrist before the shot could go off, taking both the hand and the gun, before hurtling back to Paris's waiting grip.

Except, he'd missed the other Hunter with the other gun, currently aimed at Lucien. Paris went to throw the blade, but the shot boomed out, nailing Lucien in the side. Blood spurted. The warrior shouted, but didn't go down. Kept fighting.

The other Lords closed ranks around him, protecting him. Good men. The best. They'd fought together a long time, in the heavens and on earth. They knew to stay close, to fight with their backs to each other and to draw tighter when an injury was sustained.

But Lucien gathered his strength and flashed himself directly behind the Hunter who'd harmed him. The man was dead before his body hit the ground.

"Look out," Paris shouted as another Hunter came at his friend. His boots hammered at the ground as he raced to intervene.

Lucien ducked. The human's dagger swiped nothing but air. And then Paris was on the guy, slamming into him, propelling him down, down. He punched once, heard bone crack, twice, *felt* bone crack, then finished him off with a swipe of his blade.

"Thanks," Lucien said, helping him up.

"No prob." He scanned the area, even as he threw himself into another fight. *Shit.* He'd lost sight of Sienna. Humans and immortals were still standing, weapons locked in battle. The injured had slinked off to the sidelines to protect themselves from further harm. Of course, warriors, being warriors, hunted them and took care of business.

Meanwhile, body parts were flying and blood was pooling. And was that a wing at his feet, white threaded with gold? Yeah. Damn. Poor angel.

Find Sienna. A command from his demon, his darkness and himself.

He barreled in the direction he'd last seen her, leaving a trail of death in his wake. This was why he'd been created, after all. To fight. To kill. He rolled with the violence, bending, straightening, darting as needed. Throwing punches, slicing through skin and into organs. He experienced several more stinging pains and trickles of blood, but still he kept going.

From the corner of his eye, he thought he saw Maddox fall. Then Reyes. And was that Sabin? They would be fine, he told himself. Like Lucien, they were strong. He would not believe otherwise.

A few feet ahead, Gideon was sliced through the stomach and bleeding like a sieve, fighting off two giants. Strider was...nowhere. Gone. But there were Kaia and Gwen, Haidee and Scarlet, hacking through enemy lines with grins on their faces.

My boys are fine or the girls wouldn't be so happy,

Paris assured himself. He quickened his steps and took one of the giants from behind, the decapitation allowing Gideon to center his efforts. There were just so many Hunters, so many immortals. If they could hurt his friends, then Sienna would be—

There! He caught a glimpse of those black wings. Blood dripped from their tips, and he wasn't sure if it was hers or someone else's. Urgency rode him, guiding him faster and faster. A war cry echoed as a male plowed toward her from the right. Paris noticed and launched himself at the man, catching him around the waist. They skidded across the floor. A swift twist of the guy's neck, and that little battle was over.

Paris hopped to his feet and headed for his woman. She took down a big bruiser of a man with a swing of her dagger. Crimson stained her arms to the elbows. Her shirt was torn, her side bleeding.

The darkness inside him thickened.

Zacharel appeared in front of Sienna, cutting a clearer path for her and challenging the Titans who clashed with other angels in front of Cronus. Big shocker, Cronus was fighting, too. Rhea's men had come from the other side, and were currently hacking at him as if he was a piñata and they wanted the candy inside him. And yet, they hadn't managed to inflict a single injury on him. He was too strong, too fast. Too damn powerful.

Then those Hunters were down, and it was Cronus against Rhea, no one standing between them, the rest of the battle raging behind them. Both held two short swords, and both raced toward each other. *Contact.* Metal clanged against metal, even sparking.

"Bitch!"

"Bastard!"

"If your man kills me, you'll die, too," Cronus spat.

"Worth it," the queen gritted.

All around, the humans and angels—and hell, even the Lords, because yeah, Paris felt it too—experienced an increase of fury. As if their emotions fed off the king's and queen's. Teeth were bared. Claws unleashed.

Paris had a strange thought that the entire world was probably shaking from this. Earthquakes, tornados, tsunamis, volcanic eruptions, storms of any and all kind. What would he find when he returned there?

Head in the game.

Kill, he thought. He threw himself back into the fray. Dagger, swinging. Bodies, falling. Sienna, close by. Finally he reached her. Of course, that's when Galen appeared. He was soaked in crimson, shaking with rage. And he swung a long broadsword at Sienna's neck.

She hadn't noticed, too busy finishing off another Hunter.

"No!" Paris leapt between the two combatants. Because he was taller than Sienna, the tip of Galen's sword cut through his chest rather than his neck. Skin, muscle, bone, all three split. Warm blood poured as his knees buckled.

A high-pitched scream of unholy rage and denial nearly busted his eardrums. Sienna had noticed. He thought maybe his heart had taken some of the impact, too, because the organ skipped one beat, then another.

His vision fogged. Bodies became blurs of movement. Black—Sienna and her ire. White—Galen and his brute force. The two engaged, a whirlwind of motion and menace.

Come on, come on. Paris wasn't going down like this.

He pushed to his feet, but was immediately tossed back down. Someone had barreled into him, was punching at his face. Got his lip but good, the tissue slicing on his teeth. Though Paris couldn't see who it was, he suspected the culprit was human, and kicked out. The weight left him, and he got back on his feet.

The male came at him again. "I've always wanted the honor of killing one of your kind."

Paris still held his dagger and swiped. Contact, gurgling. Another body joined the ever-growing pile.

Sienna…Sienna… There! Still fighting Galen. Her motions were slowing, and there were seemingly thousands of new streaks of red interspersed with the black of her broken wings. She was hurting, weakening. Eyes narrowing, homing in on his target, Paris kicked forward. More Hunters rushed him, but he kept his eye on the prize and hacked at whoever got in his way. Then it happened.

Galen pinned her to the floor, ready to render the final blow.

"Where is Legion?" the keeper of Hope shouted, going to his knees, putting his weight on her shoulders.

"Never…tell…" Her voice held no trace of Wrath. Which meant the demon wasn't guiding her right now. *She* was in control. She would feel every injury.

Hurry! Get to her! Paris stumbled, righted himself, kept moving. Closer…but not close enough…so damn far away.

Another human, tossed aside.

"Where is she?" Galen.

"Where you'll never find her." Sienna.

Just beyond them, Cronus drilled Rhea's sword with so much force, the queen lost her grip. The king pounced, fisting her hair and forcing her to her knees. And there was nothing she could do about it, weaponless as she now was.

With his free hand, Cronus withdrew a thin link of

chain from the pocket of his robe and bound her wrists behind her. Struggling the entire time, she spat curses at him. He hooked the chain around her ankles. A hog tie. A good one. The queen wouldn't be going anywhere until he let her.

A sharp lance of pain seared between his shoulder blades. Someone had just stabbed him in the back, Paris realized distantly. Once again his knees gave out. This time, he couldn't get to his feet. Commanding his crystal blade to elongate, he shoved the length backward, nailed the one who'd taken him down, then he began crawling. He *would* reach Sienna. He would, even though every inch he gained left a thick trail of blood behind. In fact, he'd lost so much he wasn't sure how he was still conscious.

Galen swung around, removing his weight from Sienna, but she stayed where she was. Prone, motionless.

What had the bastard done to her? "No. *No.*" On his hands and knees, Paris worked his way to her. "Hold on, baby. I'm coming."

Cronus and Galen circled each other. Both were cut and bleeding profusely. Both were limping.

"Well, well. Our showdown at last," the king said. He coughed and spit out a tooth. He was without a weapon, having dropped them to confine his wife.

He couldn't flash away, too injured to do so.

Galen raised his sword. "Well, well, indeed. You didn't bring what you promised me, and now you are defenseless."

"Am I? I think not. If you want your woman," the king continued, "you'll walk away now. I will bring her to you, and you may keep her. But you are never to defy me again. So walk away. *Now.*"

Sienna twitched. Twitched again. Relief consumed

Paris. Almost there, almost… Slowly she rose, shook her head and took stock of the scene playing out in front of her, clearly still consumed by Wrath's influence after all. Cronus had his back to her. Galen was in front of Cronus, but paid her no heed.

The crystal dagger she held glinted in the light. And it elongated as his had just done, thickened, the end becoming a hook. Becoming a scythe. Becoming the only weapon capable of killing the man who ruled from the Titan throne. Paris realized what was about to happen and froze.

Oh, damn. Anyone looking from behind Galen, which was the view from Danika's painting of this moment, would see only Cronus. They wouldn't see the slight female behind him. The female who would change the world with her next action.

"I will never bow to you," Galen snarled. "And I will get my woman on my own."

"You'll get her after I kill her, then."

Galen roared, his weapon shaking in his grip.

"Actually," Sienna said, even as Galen swung, "*you'll* be the one dying." She, too, swung.

Her weapon was longer, stronger, and far more powerful, and she beat Galen to the punch.

Cronus never knew what hit him.

His head detached, flew, and his body collapsed. Rhea screamed, but for a split second, she looked nearly triumphant. "Worth…it," she whispered, and then she, too, went silent, suddenly motionless.

My woman. Pride joined Paris's relief. *My woman did this. Won this.*

As the throngs began to shout in revelation, a dark, screeching form rose from the king's body, its crimson eyes glowing, its fangs long and sharp, and a tail swishing behind it. A similar form rose from Rhea, only hers had a stooped back with horns and claws so long they could have been sabers.

Their demons were escaping.

Crazed, Greed and Strife shot high into the air, disappearing into the night. Two of Pandora's demons would once more be unleashed upon the world.

"Someone should go after them," Paris tried to say, but then Sienna screamed, hitting her knees, and he no longer cared about anything else. Her arms spread wide, her back arched, contorting her. Her head fell back, and she released another scream, then another and another.

At last Paris reached her. At last she quieted, her voice box razed. She remained in that position, shaking, shaking so badly. He wanted to gather her into his arms, to offer comfort, but he put himself in front of her. He was her shield. Now, always.

Galen stood there, panting, and maybe he would have attacked, but the battle had ended as suddenly as it had begun. The few remaining Hunters realized they were outnumbered and took off in a dead sprint, though where they thought they could escape to up here, he had no clue. Bloody gods and bedraggled goddesses sank to their knees. Some bowed their heads; others simply looked stunned.

The angels came up to flank Sienna, daring the keeper of Hope to make a move.

"All hail the new queen," a goddess suddenly said.

The rest of the Titans repeated the phrase, their voices rising in fervor, as one by one, they kneeled in front of Paris. He wasn't sure what was happening; surely they would not refer to him as the new queen. He had his moments, sure, but maybe it was a Titan thing, like how Viola called her male pet "princess."

"They speak to the girl behind you," Zacharel said, moving to stand beside him.

Sienna? Sienna was *queen?* Of the Titans? Still crouched, he swung around to check on her. The dizziness increased, and he realized his line of sight was completely blown.

The angel added roughly, "Choices decide our fate. And though I was not made aware until now, she was to be the king's greatest asset—or his only downfall, depending on the choice she made."

"But *he* would...have known. His Eyes...would have...told him." Every word scraped his throat, burning. Every word weakened him further.

"I am sure they did," Zacharel said. "In their own way. Perhaps he did not look closely enough, or perhaps they did not show him everything. And now Sienna has taken the godly throne. *This* is why we wanted her on our side, why *everyone* wanted her on their side. The powers Cronus stole from so many others over the centuries have now become hers."

Do I know how to pick 'em or what? This was one more hat for her to wear, he thought with a faint laugh that caused blood to bubble up his throat, spilling out of his mouth.

A fog drifted through his mind, but it couldn't hide the revelation that he was dying. Already he'd lost too much blood, and with every second that passed, breathing became more difficult. But Sienna would be safe, always safe, and that was all that mattered. He couldn't ask for more than that. Except for a future with her. He would have liked that.

The rest of his strength draining, he allowed himself to fall backward, his head landing in her lap.

"Paris?"

Darkness that had nothing to do with his anger closed in. "I...love...you," he croaked out.

"Paris!"

"Save...friends...don't let...die." The darkness consumed him, and he knew nothing more.

Except...

"Paris!"

Her voice jerked him back. A flash of white. Darkness. A flash of white, lasting several seconds longer. Another flash, lasting...lasting...his body and demon seeming to stretch apart, disconnect...until he heard Sienna's voice and everything snapped back together.

"—not leaving me! I won't let you. Remember when we talked about having someone to die for? Well, you're mine. You're my someone. If you pass, I'll follow. Somehow, I'll follow." Oh, was she pissed. That temper of hers was coming out to play. "Do you hear me?"

The ground rumbled beneath him.

He smiled, because in that moment he realized something wondrous. Everything was going to be okay. Sienna was stubborn to her core. She had defeated Cronus, outwitted Galen. This was nothing.

They would be together, one way or another. She would make sure of it.

CHAPTER FIFTY-ONE

SIENNA HATED TO LEAVE PARIS in bed, and didn't want him to wake up without her by his side. His body was in the process of healing from the massive wounds he'd sustained during battle, and when he opened his eyes, he would want answers. Answers she would happily give, just as soon as she learned them.

So, after brushing her knuckles over his beautiful face—though he turned toward her, he gave no other reaction—she hurriedly left the chamber they shared in the Realm of Blood and Shadows. Then she stopped. Wait, wait, wait. She could flash now, couldn't she?

In fact, that's how she'd gotten Paris and all of his friends back here. She'd entertained a simple thought: *I wish we were home,* and boom, she'd blinked and every single one of them had materialized at the castle. Shock had drilled her to her knees, and her mind had gone into a tailspin. For hours after that, her mind had reeled with the possibilities—Hawaii, Russia, Ireland, Key West, plus everywhere else she'd ever wanted to visit—and she'd ended up flashing all over the world by accident.

That had been, what? Two days ago. Two days that seemed like an eternity, but she'd finally gotten control of that particular ability. She didn't think she would ever get used to some of the others.

Power swirled inside her, so much power her skin felt too tight for her body and her pores felt stretched, as if at any moment she could shatter into a thousand pieces. Apparently, taking Cronus's head meant she was entitled to nearly all of his powers, and definitely all that he'd owned. Like, say, his home in the heavens and even his harem—from which she'd promptly freed everyone.

One of the females inside—Arca—had asked her if Paris had sent her. In exchange for Arca's aid, he'd vowed to free her after saving Sienna. She'd said yes, and now that debt was paid.

On top of everything else, Cronus's allies were hers—as were his enemies. But she wasn't worried.

She could also *feel* the darkness inside her now, the darkness Zacharel had told her about, the darkness Paris had given her—a darkness Wrath loved to devour. He'd never fed from her, but had begun to feed from Paris, taking that part of him and lessening its hold on him. Zacharel would have to approve.

With a sigh, she flashed into Lucien's room, ready to begin her daily checkup on all of Paris's friends. He and Anya were in bed, sleeping peacefully. His injuries were less severe than Paris's, and he had finally crawled out of bed this morning, only to stalk into the entertainment room, toss Anya over his shoulder, and vanish them both.

Maddox and Ashlyn were also in bed, but they were cooing to their babies, who kicked and gurgled in their adoring parents' arms. Maddox was bandaged pretty heavily, was pale and bruised, but he was smiling. The little boy, Urban, met Sienna's gaze and winked.

Winked? Surely not.

Strider and Kaia were—having sex. Oh, oh, ick! *My eyes.* Sienna moved to the next room.

Sabin and Gwen—*someone save me.* They were also going at it. What was with the people in this castle? Had Paris's demon somehow rubbed off on all of them?

Gideon and Scarlet were snuggled together, talking. And a stranger conversation Sienna had never heard.

"I hate you."

"I hate you more."

"I hate you most."

Moving on.

Amun and Haidee were in the kitchen, baking cookies. Haidee had flour streaked on her cheeks, prints on her breasts and butt, all courtesy of Amun and his wandering hands.

Reyes and Danika were in their bedroom. Like Paris, Reyes was sleeping off his injuries. Danika was painting.

Sienna knew Danika was the current All-Seeing Eye, and purposely didn't look at the colorful scene being created. She didn't want to end up like Cronus, obsessed with what was to happen and doing everything in her power to prevent it, all while forgetting to truly live in the present.

All she'd been willing to listen to was Danika's claim that the Lords' fortress in Budapest would soon be too dangerous to occupy, though she didn't know why, and that the whole crew needed to stay here for the time being. Sienna had, of course, given her blessing.

Cameo was in the entertainment room, polishing her daggers while the TV played an episode of *1000 Ways to Die*. Yes, the warriors had found a way to rig the immortal realm to receive a satellite signal.

Aeron and Olivia— Not again! Seriously. The castle was more like a zoo with monkeys. Wrath gave his customary heaven/hell coos, and there was still a hint of yearning in his tone, but no more of the whimpers.

Happy to be with me? Sienna asked the demon. *At least a little?*

You aren't so *terrible.*

She laughed. Wrath talked to her more and more now, real conversations rather than a spew of single-minded words. He'd helped her on that battlefield, guiding her actions but not overtaking her completely, just as he'd done with Fox, allowing her to work with him and do what was needed. She suspected he felt that this way, he helped protect his Aeron and Olivia.

Legion was in the room they'd chosen for her, as well, but one of her wrists had been chained to the wall. A long link allowed her to move freely about, but the cuff itself kept her from flashing to Galen to keep her vow to him.

I'll have to fix that, Sienna thought.

Hope will fight to the death to win her back, Wrath said.

Yeah. Probably. But that was a worry for later in the day.

Viola and her princess dog thing were in there with Legion, and Viola was regaling the chained girl with stories about herself. A captive audience. Seemed about right. Poor Legion, though. The princess was licking her feet.

Torin was in his room, sitting in front of a bank of computers. There was a faraway expression on his face, and she wondered what he was thinking about.

In a snap, she knew. Could actually hear what he was thinking.

—supposed to do with the All-Key now? Cronus won't be asking for it back, he's dead, and crap, what's up with Paris's woman being queen of the Titans? Are you kidding me with that? She's a former human and dead besides. Not to mention a former Hunter. And we already know how whacked it is to be ruled by those with demons

inside them. Do we bow to her now? Damn, this is weird and I have no clue—

Enough! she thought, and the volume on his mind was completely shut off. Much as she didn't want to know the future, she didn't want to know more than her fair share about the present, either. Invading people's thoughts was so uncool. Mrs. Manners would not approve.

Sienna hadn't spoken much to the Lords in the past two days, too busy tending Paris and adjusting to her new position, but now she knew most of them were still uneasy about her. Fine, whatever. That would take time. Time she was willing to give them. Anything to be with Paris.

Next, she appeared in front of the three rooms occupied by Cronus's immortal prisoners. Cameron, Winter and Irish. Unlike all the times before, she saw no flashes of their crimes inside her mind. During the battle in the heavens, Wrath had fed to the point of sickness and currently had no appetite.

Cameron spotted her first, and alerted the others. She wasn't surprised that they could see her now. Everyone else could, too. They strode to those air-shielded doorways.

Cameron sniffed, caught her scent and growled. "Ambrosia. Again. I know you. You're that bastard's invisible spy."

"Well, good news," she replied. "That bastard is dead, and clearly I'm no longer invisible."

All three blinked at her. Irish gave no reaction, but the other two laughed without humor.

"Yeah, right."

"Whatever."

"I'm going to set you free," she said, and that shut them up fast. They stared over at her, suddenly serious.

She hadn't done this earlier because she hadn't been sure it was the safest course of action. How would they react to her as queen? Try to kill her? But then she'd decided, so what if they did? *My powers are greater than theirs.* "If you harm the Lords of the Underworld, your brothers by circumstance," she stressed, "you will regret it. They are mine, and I protect what's mine. Do you understand?"

Stiff, disbelieving nods.

"Ask around," she said. "You'll discover that I can hurt you in ways that will haunt you for eternity."

She stepped forward, touched Winter's door. The shield fell away, and Winter gasped. A second later, the girl was gone. She repeated the process with the men, and they, too, left in a snap.

So easy, when only a few days ago, such a thing had been impossible. Go figure.

Sadly, she still was not done with her chores.

William was not in his room, but a human girl—Gilly, she recalled—was sleeping soundly in his bed, her dark hair spilled out over his pillow. The scent of sex was *not* in the air, but fear was, with an overlay of comfort. Gilly had come here, afraid for William, who had also been injured during the battle. He had soothed her until she'd fallen asleep beside him, then he'd left.

Now he was perched on the rooftop of the castle, popping gummy bears into his mouth and talking to another man in hushed tones. Hades. Instantly both males sensed she was there, as proven when they glanced in her direction.

"Hello, girl I helped time and time again," William said, his sly humor evidently intact despite his battle wounds.

"Hello, girl who owes me many favors," Hades added.

Black mist enveloped him, veins of fire running through what appeared to be wings.

Maybe her new powers had improved her vision, because suddenly she could see things she hadn't noticed before. He had long jet-black hair, eyes of pure black, no pupils evident, and a face even more handsome than Paris's. Well, a face that other women might consider more handsome than Paris's. She didn't.

His muscles were huge, and there appeared to be tiny stars tattooed all over his chest.

I like him, Wrath said.

That kinda scares me, just so you know.

"If two equals many in your world, yeah," she replied dryly. "Have you decided what you want me to do yet?" What left her uneasy was the fact that he could ask for the world and she would have to give it to him, as long as it didn't harm Paris or his friends.

Hades shook his shadowed head, his grin serial-killer wicked. "Soon," he promised.

"Great," she said, and left them to their secret conversation. A blink, and she was up in the heavens, standing inside Zacharel's cloud.

It amazed her that the angels lived in the clouds, and those clouds were actually like homes. Furniture, hallways, gardens. Whatever the owner desired. Zacharel's had the requisite bed, but it had a man with pink hair and blood-inked tears chained to it. A blindfold was wrapped around his eyes, a gag stuffed in his mouth, and a sheet draped over his waist. The rest of him was naked.

Don't look. Not my business. On that nightstand was an hourglass-shaped jar with some kind of gooey substance in it. She did not want to think about what he did with the stuff.

"Zacharel," she called, gaze already returning to the

pink-haired man. Her eyes narrowed. This was Paris's assailant from the cavern...and, she saw with her new and improved vision, he was no man at all, but a fallen angel. Since when were his kind held hostage in the very place they'd chosen to escape from? She watched as he struggled for freedom.

Zacharel walked through the far doorway, and he was naked and wet, and oh, sweet Lord, he was gorgeous. Just...wow. A muscle mass to rival Paris's, and he must be smuggling tube socks in his stomach, because damn. He had muscled roll after muscled roll. Small brown nipples, and some serious man business, and no body hair.

Only flaw that he possessed was a black spot as big as her fist on his chest, just above his heart. The spot bled out in a few places, as if ink had been smudged. Wait. Nope. Not the only flaw. Whip marks seemed to wrap around his ribs, red and raw. And could she really call the snow still falling from his wings a sign of perfection?

He stopped when he spotted her. A second later, a white robe draped him. Also, his bed—and its prisoner—had vanished. "I had a do-not-disturb barrier outside." His emotionless tone had returned. "How did you get in?"

"Um, sorry about that," she said. "I just, uh, kind of willed myself here."

No chastisement. Just a tight "What do you want?"

"I wanted to thank you." He was the reason Paris and company lived. "You gave me water from the River of Life. I didn't know what you had to do to obtain that water at the time, but I do now, and I'm aware you had to make some sort of sacrifice."

Tidbits of information came to her at the oddest times now, and only this morning, she'd realized angels had to give up something they loved to even approach the water. And to leave with a vial? They had to bleed. A lot. Maybe that's why he'd been whipped.

After the battle, as Paris's energy had drained right along with his blood, Zacharel had traded her a vial of the stuff for a simple promise to help the angels in the coming war. Apparently, the battle against Cronus was not the one he needed help winning.

"I will do everything I can for you," she finished. There were limits to what she could do, of course. She couldn't bring her sister back, though she'd tried. She couldn't find Kane. She couldn't heal others. Cronus had never been the all-powerful entity he'd made himself out to be.

"You have much to learn about yourself," the angel said. "You will spend the next few weeks with us, and we will teach you what you need to know."

"As soon as Paris is up and around. He'll be coming with me," she said. And she prayed she was right, that he would want to.

"He shared his darkness with you, and you want him still?"

"Of course. I am a light for him, a way out, and somehow his darkness is my light."

"That is—"

"Enough about this, I know. I want him with me, and that's that." She disappeared, having one more stop to make before she could return to Paris.

Galen's home.

He and Fox were seated at their kitchen table, piles of guns and ammo spilled out around them. They were polishing metal, checking clips, fitting bullets.

Wrath growled, but didn't say anything.

Galen looked upset. Fox looked strung-out. Her nostrils flared, and she sniffed, hard, and then her head was whipping around. Her gaze landed on Sienna and she jumped to her feet, about to lurch in Sienna's direction, obviously craving another taste of her.

With a flick of her wrist, Sienna willed the female to the very table where Sienna herself had been snacked on, chaining her there.

Galen jolted to his feet, his chair skidding behind him. "You!"

"Me."

"I want my women back. Legion *and* Fox."

"And I want you to release Legion from her vow to you."

"Never."

"I thought you'd say that." She glided over and eased into Fox's seat. He made no aggressive moves toward her, but then, he knew what she could do now.

Maybe she should have killed him for all the wrongs he'd committed. But most of his Hunters were dead, decimated in the battle, so perhaps he'd suffered enough. Also, she didn't want his demon loose, like Greed, who had belonged to Cronus, and Strife, who belonged to Rhea, the two now out there somewhere, no doubt plaguing the world.

"As you know, the Unspoken Ones were bound to Cronus. Now that he's dead, they are free. I tried to keep them chained, but by the time I realized who and what they are, that I, too, could bind them, they were long gone." Her gaze was piercing. "They want your blood, Galen. They want it bad. They'll be coming after you hard-core." And really, she was surprised they hadn't gotten to him already. "Do you really want to put Legion in that kind of situation? That kind of danger?"

A long moment passed. His answer would reveal his true feelings for the girl.

His shoulders sagged. He sank back into his seat. "No. I do not."

He cared for her, Sienna realized. Truly cared for the girl.

"I...release her," he gritted out. "Release Legion from her vow to remain with me, obey me."

Double wow, but she didn't comment. She didn't know what to say. So she moved them on to their next order of business. "You have something I want."

He didn't pretend to misunderstand. "The Cloak of Invisibility."

"Yes."

"It's mine. *Mine*."

How she wished she could make him give her the artifact, but free will was a greater power than what bubbled inside her. Whatever Cronus had told her, that's why he'd worked so hard to convince her to do what he wanted. Immortal or not, king or not, you messed with free will, and you would be punished. Severely. She was pretty sure that's why she had ultimately defeated him. Because he'd taken hers, he'd lost his own in turn.

"What will it take to convince you to give me the Cloak?" she asked. She'd learned a thing or two about bargaining.

His eyes narrowed on her. "Protection. You must protect me from the Unspoken Ones."

And wouldn't the Lords just *love* that? "For a year," she said.

"Eternity."

"Two years."

"Eternity."

"One year," she said, her own eyes narrowing.

He popped his jaw. "Very well. Two years of protection. Maybe in that time, I'll kill you and take those kingly powers for myself. Protect myself."

By that time, she would have found Pandora's box, but she didn't tell him that. "Make a play for me, Galen, and you'll find yourself in a special prison for immortals for the next two years."

He paled.

Yeah. He caught her drift. He'd be rotting next to the Greeks he'd once betrayed. "Give me the Cloak."

His motions jerky, he pulled a small square of gray material from his pant pocket and tossed it at her. "There. Yours."

There was no time to bask in her victory.

"Sienna!"

She heard Paris's bellow across the vast distance between them. Her cheeks flushed with pleasure as she stuffed the tiny, folded Cloak in her bodice. He was awake! "Gotta go," she said, and willed herself back inside her bedroom.

CHAPTER FIFTY-TWO

PARIS WAS JUST ABOUT TO GO on a rampage when his woman appeared beside the bed. He caught his breath and fell back against the pillows. Her dark hair tumbled over one shoulder. She wore a gown threaded with gold and emerald, jewels sparkling in the material. Her hair was brushed to a luxurious mahogany shine. Those black wings arced over her shoulders.

She had never looked more beautiful.

He sighed with happiness as she threw herself on top of him. "I'm so glad you're awake!"

Her slight weight settled on him, her hair creating a curtain that made them the only two people in the world. He rejoiced. They belonged together.

"Is it true you're now the boss of us?"

She snorted. "You have such a way with words. But yeah, I am kind of the boss of you. Titans kept appearing out of nowhere to pay their respects, and I finally had to make a royal decree for space."

Queen Sienna. He liked it. "I guess that makes me King Paris."

A tinkling laugh escaped her. "I've always known you were destined for greatness."

"I'll get to boss my boys around, of course."

"Of course."

He grinned, so damn happy he could burst. "I knew you'd bring me back, baby. So, am I an undead soul?"

She lifted her head, a soft smile lighting her delicate features. "No, you're very much alive, and you still have your demon."

Yeah, he could feel the bastard waking up, stretching, demanding Sienna, only Sienna. Sex wasn't after random grind anymore. The demon had embraced Sienna and all the different facets of her personality, and didn't want to lose her. She was their lottery ticket.

Maintaining his grip on her with one hand, he patted himself down with the other. No injuries. He was completely healed. "What happened up there?"

She kissed his cheek, his neck. "After you passed out and I flipped my ever-loving lid, Zacharel calmed me down and told me about my new status and abilities. He also gave me a vial of water from the River of Life. For a price. I gave you and all the Lords a sip and you guys have been healing ever since."

"What price?" he asked.

"Well, all along the angels have wanted me in the heavens, helping them with their war. I told him that I was willing to help, but I wouldn't be living there. I will stay with you. If you'll have me. Except, we do have to stay up there for a few weeks so I can learn how to use my new powers. There's where I was just now. And I'm rambling, aren't I?"

"I love when you ramble. But did you really just say the words *if you'll have me?*" He couldn't help himself. He kissed her hard and fast, staking his claim. "I will have you today and every other. And I will help you help the angels. And yes, I will go with you, wherever you need to go."

A relieved breath left her. "I'm glad. Oh, and just in case it comes up, the darkness inside of you is now inside of me, too."

"What?" He sputtered, paled. "I'm sorry, so sorry. I didn't—"

"Don't worry about it…*husband*."

Everything stilled inside him. His heart, his lungs, the synapses in his brain. "You know I married you?"

"Of course." A sly smile lifted her lips. "I know a whole lot of stuff now. Like, world-changing stuff."

"World-changing, smorld-changing. You're okay with being bound to me forever? Because I get the impression it's not a two-sided marriage until you say so."

"I'm saying so, and I'm better than okay with it."

He *so* loved this woman. "Good, because I feel the same. *Wife*."

Her smile quivered as if she were fighting tears. She told him about Arca, and rather than displaying his customary guilt and shame because of his past actions, he kissed her tenderly. She loved him, too, and she had forgiven him. She saw the best in him.

"Thank you," he said. "With all of my heart, thank you."

"Welcome. Now, back to the darkness," she said, probably trying for a business tone but failing. His woman was a softie, a Twinkie with a cream filling, and he loved that, too. "Wrath feeds on it, and that helps keep him calm. And you know what that means, right? We're perfect for each other in *every* way."

"I so agree with that. We're a family, you and me, and I love you more than I can ever say."

"That's good, because that's how much I love you."

He planted a quick kiss on her mouth. Anything more, and he'd be all over her before he had all the information he needed. "So where are we right now?"

A wicked glint in her eyes as she said, "Back in the Realm of Blood and Shadows. All the Lords but Kane are here. Amun and Haidee found him, fought for him, but then they lost him again somehow. But don't worry, I'm on the case now. I'll find him once and for all. And I'm, uh, kind of a big deal."

He grinned.

"Now, on to the next topic. I want to show you something," she said. Rolling to her side but remaining within his embrace, she swirled her hand in the air above them. Shimmers of light, a thickening of the particles, and then colors bloomed around a mist.

He saw Baden. Red hair, muscled body.

Joy and grief bloomed inside him.

He saw Pandora. Black hair, leanly honed body.

Guilt and shame.

He saw Cronus. Brown hair, muscled body.

Smugness.

He saw Rhea. Black hair, slender body.

Vindication.

Their mouths were moving, but he couldn't hear them. They stood between thick, white pillars in a temple.

"I'm dead," Sienna said, "but I live. So I can do what even Cronus could not when he had the throne. I can travel there. I can talk to them. And I think I can even get your Baden back."

Tears suddenly burned his eyes. A puss once again, but whatever. This was a dream come true, all of it. "I would love that. *Thank you.*"

Her eyes misted, and she cleared her throat. "Okay, so do you want the good news or the bad news next?"

There was more? His chest constricted. "Bad. Give me the bad, no matter what it is."

"With Cronus dead, his enemies are now mine. I'm not exactly sure who they are, so I'm not exactly sure who to trust. Also, the Unspoken Ones are free, and I have to protect Galen from them."

He breathed out a gust of relief. He wasn't sure what he'd expected, but that wasn't it. "We'll deal with the enemies as they come. As for Galen, we'll discuss it."

She planted another kiss on his neck. "Great, because that's the perfect transition into the good news."

He would never grow tired of her caress and angled his head so that she'd kiss him again. "What?"

"Well, this is a two-parter. First, the Hunters have been all but obliterated. Second, Galen gave me the Cloak of Invisibility."

"Wait, wait, wait. Back up. *What?*"

"You are currently enemy-free."

"I don't…" Have any words, he realized. He experienced shock, then excitement, then disbelief, then shock again. He'd been fighting the Hunters for so long. *Thousands* of years. To suddenly find out he would never have to battle another? Almost too much to take in.

When he found his voice, he managed to croak, "Why would Galen give you his only artifact?"

"Well, when Cronus and Rhea died, the Unspoken Ones were freed, as I told you. They are now after him. He gave me the Cloak and in return, I offered him my protection. He hated doing it, and I whittled him down to only two years."

"You should have saved yourself the hassle. One, everyone here wants him dead no matter what, and two, with the Hunters out of the picture, we're good without the Cloak. We won't need to use it to sneak into enemy territory."

"You're welcome," she said, chin going in the air.

"Sorry, sorry. I'm grateful, I swear. That came out wrong. I just hate the fact that you were around him, and now you have to protect him." Which meant *Paris* had to protect him, too.

She softened. "You still need the Cloak. You can't be sure no one else will rise up against you, and it's better for you to have every weapon at your disposal, rather than someone else's."

"Such a smart girl."

Our girl.

Definitely.

"Besides, we can now search for the box," she said, beaming.

All four artifacts, he mused, awed by this woman of his. She was right. They needed the artifacts, not only to keep them out of enemy hands but to find Pandora's box and destroy it before anyone could use it against them. The goal they had been working toward so single-mindedly and for so long was nearer than ever to being met. "Let's not go searching for the box just yet," he said, tugging at her clothing.

"Such a smart boy." She met his waiting mouth with her own, licking and kissing and sucking on him. "We'll search later. Much later."

Yes! I'm on board!

IN A CORNER OF SIENNA'S MIND, a man's thoughts bubbled up. *What's up with this crap? Here comes another apology I have to make.*

Strider's voice, she realized. He was walking toward their bedroom, even then.

I tried to talk Paris into booting his girl, just like I tried to talk Amun into booting his, and both of them suffered for it. Not to mention how their women must have felt. So that's it for me. I'm done. No more getting involved with my boys and their women. But then, the

*only single ones left are Kane and Torin, but Torin is a
recluse so he doesn't count. And if ever Cameo brings
home a guy, well, all bets are off. Guy will have to prove
himself worthy, no matter what. And damn, I'm almost
there. Kaia better thank me properly for this, since she's
the one who insisted I do it. I hate apologizing, and Paris
is the vengeful type. He'll make me get on my knees and
beg, I know it. This is gonna be embarrassing. And painful!*

Knock. Knock.

"Go away," Paris shouted, hands clenching on Sienna's
ass.

"I need to talk to you, man," Strider replied, voice
muffled through the doorway. "Also to Her Highness,
who I assume is in there with you. I don't really have to
call her Your Highness, do I?"

"Yes, you do. But talk later."

"Now. So, uh, yeah. I'm sorry. See ya." *Yep, hurt just
as bad as I thought it would,* Strider thought.

His footsteps faded away.

"What was that about?" Paris asked.

Sienna's own thoughts filled her head. *I will not laugh.*
"Me. He was saying sorry for the way he messed with
you about me. Apologizing to both of us, actually."

"I love you, baby," Paris said.

Her lips stretched into another grin. "I love you, too."

When they were both naked, he sank inside her.
He was home, finally home. And he was at peace. His
woman was with him, and she wasn't leaving him. They
were going to be together.

Whatever else came, whatever else happened, they
would be together, just as he'd wanted since the beginning.

EPILOGUE

ONCE AGAIN ZACHAREL found himself high in the heavens, Lysander beside him, the pair of them peering down at a very content Paris and Sienna.

"I gained her cooperation," he said, "but not the way you wished. Paris will be joining her here."

"This is not the travesty I had feared it would be," Lysander replied. "When dealing with people and their emotions, allowances must always be made. I sometimes forget."

Emotions. A waste of energy in Zacharel's estimation. You lived, you warred and one day you died. Anything else was unnecessary.

Lysander continued, "I am surprised they complement each other so well, even more surprised they actually aid each other both emotionally and physically. I never would have guessed."

Nor he. Paris should have dragged Sienna down. She should not have had the determination and strength to pull him up. "What happens now?"

"Now, I will begin Sienna's training, and take responsibility for Paris. And you, in turn, will heed the Deity's newest order."

"Very well." The Deity's newest order—or rather, sentence—had come only this morning. Zacharel had been summoned to the Deity's temple, where a second punishment for his prior sins had been heaped upon his head, as if the eternal snowfall wasn't enough. "You must admit you have the easier task."

"True. I do not envy you, my friend."

Zacharel was to lead his own army of warriors. Warriors just like himself, only far worse. Men who had defied the rules one too many times. Men who would—supposedly—teach him the value of following heavenly laws.

They were like no other angels he'd ever dealt with. Some took lovers. Some cussed and drank. Some were tattooed and pierced, and as dark in spirit as many humans.

If he trained them well, the Deity had proclaimed, the snow would cease to fall from his wings, and he would be allowed to remain in the heavens himself. If he failed, if they failed, they would all fall together, forever banned from the only home they'd ever known.

Whatever it took, Zacharel *must* remain in the heavens. His greatest treasure was here, and he would rather die than be parted from it. He did not consider his attachment emotional, but rather, essential to his survival.

You might not survive even if you remain up here, he thought, rubbing the dark spot growing on his chest.

"If ever you need me," Lysander said, pulling him from his musings, "you have only to call."

"Thank you. I feel the same. If ever you need me…" *I might not be around to help.* At that moment, the Deity's parting words echoed in his mind. *Your life will soon change in ways you cannot even imagine. I hope you are prepared.*

Was he? He and his men would find out together, he supposed.

* * * * *

Lords of the Underworld
Glossary of Characters and Terms

Aeron—Former keeper of Wrath

All-Seeing Eye—Godly artifact with the power to see into heaven and hell

Amun—Keeper of Secrets

Anya—(Minor) goddess of Anarchy; beloved of Lucien

Arca—Messenger goddess

Ashlyn Darrow—Human female with supernatural ability; wife of Maddox

Baden—Former keeper of Distrust (deceased)

Bait—Human females, Hunters' accomplices

Bianka Skyhawk—Harpy; sister of Gwen and consort of Lysander

Black—A Horseman of the Apocalypse

Cage of Compulsion—Godly artifact with the power to enslave anyone trapped inside

Cameo—Keeper of Misery

Cameron—Keeper of Obsession

Cloak of Invisibility—Godly artifact with the power to shield its wearer from prying eyes

Cronus—King of the Titans, keeper of Greed

Danika Ford—Human female; girlfriend of Reyes

Dean Stefano—Hunter; Right-hand man of Galen

dimOuniak—Pandora's box

Ever—Daughter of Maddox and Ashlyn

Fox—Current keeper of Distrust; servant of Galen

Galen—Keeper of Hope and Jealousy

Gideon—Keeper of Lies

Gilly—Human female

Greeks—Former rulers of Olympus, now imprisoned in Tartarus

Green—A Horseman of the Apocalypse

Gwen Skyhawk—Harpy, daughter of Galen and wife of Sabin

Hades—Father of Lucifer and William

Haidee—former Hunter; beloved of Amun

Hunters—Mortal enemies of the Lords of the Underworld

Kaia Skyhawk—Harpy; sister of Gwen and Bianka; wife of Strider

Kane—Keeper of Disaster

Legion—Demon minion in a human body, friend of the Lords of the Underworld

Lords of the Underworld—Exiled warriors to the Greek gods who now house demons inside them

Lucien—Keeper of Death; leader of the Budapest warriors

Lucifer—Prince of darkness; ruler of hell

Lysander—Elite warrior angel and consort of Bianka Skyhawk

Maddox—Keeper of Violence

Olivia—An angel; beloved of Aeron

One, True Deity—Ruler of the angels

Pandora—Immortal warrior, once guardian of *dimOuniak* (deceased)

Paring Rod—Godly artifact with ability to render soul from body

Paris—Keeper of Promiscuity, also known as the Lord of Sex

Princess Fluffikans—vampire Tasmanian devil; pet of Viola

Púkinn—aka Irish; keeper of Indifference

Realm of Blood and Shadows—A sinister, hidden section of Titania

Red—A Horseman of the Apocalypse

Reyes—Keeper of Pain

Rhea—Queen of the Titans; estranged wife of Cronus; keeper of Strife

Sabin—Keeper of Doubt; leader of the Greek warriors

Scarlet—Keeper of Nightmares, wife of Gideon

Screeching—Immortal equivalent of tweeting

Sienna Blackstone—Deceased female Hunter; current keeper of Wrath

Skye—Sister of Sienna

Strider—Keeper of Defeat

Tartarus—Greek god of Confinement; also the immortal prison on Mount Olympus

Titania—The city of the gods; formerly known as Olympus

Titans—Current rulers of the heavens

Torin—Keeper of Disease

Unspoken Ones—Reviled gods; prisoners of Cronus

Urban—Son of Maddox and Ashlyn; twin of Ever

Viola—Minor goddess of the Afterlife; keeper of Narcissism

Warrior Angels—Heavenly demon assassins

West Godlywood—Titania's premier hotel

White—A Horse(wo)man of the Apocalypse

William the Ever Randy—Immortal warrior

Winter—Keeper of Selfishness

Zacharel—A warrior angel

Zeus—King of the Greeks

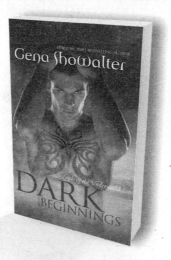

There's something different about the new guy at Crossroads High...

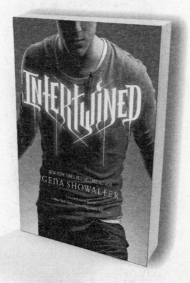

With four undead souls living inside him, Aden's about to discover just how different he is. Helped by his new friends, Mary Ann, a human teenager with powers, werewolf shapeshifter Riley and especially vampire princess Victoria, Aden enters a dark and dangerous underworld.

When one of the souls in Aden's head foretells his death, Aden must uncover his own supernatural skills if he hopes to survive.

www.miraink.co.uk

Sixteen-year-old Aden Stone has had a hell of a week.

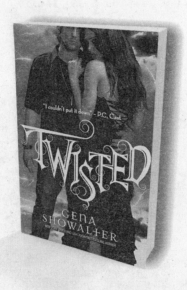

Tortured by angry witches.
Hypnotised by a vengeful faery.
Spied on by the most powerful vampire in existence.
And, oh, yeah. Killed—twice.

His vampire girlfriend might have brought him back
to life, but he's never felt more out of control.
There's a darkness within him, something taking
over…changing him. Worse, because he was meant
to die, death now stalks him at every turn.
Any day could be his last…